Bad Mothers United

Kate Long is the author of *The Bad Mother's Handbook*, *Swallowing Grandma*, *Queen Mum*, *The Daughter Game*, *Mothers & Daughters* and *Before She Was Mine*. She was born and raised in Lancashire and lives with her husband and two sons in Shropshire. Visit her website www.katelong.co.uk

ALSO BY KATE LONG

Bad Mothers United

Kate Long

**SIMON &
SCHUSTER**

London · New York · Sydney · Toronto · New Delhi

A CBS COMPANY

First published in Great Britain by Simon & Schuster UK Ltd, 2013
A CBS COMPANY

Copyright © Kate Long 2013

1 3 5 7 9 10 8 6 4 2

Simon & Schuster UK Ltd
1st Floor
222 Gray's Inn Road
London WC1X 8HB

www.simonandschuster.co.uk

Simon & Schuster Australia, Sydney
Simon & Schuster India, New Delhi

A CIP catalogue record for this book is available
from the British Library

PB ISBN: 978-1-84983-793-4
EBOOK ISBN: 978-1-84983-794-1

Typeset by M Rules
Printed and bound by CPI Group (UK) Ltd, Croydon, CR0 4YY

For Damian McClelland, Jon Dwyer,
Carys Roberts MCSP, Sister Lease and the team on
Ward 121 at the University Hospital of North Staffordshire,
for Midlands Air Ambulance and everyone involved with
saving my husband's life and limbs in 2010.

All t'world's queer 'cept for thee and me.
And I'm not so sure about thee.

Spotted this woman walking towards me in BHS, right miserable face on her, thick waist, bad hair. I thought, Eeh, you've let yourself go, love. Then I realised it was a mirror.

CHAPTER 1

On a day in January, 2000

Some things change, some stay the same.

The day our Charlotte went back to university it was lashing down. I watched her dodge along the front path, twirling her umbrella, while Daniel struggled behind with her bags and cases and coats and poster tubes – all the rubbish she reckons she can't survive the term without. I'd brought Will up to the window so he could wave to his mum – *Bye bye, Mummy, you buzz off and enjoy yourself, don't bother giving us lot a second thought* – but after thirty seconds he'd wriggled out of my arms and gone to sit in front of the TV again. I left him where he was. We don't make a big deal of these partings in case it upsets him.

When Charlotte reached the car she stood back and let Daniel open the door for her, even though it meant that to do so he had to squash one bag under his arm and balance a holdall between his hip and the rear wing. Then he'd somehow to take the umbrella carefully off her while she climbed in, mustn't for God's sake let any moisture get to that swinging mane of straightened hair, and meanwhile there's water pouring off the umbrella canvas and dripping from the spokes onto his shoulder. That lovely lad. Devoted isn't the word. I wondered whether he'd noticed she wasn't herself this holiday.

I saw my daughter rearrange whatever was in the footwell, then pull down the vanity mirror to check her fringe. Daniel began wrestling to close the umbrella. Across the road, two kids in anoraks cycled figure eights round the Working Men's Club car park. The rain was coming in waves now. And I thought, Well, it's been raining all my damn life, hasn't it? How many days has it NOT rained? My first morning at the big school, a passing car splashed mud nearly up to my knickers. My sixteenth birthday, a bunch of us were supposed to be going up the Pike to get drunk, only it drizzled non-stop and we ended up stuck in Rivington Barn tea room, trying to swig cider without the waitress seeing. It was coming down in stair-rods on that third date with Steve, which meant we had to stay in, which meant we started having sex before I was ready, which meant I got caught with Charlotte and ruined my entire future, never even got to take my A levels. There were flood warnings on my wedding day, and the week my decree absolute came through, the Irwell burst its banks. It was pouring the afternoon I moved in here, Mum standing on the doorstep going, 'We'll work things out, you'll see.' Me going, 'Twenty bloody one and I can't believe I'm back home where I started.'

Of course at school we were taught that there was actual science behind all the wet. Clouds sweeping in off the Irish Sea had to rise to get over the Pennines and as they did, they cooled and condensed, dumping their load on the Lancashire side. By the time they got to Yorkshire, they were wrung out. All I can say is, Barnsley must be parched. I can remember the teacher making us sketch diagrams of fat clouds, landscape in cross-section, notes below about how soft water was a crucial component of the textile industry and how without it, our local economy would never have got going. No hills, no mills.

So we're used to unkind skies in this village. But sometimes it feels more personal. Certain people are born to be rained on.

After Daniel had driven off, after I'd waved and waved, watched till the car reached the end of the street and turned, I had this sudden sag of tiredness. It's the holding myself together that does it. Trying not to start a row every five minutes. Whatever I'm doing with Will, it's wrong, she wants it her way. Except she's not around then to follow anything up. All right for her to decide he's having an extra story at bedtime, or encourage him to throw his fifty-odd teddies round the room as a fun game. It's me who's left to settle him again, mauling up and down, trying to keep the house safe and tidy. Ask her to rein him in and that makes you Mrs Miserypants. 'Let him have FUN,' she says. Subtext: *Because you never let me have any, did you?* This deprived childhood she's supposed to have had.

So always after she's gone an emptiness takes over my insides and all I want to do is flop on the sofa with Will. This time was worse, though, because I knew something else was wrong, something new, but I hadn't dared ask and now I'd lost my chance.

What would *you* have done with her, Mum? I thought. You always knew how to get round Charlotte.

On the windowpane a cloud of my misty breath shrank away to a smudge.

There was always Steve – I could ring him, talk it over. He

was her dad, after all. He might have an idea. But no, not that. Mustn't call Steve.

I said to Will, 'Right, work to be done. Grandma's just going to be in the bathroom,' and his big eyes rolled briefly in my direction, then back to the screen where the Teletubbies danced. I went through to the kitchen, paused to put away a few plates that had been left out on the drainer, then pushed open the bathroom door. The usual chaos greeted me: towel slung over the bath side instead of hung up on the rail, empty box of eyelash dye stuck between the taps, toilet roll finished but not replaced, Will's colander of plastic toys knocked over, spilling across the bottom of the sink. For me to pick up, because I've nothing else to do. Ruddy students.

I had meant her to take some Vim back with her because, heaven knows, that manky old suite they all use in York could do with a scrub. But here the bottle was, sitting on the windowsill. I grasped it by the middle, gave it a vigorous shake and squirted five or six thick gouts of scouring cream across the inside of the bath. Then I plucked the sponge from behind the water-pipe and got down on my knees to start cleaning. Thought of my mother in her apron and slippers doing the same job, looking up and smiling as I came in. *You'll have t'cross your legs a minute, love, till I'm finished.* Remembered the old wall-mounted toilet cistern we used to have when I was little, with its swinging chain and extra piece of string tied on so I could reach it. The soap in the dish always multicoloured, all ends of bars squashed together because we'd never to waste anything. I suddenly had an image of Steve's maroon bath, me sitting with my feet under the running tap while he poured half a bottle of Radox over my legs. God. *God.* It was vital not to phone Steve.

'Where Mummy?' Will was standing in the doorway, swaying.

'Mummy's gone to York,' I said brightly. I opened my arms to give him a hug but he stepped back into the kitchen again, out of sight.

'Kit Kat,' I heard him mutter.

'Hang on a sec, sweetheart.'

The cupboard door clicked, rattled, then banged as if it was being kicked.

'Will, stop that.'

I placed the sponge on the side and hauled myself to my feet. Every damn stick of furniture in this house has some sort of child-lock on it, every domestic task's an obstacle course.

When I came through, he'd given up attacking the cupboard and was laid flat out on the lino, holding his breath and drumming his heels. First time Charlotte saw him do that she thought he was having a proper fit, wanted me to ring for a doctor. I told her, 'It's just the Terrible Twos. No need for panic. You were a nightmare at that age. You used to knock your head against the wall if you didn't get your own way.' (She used to pee herself on purpose as well, but I didn't say that.) She went, 'What should we do, Mum?' and I said, 'Leave him to get on with it.' But she wasn't having that, so we ended up distracting him with a glove puppet I'd picked up at the Christmas Fair. That brought him round. Except then she started with, 'How come you're so much nicer with him than you were with me when I was that age?' I must admit, at that point I went upstairs and left her to it.

I looked down at where Will lay. 'Hey, tell you what, how about a nice banana instead?'

'No narna! No.' He rolled up onto his feet in one fluid action and ran to tug at the cupboard door again.

'OK, just one finger of Kit Kat then. And we'll see Mummy soon, yes?'

He didn't even turn round.

With a flick of my thumb I undid the child lock and pointed to the biscuit tin. Daft move because there was a stack of bowls at the front, but Will being Will he just dived in and tugged. Out tumbled the bowls, plus a box of Cheerios that Madam must have opened even though there was one already on the go. Finally, as a sort of encore, a tower of ancient canned salmon toppled and fell. The cans rolled across the floor tiles unharmed, but the dishes weren't so lucky. The first shattered, the second split into two neat halves and the third lost an inch-wide chunk from the rim. Cheerios flowed and settled around the debris. So now I'd a floor covered in smashed crockery and cereal, and a toddler in the middle trying to bite off the lid of the biscuit barrel.

Eeh, keep your hair on, Karen, went Mum's voice. *It's nowt a dustpan and brush can't sort.*

Sighing, I picked up Will round his waist and carried him to the doorway of the lounge. 'Stay there,' I said. I prised the biscuit tin open and plonked it down in front of him, then went back to consider the mess. One of the cans had wedged itself under the gas cooker; I knew without looking that all the salmon would be out of date. There was only ever my mother who ate the stuff.

'Juice, Grandma?' said Will, rummaging around inside the barrel as if it was a bran tub.

'Can it not wait a minute, love?'

'Juice!'

'All right. Where's your cup?'

Shrug.

You never do get to finish a job in this house. I thought perhaps I'd last seen his lidded beaker in the lounge, but a quick hunt turned up nothing except one of Charlotte's magazines (must be nice to have time to sit and read), plus a stray sock. I pocketed the sock and came back into the kitchen to check the sink and drainer: empty. The unit next to the cooker contained only my mother's collection of floral mugs. Fridge: fat-free mousse, mayo-lite, Diet Coke, low-cal spread, monster bar of Dairy Milk. On the inside of the big cupboard's drop-down flap I discovered a trail of golden syrup and a scrawled Post-it from Charlotte saying *TROLL*. Charming. What had I done to deserve that?

I banged the flap shut. 'OK, I'm going to have to pop upstairs, see if it got left in your room. Looks as if you might need a clean top too, doesn't it?'

He glanced down at his crumb-smeared vest.

'So you go and sit on the sofa, watch TV a minute till I—'

The phone began to ring.

And that must be Charlotte, forgotten something, or wanting to speak to Will which I've told her before isn't helpful, not straight after she's left. Or Daniel to say she's upset again. That used to happen a lot. Although not so much lately, thank God. Five terms on, we're pretty much into a routine.

I ducked into the hall and snatched at the receiver.

'Hey up, sexy,' said Steve's voice. 'How's tricks?'

Bloody hell. You try and try to keep out of the way, but trouble still finds you. I slumped down on the bottom step, my back against the stair gate. 'What do you want?'

'Our Charlie gone?'

'About half an hour ago.'

'All right, were it?'

'Well, the usual stropping about. But also this vagueness about her. I'd be talking and I could see it wasn't registering at all. She'd be playing with Will one minute, and the next she'd be frowning and gazing off into the distance, like she'd something on her mind. It's got me worried. She's not spoken to you, has she?'

'To me? You must be kidding. When does she ever confide in me?'

'Oh no, I've just had a thought – dear God, let her not be pregnant again.'

'Pregnant? Come off it, Karen. If I know Charlie, she won't be going down that road again in a hurry. Is she not just fretting over her exams?'

'I don't know. I hope so.'

'Aye, I bet that's all it is. Don't wind yourself up over nowt. Anyway, I was wondering, are you busy? Can I pop round?'

I knew what that question meant, and what my answer was. This time I was resolved. You don't sleep with someone just because they pick your grandson up from nursery occasionally, do you? Or once-in-a-blue-moon babysit? Or because they mop your tears when your daughter's left or you're missing your mother, or because they tell you you're looking great when you're actually feeling like death? Hopping into bed for stuff like that isn't even gratitude, it's desperation. If Charlotte ever found out I'd been sleeping with her dad she'd tear a right strip off me.

'I'm in the middle of tidying the kitchen,' I said. 'We had an accident.'

'A bad 'un?'

'Only broken dishes.'

'I can help.'

'No.'

''S'no bother.'

'No, really.'

'I can be there in thirty seconds.'

Through the frosted glass panel of the front door I could see the gate swinging. A familiar thin figure, his hand clamped to his ear, was trotting up the path.

'Steve, I'm fine.'

'Yeah? I don't think y'are.'

The doorbell rang and his face appeared against the glass, grinning. 'Come on, Karen, let me take your mind off housework for half an hour, eh?'

It acts as a kind of decompression, the journey between home and uni. As we drive over the Pennines, mentally I'm swimming up through the depths of one identity to surface as someone else. It's exhausting, horrible. Each time I think I'll never manage it.

We were on the M6 before I tuned into what Daniel was saying, and it turned out he was considering the implications of human evolution and how, in a million years or so, women might not be able to give birth naturally because our skulls were getting bigger. 'Too big to fit through the pelvic girdle,' he was saying. 'Reaching a critical diameter. Which wouldn't necessarily be a problem if society retains or improves its current level of technology, so that medical intervention becomes the norm and babies can routinely be extracted via Caesareans. But in the event of an apocalypse, the collapse of civilisation, that type of thing, we'd be stuffed. We'd pretty much die out within a handful of generations.'

I glanced across at him, at his mad hair and wire-framed glasses, his earnest grip on the steering wheel.

'Do you mind if we talk about something else?'

'Oh, OK.'

It was pissing down. The windscreen-wipers were squeaking in a really annoying way and I wanted to wind the window down, lean out and wrench one off.

'Are there any paracetamol in this car?' I asked.

'Possibly. Mum might have left some in the glove compartment. Got a headache?'

'Yes.'

I opened the flap and gave the contents a half-hearted poke. A load of Glacier mints tumbled out but I didn't bother to pick them up. Little minty bastards, they'd only done it to spite me. By now there was so much spray coming off the lorry wheels around us it was like sitting inside a carwash. Mum must have told Daniel about twenty times to go carefully, as if he's ever anything other than careful – he's Mr Careful – but it's other drivers you have to watch out for. Despite the rain there were guys in the fast lane dicking about, tailgating and flashing their headlights as if they *wanted* to cause an accident. I mean, fine, they can go ahead and smash themselves to bits for all I care, but I'm damned if they're taking me with them.

'Well, I can't find your bloody tablets,' I said, whacking the glove compartment shut.

'No? Not to worry. We'll stop at the next services.'

Somewhere during this last hour or so I'd ripped my own heart out and lobbed it onto the tarmac behind us. Splat, it had gone, a lump of wet offal disappearing under the tyres of some massive lorry, blood smearing across the greasy surface of the road and mingling with the diesel. I thought, If only I was able to drive, I'd grab that steering wheel and take us straight home again. Then I could be back with Will, cuddling him. The memory of his small hands made me shiver with longing.

'Shall I turn the heating up for you, Charlotte? Are you too cold?'

'I'm FINE.'

Not that I ever would learn to drive, with Dad teaching me. Casual isn't the word; he thinks an amber light means *Put your foot down.* I've said to Mum it's the blind leading the blind, but she lets him get on with it because of how much real lessons cost.

'How about I switch the radio on. Is that OK?'

I shrugged unhelpfully. Now Daniel wasn't sure what to do. I knew I was being mean but I didn't care.

He pushed the button anyway. Unluckily we got Westlife singing 'Seasons In The Sun'.

I said, 'If I have to listen to another verse of this I'm going to undo the seat belt and hurl myself out.'

'Seems a bit extreme. Five minutes and we'll be at Hartshead Moor. If you still want to fling yourself around, they have a nice car park.'

'How is this song entertainment anyway? Wailing deathbed confession.'

'So turn it off.'

I think I hate him most when he's being reasonable.

Inside the motorway services it was warm and bright and they were playing All Saints over the Tannoy, which was a marginal improvement.

'Great levellers of humanity, service stations,' said Daniel as I loaded a basket with Panadol, a magazine, jelly snakes, Coke. 'Everyone comes here and gets ripped off in equal measure.'

There was a rack of scarves by the till; I spun it, took down a length of black and red chiffon to examine.

'I'll buy you that if it'll cheer you up.'

''S'OK,' I said.

'Let me.'

I handed him the basket.

After he'd paid, I said, 'Look, Dan, go and grab a cup of tea or something. And one for me as well. I won't be long.' Then I took myself off to the toilets because I knew I badly needed to sort my head out.

Sounds feeble but the first thing I did was stick some make-up on. At home, what with looking after Will, I barely have time to bother, whereas in my student life it's kind of essential, it's who I am. I pulled out all my cosmetics from my bag and lined them up along the edge of the sink. Pouting, I re-drew my lips in scarlet, blotted them, set the colour with powder. Lined the rims of my eyes in thick black pencil, neatened the edges, did them again. Pressed my lashes up against my lids to make them stick up, and piled on some high-gloss mascara to lacquer them into place. Slicked on gold eyeshadow, swept the same brush up each cheekbone. Posed while I considered the effect. I caught the disapproving glance of an old biddy drying her hands at the towel dispenser and thought, Excellent. Somewhere in the background Lenny Kravitz was singing 'Fly Away'.

I felt around in the plastic carrier and found the scarf, drew it out, de-tagged it with my teeth, then wound it round my brow, letting the ends trail down over my shoulders. *What a state to get into*, went my mum's voice. *You look a right trollop*. To which I might say,

'Trollop is as trollop does. People in glass houses should keep their middle-aged mouths shut.' I know what she gets up to with Dad when I'm not around.

By the time I got to the café my tea was cold but it didn't matter.

'Transition accomplished?' Daniel asked.

'Pretty much.'

'How's the head?'

'Still attached to my neck.'

'Always a bonus. Drink up and we'll get going again, shall we?'

Back in the car I unpeeled the sample bottle of pink varnish from the cover of the magazine I'd bought and attempted to paint my nails. Knew even as I was unscrewing the lid that I'd never have dared risk this in anyone else's car.

The rain became blinding and we slowed almost to a crawl. 'This is all a bit tedious,' said Daniel. 'Go on, read me some of your celebrity headlines.'

'Really?'

'Yeah. Amaze me.'

The pages flopped apart, revealing a gallery of stars. 'OK, let's see. *Entertainment Round-up*: Michael Owen's been filming an ad for British Airways. Shania Twain's been slightly injured by a firework. Adam Rickitt keeps locking himself out of his Manchester flat.'

'All earth-shattering stuff then.'

'You asked. In other news, Leonardo DiCaprio was forced to swim in shark-infested waters for his new film, but escaped without injury.'

'This is why I read science journals.'

'OK, geek-boy. But I bet you don't get exciting free gifts stuck to the front cover. Or do you? "New with January's edition, this attractive pipette".'

'We don't need add-ons. The brilliance of the content's enough. In fact, my tutor's got an article in this month's *Nature*. It's about the structure and mechanism of the kinesin motor protein, how it's able to move along these long filaments called microtubules. It's actually very cool because what he's found is, the kinesin motor protein seems to *walk* along under its own steam.'

'Astounding. My day is complete.'

'No, this stuff's critical. Human life can turn on what you see down a microscope.' Daniel nodded dismissively at my mag. 'What's Britney Spears contributed to the sum of world knowledge?'

'Dunno. Hang on. Oh, it says here she recommends dipping your fingernails in pepper to stop yourself biting them.'

A petrol tanker drew up alongside us, gigantic wheels slashing through the surface water. I tried not to picture it skidding, exploding. Instead I turned the radio back on. This time I got 'Perfect Day'.

And instantly I was back in the weeks after Will was born, when the song was everywhere, and I'd be changing his nappy to it or bathing him or walking him about the house to try and stop him crying; a song about summer, in the depths of winter. A jolt of hideous longing passed through me. What the hell was I doing, letting myself be driven away from my son? How could that be right? Less than sixteen hours ago I'd sat and read him his bedtime story, pulled up his covers, made his toy monkey dance – Mum claims it's the penguin he likes best but she's wrong – kissed him night night. Earlier that day we'd gone stamping puddles on the rec. Late afternoon we'd lined his teddies up on the edge of the bed and thrown a beach ball at them till they were all knocked on the floor. He thought that was so funny. No one else can make him laugh the way I can. Afterwards I'd heated up his spaghetti hoops, run his bath. Even this actual morning I'd warmed his porridge and sat with him while he ate it, mopping up the flood of milk from his overturned cup – and there was a lot, it had taken the entire toilet toll. When he'd finished I'd lifted him down and washed his hands and face – tried to replace the toilet roll, couldn't find a new one, couldn't ask Mum because she'd swanned off down the village, had to scribble *T.ROLL* on a Post-it and stick it inside the cupboard door – by which time Will had managed to walk into the edge of the sideboard and bump his head, entirely not my fault. Mum's fault for having ancient knobbly furniture. It rips me up when he cries.

And I remembered those first two weekends at York when they brought him to visit, and what total bloody hell it had been. Everyone upset. Will screaming, Daniel pleading, Mum shouting, me threatening to jack in the degree and come straight back with them. Daniel phoning afterwards to suggest we stop the trips altogether. I'd said, 'For God's sake, that's just a line Mum's fed you.' He'd insisted it wasn't. He said he just couldn't bear to see me in such distress. 'But the plan was to see Will every weekend, either here or at Mum's,' I'd raged. 'Otherwise he'll forget me!' Touch and go it was, for the whole of that first half-term. So they ganged up together, Mum, Dad and Daniel, to convince me that wouldn't happen. It was like an assault of positivity. 'You're Will's mum,' people kept saying. 'No one's trying to take that away from you. This way, you get the best of both worlds. Don't waste your chances.' I'd said, 'I could try and get a college place nearer.' And Mum went, 'What – walk away from one of the top courses in the country, lose a year, have to start all over again?' I said, 'Nan wouldn't want me to leave him.' And Mum said, 'Nan's too poorly to understand. She wants the best for you, we all do.' In the end they wore me down and I stayed put, and now it kind of works, me coming and going, Mum standing in for the day-to-day stuff.

Partings are still shit, though. When Will was about eighteen months he became incredibly clingy, and I'd be carrying my suitcases down the path while he shrieked his head off. Once or twice I did try sneaking away while Mum kept him busy, but apparently when he realised, that made him even worse. Now I tell him I'm going and he's mostly OK. The hard truth is, *I* have to try and forget *him* while I'm away, or I'd never survive. Selective amnesia's the key to long-distance motherhood. I don't ever admit that to anyone, though, in case it sounds like I don't love him enough.

Daniel broke into my thoughts with his usual irritating brand of telepathy. 'You know, I miss him too, Charlotte.'

Oh yeah? I wanted to shout. *You have NO idea. You're not even his DAD. NO one understands. This is MY pain!* Some moments there's nothing worse than sympathy. It falls like a branding iron across your skin.

I reached forward to retune the bastard radio and noticed I'd left a smear of pearly-pink nail varnish on the dial.

What I needed now, where I really needed to be was in the student house on St Paul's Street, with Gemma and Walsh and Roz and Gareth. Crashed out in front of the TV, drinking and chatting, with my books lined up in my room and Professor Martin Eavis waiting for me at the English Department. Another twenty-four hours and it would be better – it would. If only Daniel would stop caring so much. The windows were misting us in, all the air was being sucked out of the car.

'Just get me to uni,' I said.

'I've been thinking.' Steve flopped down on the sofa next to Will and flashed me one of his winning smiles – not that it's ever won much off me. If only he could see himself. That damn moustache needs to go, for a start.

'Exhausting for you.'

'No, hear me out, Karen. I need you to give me some cash.'

'That's why you came round?'

'Well, to see you and Billy-boy here.' He gave Will a manly nudge.

'I haven't time for this. Some of us have work to do.'

I left them watching *Story Makers* and ran upstairs. Will's cup I eventually located on Charlotte's pillow so I grabbed it, unhooked one of his hooded tops which was hanging off the back of her chair, and was about to whizz back down to Steve when I caught sight of Charlotte's mobile phone propped on the windowsill next to the landing mirror. How in God's name had she managed to leave that? Distracted by last-minute fussing, no doubt. That meant something else for me to sort out, hunting down a Jiffy bag, paying for Special Delivery.

My own reflection was disastrous. I looked like one of those 'before' women in a makeover programme. My cheeks were flushed, my hair frizzy and unstyled, and the more I tried to smooth it down, the wilder it got. If Charlotte had been about I could have asked her for help, she knows about these straightening sprays and tongs and what have you, although she'd definitely have taken the opportunity to have a laugh first. That's how she is: unsympathetic. I gave up on the hair and instead went back into my bedroom, wiped some powder across my face then slicked a bit of gloss over my lips. That was better. Then I thought, Bloody hell, it's only Steve, why are you bothering?

I stuffed the phone in my pocket alongside the sock and stomped back downstairs. 'Right, then, what do you want this money for?'

'Just a sec,' Steve said, waving his hand for me to be quiet. On the TV screen, Bob the Builder lectured a blue digger. 'We're seeing whether they get the bunkhouse built in time for the Scout camp sing-along.'

I swept past and left him to it. There was the kitchen floor yet to deal with, never mind the immediate danger that if I hung around I might try and stove his skull in with Nan's biscuit barrel.

By the time he did come through I was almost finished. 'Do you need a hand with owt?' he said, surveying the dustbin bags and kitchen roll and bowl of soapy water.

'Perfect timing, as ever. It's done now.'

He stooped to pick up an escaped Cheerio. 'You should have shouted me.'

I said, 'This money.'

'Oh, aye. Yeah. Well. It is mine, Karen.'

'I know that. But you asked me to look after it for you. You told me to hang on to it like grim death and not let you blow it on some spree.'

'Yeah. Only, I've got it into my head I wanna buy a bike.'

'A bike?' True he was on the skinny side, but there were the beginnings of a middle-age paunch under that T-shirt. Not surprising when you considered the amount of beer he put away at weekends. 'I suppose it'll keep you fit.'

'Nah, norra pushbike. A motorbike.'

'You what?'

'I've seen this Kwacker up in Chorley—'

'Talk English.'

'This Kawasaki ZXR 750. The guy's keen to get rid before his bank has it off him.'

'You want to buy a motorbike. You.'

'I had one before.'

'When? I know when you left school you had that scooter, used to conk out if you went up a hill. You're not counting that, are you?'

His moustache bristled. 'Course not. I had an RD 250 LC. It was after we split up, you never saw it. I did my test and I bought it straight after.'

'Oh? News to me. However did you afford that?'

'Aw, well, it weren't a right lot. I got it for cash and it was pretty old. And what it was, I'd done a spot of extra work for a mate. Nothing illegal, it were just holding on to a few bits and pieces, summat he'd come across unexpectedly, till he—'

I waved my hand at him. 'Stop there.'

'I'm only saying. I needed that bike, it were special. It got me through a grim time.'

'Don't talk to me about grim times.'

Will appeared in the doorway. 'Juice, Grandma.'

I handed the beaker to Steve. 'There you go, that's something you can do to help.'

Meanwhile I wiped down the sink and bleached it, pushed swollen Cheerios through the plughole. Outside, the bare hedge next to the coal shed shivered with sparrows. Will's yellow wheelbarrow lay and mouldered on the scruffy lawn.

Steve came to lean against the unit next to me.

'So can I have that money, or what?'

'No. It's your redundancy package. It's supposed to last you. Don't make that face at me.'

'What face?'

I dried my hands and looked at him. 'The payment was a one-off, and you've already had a car out of it. You're not going to get another lump sum next week, are you? I mean, not that I wish to be picky, but you'd actually have to be employed for that.'

'Well, *I* wanted you to use the cash for your teacher training, if you remember. Only that particular plan seems to have gone off the boil.'

'Not my fault, is it? Two years to do A levels, three to get a degree, one more for my teaching certificate, I'd be about ninety by the time I'd finished. And I'm lucky to have that classroom assistant post as it is; there's any number of mums waiting to jump into my shoes if I give it up and slope off to college.'

Steve scratched his head. 'It sounds daft to me, having to pass all them extra exams when you already know what you're doing. Can't that headmaster of yours swing summat for you?'

'Leo? Don't talk soft. It's not up to him. He can't magic me up a teaching qualification.'

'I don't see why not. It's his school.'

'Have you any idea, Steve, how the actual real world works? Anyway, how could I start a college course when I've Will to look after?'

'I've told you, I'll have him. I'll help.'

'Then how would *you* have the time to look for another job?'

He reached out to put his arms round me and, damn it, I didn't step away.

'Eeh, we're a pair, aren't we, Karen?'

'No. We very much aren't.'

'Aw, come on.' He tightened his grip around me. I laid my head on his chest, wearily.

I said, 'You're having a mid-life crisis, aren't you? Middle-aged men and motorbikes. I've read about it. Trying to claw back the past.'

'Nowt wrong with that. Everyone wants to hold onto a bit of their youth. What about you and your family history project, all your tapes and family trees and old photos?'

'That's to do with the future. It's for Will, so he'll know where he came from.'

'Well, there you are.' Steve's hand on my back, roaming. 'What's so bad about taking the best from what you had and bringing it into the present?'

'I'm not sleeping with you again. I always hate myself after.'

'Shh. We're having a little cuddle, that's all.'

'As long as you know.'

'Course.'

He moved in for a kiss. A ringing started up in my ears.

'That's Charlotte's mobile,' I said.

By the time we reached the ring road, I'd pretty much shed the mother-gloom. Funny, it's like taking off a massive old coat, all heavy and comforting and stifling, and you're ages fighting with the sleeves and you think you'll never get out from under it and yet once it starts to go, it slips off fast.

Then came a rush of light-headedness and excitement. I started thinking about my plans for the term and my reading list, essay topics to cover the Augustans through to the Romantics, and what I was going to talk about with Martin Eavis. What I was going to talk about with the others, the holiday gossip and news. This term it would all be comparing millenniums, who'd been having the craziest time the moment Big Ben chimed. Gareth and Roz I knew had been headed for Cardiff to see the Manics gig. Gemma had a rave planned in Glastonbury. Walsh's dad was supposedly flying him to Prague for some bash there.

As for me, I was right outside the competition because I'd spent the Ultimate New Year's Eve sitting in front of the TV watching *Goodbye to the '90s* with my parents. I've checked in the Encyclopaedia of Sad and it doesn't get any sadder than that. 'Mum, what were you doing as the millennium dawned?' Will is going to ask me at some point in the future. And I'll have to say, 'Arguing with your grandma about whether or not you should be allowed to stay up.' And he'll say, 'Whose side were you on?' And I'll say, 'Yours, of course, because I am the best mum ever.' And we will high-five, or whatever it is twenty-first-century youth do to express solidarity.

In the end I'd got my way and carried him back downstairs in his pyjamas, but by nine o'clock he was conked out on the sofa so Mum sort of won that one. At five to midnight I jiggled him awake, and at 12.01 a.m. Daniel rang the front doorbell and brought a lump of coal across the threshold, which Will then tried to eat. Afterwards, while Mum put my son to bed, I went out on the lawn and watched the fireworks explode over Rivington Pike. Daniel said, 'I wonder what the next thousand years will bring?' and I said, 'Mortgages, wrinkles and death.' When we went back inside, Dad was trying to kiss Mum although he pretended he wasn't. Daniel left, and I lay awake till two, listening to a woman in the street shouting, 'Please, Barry, please,' over and over. In the morning our front garden was full of silly string.

'Why don't you ring your mum,' Daniel was saying now, as we pulled into St Paul's Street. 'Let her know you've arrived safely.' Sometimes I suspect he's a forty-year-old man trapped in a twenty-year-old's body.

'Yeah, all right. Well.' I was patting my pockets, shifting bags with my feet. 'I would if I could find my phone.'

'You haven't left it behind?'

'I don't *know*. No. I had it when I got in the car.'

'Did you?'

'Not sure. No, I didn't. Oh, it's no good. Give us your mobile. I can ring myself and then we'll hear it.'

He passed it across and I keyed in my number. An ominous silence followed.

'Maybe you're out of signal range.'

'I'm not.'

'Ah.'

'Fuck.'

'Your mum'll pop it in the post for you.'

'Yeah, and have a trawl through my texts while she's at it.'

'She wouldn't do that.'

'Shows how well you know her, Daniel. Honestly, the less you tell her, the nosier she gets. It's really infuriating.'

'She's only trying to watch out for you.'

'Stop bloody defending her, will you? Oh, hang on, here she is.'

I held the little phone to my ear and she went, 'Mum? Mum?' all cross, as though it was somehow *my* fault she'd left her mobile sitting in Bank Top.

I said, 'You put it down by the landing mirror. I can post it first thing tomorrow.'

'Not this afternoon?'

'The health visitor's coming. You know that.'

There was some muttering, then she said, 'All right. But while you're here, can you check if my Dryden notes are in my bedside drawer? I meant to clip them in my file but I don't think I did. I need them as well.'

'What, you want me to go and look now?'

Obviously. Everything always has to be right that minute with our Charlotte. I handed the phone to Steve, who took it off me as though it was a live scorpion. 'Say hello to your daughter,' I ordered.

After Mum had rung off I had to stop myself flinging Daniel's phone down and grinding it into its component parts with my boot heel. 'Are you still remembering to take your pill?' she'd asked me. For fuck's sake. 'Are you remembering to take *yours*?' I should have said.

'Sorted?' Daniel enquired.

'Uh-huh.' I took some deep breaths. I needed to remember it was Mum I was angry with, not him. An effort was needed. 'Look, do you have to get straight off or can you come in for a brew?'

He switched off the car engine and sat back, his brow furrowed.

'No, I'll pass. I have to get back to Manchester. There's a lot of stuff to set up in the lab before term starts. And I need to check in with my mother—'

'Course.'

'So I'll give you a hand with your bags but then I've got to be straight off. '

Rain dribbled down the windscreen in jagged paths.

I said, 'Dad's there. Round at ours.'

'Thought the conversation sounded a bit stilted.'

'I suppose now the coast's clear they'll be all over each other again. It's ridiculous at her age. She should be past it. And what does she think she's doing, raking up the marriage when it died bloody years ago? I mean, either she wants him or she doesn't. She should make up her mind. The worst thing is this ludicrous pretence that nothing's going on between them. Does she think I'm stupid, or what?'

'Put her out of her misery, then. Talk to her.'

'About her sex-life?' I mimed extreme horror. 'Oh, yeah, top idea. Tell you what, I'll book us on *The Jeremy Kyle Show* and we can have it out in front of a live studio audience.'

Daniel closed his eyes for a moment. 'Give it a rest, hey, Charlotte?'

We sat side by side with the water drumming on the car roof. The drainpipe between our house and next door was sputtering onto the pavement furiously.

I said, 'I'm really sorry. It's not you. You get that, don't you?'

I just feel as if my insides were fish-hooked to a bungee cord, and the further away from Bank Top we drive, the more it pulls my guts to ribbons. And I'm sick of feeling this way and not being able to keep saying it for fear of boring everyone.

He sighed, pushed his glasses further up the bridge of his nose. 'Look, go and see your tutor, Martin Whatshisface. He always straightens you out, doesn't he?'

'Martin Eavis. Yeah, I will.'

'Tell him to read poetry at you or play you Telemann till you cheer up.'

'OK.'

'OK, then.'

'Do you really have to go?'

'I do.'

'Why the hell do you put up with me, Daniel?'

He only leaned across, kissed my forehead, and opened the driver's side door.

As soon as Steve left I got the mobile back out and began to fiddle. After all, if Charlotte was in bother, I might be able to help her. In fact, the more I thought about it, the more I decided I had a right to know. Where was *Contacts* on this phone? Where was *Call Log*? Why did they have to make every model different? Mine was a Nokia too, but nearly twice the size. Fiddly bloody buttons, teeny screen. Right, *Messages*, that would do. You see, if my daughter *talked* to me, if she was more open, I wouldn't be forced to snoop around like this.

The last text she'd received was from me, asking why she hadn't got her phone switched on. Message two was from Daniel: Abidec Toddler Vitamin Drops, his father recommended. Well, his dad was a doctor, he'd know. Another message from Daniel: running a half-hour late because his mother had banged her head. From Daniel again: *Big kiss for Will. Bigger kiss for you.*

Such a lovely boy.

Raft of messages from before Christmas, mainly indecipherable rubbish from her flatmates, Gemma and Roz. None of them seemed to be able to spell, for all they were at university. Also, how many hours a day did Charlotte waste answering these nuggets of gibberish when she should've had her head down, working? That wasn't what we got her the phone for. God, if she veered off-track now, in her second year, after all that effort, I'd never forgive her—

Wait, what was this one now: *Soz abt lst nt. Cn stll b frnds?* My heart speeded up and I scrolled down quickly to see the name at the bottom: *W*, it was signed. Dated a week before she came home.

I could guess who W was: Walsh, or Walshy, or Walshman, she called him, the other member of the house. Not Roz's boyfriend, because he was called Gareth Thomas, like the rugby player. Walsh was Charlotte's landlord, if you please.

I'd said over the summer, 'One man sharing with three girls? What's going on there?' And she said it was his house and he could let it to whoever he liked. And I said I didn't like the sound of that either. What was a lad of twenty doing owning property? What would happen if any of them couldn't pay their rent – what would he ask for in lieu? And she said I had a nasty mind and that he was nice and a mate of Gemma's. 'You don't know what it's like to share a house. It's a different relationship with flatmates,' she'd said.

You know nothing, Mother, is what she meant. I knew enough to count one man and three girls.

I read the text again. *Soz*, was he? For what, exactly? I navigated back to *Sent Messages* to see if she'd replied, but there was nothing. No, well. I may not be on top of my Text Speak, but I'm not a fool. I get what sorry about last night means when it comes from a lad. And it proves I was right to check her phone. Call it mother's instinct: I *knew* she was unsettled. I pick it up like a radio signal.

So now there's Daniel, our smashing Daniel, a GP's son, always available, always accommodating. Wonderful with Will, super-polite with me, comes into the house like a ray of sunshine. I've told him he needs to stand up for himself more, but he's not made that way. Love seems to have filleted him.

Then there's this Walshy, wide boy, stirrer. Once went to a

lecture so hungover he fell down the theatre steps, apparently. Famous for catching a seagull under a towel and letting it loose in Woolworths. He's a show-off and a twit, the last kind of male I want anywhere near our Charlotte. I bet his dad's not a doctor, either.

Always there's this destructive streak in her, always she manages to scupper her own chances. Where in God's name does she get it from?

NAN: What have you got there, Karen?

KAREN: Hang on a minute, Mum. Is it working? How can you tell it's working?

CHARLOTTE: There's a red light.

KAREN: Oh, I see. Right. And it's this button to pause, is it? Which one do you press to play back?

CHARLOTTE: Did you hear about the businessman who asked his boss if he could use his dictaphone? And his boss said, 'No, you can use your finger like everyone else.'

KAREN: You're not helping, Charlotte.

NAN: Is it a cigarette-lighter?

KAREN: Ah, right, I see now. I get it. You hold both buttons down at the same time. OK, Nan, we're ready to go. This is a tape recorder, only it's a lot smaller than the one we had before. I'll pop it here on the chair arm, OK? And then you just forget about it. And we'll carry on chatting, yes? About the family, the past, whatever you remember.

CHARLOTTE: Can *I* ask Nan something?

KAREN: No one's stopping you.

CHARLOTTE: OK, Nan? Nan? Can you tell us about how you met Granddad?

NAN: Oh, well. Your granddad. Aye. Well, I were carrying a basket o' washing back to t'doctor's – my mother did his laundry for him – and it were blowing about and I were worried it'd end up on t'ground and get mucky – because it were all day of a job, washing then, and hard work – and Bill come over, crossed t'street and laid his coat on top. Then he took a handle and walked alongside me. It were a lot easier to carry wi' two.

CHARLOTTE: Aw, that's lovely. And what happened then? Did he ask you out? Did he kiss you?

NAN: He went off to t'convalescent home in Blackpool. He had TB. I didn't see him for months.

CHARLOTTE: Oh no! How awful. Could you not go up and visit him on the train?

NAN: (laughs) I were only nineteen, I'd never been further than Harrop. We hadn't the money to be getting on trains.

KAREN: No, and you couldn't even speak to him because you had no telephone in those days.

NAN: Aye, so he met this girl there—

KAREN: Alice Fitton.

NAN: That were her name, a bonny woman. Older than him. From up Chorley way – her father ran an ironmonger's.

KAREN: And you were working at the mill.

NAN: At Jarrod's, aye.

KAREN: And then what happened? She had an accident, this Alice Fitton, didn't she?

(NAN laughs guiltily.)

KAREN: What happened, Mum?

NAN: It were a shame. She'd come t'have her tea with Bill's mother – now she was a fierce woman, old Mrs Hesketh.

Very religious, wouldn't even knit on a Sunday. Did I ever tell you about her?

CHARLOTTE: What happened to Alice, Nan?

(NAN laughs again.)

KAREN: Didn't she come a-cropper by the butcher's?

NAN: Aye, well, what happened was, she were walking past t'shop door and t'butcher threw a pail o' swill all over her legs.

KAREN: That's the water they use for wiping down the surfaces at the end of the day, Charlotte. Water with blood and scraps of meat in it, basically.

CHARLOTTE: I know.

NAN: All up her dress, it went, over her stockings and shoes. So when she got to Bill's house—

KAREN: I don't suppose his mother was very impressed when she turned up in that state.

CHARLOTTE: Oh my God. Bet she stank!

NAN: It were a shame, aye.

CHARLOTTE: So why are you smiling?

(NAN laughs.)

KAREN: And it finished? They had a row and she broke off the engagement?

NAN: Aye.

KAREN: So you and Granddad started courting.

NAN: We did.

KAREN: And he was cured of TB by then?

NAN: Well, he allus had a weak chest. That's what killed him in t'finish, his lungs.

KAREN: But he played the tenor horn in the pit band.

NAN: Oh aye. For a bit. He'd a beautiful tone.

KAREN: And you were married how long?

NAN: Forty years. He died in seventy-nine.

CHARLOTTE: That's amazing. So how did you know he was The One?

(NAN laughs.)

CHARLOTTE: Seriously, Nan, how did you know you wanted to marry him? What made you wait?

KAREN: Don't pester her if she doesn't want to answer.

CHARLOTTE: I just wanted to know.

(Sound of knocking on the door.)

CARE ASSISTANT: Mrs Hesketh, it's time for your – oh, I didn't realise you had visitors. Can I just get these tablets down her? Is that OK? Won't be a tick.

KAREN: It's all right. We were only really experimenting today.

CHARLOTTE: Shall I switch the tape off?

KAREN: No, I'm nearest. I'll get it.

CHARLOTTE: Oh, have you brought that photo of Will, Mum, or did we leave it on the—'

CHAPTER 2

On a day in February

Yorkshire sun streamed through the window of my student room, making even the shabby wallpaper look cheerful. Nan's kittens-in-a-basket picture, which I'd hung over my desk next to a sheet of Will's mad daubs, was positively illuminated. Shards of light from my hanging crystal crossed and re-crossed the duvet, my planner, my waiting backpack. Thank God the night was over. The dark hours.

And I was getting ready to see Martin again. Not that I was due for a tutorial, but I wanted to ask about extending my reading and also for some thoughts on the next essay title. I doubted he had any idea what a treat it was for me to sit in his office, inhaling the wood polish and admiring the shelves of books. He'd pour me a cup of real coffee which I thought tasted disgusting but drank anyway so as not to appear common. He might ask – I hoped he would – how things were going, four weeks into the new term. Then I could tell him about the Will-dreams: how quashing thoughts of my son during the daytime only made them resurface later, in super-horrible form. Because in these dreams I'm never doing any normal activity with Will. No squirting woodlice off the entry wall, or building towers of custard creams. No making hedgehogs out of mashed potato. Instead it's always some really sinister, upsetting scenario such as last night's special, which was that Will was trapped on a rollercoaster on his own and the man who owned it wouldn't pull the lever to make it stop. And it was *Mum's* fault – that's right, now the detail was coming back to me – Mum had paid for him to go on the ride even though the rules were that you had to be over six and accompanied by a parent, but she'd stuck him in a seat, pulled down the bar and then buggered off to buy some Vim. And I had to fill in some kind of special form before the man would let Will off. I can't remember what happened next, just it was the morning and I was awake.

Martin, I knew, would listen to these ramblings and be sensible and kind. He understood about being apart from your child because his wife had left him last year and taken his nine-year-old daughter with her. He had a picture on his desk (of the girl, not the mother) and in the past I'd pretended to admire it and said how sad it was when families broke up. I'd told him about Dad living at the other end of the village, and how Mum and I had managed to muddle along without him OK. For Martin's sake I'd stressed how, although things were sometimes tricky, e.g. with money, I hadn't been in any way *damaged* by growing up in a dad-free home. I didn't really feel I'd missed out in any way. Dad was only at the end of the village if I wanted him. And I think Martin appreciated my telling him that. He wasn't just a brilliant tutor, we really talked to each other, adult to adult.

Which was important because, although the student house was fun, there wasn't a right lot of serious discussion went on. Roz was good for a chat but she could be a bit silly, especially with a drink inside her. Her parents were Methodists and very strict; Lord knows what they'd have thought if they could have seen her on a Saturday night outside the union, so wrecked she had to lean against a wall to keep from falling over.

Gemma was cooler. Her mum was French, which gave her an edge straight away. She was smarter at handling the booze, she went out most nights and she dressed sharper than me and Roz. She spoke less, was more reserved. It had been a surprise when she and Walshy got together. 'Chalk and cheese,' said Roz to me privately. 'I just don't get it.' I'd said, 'I suppose they're both nice-looking.' And Roz had rolled her eyes as if to suggest she was glad *she* wasn't afflicted by physical beauty. She said, 'It won't last. He collects women.' She didn't seem to notice how quiet I went after that.

So there was another reason for getting out of the house this morning. I knew the girls were at lectures, and it made me twitchy when it was just him and me on our own.

I reached for my backpack, squinting against the sunlight, and unhooked my jacket from the chair. But as I did so, one of the shoulders caught and the chair toppled over with a massive crash. 'Fuck,' I said.

'Chaz? Is that you?'

Too late, he'd heard me. 'Yeah. I'm going out.'

'Just come and have a look at this.'

'I'm in a hurry,' I lied.

'Won't take a minute. You'll be impressed.'

I drew in a long breath and stepped out onto the landing. From there, a sharp chemical smell hit me. 'Jesus, Walshy. What the hell?'

'Come and see.'

The door of his room was wide open. I looked in and saw that he was kneeling by the open window, painting the sill a violent acid green.

'God's sake,' I said, stepping through the door. 'What have you been doing?'

'Shaving a poodle.'

'Oh, you're killing me.'

He was wearing his University of Central Yorkshire T-shirt with its *You See Why (UCY)* slogan. We'd all bought one during Fresher's Week, before we realised they were naffer than naff and only fit for covering your nakedness when everything else was in the wash.

I said, 'If you carry on with that, you won't get your deposit back.'

'Yeah, that landlord, he's a bastard.'

'Seriously, though, what? That colour's vandalism in a tin. What's it called? Burnt Retina?'

'This is home improvement, this is.' He propped the brush across the pot and stood up to survey his progress. 'The paint was all flaking off before.'

'Did you strip the wood before you started? Or even sand it? Tell me you at least wiped the dead flies away.'

He flashed a roguish smile. 'It's created a nice textured effect.'

I watched him overload the brush, gloop paint in a pool onto the windowsill, then try and persuade it evenly over the lumps and ridges. In places it was so thick I knew it would take weeks to harden. Bristles were detaching themselves at every stroke. At least he'd thought to rest the pot on a magazine.

I sat down on the end of the bed. 'You know, if you'd been after some home improvement, you could simply have cleared the floor.'

Next to the rucked-up duvet a drawer of socks lay tipped on its side. There was a scattering of pens over the carpet as if someone had emptied them there deliberately. A beanie hat was lodged across his bedside lampshade. Unpaired footwear lay distributed at odd intervals, like a children's picture puzzle: *How many trainers can you spot hidden around the room?* The more I looked, in fact, the more I could see out of place. There were bright squares in the dust on top of the table where objects had been recently removed, a desk tidy slung underneath a chair, empty hooks on the wall. 'It's a bit chaotic today, even by your standards. Has Gemma been having a clear-out?'

'You could say that.'

'Meaning?'

'She's moved back to her old room. We've broken up.'

I stared at him. 'No. When? Why?'

'Last night. Late, late last night. Morning.'

'My God.'

'Don't look so worried, Chaz.'

'It wasn't—'

'—anything to do with you. Or me, actually.'

'You sure?'

'Uh huh.' He glanced up. 'She reckons she's gay.'

'Eh?'

'Woke up one morning, found she was a dyke.'

'Don't use that word. It's horrible.'

'She used it herself.'

My head was reeling. 'Is this a wind-up, Walshy? Because if it is, it's in really poor taste.'

All the time he never stopped his painting, the brush sweeping backwards and forwards through the ugly-bright mess. 'Go ask her. If it *is* a wind-up, it's hers.'

I thought, No, even you wouldn't set up a joke like that. He must be telling the truth. 'Blimey. So is there someone else? A girl, I mean.'

'Dunno. There's no need to get stressed over it, though. Me and her, we're not going to turn into the housemates from hell, throwing plates and screaming down the stairs at each other. We'll just go back to how we were when she first moved in – you know, friends. It was probably time we wound it up anyway.'

'And have I to tell Roz?'

''S'up to you. Fuck, I've dripped on the curtain. Pass us that towel, will you?' He frowned at the curtain hem, spat on it, then scrubbed vigorously. 'I suppose you'll be saying I should have taken these down before I started.'

'It makes no odds now. You need proper paint-remover on that. Have you any white spirit?'

'Is that like absinthe?'

'No.'

'Oh. Can we not just stick it in the washing-machine?'

'I wouldn't have thought so. It's gloss you're using, isn't it? Not emulsion.'

'Search me. I asked for a tin of paint, that's all I know. The guy in the shop never said.'

I went over to his desk and grabbed the chair, dragged it across to the window.

'What you doing, Chaz?'

'Saving your curtains.' I stepped carefully up till my head was level with the rail. 'If Gemma or Roz have any nail-varnish remover, we might be OK. So long as we act fast.'

'Not Roz. She bites her nails to stumps.'

'Gemma, then. Look, can you at least take hold of the hem end for me, stop it falling in the paint?'

One by one the plastic hooks clicked off neatly under my fingers. When I glanced down, however, I saw that in stretching across, he'd managed somehow to press the other curtain up against the wet paint. 'Ah,' he said when I pointed.

'It's on your jeans too. Stay where you are and I'll unclip that side while I'm up here.' My arms were aching and I was desperate not to mark my own clothes. 'Just watch you don't knock that tin. Oh, shit. Too late. Right, stand still and *don't* step off that magazine. Don't! Yes, it's on your shoe as well. But if you stay on the paper you'll save the carpet.'

He stood quietly with his head bowed while I finished and climbed down. The curtains I balled up, paint smudges tucked away inside, and thrust against his chest. Then I knelt, the way I do to help Will with his shoes, and eased Walshy's feet out of his trainers; guided him off the island of magazines and made him sit on the bed and remove his T-shirt. 'You'll need to take your jeans off too. We'll stick them all in a hot wash together after we've had a go with the varnish remover. No promises, but it's worth a try.'

I could feel his eyes on me throughout. Eventually he said, 'You always know how to fix everything. You're like our mum, the House Mum.'

His pale bare shoulders gleamed under the electric light.

'Get stripped,' I said. 'I'll see you down in the kitchen.'

The morning began with body parts in the garden and ended with a dead neighbour.

It was Will who spotted the debris. There were tiny plastic limbs strewn across our back lawn, a 9-inch propeller lodged in the flowering currant. He came running to me with a fistful of pieces he'd gathered. 'Little man broken,' he said, which was a pretty accurate assessment.

Together we hunted down the rest and brought them inside to reassemble. It helped that I knew what I was making. Old Mr Cottle's lumberjack windmill has been poking up over the top of our back fence for at least two years. The structure sits on a pole, like a bird-table, and with every passing breeze the blades rotate and the miniature man bends forward and mimes a chopping action. Pointless as well as ugly, not to mention way too light and flimsy for the job. Three times now the lumberjack's ended up on our side, blown from his moorings *Wizard of Oz*-style. Sometimes he arrives intact, sometimes he's been blasted apart. My impulse today was just to bin the bloody thing, put him out of his windy misery.

I didn't owe Tommy Cottle anything, either. He wasn't a nice man. Never one of these grandfatherly types who handed out sweets and smiles and liked to pass the time of day. If he spoke at all it would usually be to moan about Will being noisy. In the last eighteen months he'd tipped grass clippings down the gap behind our currant bushes, phoned the council to say we were breeding rats under the shed, and prised a fence panel apart to help his bag-of-bones cat use our flowerbed as a toilet. Not so much a character as an old git. Once he even made the front page of the local paper for trying to nick crocus bulbs from round the War Memorial.

So basically he's been a crap neighbour from the moment he arrived, and no court in the land would have convicted me if one night I'd set his lumberjack on fire and danced round the flames cheering. But I knew he'd been in hospital again recently and that nobody had visited him – he told me that himself, as if he'd been expecting me to trot up there with a bag of fruit and a copy of the *Racing Times* – and overall my feeling's been I've enough on my plate without encouraging a war in my own back yard.

For this reason Will and I took the trouble to snap the plastic lumberjack into working order, spent a fun time testing him out, then put on our coats and trooped round the corner to Mr Cottle's front door.

There was no reply to our ringing or knocking, but the car was in the drive and I could see his mobility scooter parked in the hall behind the bevelled glass. Given he can't walk to the end of the street these days unaided, I guessed he must be inside. I opened the letterbox and shouted his name.

'Watch, Grandma,' said Will, running down the metal disability ramp with thumping, clanging strides.

'Shh,' I told him.

All I could hear from inside was the muffled sound of the TV.

'Let's try round the back,' I said, laying the lumberjack on the gravel next to the ramp and taking my grandson's hand. I had a sudden prickle about what we might find, and though I'd rather Will had stayed outside, he was just too young to be left unsupervised.

At the rear of the house the garden was neat, wheeliebins labelled, planters and tubs emptied ready for spring. Will poked at the cat-flap and I tried the door handle. It gave, and we were in. The kitchen smelled of toast overlaid with menthol and chemical toilet; in the sink sat a milk pan half-full of water, but aside from that the room was fairly tidy. A clutch of money-saving coupons was bulldog-clipped to a *Bonnie Scotland* wall calendar, pots of Brylcreem were stacked into a tower, his mugs hung symmetrically from a wooden rack. Even his pan scourer was tucked into the mouth of a china frog sitting on the windowsill.

'Here, play with this,' I said, picking up the frog and handing it to Will. Needs must as the devil drives.

I could see across the hall into the lounge. On the TV screen, a blonde presenter was helping a middle-aged woman step onto some weighing scales. The top of Mr C's head showed over the back of an armchair. I led Will into the hall, closed the kitchen door behind us, set him to feed his frog on the floor. Then I made myself walk into the room.

Tommy Cottle was sitting upright with his eyes open, and for a split second I thought he was OK. I'd been a fool crashing in, over-dramatic. Words of apology formed on my lips. But the next second I knew.

'Mr Cottle?' I said hopelessly. A quick glance at Will to check he was occupied, then I leaned forward and pressed the old man's shoulder. 'Mr Cottle? Tommy?' There was no response. His face was perfectly peaceful.

'OK, Grandma has to make a phone call, we need to go,' I said. I stepped backwards and, though I was trying to be careful, my leg caught against a small table with a mug of coffee on top. The mug slid off and bounced onto the floor, sloshing beige liquid across the beige carpet.

Will looked up, only mildly interested. 'Frog's hungry. Yum yum.'

I knew it wasn't the time to be worrying about stains, but I couldn't stop myself picking up the mug and placing it back on the table. The action made me shiver and almost drop the mug again: the china was still very slightly warm. However Mr Cottle had died, it had been both recent and quick.

I stood in Gemma's doorway and scanned her room. Huge black and white poster of Jean Harlow over her bed, tumble of shoes under the window, clutch of Aldi carrier bags dumped on her dressing-table. The wardrobe was open a crack and I could see clothes spilling out from the bottom. I had this sudden picture of her scooping her belongings together and making trip after trip up and down the stairs while Walsh sat by and watched. Gemma staggering in here, dropping things, rooting through them, throwing armfuls into the cupboard, not bothering with hangers or folded piles and then trying to jam the door closed, swearing, leaving it. My mum's like that. She believes inanimate objects are in league against her.

I made my way between the piles of Gemma's history books and poked around the dressing-table. One of the plastic bags I could see straight away was full of make-up, so I had a rummage and brought up two bottles of nail polish. The second bag was all hair products, and the next, Ventolin inhalers, painkillers, eczema cream, tampons. Finally, at the bottom of the fourth bag, a pot of varnish-remover pads.

There was no time to waste. I'd run to the kitchen now, scrub the paint-marks, then put the pot back before she came home from lectures.

And yet I stayed a few moments, staring at Jean Harlow and trying to work out what I felt. Gemma gay and Walshy free. Us all together, in the same house.

Just thinking about it made my head spin.

After the ambulance men had been and gone, the niece turned up. She was what Mum would have called hard-faced. Older than me, bone-thin, dyed black hair. 'You're the one who found him?' she asked.

'I'd fetched his little chopper.'

She narrowed her eyes. 'Eh?'

'He has this . . . thing, plastic, windmill. A man.' I seemed to have lost the power to construct a sentence. 'A garden orna-ment. It blew over. Our fence.'

She was only half-listening, her gaze roving round the room, and I thought, She's doing an inventory. She's thinking, What did he leave me in his will? I felt like saying, 'Sorry, am I in your way?'

'And he was in this chair?'

'That's right.'

'What's this mark here?' She pointed to the carpet. 'Did he wet himself?'

'That was me,' I said.

'Eh?'

'I mean, I knocked over a drink. He'd made a drink. Before he died. I don't mean I made a drink while I was here.' *I haven't filched anything, you grasping cow.*

'You live over the back?'

'Yes. With my grandson.' Will was at the table, good as gold, scribbling over a colouring book. 'We didn't see a lot of Mr Cottle. I know he'd had a spell in hospital a while ago.'

'Creaking gate. It was a shock, though, I thought he'd go on forever.'

'Well, you do. When my mother died, we knew she was ill, but even so—'

'Can you take the cat?'

She took me completely off-guard. 'Cat?'

'He has a cat.'

'Oh, yes, I know, but I don't think—'

'Otherwise we'll have to get it put down. Which would be a shame.'

'Can't you have it?'

'Not allowed. I'm allergic.'

Bet you aren't, I thought.

'It can't have that much longer to live. Six months tops, I'd say. It'd be nice for your little lad there, to have a nice pet. You'd like a cat, wouldn't you, love?' she called across to Will.

Straight away I should have said, *Sorry, I can't manage that, but shall I look up the vet's number for you?* There was this small window of opportunity where I could have turned my back and not left the house seething at myself, a tatty basket under my arm. 'What about the RSPCA?'

'I don't think it would survive. On its last legs, that one. It'd be cruel to stick it in a pen at this stage.'

'And Mr Cottle's got no other family?' Because who were all these framed photos of? I'd barely registered them till now, but suddenly they were everywhere, the same dark-haired woman over and over. She looked familiar, too. Then the penny dropped. It was Carol Vorderman.

'No, he had no one. Just me.'

Poor beggar, I heard Mum say. *Take his cat. It's t'least you can do. Don't you remember our Chalkie? You loved him. He was never any bother.*

'I suppose we could look after it till you find a proper home,' I heard myself saying.

The deal was done. She relaxed visibly, even allowed herself a slight smile.

I said, 'I'm sorry about your uncle. My mum died last year and it's hard, incredibly hard. Adjusting, coming to terms with the fact they've finally gone, that you'll never speak to them again. All the things you meant to say . . .'

The room was hushed. Somewhere a tiny clock was ticking. I searched her face for some flicker of sympathy.

She said, 'Yeah. Anyway, there's some tins of Whiskas in the kitchen if you want them. Daft to let them go to waste, isn't it?'

Walshy wandered into the kitchen just as I clicked the washing-machine door shut. He was wearing a black kimono that barely reached mid-thigh.

I said, 'I hope you've at least put some knickers on under that.'

'Don't worry, I'm safe inside my boxers.' He twitched the kimono aside to demonstrate.

'Lovely. And the reason you're still trouserless is . . .'

'Thought I'd take a shower.'

'Go take one, then.'

'In a minute. Don't rush me.' With infuriating slowness he opened the fridge, extracted a bottle of Yazoo milkshake and began picking at the silver-foil cap.

'Is that even yours?'

'It's Gemma's. She won't mind. You're using her nail-polish remover, so you can't say too much.'

'It's not the same. God, you're annoying.'

I watched him puncture the foil with his thumbnail, hold the bottle to his lips and drink. Then he stuck the bottle back in the fridge, wiped his mouth with the hem of his kimono – another nice flash of his pants – and hoisted himself up onto the unit where he sat with his bare legs dangling.

'Why *do* I annoy you so much, Chazbo? What is it about me that squeaks your inner polystyrene?'

Because I fancy you, you git, I thought. I fancy you beyond reason and I hate myself for it.

'Well, see the state of you. At least tie your belt. What would Gemma say if she walked in? What would it look like?'

'It doesn't matter now.'

'It matters to me.'

'Why?'

'Oh, fuck off, Walsh.'

The machine choked and spat and juddered. Walshy picked up a jam-smeared knife that someone had left out and began to lick it. I shunted together a few dirty plates and lowered them into the sink.

'So when's Dan the Man making his next appearance?'

I ignored him. Scummy water was backing up from the plughole, which meant the u-bend was blocked again. Possibly a wiggle with a spoon handle might do it, but more likely it would need chemicals and a blast with a plunger.

'Oh Danny Boy, the pipes, the pipes are calling,' sang Walshy.

'Act useful for once and find the Mr Muscle.'

'Aren't I muscly enough for you?'

'Only if you can unblock the sink with your bare hands.'

The appeal to his manliness worked. He oozed off the counter in a slither of silk and began to roll up his sleeves. I knelt to open the cupboard where the plunger lived.

I said, 'Did you honestly have no idea about Gemma?'

'About her being gay? Nope. Did you?'

'Why would I?'

'I dunno. Girly sixth-sense or something?'

48

'Sorry, passed me right by.' I lifted the plates out of the way and passed him the plunger. 'Right, you know what to do with this.'

But he shook his head. 'My sleeves won't stay up. They're too floppy. I need to take my robe off.'

'Oh, no, you don't.'

In the drawer by the back door we kept a handful of clothes pegs. I fished out two, snapped them in Walshy's face like miniature crocodiles. 'Hold out your arms.' I gathered his cuffs up concertina-style and clipped them above his elbows. 'There. Now off to work you go.'

'I bet I look a right knob.'

'No change there, then.'

While he assaulted the plughole I went and sat at the table. Suddenly a memory of bathtime Will swept over me: Will sitting behind a wobbling mountain of bubbles, shrieking and blowing foam up the tiles. What would he be up to right now? It was too early for his nap. Had Mum taken him up the shops or to the library? Was she clicking him into his toddler reins, wiggling his weeny hands into stripy mittens, persuading his boots over his socks? *But it should be me! I should be doing that!* For a moment I felt stricken, wanted to run out of the front door there and then and jump on the nearest train – but I breathed calmly and made myself sit.

There was a drainsy sound like a troll clearing its throat, then some sputtering, followed by a huge burp from the plughole.

'Aha,' Walshy said.

'Have you done it?'

'I have.' He peered one last time over the sink then laid the plunger on the worktop, where it began to drip filth into the cutlery tray.

'Bloody hell, Walshy, watch it.'

'What now? Oh.'

I came over and pushed him out of the way. There was a bottle of Parazone somewhere in the cupboard. 'The whole area needs bleaching now. Unless you want to contract galloping salmonella. Remind me again why we moved in with you?'

'For daily glimpses of my excellent pecs, of course. And because I'm the only one here who doesn't have a complete sparky fit if I see a spider. Because of my even temperament, my ability to knock up cocktails from limited means, my—'

'Because you don't mind if we're late with the rent and you let us use drawing pins on the walls.'

As I wiped bleach round the worktop and drainer I remembered the night Gemma had first mentioned him to us. 'There's this guy on my course with a house looking for people to share. He doesn't mind boys or girls, but we've got to move quick. Are we interested?' And Walshy had been charming at that initial meeting, shy and hesitant. A total act.

I said, 'You promise it won't be a problem, you and Gemma now?'

'It's fine at this end. I can't speak for her. Although she seemed all right last night. Honest, she did.'

'As far as you could tell.'

'I'm just a man, what would I know? You'll claw it out of her, over one of your girly chats.'

That was going to be an interesting conversation, I thought.

'Anyway,' he went on, 'enough of my love-life. What about yours? How's it really going with Desperate Dan? I haven't seen him for weeks. Nothing wrong, is there?'

Nothing wrong that wasn't wrong before, no.

'It's fine, thanks for asking. He's coming up this weekend.'

'Ah. That'll be nice for you.'

'Yeah, it will, actually.'

'Cool. Hey, fancy sharing brunch? I've a malt loaf and tin of fruit pie filling somewhere.'

Walsh pulled off his clothes pegs, snapping one onto the kettle flex and the other onto the rim of Gemma's Churchill mug.

'I'm afraid I have to go see my tutor now,' I said crisply.

'Oh, deep joy. Mmmmartin. Mmmm. I *heart* Martin Eavis.' He drew the shape in the air.

'Take the washing out as soon as it finishes and hang it up,' I told him. 'And if those pegs aren't back in the drawer when I get in, there'll be trouble.'

'Yes, ma'am.'

I gave him the finger, and left.

Wet playtime in primary school: what joy. Normally Leo herds the kids into the hall and contains them there, but we were having building work done and it was temporarily off-limits. Glum teachers had been forced to take their afternoon coffee and sit in classrooms to police the mayhem. Which left just me and Sylv the secretary with the staff room to ourselves.

'Well, it was bound to be a shock for you,' she was saying as she tipped sugar into her mug. 'Lying there all dead and that. Eugh. I think I'd have fainted.'

Not known for her finesse, isn't Sylv. I don't know why I always end up telling her my private business.

I said, 'It wasn't the body; he just looked like a tired old man. What got me churned up was how cool the niece was. She obviously wasn't fussed at all. And all right, yes, Mr Cottle wasn't the most likeable person, but no one deserves to be unmourned like that. Sitting there dying with only Carol Vorderman for company.'

'And his cat.'

'Oh, heck – yeah, the cat. I'm so cross about that. The last thing I need right now is to be taking on an ailing pet. Pringle, he's called. Moth-Eaten would be more like it.'

Sylv arched her pencilled eyebrows. 'I thought you used to have a cat? You've talked about a cat.'

'Chalkie. That was ages ago, when I was a kid. But that was then, this is now. I haven't the time to be homing strays. I've enough on, what with looking after Will.'

'So drop the cat off at the vet's, have him put to sleep. You said he's on his last legs. Problem solved.' When I glanced across she had her handbag mirror out and was inspecting her lipstick. A hard woman. She's our designated first-aider, but the kids don't go near her unless they're on the verge of collapse.

'Thanks for that.'

'No problem. Your trouble, Karen, is you worry too much. It's putting years on you.'

'You really speak as you find, don't you?'

'I do, yeah. That's why I'm a good friend to have.'

'Right-oh.'

On the wall above Sylv's head a cheery poster spelled out *Have a great day!* in twenty-four different languages.

I said, 'The thing is, I've no choice but to worry. Seems to be one crisis after another at the moment.'

'Yeah? Such as?'

I blew out a long breath. 'Well, for one, I think our Charlotte might be mucking about with a boy up in York.'

'No. Are you sure? I thought her and Daniel were practically engaged. How long's it been now – three years?'

'Coming up to that. And they were fine, it was love's young dream till last autumn. Now, though . . . she's restless, I can tell. Something's happened. I'd try and talk to her about it but she'd only go off in my face.'

Sylv smoothed her skirt and considered. 'Hmm. There's probably nothing you can do about that one. I mean, she's grown-up, she's got her own life. You can't *make* things work out between them. Either they will or they won't; you poking about isn't going to solve it. Anyway, you might be wrong about the York lad. They might just be flirty-friends. Loads of people have those. Haven't you ever had a flirty-friend?'

'No.'

Why am I not surprised, said her expression. 'OK, what's next on the list?'

'Just the usual fretting about Will, whether I'm doing a good enough job. Because Charlotte's very particular, everything has to be her way, even though she's not here. I do my best with him but he's got so much energy it's exhausting, and then at night when I should be sleeping I'm all strung out. Recently I've started forgetting things, and that causes extra hassle. I forgot where I'd put all those Year Four reading tests the other day, and twice I've left my car lights on and drained the battery. What I really want to do is to go lie in a darkened room for a month, but there isn't time to flake out, or be ill, anything like that, because I've people depending on me. Even the children here, kids like Lucy Medlock and Felix Burrows who struggle in that big class of Pauline's need my little group or they'd sink without trace. I mean, don't get me wrong, I enjoy my job but it's like there's never any break from the pressure. I feel like Atlas holding up the sky. And some days I can't cope. Except I have to.'

Through windows running with water I could see young Robbie Talbot being led across the rec by his mum, bound for one of his speech therapy sessions. The tarmac was so wet you could see his figure reflected below, sole to sole. Rain swept by in sheets. The gutters foamed.

Sylv lowered her compact mirror and dropped it in her bag.

'You know what the root of it is? You're missing your mum still. That's why you're all over the place. You're depressed. You want to get yourself to the GP and ask for some tablets.'

'I'm not taking tablets.'

She wrinkled her nose. 'Nothing wrong with a few happy pills to help you through a rough patch, loads of people take them. At least two members of staff here. Not that I'd name names.'

'I wouldn't ask.'

That made me wonder, though. How many of us were silently struggling, under the surface? It was like the way we covered the tatty school paintwork with cut-out caterpillars and poems and paintings of poppy fields, and then, at the end of every term, when the work was taken down, you saw the real state of the building. The chips, the flakes, the sinister cracks.

I said, 'I just find myself stressing over what constitutes normal grieving and what crosses the line.'

'How do you mean, Karen?'

I hesitated for a second. 'Well, I know it's mad but I have this really strong sense Mum's still around. I mean I *understand* that she isn't, I'm not delusional, but at the same time I can't quite make myself believe it. I often feel like she's in the house with me. Maybe in the next room, or on the other side of a door. I can smell her perfume. I think I'm going to hear her calling.'

'Ooh. As if you're being haunted?'

'I don't know. As if – and this does sound unbalanced – she might have something to tell me.'

Sylv leaned forward in her seat. Now she was properly interested. 'Like a message? There was this woman on TV a couple of nights ago who reckoned her late husband was making fruit jump out of the bowl. Apples plopping out and rolling across the floor all on their own. She didn't know what it meant, though. And I said to Gavin, "You'd think the dead would have something better to do than shunt fruit around, it's a bit obscure." Have you thought about consulting a medium and asking if there are any communications for you from beyond? Your mother might have a warning for you, something along those lines. And then there are these psychic shows where the audience can shout out requests.'

'I wouldn't like that at all.' No way was Mum being turned into a stage act.

'But if she did have something she wanted to tell you?'

'No, forget it. I'm being silly. I should never have said anything. It's probably just that she's on my mind a lot what with putting together this family history project. And because it was her house and she lived in it all her married life, she's everywhere. I went to dig out Charlotte's spare phone charger the other day, and I pulled open the cupboard and there's one of Nan's old moustaches from her Mothers' Union plays.'

'No wonder you're upset, all those reminders.'

'I know. I ought to clear out some of it. I suppose what's really getting to me is how death leaves things unfinished – ideas go round and round my head. I think, if I could just, if I could just have ten more minutes with her . . .'

And right there the sequence unravelled in my mind: the night I found Mum on the kitchen floor ill and rambling, and she let slip I was adopted. Not hers, she said. Not who I thought I was. My struggle over the following weeks, the appointments with counsellors and social workers. Setting out on the sly in search of my birth mother, lying to everyone about where I was going, telling my own daughter I was having a seaside break. Seaside break! The reality – cold station platforms, cold London streets, cold eyes peering out at me, a door slammed in my face. Cruel words branded across my memory. A hidden history I'd dragged up that I could never un-know, or share. And the continual battle now to blot it out, the guilt I carried round. *Mum, I'm sorry, I'm sorry, I wish I'd left well alone.*

Sylv was staring at me.

'. . . I'd tell her that I loved her, I suppose.'

'Oh, she'll have known that.'

'Will she, though?'

'Don't be daft. My God, Karen, is that what's really getting to you?'

I made myself nod. I wanted to say, *What do you think the rules of the afterlife are? If Mum is still about, how much is she able to see? When you pass over, do you find out stuff that people kept hidden from you while you were on earth? Can the dead look down and see the secrets of our hearts?*

Without warning the electric bell went off above our heads, jangling at top volume and making me jump and spill my coffee. Break was over. It was time for Phonics with Year Three.

Sylv snapped her handbag shut and stood to watch me dab my skirt with a hanky.

'Listen, I can't begin to untangle your head right now. But here's an idea. Why don't you come out with me and Maggie one evening? Or join Pauline's salsa class? It's a giggle. Let your hair down, have a night off? It'd do you the world of good. Stop you brooding so much.'

I blinked at her. 'Salsa?'

'Why not?'

'Me doing Latin dance? Thump thump crash.'

'It's not a serious class, it's not competition standard or anything. Just a bunch of us having a laugh.'

'Oh? OK. Sounds fun. Maybe I will.'

I think we both knew I was lying.

'The offer's there anyway. And you know me, Karen: I wouldn't ask if I didn't mean. Think about it.'

And with a squeak of the fire door she was gone, spiky heels tap-tapping down the lino.

So I'm on my way back from the library, replaying my session with Martin and feeling a whole lot better about the day, when Mum rings and starts blethering on about some neighbour she reckoned I knew. I kept saying I didn't, and even if I had I wasn't interested. Then I catch the words 'sitting there dead' and 'windmill'. I said, 'Hang on, who's dead? What's going on? Is Will OK?' and she said, 'He's fine, he didn't see the body.' So then I totally freaked because it dawned on me she'd taken him right into this man's house, had him playing just a few feet away from a corpse. I felt sick, actually.

'He didn't touch anything, did he?'

'No,' she said. 'I gave him a pot frog.' *Pot frog*? I mean, honestly, if that had been me saying something like that, she'd have been calling the drugs helpline.

Eventually I got the full story out of her and it was just so bloody weird, and she was gabbling about Nan's moustache and then a cat, and I said, 'What cat? What are you on about, Mum?'

And she said, 'I've taken in Mr Cottle's cat; it was homeless.'

I said, 'You got a pet and you didn't think to ask me first?'

Why? she wanted to know. What was wrong with having a cat?

'Because of Will.'

'He's not a baby,' she said. 'It's not going to sit on his face and smother him.'

'But you should have asked me. It might not have been suitable.'

And she went, 'We're not talking about a bloody tarantula, Charlotte. Get a grip.'

And that's when I really lost it.

'DON'T go installing any more animals in the house without consulting me,' she was yelling down the phone at me. 'And don't keep dragging him round to see corpses either.'

I was that gobsmacked I just said, 'No.' Then the phone went dead.

Why does she feel she can speak to me like that? Why do I let her? Who is it looking after her child two-thirds of the year? I sat and stewed for at least an hour afterwards, TV on and no one watching.

I heard the engine revving outside our house but I didn't take any notice. Why would I? The curtains were drawn, Will was in bed, the day was practically over as far as I was concerned. How could I ever get myself to a salsa class feeling as drained as I did? It took me all my time to stagger to the biscuit tin and back.

Then the doorbell rang.

Bad news, I thought, the way I always do now Charlotte's so far away.

When I opened the door I nearly screamed. Right there on my step was a man in a leather jacket and a motorbike helmet with one of those scary blacked-out visors. I thought he'd come to burgle the house. We'd had a policeman round two weeks ago warning us about gangs selling counterfeit dusters.

'What do you want?' I snapped. 'I've a big pit bull in the back.'

The visor flipped open to reveal Steve's squashed-up features. 'Have you heck as like.'

With a monumental effort he prised the helmet off his head and stood grinning at me. His skin was flushed and marked from the straps. Behind him, lit by a pool of streetlight, was parked a blue and green motorbike with a jumbo chrome exhaust.

'Oh my God. You bloody well haven't, have you?'

'I bloody well have. Smart, int it? One hundred and fifty horses.'

'And how have you managed to afford it?'

'Cashed in some assets.'

What assets did my ex-husband own? His house was full of junk, and I mean genuine tat. Flammable sofa, temperamental TV, ring-marked tables, buzzing fridge. All the taps dripped, and you had to turn the cooker on with a pair of pliers because the knob had come away. Not even a charity would have touched his stuff. 'You've flogged your Linda Lusardi mug?'

'I've sold my Escort.'

'You've what?'

He turned and eyed the bike lovingly. 'I did a part-exchange. The car weren't worth a stack, but it was worth more than this.

And don't worry about our Charlie's driving lessons. With the bit of cash I got over, I'll pay for her to have professional ones. Be better than me confusing her. I teach it all wrong.'

'But you were really suited with that car.'

'I'm really suited with this Kwacker. It is a belter. You should hear the engine when it starts up. Magic. I thought you'd want to see. Shall I give you a demo?'

'Only if it heralds you climbing on the thing and riding away. Preferably forever.'

I'll say this for Steve, he's not easily knocked back.

'OK, great, listen to this.' He squeezed the crash helmet on again, and gave me the thumbs-up. Then he sauntered down the path and through the gate. I leaned against the door jamb with my arms folded, watching. For maybe two minutes he was twiddling keys and knobs and tweaking the handles, for all the world like someone who hadn't a clue. Out of the corner of my eye I noticed a small dark shape skulking at the edge of the lawn: that would be Pringle doing a poo. Marvellous.

At last Steve climbed onto the Kawasaki, twisted his wrist, and the bike roared into life. He revved a couple of times experimentally. Then he was off, weaving down the road, the exhaust growling and sputtering. Ex on a death-machine. Something else for me to add to the worry-list.

I stepped back inside, my insides wound tight as a watch-spring. Suddenly, for the moment before I pushed open the lounge door I had the strongest feeling I was going to see Mum sitting by the television, methodically unravelling the wool from an old jumper into a ball. Her face would lift, showing her soft wrinkles and her brown eyes, and she'd look right at me. My skin prickled with the certainty of it.

What, Mum? What is it? I'd say.

Don't fret, Karen. It'll come round. It allus does.

The door swung forwards. The room was empty, the TV playing to itself.

NAN: Eeh, you love. You little love.

CHARLOTTE: Hasn't he grown, Nan? His trousers are showing his ankles, and before they were hanging right down over his toes. And they're nine-months-plus. The health visitor reckons he's going to be really tall.

KAREN: Pop him on the bed next to her, Charlotte.

NAN: That's right. Come and sit here wi' your nan. That's a lad. Soon be spittin' in t'fire, eh? Who's bonny? Who's a little bonny brid?

CHARLOTTE: Why does she call him that?

KAREN: Bonny brid?

CHARLOTTE: Yeah.

KAREN: It's a poem, she used to recite it at Mothers' Union concerts. 'Th'art welcome, little bonny brid, But shouldn't ha come just when tha did.'

CHARLOTTE: Charming.

KAREN: No, it's nice. About how times are hard but the baby's loved anyway. I'll look it out for you when we get home.

NAN: He does favour Bill, dunt he?

CHARLOTTE: (whispers) She always says that and he can't do, can he?

KAREN: Ssh. Mum, we've found this photo of a little girl with no name on it and we were wondering if you knew who it was. Can you reach across with it, Charlotte? Ta.

NAN: Oh, that's your dad, that is.

KAREN: What, in a lacy dress?

NAN: Aye. They put all babies in dresses then. My little brother Jimmy, all of 'em, all t' lads. I think it were easier. Or cheaper, passing clothes down. Y'ad to count every penny.

KAREN: I see. Blimey. Was it tough when you were growing up?

NAN: Well, it were for my mother because my dad were never around. He were in and out like a cat, and then he'd turn up and Grandma Florrie'd be wanting to bolt the door against him and my mother'd be weeping and shouting for her to let him in. It wasn't her house, see, it were Florrie's. She never had a home of her own. And I loved my dad, he were my dad, but he led my mother a terrible dance. It was very shaming for her. And we had no money.

KAREN: Did you go hungry, ever?

NAN: There was allus food on t'table. I don't know how my mother did it. But it weren't what *you* eat. Nettle pop, we had, and cow heel. Tripe, that come round in a cart.'

KAREN: Belly pork. You still like your belly pork, don't you?

NAN: Belly pork, aye. Prayta Pie. Once our Jimmy were messing about lobbing bricks in t'farmer's pond an' he killed a duck. I were for running off, but he waded in and fetched it home and my mother plucked it and put a crust on it. Oh, and charity loaves you could get, off t'church, two a week. And you'd barter, so's if you grew goosegogs like Grandma Florrie did, she'd swap 'em for someone else's onions. There were a lot of that went on. A bit of scrumping, on t'side. (Laughs.)

KAREN: And how did you manage for clothes?

NAN: My mother used to say, 'If it weren't for our backs and our bellies, we'd be rich.'

KAREN: I'm thinking shoes, for instance. Kids grow out of them so quickly.

NAN: Aye. Well, your clogs lasted forever. You could pass a pair down four or five times – just put new irons on t'soles and they'd be grand. Everybody wore 'em. And a chap used to come round every few months wi' a cart full of clothes – second-hand, like – and we'd get fixed up off him. Sort of a mobile jumble sale. I did have a new dress for Walking Day – that would have been 1930 because I'd turned thirteen and I had a bit of a bust coming; nowt fitted. (Laughs.) But I think even then my mother just ran it up out of material from Grandma Fenton's bedcover – that were my dad's mother.

KAREN: Times were tough?

NAN: Y'ad to be inventive. There were a lot worse off. Miners out of work, begging on t'streets, squatting on t'corners. They say people are poor nowadays, but in them days . . . See, we were only childer, we didn't feel t'worst of it. I think it wore my mother out, though, shielding us.

KAREN: You don't know you're born, Charlotte.

CHARLOTTE: Yeah, and I'm glad about that, aren't you?

CHAPTER 3

On a day in March

'There used to be this sitcom on TV,' said Daniel as we climbed the stairs to his first-floor flat, 'called *My Wife Next Door*. About this couple who'd split up only to find they'd accidentally bought adjoining semis.'

'I don't remember that.'

'It was ages ago, right back in the Seventies.'

'How come you've seen it, then?'

'My dad had it on video. We used to watch it when I was little. Wishful thinking on his part, probably.'

We stopped on the landing and he fumbled for his key. Music boomed down through the ceiling, some wailing female vocal.

'And your point is?'

The key turned, and Daniel cast a nod towards the ceiling. 'I could probably write some kind of hilarious sequel. *My Mum Upstairs.*'

It was a slightly weird set-up. When Daniel's parents had divorced last year his dad had got rid of the family pile and invested in this three-storey Victorian terraced house, installing his ex-wife on the top floor and Daniel in the middle, plus some Ukrainians on the ground floor. Meanwhile Dr Gale himself moved into a flat across the other side of the city. The idea was sold to Daniel as rent-free student accommodation plus on-site domestic support – his mum could help with cooking, cleaning, shopping and washing, leaving Dan free to concentrate on his studies. He'd have his independence, but as a sort of, ha ha, payback he could keep half an eye on his mum. Provide her with a bit of company from time to time, make sure she was coping. Everyone a winner. Dr Gale walking away, dusting his hands and smiling. We all knew the real score, but none of us was saying.

Daniel pushed open the door cautiously. His mother has a key; I suppose he's never quite sure what he's going to find on the other side.

But the flat, when we walked in, was tidy and freshly hoovered. The cushions on the sofa were square and plumped, and the window open to air the room. Evidently Mrs G hadn't been necking Chardonnay the whole day. Upstairs, the music rolled on in sentimental waves.

'What *is* that?' I asked, pointing upwards.

'Rita Coolidge.'

'Who?'

'Mum filched the CD off Dad before she left. It's one of his favourites.'

'Why would she do that? To annoy him? Doesn't it upset her, listening to it?'

'Yup.'

'So why doesn't she put a sock in it?'

Dan sighed. I know I should keep my mouth shut. The thing is, though, Mrs Gale was such a prize cow to me after Will was born. Like, I'd bring the baby round and she'd bugger off into a different room, out of the way. Once we were in the kitchen and I asked if she wanted to hold him and she actually shuddered, a big dramatic shiver. I mean, for fuck's sake, my little baby. Then these thought bubbles started appearing over her head: *Don't forget, that child's got nothing to do with this family. Why don't you go and see his biological dad's mother and foist your infant on* her? *Or perhaps you aren't even sure who the father is.*

To which I could have replied: *OK, first off, I DO know who the father is, and second, he was the only boy I'd ever slept with, and third, we did try and use contraception, and fourth, it wasn't my fault he turned out to be a git. Also, Daniel's free to choose who he goes out with – do I look as though I've got him in an armlock? Anyway, it was your affair ruined your marriage so you're hardly in a position to preach to anyone. Look to your own house, Mrs G, look to your own house.*

Obviously I never said any of this out loud, which makes me some kind of saint.

From time to time Mrs G and I did manage an ordinary civil conversation – we saw each other too much not to – but always she'd find a way to turn the topic onto Daniel's university place, Daniel's glittering career path. Like I was just destined for the gutter. As far as she was concerned, I was some council-estate slapper out to snare the first sap who wandered past. 'It's not that she's against you personally,' Daniel had once said. 'She worries about me, that's all.' But I knew that even without Will on the scene, she'd have been anti. Essentially I was just too common.

So, now that life had brought her down, some devil in me couldn't resist prodding, drawing attention to the fact she was struggling.

Because it's supposed to be us young mothers who screw up our lives, isn't it? Feckless teenage mums perpetually on the scrounge, draining the economy. We're the root of all evil: morally corrupt, educationally impoverished, greedy, casual, selfish. Slated in the papers every day (or at least the papers Mrs G reads). Yet here, in front of me, was this doctor's wife – smart, middle-aged, wealthy, Oxbridge-educated – threshing around in a total fuck-up because she couldn't keep her hands to herself and the screw cap on the bottle.

'Right, here you are,' said Daniel, reaching behind the sofa for a plastic bag.

'You genius. Is it purple?'

'As you ordered.'

I opened the bag and drew out the velvet jacket, unrolled it, shook it by the shoulders. The colour was rich and gorgeous.

'Ooh, smart. How much do I owe you?'

'Twenty-five. You can give it to me later. It's a nice jacket, no flaws in the pile that I could see. The lining's frayed near the collar but I didn't think that mattered.'

I turned the jacket this way and that. The light caught the velvet in a wavy sheen down the sleeve.

'Eew, though, it's not her size.'

'The measurements are exactly what you told me.'

'But it'll be too big. Wait.' I pulled off my jumper, dropped it on the sofa, and slipped the jacket on over my shirt. It hung loose on me but it wasn't completely enormous. 'Hmm. Actually, I think it will be OK. If you've got some scissors handy, I can cut the label out.'

'Sorry, no can do. My mother borrowed them last week and now she can't remember what she did with them.'

'Oh well. Have you got the photo?'

'Uh-huh.' He took the bag off me and rooted round. 'Here.'

The picture still made me smile. Mum, about fifteen, in a jacket almost the spit of this one plus a gypsy-style skirt and wedges, her hair all flicked and lacquered. With her were two girls, one plump and one skinny. The plump one was wearing a checked shirt and jeans and the skinny one was kitted out entirely in black. They were standing against a brick wall – could be the side of our coal shed – smiling self-consciously.

I'd found the photograph stuck between the pages of one of Nan's ancient books, *The Altars of Sacrifice*. Mum had screeched when I showed her, then she'd gone quiet, studying the detail for ages. I'd asked her who the other girls were and she said the thin one was Dee, her best friend who'd moved away straight after O levels, and the plump one was Donna. 'Works for the Halifax in Exeter now, does Donna. Getting on very well, her mother says.' And she'd pulled a strange face, half-wistful, half-jealous.

But staring at the photo afterwards I'd felt sorry for her because once upon a time, before me, she was oblivious to the future, and hopeful. 'I did love that jacket,' she'd said. So I thought, her birthday's coming up. Get Daniel down to Affleck's Palace in Manchester, he might be able to root around the vintage clothes stalls there and dig me out a reasonable substitute. And he had. Good man.

'Brilliant, you're brilliant. Thanks,' I said warmly. He looked surprised and pleased.

'No problem. Though the leather and bondage stall right next door was a touch intimidating.'

'Really? I was going to ask if you could pop in there next week and get me a new gimp mask.'

He reached round and gave me a light smack on the bum. Then

he kissed me. I kissed him back. I stroked his hair and traced his jawline with my finger while he closed his eyes. Above us Rita warbled on. *We're all alone, we're all alone.*

I'd have gone on with the kissing, but after a few moments Daniel broke away. 'Sorry, do you mind if we just nip up and see Mum before we go?'

That's the problem. Just as I think I'm into him again, he does something to break the spell.

So, close the bedroom door, open the wardrobe mirror and let the thirty-eighth-birthday inventory begin.

Face: OK, no deep lines yet, no under-eye bags, jawline coming a bit loose but not horrific. None of the appalling white chin bristles my mother developed in her later years. I've decided I'll shoot myself if I find I'm sprouting any of those.

Hair: quite nice when it's just been dyed and styled, otherwise greying at the temples and suddenly tending to wiry at the front. Keep changing shampoo, conditioner, waste of time. It goes mad in damp weather.

Body: honestly, not great. I put on a stone in weight after Charlotte first went to York, then another last year after Mum died. I'm not fat-fat, but I'm not myself. This shape isn't me. I hold my arms out and the loose skin underneath goes wibble wibble, makes me look like a flying squirrel. Perhaps by the time I reach forty I'll be able to take off and soar away into the sunset.

My legs are quite good, except no one ever gets to see them. Well, Steve does, but I mean no one who counts. There's a funny thread vein popped up above my knee, could have done without that. It doesn't seem to have put him off, mind.

It is amazing what the years do, how they strip your power. When I was a teenager I could climb on a lad's lap, wriggle a bit and straight away feel a lump rise up in his trousers. That was all I had to do to turn him on. If I plonked myself on someone's knee these days, they'd probably just moan I was too heavy.

Sometimes, in the long evenings after Will's gone to bed, I watch these TV programmes where young girls fret over their appearance, confiding how they're desperate for bigger breasts or liposuction or nose jobs, and they're crying, a lot of them, over how disgusted they feel at their own bodies. Radiant, beautiful, glossy and firm these girls are, but they just can't see it. And I find myself shouting at the screen, *Don't start already, love. Believe me, this is your high point!*

I stand here now in front of this wardrobe mirror in my bra, tights and knickers, jiggling my revolting bingo wings, and I wonder, Why *do* we women hate ourselves so much? Who was it implanted this soundtrack in my head? Not Mum, she always used to say I looked nice whatever state I was in. And Steve was never one to pick holes. In fact, he laughs when I whinge about my figure. He says women are daft to worry so much. He says boobs are the most brilliant things ever invented, and I could wear an old sack and a pair of wellies and he'd still want to go to bed with me.

As though that's supposed to cheer me up.

Maybe it's something he plans on asking me to do.

I really must stop these birthday inventories. They're much too disturbing.

As we climbed up the stairs to Mrs Gale's flat, I wondered what state she'd be in. Part of me hoped to catch her out, that we'd find her sprawled and raving with an empty bottle clasped to her chest. Then I could say it out loud: *Your mum's a drunk, Daniel. She's a useless lush, see the state of her. And this is the woman who's had the nerve to judge me over my life choices.*

But mostly I was hoping she'd be all right because then we could be in and out and on our way to Bank Top. I couldn't stand for there to be any more delay. I had to be with my son.

Rita must have been playing at top volume because when the door opened I was nearly blasted off my feet.

'Oops, sorry,' Mrs Gale mouthed over the din. She did this silly half-run across the room to turn off the stereo, then stood by the window with her thumbs in her jeans pockets, smiling at us. At Daniel, anyway. 'I almost didn't hear you knock. I was away with my music.'

'No shit, Sherlock,' I said under my breath. Dan shot me a warning frown.

'Did you see I'd got you some more milk, darling? You were running low.'

'Thanks, Mum.'

'And I emptied your bin.'

'Great.'

'Fancy sharing a pizza tonight? You can choose the topping. We can go mad and have garlic bread, what do you say?'

That's another annoying thing about Mrs G: she's developed this girlish manner, completely inappropriate for a woman her age. Since she split with Dr G she's gone really thin and she's grown her hair past shoulder-length and taken to wearing scarlet lipstick. Because she's long-limbed she can almost get away with it, but it's the body language that irritates me. Playful shrugging of the shoulders, flirty winks. It's how you'd behave towards a boyfriend, not a son. With me she's simply dead-eyed and flat.

'Sounds good, Mum. Everything else OK?'

'Fine.' Brows well up, bright showgirl grin. No bottles of plonk hidden away behind *my* curtains, thank you.

She had made the place smart, I'd give her that. According to Daniel, Dr G let her take all the furniture, whatever she wanted. I bet he reckoned it was worth it to get her out.

'OK,' said Daniel, adjusting his glasses. 'Just wanted to check in. So, we'll be off. Charlotte's itching to give her mum her birthday present.'

'And tonight's a date,' said Mrs Gale, coming forward to embrace her son. As I would have expected, there was no acknowledgement of my presence or concerns. I might not have even been in the room. Then: 'Oh, while I remember, someone called Amelia came round.'

Daniel's face was turned away from me so I didn't see his reaction. 'Oh?'

'To ask if you'd help with the concert. She said you'd spoken about it and you'd had some ideas.'

'Right.'

'She says she has plans for you.'

'OK. Like I said, we'd better get moving.'

'She's going to come and find you next week, in the lab.'

There was this crackling charge going between us all. *Got you there, madam*, Mrs Gale flashed at me. *You don't know who Amelia is, do you?*

Well, I'm not giving you the satisfaction of asking, you old witch, I vibed back.

Get me out of here, went Daniel.

'Come on,' he said, taking my arm and steering me to the

door. 'I'll see you tonight, Mum. I'll give you a ring when I'm setting off.'

'I thought she seemed a really lovely girl,' I heard Mrs Gale say as we closed the door on her.

In the end I solved the frizzy hair problem by just tying it back and actually, it looked better. Will played on my bed with his *Methods of Transport* jigsaw while I did my make-up, took my time and went for the full works rather than the usual rush job. Then I slipped on my new dress, actually a cast-off from Leo's girlfriend, but Alexon so I wasn't going to say no.

'What do you think?' I asked my grandson. 'Do I look nice today?'

'Plane's crashed,' he said, flinging a jigsaw piece against the headboard.

Pringle slunk past the doorway carrying something in his mouth.

'Oh, for God's sake, what have you caught?' I shouted after him.

'God's sake,' said Will.

This is why I didn't want a cat again: it's the associated slaughter. Pauline from school once put her bare foot in her slipper and found half a shrew laid across the insole. And I remember years ago, when I was a little girl and we had Chalkie, coming down one morning and finding this rabbit unzipped on our back lawn, innards strewn right across the grass. Headless baby birds on the doorstep, we had, mutilated frogs. Mum used to fetch a shovel and newspaper and put them to rest while I hyperventilated in my bedroom.

I dreaded what I was going to find this time. I'd assumed

Pringle was too old to catch anything, but maybe he'd stumbled across something as sick and elderly as himself. I thought, Let it at least be dead. I really couldn't cope with tiny heaving flanks.

When I came out of the bedroom, the first thing I clocked was a trail of horrible skin-coloured flakes coming up the stairs and along the landing. 'Pringle!' I yelled sternly. As if he'd turn right round and come trotting up to me. I don't think he even recognises his name. The only time Pringle shifts is when he hears the rattle of cat biscuits.

I checked in Will's room, then in Charlotte's. Couldn't see anything at first glance, but I could make out a hawking, huffing noise coming from under the bed. When I dropped to my hands and knees, Pringle was hunkered down between two cardboard boxes, bolting what looked like a child's limb.

'Drop!' I commanded. He carried on chewing.

'Naughty cat,' said Will helpfully.

I laid myself flat on the floor and stretched my arm out as far as it would go. Pringle edged away, out of reach. 'Grandma needs a stick or something,' I said, half to myself.

I sat up and scanned the room, but without luck. Charlotte didn't appear to keep a stock of cat-poking devices handy. In a temper I snatched at the long Indian scarf trimmed with stiff tassels and bells that she keeps draped over the headboard, dragged it onto the carpet alongside me, then flattened myself once more and attempted to flick the cat with the tasselled end. The first flick went nowhere near but the second clipped him on the nose. He stopped eating. I flicked again and his paw came out automatically and grabbed for the scarf. 'It's not a game,' I told him, tugging crossly. Pringle's eyes narrowed. *Oh ho, Mrs Cooper, I think you'll find it is*. I gave another jerk. Quick as lightning he fastened both sets of claws into the fabric and rolled onto his side.

'Right, my lad, I've got you now.' I began to reel him in like a fish on a line. Like a fish he threshed about, twisting and writhing and gnawing at the little Indian bells – what would Charlotte say when she saw the state of her scarf – till I'd drawn him from under the bedframe. Then, the second he was out, he let go of the material and made a dash for the door.

'Cat's fast,' said Will.

'When he wants to be.'

With the cat out of the way, I shoved the bed over a few inches and got back down on the floor. I patted about, straining my arm and shoulder muscles and trying not to breathe in the dust of ages. Or to panic, or imagine all the nasties Pringle might have dredged up. Mum would have just rolled up her sleeves and got stuck in without a second thought.

Suddenly I made contact. My hand brushed something soft, squashy and cold, oddly crumbly. I took a deep breath, closed my fingers and drew the thing out, dreading what I was going to see.

Will leaned forward, blocking my light. 'Sossy roll, Grandma.'

'Good grief, so it is.'

I heaved myself upright. Clumps of pastry came away in a shower. It was one of those giant sausage rolls, half the length of Pringle's body. He must have had to drag it up the stairs; I had an idea what state the kitchen and lounge would be in. I thought about Sylv urging catty-euthanasia, about Steve sawing a damn great square out of the bottom panel of our back door. Next time Pringle showed his pointy face I was going to grab him by the scruff, phone that damn niece and get her to take him back. Except I didn't have her number. Hell.

Will was prodding hopefully at the sausage roll. I snatched it away. 'Eugh, dirty. This is going in the bin. Then we'll wash our hands.'

'Have a Kit Kat?'

'After Grandma's cleared up, all right?' I looked at the mangled sausage roll.

The doorbell rang.

If this was Steve with some daft-bollocks present, he wasn't coming in, I couldn't be doing with him right now. It might be one of Mum's old friends, Ivy or Maud, popped round with a box of Quality Street for me. *Eh, your carpet's a state, love. Do you want me to run t'Dustbuster over it for you?* Or perhaps it was the owner of the sausage roll who'd followed the trail of crumbs to claim back his property. Obviously he'd be welcome to that.

I peeked out of the bedroom window and saw a familiar balding head, big round paunch, denim jacket, steel toe-capped boots.

'Postman?' said Will.

'No, not the postman. Someone else. We don't have to answer the door.'

At that moment, the balding head tilted and a pair of pale blue eyes met mine. A chubby hand waved.

Sometimes the hardest part of childcare is the not-swearing.

'So who is Amelia?'

I'd managed to last till we were on the motorway.

Daniel took his left hand off the steering wheel for a moment to straighten his glasses. 'You know my mother's just stirring.'

'I do, yeah. Who is Amelia?'

'A girl.'

'And there was me thinking she was a big hairy bloke.'

'She's a student. Sometimes she works in my lab.'

'And?'

'Nothing. That's it. She's organising a charity event, *Twenty-First Century Rocks*, and she's trying to round up as many helpers as she can. She's very enthusiastic. Goes on at you till you capitulate.'

'Have you capitulated?'

He laughed, and I thought I heard a slight awkwardness there. 'I've said I'll help sell tickets and do marketing, but I'm not taking part in any performance. I'm not the on-stage type.'

'Unless they wanted a short lecture on microtubules, or whatever it was.'

'Now there's an idea. *Microtubules the Musical*. Do you think the world's ready for sing-along-a-biochemistry?'

'You may be ahead of your time.'

I hugged the bag containing Mum's jacket and thought about being with Will. His face at the window as we drew up, maybe. My scramble to get out of the car, running up the front path, leaning on the bell. His small solid body slamming into mine. He knew who his mum was.

'Another twenty minutes and you'll be there,' said Daniel.

'I know.'

'How's things at the house? How's Gemma doing? Has Roz got over herself yet?'

'Oh, that.' I had to drag my mind back to student-world. 'Well, sort of.'

When I'd first told Roz about Gemma being gay, she'd seemed OK about it. Startled, yes, like I'd been, but I thought that was just because the news had come out of the blue. She too had wanted to know if there was a girlfriend on the scene, and if Gemma would be bringing her round. I said, 'I've no idea. Why don't you ask her?' Roz had dissolved into a fit of giggles and put her hands over her face. 'I couldn't. I couldn't!' Then she said, 'Imagine them on the sofa together.' More giggles. She had been drinking.

Then a few days later I'd walked in on her and Gemma having a Talk. Gemma was making toast and Roz had been standing by the sink looking sympathetic. 'I was saying,' Roz blurted out when she saw me, 'how it doesn't matter, the gay thing. If you want to, you know, date girls instead of boys, that's your choice. It doesn't matter to either of us. It's fine.'

'Glad to hear it,' said Gemma.

'Because at the end of the day, we're your *friends.*' And without any warning, Roz had launched herself at Gemma and given her a huge dramatic hug, Gemma mouthing, *Get her off me.* I was about to act when the toast popped up and broke the moment. Roz loosened her hold and I went, 'Is that your phone?' which sent her scuttling off. Ten seconds after that, Walshy flounced into the kitchen, smirking.

'I want you to know, Gemma,' he said in a silly high voice, 'that if you choose to put peanut butter on your bread instead of jam, that's fine. Not everyone likes jam, and it's a free country. We're all mates here. We're cool with it. You go right ahead.' She'd thrown her toast at him, and he'd picked it off the floor and eaten it.

So the answer to Daniel's question was, I didn't really know. The house felt unsettled, but that was as much down to Walsh as anything. Walshy floating free, unattended. 'It's kind of hard to know how Gemma's coping because we never see her.'

'She only lives in the room under yours,' said Daniel.

'I know, but she's really self-contained. She's always been that way. Plus she goes out a lot, and when she's in she sometimes puts this sign on the door and then we're not supposed to disturb her. I'd like to speak to her about things, though. I don't want her thinking I'm as crap as Roz.'

'I'm sure she doesn't.'

'Martin says the atmosphere'll settle down in a few weeks. He says even the most surprising things stop being surprising in the end.'

Daniel pursed his lips. 'Oh, *Martin* says.'

'Bugger off.'

'Does *Martin* say if there are any mints in the glove box?'

I opened the drop-down door and fished him out an Altoid. 'Hoping for a snog later on?'

'Could be.'

Lorries roared past. The windscreen began to spot with rain. Fifteen minutes till I was with my son.

'Is she nice-looking, this Amelia?'

'Hideous. Foul. A face only a mother could love.'

'That's all right, then,' I said.

I don't think of him as Will's granddad, the same way I don't think of his son as Will's dad.

'I've come with your cash,' said Terry Bentham, shuffling on the step.

'Not my cash. Will's.'

'Yeah. From our Paul, like.' He reached round and took an envelope from his jeans back pocket. I knew it was out of his own wages. Paul had nothing to do with it.

'You could always pay it into the bank. You don't have to come mauling round here every month.'

'Aye.' He just stood there, waiting.

'How's Paul?' I made myself ask.

'Still up in Blackpool. It suits him, he's near to his mum's, he makes a fair bit in tips. There's a lot of youngsters around his age work there.'

A *hotel kitchen washer-upper. You must be so proud*, I wanted to say. But you don't kick a man when he's down. I noticed he was missing two buttons off his shirt.

'You're looking . . .' Mr Bentham waved his hand but didn't finish the sentence.

'It's my birthday.'

'Oh, well. Have a nice one.'

'I intend to.'

He wasn't showing any signs of shifting off our path. His eyes flicked over my shoulder into the hall. 'Is t'littlun in?'

'He is.' Grudgingly I stepped back and let him four foot over the threshold, into sausage-roll hell.

'Ah, I see him. Growing, int he?'

I nodded.

Mr Bentham swayed forward. I knew he wanted to go over, examine Will close up, but I wasn't going to lay out the welcome mat. The way I saw it, if he'd brought up his son decently in the first place, Charlotte would never have had to go through what she did, and on her own. I mean, anyone can slip up – I did, for one – but the point is you should stand by your responsibilities. When I fell pregnant, Steve married me, we gave it a shot. And even after we fell out and divorced he was always around for Charlotte. Paul, he just buggered off like it was nothing to do with him. Even Steve going round to his house and threatening did no good. The year Will was born, we had no help from the Benthams, not a scrap. Then, some time down the line, up pops Terry, after access rights. I said, 'For Paul? Because he can take a running jump.' He said, 'No, for me.' I said, 'OK, *you* can see him, but you owe us.' Fair dos, he put his hand in his pocket then and he's not missed a month since. I suppose we could have gone to court for maintenance, made it all official, but Charlotte wouldn't have it. She wanted to cut all ties. Except she's not the one forking out for endless toddler shoes and nursery fees.

Mr Bentham cleared his throat noisily. 'Well. He's a grand lad.'

'He is.'

'Can he kick a ball yet?'

'After a fashion.'

'Great, great. I'd like to see that sometime.'

'Yeah.'

'So I'll tell Paul I've seen him.' He let out a sad laugh. 'It's quiet at home these days.'

I turned deliberately towards the hall. 'Anyway . . .'

'Anyway. Yeah. You'll be busy, your birthday. Tidying and that. I'll see you next month.'

And I closed the door on his uselessness.

It was only when I went to the toilet afterwards I realised I had flaky pastry all down the front of my dress.

When we arrived, she had Will stuck in front of the TV again. I'm going to have to say something. He needs intellectual stimulation while his brain's developing. Plus I spotted straight away this chewed-up bit of old sausage roll or pie or something balanced on top of the banister. Hardly hygienic, is it? I went, 'What the hell's this doing here?' and she said, 'Oh, I forgot where I'd put it,' and I said, 'You're getting as bad as Nan.' She snatched it off me and flung it at the bin. She said, 'You don't know what kind of a morning I've had.'

Ancient Ivy Seddon appeared in the kitchen door holding the hoover by its nozzle. 'Where do you keep your spare bags, love?'

I said to Mum, 'What, you've got Nan's mates cleaning for you now?'

Daniel put his hand on my shoulder. 'Come and help me unload the car, yeah?'

When we were outside the front door he said, 'It's her birthday, Charlotte. Don't wind her up.'

'I wasn't. She winds *me* up.'

He carried on down the path.

'She winds ME up,' I repeated, louder.

Across the road, a bright blue and green motorbike pulled onto the Working Men's car park and came to a halt, revving. The rider cut the engine. Then he climbed off stiffly, like an old man, and pushed his crash helmet up off his face.

I did a double-take – it *was* an old man. It was my dad. 'Hey up, Charlie,' he shouted. 'What do you reckon?'

Mainly I reckoned his top half looked way too big for his body, with his big-shouldered leather jacket and thin-leg jeans, a Lego-style figure. I made a gesture like I was being dazzled, then I grabbed Mum's present off the car's back seat and left him to it.

'Dad's here,' I announced to no one in particular.

'That's nice,' said Ivy.

'Bloody hell,' said Mum.

Will rolled onto his front and farted.

As usual Daniel was making a fuss of Mum. 'Lovely to see you, Mrs Cooper, you're looking extremely nice today.' She laps it up, of course.

Meanwhile I threw myself on the sofa with my son and began to tickle him. 'Mummy's home now, there's no escape,' I said. He giggled, his head butting against my stomach and his legs flailing. Having him close again was pure magic. I wanted to bury my face in his T-shirt and shut out the world. 'So, have you been a good boy for Grandma?'

'Yeah.'

'What's that? You haven't been good? You've been very naughty? Well then, I'm going to have to eat you up!' I growled, bent over and pretended to bite his tummy. He shrieked with laughter.

Mum said, 'When you've finished, Charlotte, there's some bread needs buttering.'

I made a grab for Will's foot and brought it close to my nose. 'Pooh, smelly. Pongy socks.'

'Smelly,' he said.

'Eurgh, take it away.' I rolled him to the other end of the sofa. He scrambled straight back, laughing.

'Smelly boy.' I pushed him backwards. He was squealing and red-faced.

'You're smelly!'

'You are. Pooh.'

'Please don't get him hyper,' said Mum. 'He'll be sick if you carry on.'

What, was I not allowed to cuddle my own child now? I mean, who did she think she was talking to? Some bloody stranger off the street? But before I could raise a protest, Dad walked in, unzipping his leather jacket.

'What's that noise, Karen? Can anyone else hear a baby crying upstairs?'

'It's the cat,' said Mum. 'I shut him in Charlotte's room to stop him getting at the sandwiches.'

'*My* room? Oh, thanks.'

'He's got his litter tray. Come and help me butter this bread, for God's sake.'

Somehow we all ended up in the back kitchen: me, Mum and Ivy slicing baps, Daniel on the floor with his back against the wall and his long legs stretched out in front of him, Will on his lap, and Dad nicking scraps of boiled ham and Wotsits. Even in here we could make out Pringle calling faintly.

'Reenie Mather had a cat, saved her life,' said Ivy. 'When she fell downstairs, it went round to t'neighbours' and sat on their windowsill staring in, they couldn't shift it. Threw water at it, all sorts. So they went round to complain, and that's when they found her.'

'What an uplifting story,' said Daniel.

'Aye. She died two month later in hospital, mind.'

'I once watched a film where a cat brought in a severed human hand,' said Dad, flicking Wotsit dust off his T-shirt.

Will had rolled himself into a ball and was pushing his head determinedly against Daniel's collarbone. I thought how natural they looked together, and how lucky I was to have such a tolerant boyfriend.

And yet, only last weekend we'd had another row.

The problem was, he didn't seem to read me any more. When he arrived at York he'd been talking about Will, something funny Will had been doing when he called round to pick up my camera. I said I didn't want to hear because I was having a bad day. I get these stretches when I'm raw with missing my son and I have to turn his photo face-down, and I'm incredibly touchy about anything to do with kids or mums.

So fair enough, Dan shuts up. But then, a bit later on, I was feeling less down and I *wanted* to ask about Will's speech development and whether Mum was making my son talk properly and not still using baby language, because I don't want him being held back. He's a bright little boy. He should be saying 'sheep', not 'baa-lamb'. By then, of course, Daniel's changed tack, is unstoppable. Wants to tell me in tremendous detail about a supersize rodent they've discovered in South America, some new genus which makes it really really important (who to? A bunch of nut-head scientists, end of). I mean, bloody hell, giant rats. Sometimes it feels as though he's *trying* to provoke me.

I said to Mum, 'How's it been, having a pet in the house?'

'A damn nuisance, if you want to know.'

Daniel glanced up. 'My dad says pet-owners live longer than non pet-owners. And they visit the GP less.'

'They visit the vet more, though.'

'I had a polecat ferret when I was ten,' said Dad. 'It stank.'

'Didn't you used t'have a donkey, Karen?' Ivy asked, reaching across for the Lurpak.

A donkey? When on earth had my mother owned a donkey?

'Oh,' she said. 'Twinkle. Yes. I'd forgotten him. He lived on a sanctuary in Devon and he used to send me photos and newsletters. Grey, he was, with a black cross on his back because Nan said that's the marking Jesus bestowed on all donkeys as a thank-you for carrying Him into Jerusalem. She set the whole thing up for me because I wanted a horse but we couldn't afford one.'

'So you never actually met this Twinkle?'

'No. And I was that disappointed when she showed me because I did really want a horse. But she was trying her best, I can see that now. I hope I was grateful enough. I'm not sure I was ...' Mum trailed off, looking unhappy.

After a moment Daniel scrambled to his feet. 'Has your mum seen her present yet, Charlotte? I'll go fetch it.'

He disappeared back into the lounge. After a moment, Dad and then Will followed.

And still Pringle was yowling. I thought, What if he's filled his litter tray in protest and then walked it over my duvet? Typical of Mum not to have thought of that. Or perhaps she had; perhaps that was why it was my room he was shut in and not hers. Meanwhile, down here in the kitchen we had about a million buttered baps piled round us, so did it matter if the cat helped himself to a few? It needed every calorie it could get, that bag of fur and bones.

'I'll start filling,' said Ivy. 'Did I see some tins of salmon in t'cupboard?'

'They're out of date,' said Mum. 'Use the paste.'

Daniel came back in holding my parcel. 'Here you are. Happy Birthday, Mrs Cooper.'

'I'll just finish here.'

'No, Mum. Leave them a minute.'

'There's drinks to make.'

'Ivy'll deal with them. Wipe your hands and then open your present.'

Dad and Will stood in the doorway to watch. Mum paused shyly, then tore into the plastic carrier with zero elegance. In ten seconds she had the jacket out, frowning, shaking it smooth by the shoulders as I'd done when Dan first showed it to me.

'Is it all right?' I asked when she didn't say anything.

'It's . . .'

'I know you had one like it.'

'I did, yes.'

'So I thought, you know, blast from the past. You never wear purple these days. You never wear any bright colours.'

Mum seemed a bit dazed. 'Wherever did you find it?'

'A vintage shop in Manchester. Daniel hunted it down. I paid for it, though.'

'... So much like the one I used to have. I gave it to a charity shop when we moved back here and I was trying to get rid of clutter ...' She turned the jacket over to see the label. 'Mine was from Clockhouse at C&A. Oh!'

'What?'

'Well, look. The size. God. I'm never that big. Honestly!'

I shot a look at Daniel.

'We did measure it,' he said.

'I'm not that big,' she repeated.

I said, 'It's vintage sizing, Mum. Just ignore what it says on the label.'

'Yes, try it on, Mrs Cooper.'

'It's a bonny colour,' said Ivy. 'Puts me in mind of Vimto.'

Mum stared unhappily at the collar again, then pushed past us through to the living room.

'Y'all right, love?' Dad called over his shoulder. There was a short silence, then a howl.

'What is it, Mum?'

We all craned to see through the doorway. She was standing in front of the mirror, shaking her head in disbelief. 'It *fits*. It bloody well fits.'

'That's good, isn't it?' asked Daniel.

'But I used to be a twelve!'

'Didn't we all, love,' said Ivy, pouring fresh-boiled water into the tea pot.

Dad picked up Will and handed him across to me, then went to put his arms round her.

'Get off me.'

'You look great.'

'I look fat.'

'Don't be daft. Open my present now.'

She began to take the jacket off. Dad reached down under one of the dining chairs and drew out a Thornton's bag. I could tell by his body language he thought he was onto a winner; what woman doesn't love a box of posh chocs? But no, he'd managed to pick the wrong moment yet again.

'For God's sake,' she said when she saw it. 'What is this, a conspiracy? Are you all *trying* to make me put weight on?'

Ivy bent towards me. 'I brought her shortbread,' she whispered. 'Have I to tek it home with me?'

Fuck knows, I thought. There really was no telling what was happening in that mental head today.

I went, 'Look, Mum, if you're not happy, just go on a diet.' Will wriggled and kicked so I let him slide down onto the floor.

'So I DO need to go on a diet?'

'That's not what I said.'

'Don't diet for me,' said Dad unwisely.

Mum scowled at him, and the think-bubble over her head went: *Oh, it's all right for you. You've no idea what it's like to put on weight, Mr Built-like-a-broom-handle, and Madam there smirking 'cause she's lean as a whippet, mind you so was I at her age and see what happened. It'll come to you, Charlotte, it'll catch up with you because it's my genes ticking in your body and you're doomed as I was, doomed.*

'Eeh, watch yourself, love,' said Ivy, from somewhere at the edge of my hearing. I glanced down to see Will pulling at the cloth under the tea pot, dragging it over the edge of the table so that the pot of boiling liquid lurched towards him.

My heart gave a massive jump. On instinct I snatched his hand away and smacked the back of it, one fluid action, before shoving the tea pot right back where it was safe. Then I flipped the overhanging tablecloth up out of the way and set a plate of biscuits on top. My fingers were tingling with the horror of near-miss. Will was crying. 'Oh, God, that was—' I began.

I couldn't believe what happened next. Within about two seconds Mum was at my side, shouting in my face. 'Never hit him! You must never hit a child! Ever!'

'But he would have been scalded. Scarred for life.'

'Then you move the pot out of the way. There was no need to smack him.'

This was outrageous. 'Hang on a minute. You used to smack *me* when I was his age.'

'And look how you turned out, thinking it's OK to teach a toddler by hurting him.'

'I barely touched him!'

'What was he crying for, then?'

'You're making a drama out of nothing. If I think he needs a tap on the wrist, I'll give him a tap on the wrist. He's my son.'

'Who you leave in my care.'

Who you didn't even want, I could have added. *Who you told me to get rid of before he was even born. Remember that, do we?* My face flushed and I swallowed with the effort of holding back the words.

I turned to Dad. 'What's wrong with her today? Is she menopausal or what?'

Suddenly she twisted away from me and made for the back door. She yanked it open, slammed it behind her. Through the window over the sink we watched as she stomped down the path to the flowering currant bushes by the fence at the bottom. It was still raining.

'Should I take her an umbrella?' asked Daniel after a minute or so.

Dad sucked in his breath. 'I wouldn't. Leave her alone, that's the best when she gets like this.'

'Like what, though? One minute she's slightly cheesed off, the next she's lashing out. It's not normal behaviour.'

'Aye, well. She has been a bit down lately.'

'She's going to get soaked.' Daniel craned to see the figure in the grey dress at the end of the garden.

'Good. Cool that temper,' I snapped.

He looked at me doubtfully.

I said, 'Sorry, but I'm not going to feel guilty for the way I handle my own son.'

Even as I spoke, though, I remembered Mum telling me once how guilt's delivered up to every mother along with the placenta. 'You can never feel easy with yourself again,' she told me. 'It's like lying on a lumpy mattress forever after.' I didn't get what she meant at the time.

I looked at Daniel, at Dad.

'I need to go upstairs and have ten minutes on my own,' I said. 'In case my violent tendencies break out again.'

I stood by the fence and felt the rain run over me. I thought, Will being born was supposed to be a fresh start. I was going to put the past behind me, everything. All the moaning about my job or because I had no love-life, push-push-pushing at Charlotte to pass her exams because I'd mucked up mine. Being furious with her for getting pregnant. Then, even worse, the other business, the horrible secret nightmare of tracing my birth mother and finding out what she was really like – most especially that. The darkest time. I'd been so grateful to come back to this house and have them all around me, our normal life. I told myself I was going to be a better mother. I was going to be the best grandma in the world.

For a while I think I almost was. I'd really made an effort to be sunnier and more tolerant, and to listen, and to count to ten before I spoke. And although Mum was ill and in a nursing home, in some ways it was a happy time because a lot of visits she was like herself and could chat and laugh and we were doing these tape recordings and she did love playing with Will. I suppose it was a bit of a golden period.

But over the past months, my best intentions had drained away. Every day I woke feeling bleak and raw. I'd hear my own voice, the snappish downbeat tone, and I'd cringe. Worse, I heard my voice in Charlotte's. What was I passing on to my daughter? You assume you can pick and choose your children's inheritance, only the reality is it doesn't work like that.

I sat on my bed and stewed. Complete fucking over-reaction, or what? Treating me like a naughty kid when *I* was the parent: *me*. It wasn't like I thumped Will or anything. Bloody hell, one smack. And so what if he'd cried a bit? He'd have cried a hell of a lot more if he'd managed to pour boiling water over himself. Two minutes later and he'd have forgotten all about it. In fact – I twitched the curtain to one side – there he was with Ivy on the car park below, running after a pigeon and laughing. See, Mum? See?

Since Will was born she'd suddenly become hypersensitive to stories of child cruelty, I knew that. But the big irony was, she used to slap my legs all the time. Once she did it in front of my friends in the playground, just because I'd lost my lunchbox twice in a row. The hypocrisy was dizzying. I couldn't be doing with it.

The voice behind me made me jump.

'Hullo.'

His accent was Scottish, low and warm. I spun round to see a man about my age looking over the fence at me, bold as anything. He was dressed against the rain in a hooded top so I couldn't see his hair, but he had a good jaw, brown eyes.

'Who are you?' I asked ungraciously.

'Eric,' he said.

I let out a squeaky laugh because in our school ERIC means Everyone Reading In Class. I thought about saying that, but realised in time how stupid it would sound. 'Karen, I'm Karen Cooper. You know that's somebody's garden you're standing in?'

'Aye,' he said. 'Mine. I'm renting.'

'Mr Cottle's house?'

'It's a woman who's letting it.'

The niece. 'I see.'

He said, 'Look, Karen, sorry to sound like a bad TV advert, but if you can spare a tea bag you might just about save my life.'

'A tea bag? I think I should be able to manage that.'

'And a splash of milk. And a mug.'

I squinted past him and saw the removals van parked in the drive. 'You want me to make you a brew?'

'That would be fantastic.' I liked the way he dragged out the vowels: *fantaastek*. The rain was letting up, and he reached in front of his face and pulled back his hood. Now I could see he was younger than me. His hair was close-cut, brown and crinkly, his eyelashes glossy and long and lush. 'I'll pay you back. It's just that I haven't managed to hunt down the kitchenware yet. You know what it's like when you're unpacking.'

'OK, then, Eric. Cup of tea it is. Oh, do you take sugar?'

He smiled. 'Naw. I'm sweet enough.'

Something small inside me went skip-skip.

Above our redundant chimney one break of blue showed in the cloud: just enough to make a pair of trousers for a sailor, as my mother would have said. Finally the rain was easing off. I felt his eyes on my back all the way up to the house.

KAREN: So what I was hoping we could do today, Mum, was fill in some of the family tree. I know we've got the big Bible and the records in there, but it's not always clear who's who. There are three Alfred Marshes, for a start.

NAN: My mother's brothers.

KAREN: What, all of them?

NAN: Aye. Florrie had five childer, but three of 'em died straight away. She passed t'name down each time.

KAREN: Really? It seems a bit morbid.

NAN: It's what folk did i' them days.

KAREN: Oh, I see. That poor woman. How dreadful. And her husband wasn't nice with her, was he?

NAN: He was a drunkard, Peter Marsh. I never knew him, he died more or less as I was born, but my mother used to say if he spilled his ale he'd put his head down and lap it up off t'table. Honest. And when he had no money left, he'd sit outside t'pub and beg.

KAREN: What, he'd spent all his wages on drink?

NAN: Oh, often on his way home from t'pit. What they

used to do, landlords, was put hot pies and such out on t'window-ledges, tempt the men in as they walked past, then some of 'em would stay and blow their pay packet. It were wicked, really. And t'women waiting at home. But he'd be having a rare old time, treating everybody. He were everyone's pal when his pockets were full. One time t'Sally Army band came round playing hymns and preaching temperance, and he was there blind drunk. No shame. He went up to t'captain and said, 'Don't you worry about me, I'm so full of Christ I could jump through that bloody drum.' And his mates were all laughing, you know. At his funeral, t'other colliers were saying what a grand lad he'd been, but I don't think Florrie were shedding many tears.

KAREN: And he died in 1917, I've got down?

NAN: That's right. So Peter and Florrie, they had two childer as lived – my mother Polly, and Uncle Jack who emigrated. But my mother lived wi' Florrie because she never married. That's where I was brought up, at my grandma's.

KAREN: And your dad was Harold Fenton?

NAN: Aye. But like I said, he'd never marry her.

KAREN: Was that not a big scandal?

NAN: It were very shaming for us. But what choice did we have? He made us take his surname for a Christian name—

KAREN: Yes. Why did he do that?

NAN: To show he claimed us, to show we were his. I'm Nancy Fenton Hesketh on my birth certificate. Brrr.

KAREN: It bothers you, doesn't it?

NAN: Jimmy felt it more than me. I think that's why he used to go wandering off. It were like he were searching for summat, I don't know. Then one day he skipped school, didn't say owt to anyone. Just took off. It got teatime and he hadn't come back . . . and he weren't one for stopping out, not when there was food to be etten. Harry Poxon come round t'next morning and towd us he'd seen Jimmy down by t'canal, playing wi' a stick. I think we knew then . . .

(Pause.)

KAREN: Mum? Oh, look, I'm sorry. I didn't mean to upset you.

NAN: Aye (voice wobbling). Funny thing is, I were only twelve meself, but it dunt seem that long ago. It still feels fresh, do you know? Like he's only just gone. Time goes to pot when you get to my age.

KAREN: Oh, Mum. Hell. I'm so sorry. Let me switch this damn machine—

CHAPTER 4

On a day in April

'By the way, I should warn you, I'm officially a Terrible Mother,' I told Martin Eavis as he poured me another cup of his tarry coffee. The tutorial was over, my Austen essay pulled apart, and I knew I had ten or fifteen minutes where he'd let me chat about general events. Other students didn't get this kind of time with him; none of my other tutors had offered it to me. But Martin was different. We had an understanding.

'I assume you're joking?'

'I am but I'm not.'

'How so? I'd have said you were an excellent parent, from the way you talk about your son.'

'Not really.' I hesitated before the confession. 'Last time I was home I smacked him.'

'And?'

'That's terrible, though, isn't it? That's what scuzzy mothers do.'

'You mean the ones who feed their newborns Kentucky Fried Chicken and give them cigarette-lighters to play with? I didn't have you down as a snob, Charlotte.'

That made me blush. 'I didn't mean—'

'I'm only teasing. Was there a reason for the smack?'

'Yeah, he was about to tip a tea pot full of boiling water down his front.'

'Ah.'

'It was a reflex. I didn't enjoy hurting him. I've never smacked him before. Mum went berserk, though, it was like she was going to phone Social Services and report me there and then. I know she's out of order but I still feel like the worst mother in the world.'

He leaned back in his chair and I heard the leather settle under him. There were piles of paper and box-files and cardboard wallets and books on every surface. On the wall behind him was a print of Ophelia drowning, and an engraving of some Gothic façade, a cathedral maybe. A row of arty postcards was propped along the mantel.

'OK. So let me ask you this: do you think he'll remember the incident when he's grown up? Does he even remember it now?'

'Knowing Mum, she'll probably coach him so he doesn't forget. Build up a nice head of resentment just in time for his adolescence.'

'She's on your side, isn't she?'

'Huh. That depends which way the wind's blowing. Have you ever smacked Isabella?'

The photo of his dumpy daughter sat on the desk between us.

'No, I haven't. The occasional wallop might have done her good.'

We laughed finally, and I felt better. I loved the way he spoke, direct and considered. Whatever we discussed, I always felt we'd cut to the heart of it.

He was built, I'd secretly thought, almost along the lines of Daniel. Wiry and tall but without the glasses or the mad hair. Martin's hair was sleek and grey-brown, and he had lovely elegant hands. Once I asked him if he played an instrument and he joked that he could 'saw out a tune on the 'cello'. And as soon as he said that, I was picturing him in his Georgian flat, sitting in front of an open sash window, some sad Elgar tune floating out into the street. I wondered what must it have been like for little Isabella growing up with Martin for a dad. How lucky was she? A house filled with classical CDs and poetry books. Had she appreciated him? I hoped so.

'So as far as you're concerned, smacking a child doesn't automatically make you a bad mother?'

'Not in isolation. How could it? Otherwise we'd have had virtually nothing but ruinous parenting since humans first stood on two feet. It's only within the last twenty, thirty years that corporal punishment's even been questioned. For almost our entire history children have been physically chastised for doing wrong. Think of our brightest and best over the previous millennium, Charlotte, the scientists and explorers and artists and tacticians who've shaped the progress of civilisation. Every one of them would have been smacked, or worse, as infants. Did it prevent them from functioning as balanced and loving adults, and as parents in their turn? Well, did it?'

'No.'

'Yet humankind's continued to progress, to nurture and create and produce great works of art which touch the sympathies of generation after generation and ennoble our spirits. How could that possibly have happened if every smacked youngster had been destroyed by the experience? It couldn't have.'

'Yeah, but you're not *advocating* smacking, are you? You're sort of joking?'

He spread his hands. 'I am and I'm not. So to speak.'

Once again he'd nailed me.

'Seriously, Charlotte, within the benign environment of good parenting there are too many other positive qualifying forces at work. You can relax. A single incident is unlikely to scar.'

'You think?'

'I do.'

'Thanks. You've made me feel a whole lot better.'

'Good. And aside from the smacking business . . .' he pursed his lips and blew on his coffee '. . . how are things at home?'

I considered. 'Still not great. We're all – it's hard to express – kind of coming loose somehow. It's since my grandma died. Mum's not really coping and it's as if she's angry with everyone. It's as if the grief is just hers. But I'm sad about Nan too.'

'Have you told her that?'

'I don't want to make things worse.'

Nowadays I never talked to Mum about how much I missed Nan, partly because I didn't want to stir up any extra household misery, but also because I was frightened she'd come out with something like, 'Well, you never saw her much towards the end. You were never around.' Yet Nan had been so important in my life. She'd been my best childhood friend, she'd been the bridge between me and my mum during those difficult early teens. Most of all, she'd been my champion when Mum was on at me to terminate the pregnancy. Dithery and ancient she may have been, but Nan had stuck up for me like a lion in the face of my mother's anger. Where Mum had pushed my scan photo away as if it was something horrid, Nan had pored over it and marvelled alongside me. She'd dangled a needle over my belly to test whether I was having a boy or a girl. She laid her hand on my skin and the baby had kicked her. She saved me from believing I'd made the wrong decision.

And I *had* been around for her, as much as I could. We'd even brought her up to York in my First Year, shown her the Department and the city walls and the union, none of which she was very interested in. Then we'd taken her to a tea shop and she'd perked right up. Kept stage-whispering about the waitress's chin, about how she 'favoured Bruce Forsyth'. When the girl came to take our order, Nan went, '*Nice to see you*,' and winked. The girl had no idea what was going on, luckily, but Mum knocked the salt pot on the floor in embarrassment and I had to bite my knuckles to stop myself laughing. Afterwards, on the drive home, Mum had asked her if she knew where she'd been. 'No, but it were lovely,' Nan said. 'Is it where our Charlotte works?' Mum said yes, and ever after Nan had me down as waiting on tables. It didn't matter. It had been a nice visit.

'The problem is, Martin, whatever I do, it'll be wrong. That's the way it is in our house right now. I'm a failed mother *and* a failed daughter, two for the price of one.'

'I'm quite sure you're neither.'

The leather chair squeaked again as he stood up. For one awful moment I thought he was coming to peer into my face or put his arm round me. But what he did was go over to the clock, open the glass and adjust the minute hand. He said, 'Bear with your mother; she obviously has some issues to work out on her own. Meanwhile your job is to love your son and enjoy him. That's what he'll remember.'

'Is it enough, though?'

His eyes travelled to the photo on his desk, the plain and treasured Isabella.

'I think we have to believe it is,' he said.

Days we'd had of hot weather. The sunlight on the concrete flags by the bins looked foreign in its brightness. Grass stopped growing. A plague of ants in the kitchen finally made me clear out the cupboards, whizz away all those ancient tins with their laughable price labels, and in turn that had sparked off a kind of frenzy to improve the whole house. I bought a nice patterned Will-proof oilcloth for the table, and washed all my cushion covers and touched up the paintwork round the doors. I papered over some blurred stencilling I'd done above the picture rail in my bedroom. The old wooden knobs on my chest of drawers I unscrewed and replaced with blue and white ceramic ones I'd seen in *Better Homes* magazine.

Now the garden wanted tidying, and I'd had this idea of replanting a flowerbed I'd let go, putting in some Michaelmas daisies and maybe some pinks the way my mother used to have it. The hydrangea near the back fence also needed replacing. There'd always been a hydrangea there as long as I could remember; as a child I used to sit under it and pick big green caterpillars off the leaves, mad things with horns on the end and yellow flashes down their sides. Then I'd take them indoors, one hand cupped over the other, to make Mum scream. Fine, she was, with dead rodents, but there was something about a grub she couldn't abide. I thought it was funny to watch her cringe. Occasionally I wouldn't even be holding a caterpillar in there, just empty palms, and she'd still have a fit. Then one time my dad was home and he cottoned on to what I was up to. He didn't shout, he was never one for shouting. He just led me upstairs and said, 'Would you like it if I turned off the light at bedtime and shut the door on you? Would you think that was funny?' Because at that time I was terrified of the dark. And that was it. No fuss, no lecture, he straight away made me see what I was doing wrong. He'd have made a brilliant teacher. Wasted, he was, at that paper mill.

I switched the hose to mist and began working my way across the overgrown bed, starting at the shed end and moving along, layering on moisture, quenching the grass and weeds so every leaf and blade shuddered with a bend-and-spring-up action. I imagined the beetles and bugs underneath scurrying for shelter. Where were the green caterpillars these days? You never saw them any more. A whole lot of things had quietly disappeared while I was growing middle-aged.

Water gathered in the hollows and trickled out onto the flags, carrying dust and greenflies with it. I let myself imagine my mother inside the house, pushing bedsheets into the old top-loader we used to have, or shaking Lux flakes into a bowl to rinse her tights. Nowadays *Better Homes* shows wooden airers hanging from ceilings with bunches of herbs tied to them or copper pans, very chic; when I was little, we used our airer to dry clothes. The maiden, Mum called it. *Bill, the maiden's stuck again, fetch a chair.* Dimly I remembered her electric mangle with marbled green rollers, and a spin dryer with an elephant trunk-style pipe you had to drape out of the window. I could almost smell the steamy laundry if I concentrated. My scalp prickled and I thought, If I turned round now she'd be there at the kitchen window. She would. What would she be mouthing at me through the clouded glass?

'Hullo, Karen.'

The voice came out of the blue, and in my shock I fumbled the hose, squirting my own crotch, chest and chin. Eric was standing at the fence, watching me. I tried to say, 'Hello,' back, but it came out as 'Hell.'

'Doing a bit of watering?'

'Watering myself, mainly.' I glanced down at my jeans, at the big dark stain across the denim. At least he'd seen how it happened, he couldn't put it down to stress incontinence.

'I think it's alive, your hose.'

'I think it is.' I flicked off the trigger and dropped the head on the ground. A last spiteful dribble squeezed out of the rose end and snaked towards my toe. I stepped nearer to the fence. 'How are you? I haven't seen you around much.'

'Ach, I've been back and forth to the old place, winding things up. There's been a lot to sort out and it's tricky when you're on your own.'

'I see.'

So no partner on the scene. That was interesting.

'Anyhow, I called you over because there's someone I'd like you to meet.'

Eric bent down for a second, out of view, and when he stood up again he was holding a boy-toddler under the armpits. He grinned, then with his arm round the child's waist for support, set him on top of the fence so his bare legs dangled over our side.

'Oh,' I said. 'Is he yours?'

Eric nodded. 'This is Kenzie.'

'Hello, Kenzie. And how old are you?'

The boy stared at me saucer-eyed. 'He's four,' said Eric.

'Is he?' That surprised me. He was only the size of our Will.

Still, you could see the resemblance between father and son: the same close-cut curly brown hair, the same set to the mouth. I pointed to the plaster on his bony knee. 'Someone's been in the wars.'

'Ach, he's always getting into bother. That one he got running full pelt into a clothes prop. Week before, he tripped over a doorstep. You canna take your eyes off them for a minute without some disaster. Well, you know yourself what it's like. I've seen your wee lad.'

'He's my daughter's.' I felt a blush rise.

'No kidding? I assumed he was yours. You don't look old enough to be a grandma.'

We started early, I nearly said, but bit my lip. He didn't want to hear about two generations of slip-ups. Exactly what age was Eric? Was he much younger than me? I wondered whether I could somehow steer the conversation so the information came out casually: *Hey, Eric, do you remember the first men on the moon? The three-day week? The night Elvis Presley died?*

'He's called Will. William. I have charge of him. His mother lives away, she's a student.'

Eric nodded, impressed. 'She's lucky to have you to look after him, then. We don't know where your mum is, do we, Kenzie? Disappeared without a word. We do all right, though, mostly.'

Kenzie picked at his plaster as my heart leaped with compassion and outrage. I fought an urge to reach out and gather him into my arms. Some women shouldn't be allowed to have children.

'Hey,' I said, 'you know what? We'll have to get them together. Two little lads. He could come round. It'd be nice for them both.'

Eric's face lit up. 'It would. That'd be great.'

'And you could come too and have a cup of tea inside.' I imagined us sitting together on the sofa, chatting, while the boys played on the rug. I could perhaps do us a plate of sandwiches, or a even a cake, make Mum's drop scones—

'Well, aye. Although I've a lot of work on here, everywhere's such a state. It would be a fantastic help if you could keep him out my way for an hour or two. Then I can make a really good start.'

'Ah, right, OK. No problem.'

'Brilliant. I'll bring him round Saturday afternoon, then?'

He hauled Kenzie off the fence and set him down behind it, out of sight. Then he laid his arm along the top and winked at me.

'I hope you don't mind my saying, you're a star, Karen.'

'No,' I said. My cheeks were tingling under his gaze. 'Actually, I don't mind that at all.'

'Hey, Charlotte, come see the show.'

Gemma was in Walshy's room, leaning against the fluorescent green window-frame, her face to the glass. I hesitated for a second, then went in and stood next to her.

On the small lawn below, Walsh staggered under the weight of what looked like a bundle of saplings, all of them taller than him. He'd lurch to one side, try to correct himself and end up half-running in the opposite direction like a drunk waltzing.

'Ding ding, round two,' said Gemma.

'What the fuck?'

She sniggered. 'It's a yurt. His dad sent it to him. You must have seen the big van pulling up.'

'I've only just got back from a tutorial. What's a yurt?'

'A Mongolian tent. Don't you know anything?'

'We're not that big on yurts in Wigan. I think Mum's boss has a gazebo, but that's about the limit. Anything more exotic and your neighbours ring for the police.'

It became clear that what Walshy was attempting to do was to make the sticks stand up on their own. Every time he got himself steady, he'd plant them squarely on the ground and step back, only they'd always fall over.

'We could go out and help,' I said.

'We could.'

Neither of us moved.

'What does he want a yurt for anyway?'

Gemma raised her eyebrows. 'Partying, he says. He's going to have lanterns and a barbecue or a mini-fridge, I wasn't really listening.'

'Most likely he'll set the thing on fire. Or no, I tell you what, it'll be like his own personal harem-space. He'll round up all the women he fancies and herd them in.'

As soon as I spoke the words, I regretted them. Tactless enough to speak about her ex that way, even if I hadn't spent a night last November rolling around on Walshy's bed with my skirt up around my thighs. I thought Gemma must surely be able to see inside my head, see the images flashing across my memory.

'Tim-ber!' said Gemma as the bundle pitched and fell once more.

I tried to laugh, but for the moment everything was drowned out by the soundtrack of my own morbid confession: *I snogged him, Gemma. While you were at a faculty party, we got drunk on shots and I let him take me upstairs. I let him and I enjoyed it. The fact it wasn't total full-on all-the-way sex is no defence. Daniel's heart would break if he knew; you'd never speak to me again. I am crap. I am Slut-Girl.*

'Oh, hang on, who's this?' Gemma craned her neck to see. 'Yaay, it's Roz to the rescue. Here she comes with her, hmm, towel.'

'A towel?'

'She's twirling it into a sausage. I can't see how that's supposed to help.'

'Perhaps she's going to hit him with it.'

'If we're playing Whack the Walsh, I might go down and join in.'

Roz obviously had some kind of plan because she kept spreading her arms out and leaning forward. Walshy yawned and stretched and pushed his hair out of his eyes, and at one point walked over and kicked the bundle where it lay on the grass.

I said, 'While I'm here, I've been meaning to say I'm sorry about Roz. All the Well-done-on-being-gay stuff.'

'Oh, that, yes. Having a bit of trouble, isn't she? It's not your fault. I should probably have kept quiet.'

'Don't be daft. It's up to you whether to tell us or not.' I mimicked Roz's slow, earnest tones. 'If you feel gay, you must say.'

Gemma grinned. The yurt sticks were finally stable. We watched as Roz and Walshy linked hands and also held an end of the towel each to support all sides.

'God, it's like a scene out of *The Wicker Man*,' said Gemma.

'As long as nobody takes their clothes off.'

Slowly they shuffled backwards and, as if by magic, the sticks began to ease apart in a trellis pattern to form a circular corral. Narrow and high at first, it widened out until the top edge of the sticks finished just above head height. The structure looked shaky as hell, but you could see how it was going to work when everything was fastened down. Roz went to grab the towel they'd dropped, and Walshy nabbed the clothes prop so he could push the roof beams up from the inside, umbrella-style. I thought how much Will would love a tent, wondered if I could afford one.

'Just the little matter of throwing the canvas over the top and mooring it all down,' said Gemma. 'And Roz'll forever claim she built a yurt single-handed.'

There was high-fiving going on now, and stepping back to admire the result, and adjusting the footings and more admiring. Roz put her arm though Walshy's and leaned against him. She clearly fancied him, despite the fact she was practically married to Gareth. Last term, for instance, we'd been shifting furniture around to make more space, and Walsh had looked across at her as she hauled the sofa and gone, 'Hey, I never noticed before but you've got a tremendous pair of boobs on you.' Instead of being outraged, or at least pretending to be outraged, she'd only sniggered. 'I'll tell Gareth on you,' she taunted. 'Fuck, don't do that, he'd snap me like a twig!' Walshy said, and made such a pathetic face he had us all laughing in the end. It was hard to stay cross with him for long because he took himself so lightly.

'It's funny, I just assumed she'd be OK with me coming out. I've known her since the first term and she always seemed cool about ...' Gemma waved her hand, searching for the right word. 'About difference.'

'It's her background. Roz *is* OK really, if she stops and thinks. It's not as if she doesn't rate you any more. It's that you've forced her to revise her world view: you know, whatever she thought lesbians were like, they weren't like you. And that's freaked her temporarily. Give her another month and she'll be fine.'

'I suppose so. She was all right about you having a baby, in the end.'

'Huh?'

'Like, she was a bit weirded out by Will at first. Not by *him*, I mean. By you being a mum.'

'Bloody hell. What did she say?'

I could see it was dawning on Gemma that she'd put her foot in it. 'Oh, nothing much. It was only that she didn't know any other teenage mums, just what she'd seen on TV really, so it was out of her comfort zone. And the point is, she's completely fine about it now. She thinks Will's great, she really does.'

My head was reeling. This was what, in the back of my mind, I'd always worried about. Because in those first weeks as a Fresher I had been shy about mentioning Will. I didn't know how other students would react. Then I had a long talk with Daniel and he'd said, 'Look, Charlotte, society's moved on. This isn't like the olden days when unmarried mothers ran off and drowned themselves in millponds for shame. No one will care that you've got a son.' I thought, Yeah, he's right, and I'd got stuck into student life and assumed they'd just accepted it. Now I realised I must after all have been the object of gossip, of finger-wagging or worse, sympathy.

Down on the lawn Walshy had started a grass fight, dodging in and out of the yurt's framework. Roz shrieked and spun on her heel, her tremendous bosom swinging. I thought, It's funny, even at school, even before Will arrived I was on the outside, never totally fitted in. Perhaps the problem was simply me.

Gemma stood up, wiping dust off her jeans. 'Everyone talks about everyone else here. That's a given. The trick is not to think about it.'

It's all right for you, Gemma. You were brought up to be confident and cool. That's just the way your brain works.

What it must be like, not to give a damn.

*

'I wouldn't have mentioned it,' said Ivy, peeling off her headscarf and folding it into triangles, 'only Maud says he were going like a rat up a pipe, whizzin' from one end o' t'bypass to th' other. How the police didn't clock him, I don't know. He's a lucky devil, your Steve, int he?'

Stupid, more like. I said, 'I don't see that I can do much about it. I never wanted him to have a motorbike in the first place, but he wouldn't be told. Not about anything. Not when we were married and even less now. Was he at least wearing his helmet?'

'I've no idea, it weren't me who saw him. I've brought you them photographs, though.' She sat herself down on the sofa and opened her handbag. Inside was an A5 brown envelope that she slit open and tipped up onto the cushion beside her. A handful of very small black and white prints spilled out. 'They're not all of your mum, I could only find two with her on. But there's others I thought you might be interested in.'

I came and perched on the sofa arm to see.

She passed across the first photo and it was a high-street view, the road surface cobbled and empty of cars. Shop signs hung from brackets; a man in a bowler hat stood under one of them. Ivy tapped a building on the extreme left of the picture. 'Now. That were t'Grapes. Where Londis is.'

'What, this is Bank Top?'

'Oh aye. So, your mother's mother – Polly, your grandma Marsh – she used t'clean for the landlord. She did all sorts for anyone, actually – laundry and fruit-picking – owt to earn a penny here and a penny there. And she'd to take Nancy and Jimmy with her on these jobs, either that or leave them with her mother, Florrie. Only Florrie was a harsh woman, what you'd call a last resort when it came to childminding. So when your grandma Marsh was working in t'pub, Nancy would play down below in t'cellar out of the way, and she'd open a window and when us kids saw that, we'd all climb in as well. We'd to be careful, like, because we'd have been in trouble if we'd been caught.'

'What did you get up to? Under-age drinking?'

Ivy laughed out loud. 'I should think not. No, we climbed about on t'barrels and threw a rubber ball and hid from each other. It were a good place for hiding because it were pretty gloomy. Oh, and there was a frog'd sit under one of t'barrels and drink beer as it dripped.'

'Get away.'

'It's true as I'm sitting here. Talking of frogs, see this drinking fountain?' She slid another photo out, again a street scene but one I partly recognised because it featured the spire-end of the church. Next to Saint Mary's, against the wall of a building long gone, was a plain stone basin and metal spout. 'Nan's brother Jimmy once filled t'bowl wi' tadpoles. He used Polly's milk pan to fetch them from t'ditch at t'bottom of the graveyard. He allus was drawn to water, that lad. And these taddies, they looked so funny, wriggling about. Us kids were two-double laughing. Well, except for Jacky Ollerton, that were t'teacher's son, who told him if a policeman caught him he'd be locked up because the fountain was the property of the mayor. Jacky said putting taddies in there was same as putting them in t'mayor's hat. And then a policeman did come! Sergeant Battersby walking up Church Street towards us, large as life and twice as ugly.'

'My God. So did Jimmy end up in prison?'

'Did he heck, we all scarpered. Hello, what's t'cat got in its mouth?'

Pringle had slunk in under the table and was gnawing at

something pink and plucked-looking. I thought briefly of the 'human hand' story – thanks for implanting that image in my head, Steve – but this lump of flesh was bulbous at one end and bony at the other, not hand-shaped at all. 'Hell's bells, it's a chicken leg.'

'Ooh, hey.' Ivy seemed impressed. 'Perhaps you could train him up, get him to bring you fillet steak next time.'

Pringle paused and stared at us, as if considering the option.

'I tell you what, Karen, he's put some weight on since he's been living here. He's like a different animal. You've got the magic touch.'

'I've got the fat touch.' I prodded my own stomach unhappily.

'Get away. You're a bonny woman. At least you've a bust.'

'I've one of those, all right.'

The photos sat between us in a spill of nostalgia. I thought of Mum's plump figure, how as a little girl I'd sat on her lap and pressed my head into her squashy bosom. In middle age she'd worn ecru corsets with diamond-shaped panels down the front; I could remember them hanging over the maiden to dry above the cooker.

'These pictures are brilliant. Can I take them to school and photocopy them?'

'You can have 'em.' She shoved two or three in my direction. 'See, you get to a point in life and you look around and it's all clutterment. You say to yourself, *What's this for? And this? Why am I hanging on to it?* You want to get a big broom and sweep everything away. It's the past, you know? It's gone. Buried. Meks no difference now.'

You're wrong there, I thought.

Walshy wanted to christen the yurt immediately. Soon as the last peg was hammered home, he sent Roz off to Spar for peanuts and

wine while he got Gemma and me to carry the kitchen chairs outside. He was after lighting a row of candles, but I told him there was
no point in the daytime and he'd be better saving them for when it
dropped dark. Instead he brought his radio down and tuned it into
some cheesy local station. By the time Roz returned with her clank-
ing carrier bag, we'd actually abandoned the chairs – too upright,
not yurty enough – and were lolling around on cushions, barefoot,
to *Wonderwall*.

Really I had an essay to be getting on with, so when Gemma
came round with the wine I only let her fill my glass halfway. I'm not
much of a drinker anyway, I just don't enjoy the sensation of letting
go and not caring. Always at the back of my mind I'm worried I
might be needed suddenly: what if there's a problem with Will and
I need to get back home pronto? Us mothers can't afford to get
wrecked. We have to stay Alert and Responsible. I've no tolerance
for alcohol anyway, I reach the jelly-legs stage while everyone else
is still just warming up. 'You need to put in more practice,' Roz told
me once, as though getting drunk was some kind of critical life-skill.
I said, 'It makes me miss my son.' That shut her up.

I watched Roz now, lying half-propped up on her elbows like a
sunbather. On one side of her Gemma sat cross-legged and on the
other Walshy hugged his knees and rocked to the music. It made
him look disturbed.

'This tent reminds me of being at the circus,' said Roz.

Gemma smirked. 'Does that make us the entertainment, then?
The Amazing Boozing Students. Hmm. I think I'd want my money
back.'

'I'd pay to see *you* in a spangly leotard,' said Roz, winking at her.

This flirty banter was a new thing. I couldn't tell whether it
annoyed Gemma or not.

'All three of you,' said Walshy, 'in sequined bikinis, on horseback. With feathered headbands. Yeah, I'd put my hand in my pocket for that.'

'In your dreams,' I said.

'You often are,' he said.

Roz snorted.

I thought, I wonder where we'll be in ten years' time. I wonder if we'll look back at this day, the Day of the Yurt, and what we'll remember from it. If we remember it at all. Perhaps we'd be too grown-up to bother with such nonsense. After all, we'd be completely different people by then, wouldn't we?

Or maybe not. Walshy already liked to talk about the city pad he was going to have, and the car he'd drive, and probably he was right because his dad would sort these things out for him. His dad would get him a rep's job in a good firm, and Walshy would wear a suit to work and have a succession of girlfriends who looked like models. Walsh at thirty would simply be an extension of the way he was now.

Roz maintained she was going to marry Gareth and go and live in a cottage on the Welsh coast, in amongst those rocks she'd spent three years studying. And I could see her, grown chunky – Gareth was running to fat already – and red-cheeked and windblown. Her hallway would be full of wellies and kagoules. 'What'll you do with your Geology degree?' I'd asked her once. 'Stuff the degree,' she said. 'I wanna keep chickens and goats.' You know, it goes through me when I hear students dismiss their courses like that.

I glanced across at Gemma; imagined a European city street lined with nineteenth-century apartment blocks, Gemma leaning out of an upper-storey window showing her bare tanned arms. Sleek as a cat, she'd be, and entirely content, chatting to locals as she did her daily shop, and drinking weird foreign brews. I knew her mum had plans for her to travel. There was a placement for her at an international school, if she wanted. Right now Roz was draping a daisy chain on her head, a tribute she accepted without a word or movement.

And where will you be in ten years' time, Charlotte?

I let my head fall back, followed with my gaze the lines of roof struts to where they met in the centre of the yurt. Such regular straightness, lifting to such a neat point. That was why they had vaulting in church roofs, to raise your thoughts beyond the here and now. We all need to stop and look upwards sometimes. I tried hard to focus on the future, to visualise what lay in store. Except when I've played at this before, I can only think of Will, and only as he is now, aged two. It's as if a blackout curtain drops down in front of me. Nan's friends like to nod at Will and go, 'Eeh, they're not young for long. He'll be grown and gone before you know it.' But I can't even imagine my son a little bit older, not even starting Reception class. The thing about children is they feel so much rooted in the present. The concept of a twelve-year-old Will seemed ludicrous.

Right now, everything seemed ludicrous. Like the degree: I travelled up to York and I sat with my books and I wrote my essays and went to lectures and my marks were good and on the surface everything was ticking along. I'd heard Martin calling me one of the most conscientious students he'd ever taught. The truth was, though, motherhood had broken my brain. There were some days when I couldn't remember the words for things, when I read the same paragraph ten times and it still didn't go in, when grasping the simplest idea felt like trying to shift a boulder with a stick. My concentration kept dipping, failing; I was incapable of making decisions. I didn't know what I wanted any more.

And yet you hear people say how teenage girls have babies 'because it's the easy way out', and that pisses me off SO much. It's the complete opposite. Having a child in the picture makes everything you do about a million times harder. There's nothing easy about the way your identity's squashed into a mum-shape, whether it fits or not. There's nothing easy about being distracted and tired and anxious, all kinds of health professionals watching you like hawks, about the massive endless weight of responsibility. Trying to frame your basic short-term plans, never mind the long-term. Where was I headed? God knows. Motherhood had taken up almost everything I was. What room was there left?

Something small and hard hit me on the cheek. 'Fuck,' I said.

'Oops,' said Roz. 'Friendly fire, sorry.' When I looked, she'd started flicking peanuts at Walshy. A lot of her shots were going wide, though. He stood the onslaught for about twenty seconds, then made a lunge for her, grabbing her wrists and forcing her backwards across a cushion.

'I'll teach you to play with nuts, missus,' he said.

She squealed and wriggled underneath him. Without lifting his body weight off her, he let go of one of her wrists and grabbed a fistful of peanuts. He raised his arm above her face. 'Now we'll see.'

One by one he let the contents of his fist fall. Peanuts bounced mainly onto her chest, trampolining off onto the grass. 'Say "Walshy, you are King of the Nuts".'

'No!' She was giggling and breathless. His face was close to hers. 'Say it.'

Gemma was sitting just a few feet away – there was even a peanut lodged in her shirt – but she'd zoned out. Her eyes were closed and her features relaxed.

'Say it, Roz.'

'No.'

'Then we're doomed to lie here, locked in combat indefinitely.'

She let out another squeak.

Walshy shifted his body down and let his head drop onto her chest. 'Actually, I'm quite happy. You make a smashing mattress. Nice and squashy. Well-covered. Lovely fleshy squashy tum-tum. Mmm.'

There was a pause while she thought about this, then without ceremony she heaved herself sideways and bucked him off so he flopped onto the grass. Before she could sit up he reached across and grabbed her T-shirt.

'Aw, what? Come back, flesh-mattress. I need you.'

'Piss off.'

'Eh? You're not in a mood, are you?'

She unhooked his fingers from the material and stood up. 'Why would I be in a mood?'

'I dunno. Girls usually are. One minute you're fine, the next, bang. It's a mystery.'

Roz ignored him. She just strode over to the yurt entrance, lifted the flap and slipped through, dropping the canvas behind her.

'What? What did I do?' Walshy turned to me.

'Called her fat, you pea-brain.'

'I did not. I called her squashy, which is a compliment. Women are meant to be squashy. Squashy bellies, squashy boobs.'

'Shut up, Walsh,' said Gemma.

He sank back down on a cushion. 'She started it.'

After a moment Gemma opened her eyes, unhooked her daisy crown and laid it across Walshy's chest like a wreath.

And this grand non-plan of yours for the future – where do I fit in? Daniel's voice came into my head, unbidden and plaintive. He would phone tonight. If I talked to him about the way I was feeling, would he listen, or would he try to tell me about membranes or capillaries or neural transmitters?

In front of me, Walshy heaved himself into a sitting position and plucked the daisy chain off his chest. He edged over and tried to hook it over my wrist, but I shook him off. He sighed, took the flowers and mashed them into a ball between his palms.

Daniel and me, ten years' time. Would we make it that far? If you really loved someone, you didn't fancy other people, did you? No, you didn't, Slut-Girl. I tried to picture a wedding day, Mum in raptures and some unsuitable hat, Will tricked out as a pageboy, Mrs G sulkily dishing out buttonholes at the back of Bank Top parish church. The idea felt bizarre, like trying to imagine myself on TV or something.

'Are you OK?' I heard Gemma say. 'You've not drunk your wine.'

I rubbed my face like someone waking up. 'Oh, yeah. I'm – I've got an essay crisis on, that's all. Sitting here worrying I'm not working instead of going up to my room and nailing the bastard. Mad, isn't it?'

She nodded. 'Go for it, then. Make a choice and then stick with it. Which is it to be, work-time or yurt-time?'

'*Othello*.'

'Good girl.'

I crossed the scraggy lawn still in my bare feet. Inside our back porch we keep a bike with a punctured tyre and a stolen sandwich board (Walshy's), a measuring pole (Roz's), a barbecue (Gemma's), a broken toy motor boat I filched off a skip, and twelve boxes of empty bottles we keep meaning to put out for recycling. I navigated past them all and placed my trainers under the kitchen table out of the way. Then I thought, before I started work I really ought to have a pee so as to minimise any distraction.

I was about to push on the loo door when it opened to reveal Roz standing on the other side. Her face was red, wet and streaky with tears.

'Oh,' I said, taken aback. 'Jesus. Are you OK?'

She glared at me and her skin flushed darker.

'Sorry, Roz. Stupid question. Can I do anything?'

Roz shook her head as if she was brushing me away.

I said, 'Look, you mustn't bother about Walshy, he's always talking bollocks. You have to let it slide over you. You're certainly not fat, if that's what's worrying you.'

I put a hand out to touch her shoulder but she jerked back angrily. 'For God's sake! It's *not* that.'

'What is it? Tell me, then I can help.'

'Just, you don't know what you're talking about. You have no idea what's going on in my life right now. *No idea.*' Her eyes were brimming with hurt. She seemed distressed beyond reason.

Then she barged me aside and ran down the hall.

'Is it Walshy, though?' I called recklessly. 'Is it him?'

No response. I heard her thumping up the stairs, the slam of her bedroom door, silence.

What the hell was happening to this house?

Once Will was safely in bed I brought the photos upstairs and laid them out on my duvet. Next I took my notepad and began to write up everything Ivy had told me.

I wrote about working in the cotton mills and Walking Day parades, about cats mobbing the fish cart and children begging ropes off the greengrocer so they could swing from lamp-posts. I wrote about scarlet fever and whooping cough, and about waking to the sound of clogs on cobbles and how in winter kids would pack the iron soles into platforms with snow and totter about. A whole other Bank Top my mother had lived in, and yet here it was, still just within reach as long as I took the time to search it out, to record and set it all down. Otherwise it would vanish, for good. More than ever I felt I had a mission. These pictures laid across my duvet, there were places and stories here that shouldn't be forgotten. And people, of course. I picked up the photo of the drinking fountain again, imagined young Jimmy trotting across the graveyard with his saucepan full of tadpoles, his round face bright with mischief. All those summers they thought he had in front of him.

A sudden chill came over me, and the urge to check on my grandson.

I'd only put him to bed half an hour before so it was a risky strategy even to open his door two inches. There was every chance he'd hear me and immediately ping awake, and then I'd never get him to lie back down quietly. Not this coming night, not for weeks after. It's the finest of sciences, toddlers' bedtime.

This evening, though, I was in luck. By some miracle he'd gone straight off and his eyes were shut, his chest rising and falling evenly. I pushed the door aside gently, then tiptoed across and bent over him, holding up his lamp to check his skin wasn't flushed or his forehead sweaty. The nights I'd sneaked in here to sit in the gloom after Charlotte left, because the weight of responsibility felt too heavy for me to sleep. A grandmother's watch. My penance for wishing at the start that he'd never been conceived.

There'd been no mixed feelings with Mum, of course. She'd welcomed Will with nothing but joy. He'd been the light of her life. Later, on days no one else could get through the fuddle of her dementia, she'd a smile for the baby, always. Despite the losses she'd suffered in her life, she never held back on love.

I wondered whether she was here now, watching over the nursery invisibly. There had been a couple of occasions, just after we moved her into Mayfield, she'd been home for a visit and we'd managed to haul her up the stairs. Then she'd sat by the cot like a queen on a throne, beaming.

'Mum?' I whispered. There followed a long silence where I traced the outline of his alphabet frieze with my eyes, *Annie Apple* through to *Zig Zag Zebra*, and then Will let out a deep sigh that ended with a whimper. Was he having a bad dream? Again I moved in to check, but already his limbs were relaxing, his breathing steadied. I pictured Mum's hand on his brow, comforting.

Years ago I'd seen a TV programme where a psychic had lit a candle in a haunted house and invited a spirit to blow it out. No idea whether it actually worked, because Mum chose that moment to mention she'd found mouse dirt under the sink, and Charlotte had gone into a five-star panic and insisted we put traps down there and then. Six wood mice we killed that winter. Every damn box of cereal was chewed to buggery.

I could almost hear Mum chuckling. *Well, see, your Pringle would sort that if it happened now. That would be your reward for tekkin' him in.*

There were tea lights in Charlotte's bedroom, and matches in the kitchen.

I stepped away from the bed. Will slept on.

Who else was there to phone when I was down, but Daniel? That's what he was there for.

'Sorry, it's pretty noisy in here,' he said when he picked up. 'You're going to have to shout.'

Shout? He could sod off, I wasn't shouting. No way was I going to bare my soul at top volume for everyone else in the house to hear. 'Where are you?'

'Pub.'

'A pub?'

'It's a building where they serve alcohol to the general public.'

'All right, clever-dick. I meant, what are you doing at the pub?'

I knew I was being unreasonable – for God's sake, he was a student, obviously he could go down the pub if he wanted. It's just that right at this minute I wanted him to be home at his flat, in the quiet, so he could give me his full attention. I needed to know we were OK.

'I'm with the planning group. You know, this *Twenty-First Century Rocks* thing.'

'Oh. The charity event?'

'Yup.'

'With Amelia.'

'Amelia's part of it. There are actually about fifteen of us here—' The receiver became muffled for a moment. '*He's not, is he? The whole lot at once?*'

'Daniel—'

A roar in the background.

'Is something up, Charlotte? I'm sorry I didn't ring earlier, only as I said, I was in this meeting. Hang on, tell you what, I'll go out-side—' Ragged cheering and a thumping noise as if something had fallen over. '*Jesus. Mainly over Rob, I think. Ask at the bar for a cloth.*'

For God's sake, I wanted to shout. I'm your girlfriend! Bloody pay attention. I need a bit of reassurance, not evidence of you enjoying yourself without me.

I caught a woman's voice, posh and slightly strident. I couldn't tell what she said but the intonation sounded like a question. '*No, it's fine,*' Daniel replied.

Is it, now? I thought.

Ten seconds later he was back with me. 'Everything OK?'

I should have said no. Straight away I should have nailed the conversation, come right out with the fact that tonight I was low and lonely and there was a freaky atmosphere in the house that made me want to pack my bags and jump on the first train back to Bank Top. But I didn't. I did that stupid stupid thing of lying and then hoping he'd guess. 'Uh-huh.'

'You sound a bit cheesed off.'

My second chance. 'No, I'm good. Just a bit bored.'

'Are you sure?'

'Yeah. I just called to chat. Don't turn it into a big deal.' And there was the hat-trick.

'OK,' he said. 'Great. Listen, I nearly called you earlier: did you hear that amazing story about the guy in Belgium with the pillars of ham? We were all just talking about it.'

'Pillows of ham?'

'Pillars.'

'Of ham? Like you'd put in a sandwich?'

'Yup, ordinary ham. He's wrapped these slices of meat, about eight thousand of them, round some columns on the university building and covered them in plastic and now he's waiting for the flies to come and turn his sculpture alive.'

'Why?'

'To contrast the permanence of science and knowledge – the university – with the fact that bodies rot, he says.'

'Sounds yuk.'

'It does, but at the same time it gets the philosophical point across. And I rather like the idea of public decay.'

'Bobbins.'

'No, people need to appreciate what is a really fascinating and vital natural process. Nature's waste-disposal. Amazing.'

'Wait till the vermin come. It won't look too philosophical when he's knocking rats away with a broom-end.' From where I sat I could see myself reflected in the window. I was pale without my make-up, and my hair needed a wash. 'What a tosser.'

Daniel said, 'Why are you always so dismissive, Charlotte?'

'I'm not. It's just, this weirdness. Why do you always go on about stuff that doesn't matter? I mean, bloody ham.' And I thought about Mum once telling me how she and Dad were never interested in the same things, and that was one of the reasons the marriage failed.

I heard him clear his throat. There was still a lot of background noise, faint music, laughter. Any minute now he would apologise. Perhaps he'd end the call and go straight back to the flat, ring from there. I waited.

The girl's voice came again, this time clearer; she must be standing closer. She was telling him she'd brought his drink through before someone had it. '*Thanks,*' he said. '*Cheers.*'

'Daniel?'

'Look, you want to tell me something but you won't say what, or you want me to come out with a particular line and I've to guess—'

'No—'

'But it's obviously not the right time for this conversation. It's too busy here and I can't – *Yeah, I'm coming, one minute* – and I'm in the middle of a meeting and I don't know how long we're going on for here. It's better if I ring you first thing tomorrow, yeah? Then we can have a proper talk. OK? Chin up, Charlotte. We'll thresh it out, whatever it is. Love you.'

And he hung up. I couldn't believe it.

I was always the one who hung up first.

I found a better candle, a scented job in a glass jar that one of the kids at school had bought me. *Alpine Fields* read the label. I took it into Charlotte's room because that had been Mum's, before Mayfield.

I struck a match and held it for a moment till the flare died down. Then I put it to the wick and placed the candle on the dressing-table, where its reflection wobbled in the mirror. I turned the lights out and went to sit on the bed.

It wasn't right to speak out loud, I decided, so I just asked Mum in my head if she'd come. For a minute or so I focused on the brightness of the flame, studying every slight movement. The shape of it varied, sometimes fat and sometimes stretched-up and thin, with a thread of black smoke coming from the tip. It stayed pretty upright, though.

I found myself thinking of the times I'd helped her make this bed, and how she liked to sing to housework even though her voice was awful, quavery and off-tune. 'Come Down, O Love Divine' was a favourite. *O comforter, draw near, within my heart appear.*

On Mondays, which was washing day, her fingers would stay reddened till teatime; on Wednesdays, which was Downstairs, they'd be marked with Duraglit. If I concentrated now, I could smell it over the top of Alpine Fields.

> *True lowliness of heart, which takes the humbler part*
> *And o'er its own shortcomings weeps with loathing.*

The flame began to quiver, then bend.

'Mum?'

Immediately it swayed upright again, then set up a juddering vertical motion. The shadows on the walls jigged in sympathy, disorientating me.

'Mum, are you there? I need to tell you something. I need to say I'm sorry for looking elsewhere. Do you understand?'

Some tiny reassurance, that was all I needed.

For maybe ten minutes afterwards I paced the room, sweeping stuff off my desk into the bin, kicking furniture that got in the way. Why hadn't I been able to tell him what was wrong? Why hadn't he tried harder to guess? And what the fuck was this Amelia up to? I was desperate to call him back, but I knew how weak that would make me look. My head felt like it was going to burst apart.

I said, 'I never wanted another mother. You were my mum, always. Going to London was a mistake. I'm glad you adopted me. And I wish I'd said that to you, I wish we'd talked about the adoption instead of pretending it never happened. Do you understand? Can you hear me? Is there something you want to say to me?'

The flame wobbled, as if under a breath. Darkness closed in from the sides of my vision and a sense of calm crept over me.

So in the end I phoned Mum. That's how upset I was.

Then the phone went.

I tried to ignore it. I let it ring for ages, willing it to stop, till it dawned on me that no normal person keeps trying for that long. This was someone with a point to make. Or a crisis, some news I had to deal with straight away. God.

Of all the times, though, why pick now?

Ring-ring went the phone, like a drill-bit through my ear, and from next door I heard Will calling.

I jerked myself up off the bed and snapped on the light. The candle burned steadily now. 'Grandma's coming, hang on a minute,' I shouted.

'This had better be an emergency,' I muttered as I ran downstairs to pick up the receiver. Hell's teeth, if it was just Charlotte calling for a moan, I was going to give her bloody short shrift.

KAREN: I was wondering if you could tell me a bit about what it was like, working in the mill?

NAN: Jarrod's?

KAREN: Yeah. Did you like it?

NAN: (laughs) It were better than picking coal on Pit Brow. That's what my mother used threaten me with.

KAREN: How old were you when you started?

NAN: Thirteen.

KAREN: And that was straight into full-time?

NAN: Well, they used t'have what they called Half-timers, where you'd go part-time to work, sometimes a morning and then swap over to an afternoon. And be at school rest o' t'day. That were when you were twelve. But they finished wi' that a few year before.

KAREN: You didn't enjoy school, did you?

NAN: That were our Jimmy – I didn't mind it much. Except for t'stick. They gave you t'stick for being late, for not knowing your lessons, for nowt, really. Our teacher, Miss Hartly, once asked the girls what you needed to check before shaking your duster out the window, and I said, 'Whether the neighbours are watching to see how dirty your house is.' Ooh, she were that cross with me. She thought as I were cheeking her, see.

KAREN: What should you have said?

NAN: Check which way t'wind's blowing. That were th' answer she were after. So I got t'stick for it. And she beat a lad who said th' equator were 'an imaginary lion running round the earth'.

KAREN: Oh dear.

NAN: Six strokes across his palm for that. They weren't nice with you, teachers. Not like they are today. Not like *you* are.

KAREN: So what did you do in the mill?

NAN: When I first started, I had to clean under four looms.

KAREN: While they were running?

NAN: No. Early on, i' t'morning, while they were quiet. And then I got put wi' a woman as taught me how to piece ends, that's tie the broken threads together, and that were called tenting. But you had to learn quick or you were in trouble. Later on, they taught me to weave in designs: you had these cards with a duck on or a lamb, only if you didn't place your card in t'right place you ended up with a duck's head on one towel and its body on another (laughs).

KAREN: And you liked the other women? You went on trips together?

NAN: We'd hire a charabanc.

KAREN: We've a photo of that. *Whistling Rufus*, it was called.

NAN: That's right. Twice we went to Southport. Lytham, we went to. Keighley.

KAREN: So you enjoyed working at the mill?

NAN: Aye, they were good times. But then again, you *had* to like it. You'd no choice, there were nowt else for you.

CHAPTER 5

On a day in May

10 a.m., Student-land. We were in the lounge, watching TV and eating our various breakfasts – yoghurt for Gemma, vintage pizza for Walshy, crispbread for Roz and a bowl of Lucky Charms for me – when Tony Blair came on the screen. He was grinning like the Joker out of *Batman*.

'God, what's he done now?' said Gemma.

The cameras cut to Cherie Blair holding a white bundle fondly in her arms.

'Dropped a sprog, by the look of it,' said Walshy.

'Whoa, that's some achievement. How old is she, about fifty?'

'Forty-five. So, ancient, basically. Respect.'

'Well, she can sod off!' Roz blurted out, throwing her plate down on the settee and unleashing about a million crumbs. We stared as she flung herself towards the door, wrenched it open and slammed it hard behind her.

I said, 'Ooh. I didn't have her down as a Tory.'

'She isn't,' said Gemma. 'Her family's Labour, very strong. Also Methodists and teetotal.'

'Which explains her moderate approach to alcohol,' said Walshy.

Not ten hours before, we'd heard her slouch in from the pub and start retching down the toilet. Another top night out.

I took her plate and knelt to round up the worst of the crumbs. 'She tries to keep up with Gareth. That's where she goes wrong.'

'Well. Someone had better see if she's all right,' said Gemma, never taking her eyes off the screen. The TV now was showing tanks and soldiers and broken buildings, could have been anywhere in the world.

'I'll go,' I said.

Walshy pushed the last of the pizza into his mouth. 'No, I will.'

'Probably best if you don't?'

He frowned.

'I'd go myself,' said Gemma, 'only, not the way she is with me at the moment. If I cornered her in her room, God knows what conclusions she'd leap to. I don't want to add to the hysteria.'

There was no answer when I knocked on Roz's door, but she didn't tell me positively to go away so I turned the handle and went in. I saw straight away that her fur-fabric cushions had been thrown on the floor and her pink bedspread pummelled into a heap on the carpet. Geology books were scattered widely, as if they'd been kicked. Roz herself was standing in front of the wardrobe mirror, staring at her full-length reflection.

'You OK?'

She shook her head miserably.

I said, 'Are you worrying about your weight again? Because

you're not fat, honest. You've got a lovely figure. Proper curves.' I made an hourglass shape with my hands.

At once she began to cry. 'Oh, Chaz.'

'What? What is it?' The naked distress on her face made me feel frightened. 'Is it Gareth?'

'No.'

'Is it – is it Walshy?'

'No!' The syllable came out like a howl. She covered her face with her hands and sat down on the bed.

'Because he's a daft flirt and you mustn't take him seriously. He's only attention-seeking.'

'It's NOT Walshy!'

'What, then? Are you ill or something?'

'I can't tell you.'

This was getting us nowhere. 'Shall I go away and leave you alone, then?'

'Oh, I'm bloody well *pregnant*, aren't I?'

My gaze slid down to her stomach. She didn't look pregnant. There was a bit of a belly, true, but she'd always had that. 'Are you sure? Have you done a test? 'Cos you can be really late sometimes and still be OK.'

'Of course I've done a fucking test. I'm not *stupid*.' I must have winced because she apologised at once. 'Shit. That was out of order, I didn't mean to snap at you. I don't know what I'm saying. It's just so awful.'

'How far on are you?'

'Don't know. Six weeks?'

'Have you told Gareth?'

Roz shook her head. 'Haven't dared. He'll go mental. He's always slagging off girls who get pregnant by accident. He says either it's deliberate, or they're too stupid to be allowed to have sex in the first place.' A quick glance up and down at me. 'No offence.'

'What about your mum and dad?'

Her eyes nearly popped out of her head. 'Are you *kidding*? They'd *kill* me. My mum would literally *die* of shame. She wouldn't be able to go to church or anything. She'd have to hide in the house – no, they'd have to move.'

'Or what? The morality police'll come round and haul them off to jail? You're talking like it's the 1960s. Look, if you really are pregnant and you go to them for help, they might surprise you. My mum was upset at first. Boy, was she upset. But she came round. Eventually.'

'You don't *get* it, Chaz. It's completely different. My parents have got really high standards.'

Ouch again.

'I don't mean your mum and dad are scum or anything,' she went on. 'It's just, they were so proud of me studying for a degree. Now I've messed it up. All my A levels, it was for nothing.'

I plonked myself onto the bed next to her. 'Not necessarily.'

'You think? Oh, Chaz. You're the first person I've told. I've been dying to talk to you because you've been through it, you know what it's like. What *was* it like? Was it hell? How did you cope?'

How did I cope? There was a question. Pretty damn badly, as I recall. First off, I tried simply to ignore the possibility I might be pregnant. Believed I could stop biology by the pure power of denial. Then, when Daniel persuaded me to take a test, I blamed him for the positive result even though he wasn't actually my boyfriend at the time. Went round to see Paul, the baby's father, and got told to fuck off. Finally Mum spotted my bump and we had the row to end all rows. If it hadn't been for Nan and Daniel I might have had a trip to Piccadilly and chucked myself under a tram.

'Well, it wasn't easy,' I said.

'Wasn't it?' Roz looked fearful.

'I mean, the pregnancy itself was tricky – people weren't always that great with me. But the point is, once the baby's born, that turns a lot of stuff around. There's no arguing; the baby's there, you're its mum, everyone has to get on with it.'

'I don't want to be "turned around"! I like things the way they are. God, how did I get into this state? It's so unfair. I'm on the *pill*.'

'Perhaps you were sick one time.'

Roz shifted awkwardly. Yup, I thought. That'll be it. She said, 'Was it that with you? The pill going wrong?'

'No. A condom came off.'

'How totally bloody awful.'

'It was.'

A sudden wave of sorrow for my past self washed over me. Seventeen, I was, when I'd got caught: humiliated, terrified, alone. And to think of Roz going through the same kind of experiences made me fiery with protectiveness. I wanted to reach up now and smooth the furrows from between her brows, kiss and shush her the way I did with Will when he was upset.

'Look,' I said, 'I'll help you as much as I can, but you have to start the ball rolling. So here's what you do. You go see the doctor and get the pregnancy confirmed, see how many weeks along you are. Then, assuming it really is positive, you go ask about advice and counselling at Student Services.'

'I can't. If people see me there—'

'Then phone up. Or I'll phone. Or I'll go along with you and sit in the waiting room.'

'Would you?'

'We girls have to stick together.'

'Promise you won't say anything to the others?'

'Absolutely.'

'Not even if they ask you straight out?'

'I don't see why they would, but no. Not a word.'

She took hold of my hand and gripped it hard. 'Thank you, thank you, Chaz. Thank you.'

'No probs. And later on you can have a chat with your tutors, ask about a sabbatical, maybe.'

Her face was strained with hope. 'It will turn out all right in the end, won't it?'

'Yeah,' I lied. 'Course it will. In the end. You'll be fine.'

I did tell her not to come home specially. I said, 'I'll be all right, Charlotte, you mustn't interrupt your studies.' I didn't expect her to go, 'Oh, OK.'

Then again, it was always going to be difficult, whoever was in the house with me. Perhaps if it had been a weekday it would have been better, but the first anniversary of Mum's death fell on a Saturday, when there was nothing to hide behind. So I decided to go with it and just devote the time to her.

As soon as we were breakfasted and dressed, I settled my grandson on the rug with some paper and crayons while I spread out my family history project on the dining-table to begin working on Jimmy's page. Three photographs I had – one of him as a baby in his lacy christening dress, a formal one of him suited and booted with Mum and Polly, and the fountain picture Ivy had passed on. And it struck me how strange it was that people in the past seemed to keep hardly anything to remember their children by. Our Will wasn't three yet, but we had a drawer stuffed full of mementoes. Charlotte had taken plaster imprints of his hands, plus we had his hospital bracelet, his first baby blanket and socks and sleepsuit, and even the plastic clip that had clamped his umbilical cord. Virtually every scribble he committed to paper, every nursery daub was dated and stored in shoe boxes. I reckoned we must already have taken about a thousand photos of him, easy. This documented generation.

'Well, we won't forget Great-Uncle Jimmy,' I said out loud.

Across the room, Will dropped his crayon and looked up.

'How you getting on, love? Have you done me a nice drawing?'

He sat back to admire the red and black spirals he'd scored in the paper. It was like a migraine in art form. 'Farm,' he said.

'I see. Where are all the animals?'

Will thought for a moment, then stabbed the crayon's point into the centre of the paper several times. 'Chickens.'

'A chicken farm.'

He nodded. There was a smear of baked bean across his cheek that I'd somehow missed when I was dressing him, and more bean-smears at the margin of his drawing. That probably meant orange fingerprints all round the house. I'd have to go round later, checking.

Then I thought, Actually, wouldn't it be nice if I decorated Jimmy's page with toddler hand prints, as a way of linking the past and the present, a sort of meeting between the two of them? They might not have the same genes but they were family. I could get Will to finger-paint on a separate sheet, then cut round the best results and stick them in, alongside the photos.

I opened my mouth to ask if he'd like to get the paints out later, but stopped, because of the way he was staring at the armchair in front of him. His gaze was fixed, as if he could see something I couldn't. For once his body was perfectly still.

I moved to one side so I was looking at the chair from more or less the same angle. There was nothing unusual about it, no inexplicable dents in the cushions or against the head rest. Only a rash of cat-plucking in the material down the arm, and a Duplo figure wedged into the corner crack along with God knew what else. 'What is it, Will?'

He flicked his eyes to me and took a sharp breath. I thought he was going to tell me something, but instead he did a massive sneeze. 'Bless you,' he said, wincing.

'Do you need Grandma's hanky?'

'*No.*'

'What was on the chair?'

'Got cows on my farm,' he said, picking up the purple crayon and squinting at his picture critically.

I sat and watched the armchair for another minute while Will added half a dozen thick dark lines across the middle of his swirl. Nothing else moved in the room, not the tremble of a curtain, not the slightest sway of a lampshade. Over the sideboard, Dad's tenor horn hung on the wall, next to the barometer he and Mum had received as a wedding present off Bank Top Brass Band. If I opened the door to the hall her mohair scarf would be hanging up yet, smelling of Coty L'Aimant.

This time last year it had been an ordinary Friday over half-term. I'd popped into Mayfield nursing home on my way back from shopping with a car boot full of frozen food – Lord knows why I did it that way round – so I hadn't stayed long, but it was all right as we were coming up to dinnertime and also Mum was pretty sleepy. The nurses had dressed her, but she'd said she felt tired and got back into bed. I'd sat by the footboard and told her about Charlotte's last text, and Will calling a frog a fish, while she lay with her eyes closed. She was lucid enough, asked if I was going to the hairdresser's and what was I having for tea. The Golden Labrador they keep at the home wandered in and let me stroke its back for a minute. Mum said, 'He's called Bertie,' and I said, 'I know. Bertie and I have been friends for a while now.' At one point she complained she was thirsty, so I moved up the bed and put my arm round her shoulders to help her sit up. I let her have a few sips of water out of a lidded beaker, and then before she lay back down I gave her a hug. I'm really glad now I did that. I could so easily not have done. She said, 'Stranger on the shore,' which meant nothing at the time. Afterwards I wondered if it was my dad she could see.

I'd not been home above an hour when the Matron rang. 'It was over in seconds,' she said. They'd brought Mum through for her dinner, were actually serving up, when she just slumped forward. A nurse came running, but there was no pulse. 'Did she cry out? Did she say anything?' I'd asked. 'She never made a peep,' said Matron. You have to be grateful for small things. Weeks later, when I popped back to fill in some forms, one of the other residents told me the confusion had proved too much for Bertie and he'd jumped up and stolen Mum's sausage off her plate. I know she'd have liked that.

'Finished,' said Will, giving his paper a final stab. He pushed it across the rug, then rolled back on his heels into a sitting position and straightened his short legs out in front of him. Once again his eyes wandered to the armchair.

'*Is* there somebody in the chair?'

He shook his head. 'Kit Kat?'

Of course there wasn't anyone there.

'OK,' I said. 'But first we're going to do some finger painting.'

I left Roz mopping her face and went and sat in my own room with the radio on. I like noise. Noise is my friend.

I thought, If only I could have reached back in time and taken my own hand, the way I'd taken Roz's. Why didn't *I* get support, advice? Before, more than after. No wonder I ended up in trouble, there was no one to ask. The girls at school I'd assumed would either mock my ignorance, or put me down as a slag. And Mum was always so touchy – about everything, but especially sex. She was always so determined I wasn't going to repeat her Big Mistake. She'd fallen pregnant before she was ready and she was damned if I was going the same way. But you know what? Sex education requires a touch more than just barking *Don't do it!* at your teenager. What I'd needed was to be able to confide in her, to know that she wasn't going to have a blue fit if I mentioned the subject. If I could have gone to her and said, 'This is the situation: my boyfriend Paul, who you didn't even know about, wants to go all the way and I'm feeling pressured. Is virginity such a big deal? How many times can you keep saying no? Are condoms really safe?'

Because I hadn't even especially wanted sex in the first place, only everyone else seemed to be doing it and it felt like the grown-up option. None of us likes to think we're a freak. Alternatively I could have taken charge of my own contraception, marched up to the doctor's and asked for the pill, except if you sat in Bank Top surgery for more than thirty seconds one of Nan's friends was bound to totter over and start asking in a loud voice what you were there for. They have no sense of boundaries, old people. The best option of all would have been if I'd never gone anywhere near Paul

Bentham, full stop. Obviously, when it came down to it, he was an utter bastard, but I didn't spot that key fact till it was too late.

And I couldn't help it, I found myself wondering: imagine if I'd never got pregnant in the first place, if Will had never existed. What kind of person would I be now? Smarter, braver, clearer-headed?

Immediately I felt scared sick at my own disloyalty. Imagine if Fate heard me and visited some awful lesson on my head, Will in a terrible accident, or struck down by disease. *Wishing you weren't a mother, were you? Well, there you go, see how it actually feels.* Mums must never ever ever admit they're anything less than thrilled at being mums, or they might be made to pay.

I knew I was working myself into a state but I didn't know how to stop. Soon I'd be forced to phone home and check everything was OK. And even if it was, the minute I pressed End Call the bad thoughts would start up again. I began to picture all the ways my son might come to harm: he could fall down the stairs, run out onto the road, stumble into a pond, choke, stab himself, stick his fingers up a rare unguarded socket.

The knock at the door made me jump as though I'd been shot. When I pressed my hand to my chest, my heart was throbbing under the palm. 'I'm busy,' I shouted. 'I don't want to be disturbed.'

The door opened anyway and Daniel peered round. 'Not even by me?'

I yelped in genuine delight, ran to hug him. 'You didn't say you were coming.'

'I wanted it to be a surprise. I thought you might need cheering up today.'

'I do.' I turned the radio-babble off, led him over to the bed and wrapped my arms around him. 'Really pleased to see you.'

'Evidently.' His hair was, if anything, madder than when I'd last seen him. He grinned, then freed an arm and patted his jacket pocket. 'And I've brought you a present.'

'Is it a dead beetle in a matchbox again?'

'That was one time, Charlotte, and it did have a spectacular carapace. No, I've got you a tin of Uncle Joe's Mint Balls. I thought we could suck a couple in memory of Nan.'

I squeezed him again, so hard he pretended to be choking. 'You're a well weird boyfriend, you are. But I love you.'

'Do you? Do you really?' He leaned backwards so he could study my face.

'Well, duh. Course.'

'It's just – it's been a long time since you said it.'

'No, it hasn't.' I drew him into a long kiss to stop him arguing. When we broke for air, I said, 'You know, I've been thinking: did I ever say a proper thank-you?'

'For the beetle? No. You were singularly ungrateful, as I remember.'

'Idiot. I mean for how you were with me when I got pregnant, and how you helped with the baby, everything. Because if I didn't, I'm saying it now. I'd never have managed without you. You were what got me through that year.'

'It cuts both ways. If you recall, you were about the only person who bothered speaking to me when I started in that bloody school. I was Billy No-mates, stuck in the corner of the sixth-form common room day after day, playing chess with myself. No one else would have anything to do with me till you took me on.'

'Yeah, well. Someone had to rescue you. And you are great with Will.'

Daniel flopped back onto the bed. 'That's no hardship, I enjoy shaping his impressionable young mind. You know I've taught him the word "protein"?'

'No, you haven't.'

'I have. Last time we were at your mum's. I handed him his chicken drumstick and I said, "That's protein." And he said it right back at me.'

'He doesn't understand, though. He's only parroting. You could have claimed it was plutonium and he'd have accepted it.' I lay down next to Daniel and nestled my head against his shoulder. 'Enough, already. I don't want to talk about Will, it'll only make me homesick. What I need right now is distracting. Quick, take off your jeans.'

With the sigh of someone incredibly put-upon, he reached for the buckle on his belt.

'God, Charlotte, it's one demand after another with you.'

As Roz once charmingly observed during one of her drunken heart-to-hearts, Daniel didn't look as though he'd be good at sex. His wild hair, the mad professor glasses, the generally dishevelled clothes – none of it suggested Mr Lover-Man. But appearances can be deceptive. Maybe it was because we'd been friends first, taken things slowly, or maybe it was because we'd now been dating for nearly three years and he just knew his way around my body. Whatever it was, this was what I needed. Martin Eavis once said in a lecture that poetry was 'the only pleasure humans enjoyed with their whole mind'; when some of us sniggered, he said, 'No, think: even when you're enjoying the most intense physical sensations, your mind goes wandering off.' But for once he was wrong. There are times I've been with Daniel when I've been so consumed with sex that there's been no room in my head for anything else at all. Only a fierce meshing of rightness and release, and that amazing blissed-out calm that comes afterwards.

When we'd finished, the room was very quiet. I could make out far-off noises from round the house – water running through the pipes, birds cheeping outside my window, a low bass beat coming from Gemma's room downstairs. I felt like I was lying in some kind of bubble, insulated from the everyday world. Right at this moment I had no doubts or fears about the future. I could look into Daniel's face and be sure I loved him and that we would stay together. If he asked me to marry him here, now, in this bed, I'd say yes.

'OK?' he asked, reaching across to the bedside table for his glasses.

'Wait,' I said. 'I like to see you without them sometimes. You look all naked and vulnerable.'

'All blind and clumsy, you mean.'

There was a small dent on the bridge of his nose where his glasses had been resting. I reached up and touched it. *What do you think will happen when we leave uni?* I wanted to ask. *Are you going to be there for me and Will? Do you promise? Are we safe?*

But before I could put any of it into words I heard Walshy thumping up the stairs, shouting, 'Cut the green bits off, then. No one ever died of cheese poisoning.'

And then I remembered. Oh yeah: I was a faithless bitch.

'I've brought your cat back.'

Eric stood on the doorstep holding Pringle under one arm as though he was a parcel. Kenzie lurked behind.

'Oh,' I said. I knew what a sight I must look. No make-up, a painty apron, bare feet with a plaster wrapped round one toe. 'Thanks.'

'He was in my kitchen. About to help himself to a packet of cheese slices.'

God. And prior to that a piece of chicken and a sausage roll, I guessed.

'I suppose it's because it used to be his home. You could do with nailing your old cat-flap shut.'

'Aye, I'll get round to it one of these days.'

I took Pringle and dropped him at the foot of the stairs where he stretched, sat, then stuck his leg in the air and began to groom his privates.

'Wash hands, Grandma?' called Will.

'Yes,' I said. 'Look, we've had a messy morning but it's clearing-up time. Come in and I'll make a drink.'

Automatically I turned CBBC on, then hauled Will through to the bathroom to wipe him clean. While he dabbled his fingers in the sink I leaned across him into the mirror and tried to smooth my hair into a normal shape. There was a spare lipstick down here, luckily, so I made use of that. My shoes were upstairs but I did keep a pair of mules by the bath, they'd hide my manky toe. The apron I would lose after I'd gathered up and binned the newspaper. If only I'd had some warning Eric was about to come round. It was all very vexing.

After the table was cleared, and my history laid on top of the television to dry, I rustled up a plate of biscuits, juice and two coffees. 'You're a big boy now, you don't need a beaker like Will, do you?' I said, bending over the sofa to hand Kenzie his cup. I expected him to boast a bit about being older, the way the kids at school do. But he didn't respond at all. I watched him sip his juice and thought again how little the age gap actually showed. Honestly, you could have dropped Kenzie in the Giraffe Room at nursery along-side Will and no one would have batted an eyelid. Then again, Will was tall for his age. Already we had him in Age 3 trousers.

While I was pondering them both, Kenzie slid off the sofa and went over to the TV. I thought he wanted to get a better view of 64 Zoo Lane, but it was my history he'd spotted and the multicoloured handprints round the border. He crooked a finger and poked one of the paint splodges experimentally.

I didn't mean to shout, but I suppose I did raise my voice slightly. 'No, love, come away from that!'

At once he shrank back as if I'd yelled down his ear.

'What's he doing now?' said Eric.

'It's nothing, he's fine,' I said, and led Kenzie back to the sofa where he sat with his shoulders hunched. What a contrast to Will, who only ever registered the mildest interest when you were telling him off. I suppose that was the difference between being two and being four. Two-year-olds live in their own world, largely.

Eric stepped forward and peered at the book. 'Looks interesting.'

'It's just a family history I'm putting together.'

'And what've you uncovered? Any highwaymen, or dukes?'

'I'm not going that far back. Really it's only about my mother's life. Charlotte started the project, but she left to go to university so I picked it up. We both of us wanted to record the family stories while my mum, you know ... While we still could. I'm glad we made the time.' I felt a lump begin to rise in my throat, swallowed it down. 'It's actually her anniversary today.'

'Ach, I'm sorry to hear that, Karen.' He was studying the photos as if he genuinely cared what was in them. 'You know, this is quite a work y' have here. No, really. I can see the care must've gone into it. I always meant to look into my family tree, except all I'd probably have found was a bunch of rogues. Maria started hers once – that's Kenzie's mum – but she didna get far. Always got distracted, y' ken? There was always something else more interesting going on. That was her all over, actually. Couldna settle.' He pointed at the photo I'd stuck to the top of the page. 'So, go on, who's this lot, then?'

I lifted the book off the TV and nodded at him to sit down. Then I perched on the chair arm next to him.

'This little girl in the pinafore's my mum. The boy's her brother, the young woman's my grandma Polly, and the old sour-puss in the black silk's my great-grandma Florrie.'

'She seems like a barrel of laughs.'

'Doesn't she just.'

'Your mother's pretty. She has a nice smile.'

I felt such a rush of warmth towards Eric for saying that. He had no need. In truth, Mum was quite a plain girl, her face too round for a beauty. I was glad he saw what was lovely in her. 'Thanks.'

'Aye, it's hard when your mum's not around any more.'

'When did you lose yours, Eric?'

'She's not dead. She lives out in Spain with her fancy man.'

There was an almighty clatter as the plate of biscuits fell onto the carpet. Kenzie glanced up, stricken.

'It's all right,' I said quickly. 'Nothing broken.'

'Jeez, Kenzie. Why can't you be more careful?'

Will carried on sucking his custard cream and watching TV, but Kenzie next to him was wide-eyed and appalled. The skin under his nose glistened unpleasantly.

I said, 'Ooh, now, I think someone might need to blow his nose. Hang on a minute and I'll get you a tissue.'

I knew full well we had no tissues in the house, but toilet

paper does the job. I scooted through the kitchen into the bathroom, and was just pulling a few sheets off the roll when I heard noisy breathing behind me. Kenzie had followed me and was standing by the sink.

'Come here, sweetheart,' I said. I held the paper to his nose, as I've done a hundred times with kids at school, and helped him blow. Then I wiped, wiped again, and went over his face with a damp towel for good measure. He stood meekly till I'd finished, then suddenly lurched forward and buried his face against my thighs. I put my arms round him and held him for a few seconds, while from the living room drifted the theme tune to *Fireman Sam*. I thought, Eeh, lad, whose is the bosom you snuggle into when you need someone squashy? I know you've got your father, but there's no mum, no granny round the corner. Where's the mother-figure in your life? Is there anyone? Because if there isn't, it's a poor do.

A tug of pain seemed to travel up from his heart to mine; I hoped I was just imagining it because of my own raw state. Only, you see these programmes on TV – documentaries and the news – about kids who look OK but are secretly in difficulties. Damaged children. It's something that I think about a lot these days. Sometimes I lie awake at night worrying about the unhappiness in the world.

'All right now, pet?' I asked.

He relaxed his grip and I peeled him gently off me. Such a quiet child. His eyes were dark as pools.

'About time he learned to blow his own nose,' said Eric as I steered his son back through to the lounge.

'Actually, he's nothing like as bad as some of the infants I deal with. We had one, it was like a permanent stream. Very off-putting when you were hearing him read and he was standing at your elbow. His mum took him to the doctor in the end and it turned out he'd a piece of sweetcorn stuck up his nostril.'

'Kids, eh? Kenzie once shoved a marble up his bum. Came out on its own, though, thank God. Which school is it you work at?'

'Saint Mary's. Behind the council offices.'

'I know it. I drive by there if I've a job out Bolton way.' He stroked his chin thoughtfully. 'Hey, here's an idea. How about, next dinnertime I'm going past, I stop and take you for a bite to eat? Kind of a thank-you for looking after Kenzie. You've really helped me out these last few weeks.'

He'd caught me on the hop. I was flustered. 'That's very – I enjoy having him – there's no need.'

'It was just a thought.'

'No, it'd be good. The Feathers is nice.'

'Grand. I don't know when you teachers have your breaks.'

'Twelve till one. But I do a half-day Tuesdays and Thursdays.'

We smiled at each other, suddenly shy.

Through the lounge window came the sound of an engine outside revving over and over, like a snarling dog. That broke the moment. I edged slightly to one side to see past Eric, and a big blue and green motorbike was parking by our front gate.

Half a minute later, Steve waved through the glass. Pulling off the crash helmet had swept his hair upwards so it stood on end, Chuckle Brother-style. He gave me a thumbs-up and raised a swinging carrier bag for me to see. Now, what might he have brought to help me get through this difficult day? A memorial rose for the garden, maybe? A nice boxed photo-frame so I could display another picture of Mum? More likely to be a four-pack of cider and a DVD. Mind, I wouldn't have said no to that.

I went to let him in.

'I thought as you might have been a bit low today, so I – bloody hell, who's that?' Steve stood in the lounge doorway and pointed rudely at Eric.

'Ssh,' I said, batting his hand down. 'He's a neighbour. That's his little lad, Kenzie. I look after him sometimes.'

Eric stood up and the two men eyed each other.

I said, 'Eric: Steve. My ex-husband.'

'Good to meet you,' said Eric, with reasonable politeness. 'That your bike, then?'

'It is.'

'Nice.'

Steve's body language relaxed slightly.

'Course,' Eric went on, 'Suzuki GSX-Rs are faster.'

I said, 'I don't want him going faster.'

'Do you ride, then?' asked Steve.

Eric snorted. 'Me? I've better things to do than scrape my own body parts up off the road. But I used to work with a guy who'd been a dispatch rider. He'd been all over, knew all there was to know about Suzukis. Came off I don't know how many times, broke half the bones in his body. You want to get a decent back protector.'

'Oh, aye?'

'Hein Gericke, they do the best ones. They do decent leathers, too. Plenty of Kevlar where you need it. What make's your helmet?'

'AGV.'

'Not bad. Arai's better.'

'I'll make sure I ask your opinion next time I go shopping.'

Eric nodded, missing the sarcasm. 'Yeah, I can come along with you, any time. Just give us a shout.'

Over my steaming dead body, said Steve's expression. He glared at me. 'Can I have a private word, Karen?'

We left Eric with the boys and went through to the back kitchen.

'Who the hell does he think he is?' Steve burst out, the minute I'd pulled the door to. '"Plenty of Kevlar"? I know where he needs some Kevlar.'

'He's only being helpful.'

'Oh, aye, course he is. Who is he again?'

'I told you, he's our back-to-back neighbour. Rents Tommy Cottle's old house. Works as a freelance painter and decorator; he's doing up the Swan Hotel off Moor Street at the moment. A perfectly pleasant man. There was no need to get so uppity with him.'

'Hmph.'

I stuck the kettle on again, for something to do. 'You all right, anyway?'

'I am, actually. I've been offered a bit of bar work up at the bowling green. And I've applied for a warehouse job at the Co-op and I've joined the Kawasaki Owners' Club.'

'Whoopee.'

'And I had a text off our Charlie, summat about a film she saw that she thought I'd like. How is she, do you reckon? Is she coping in York? She getting on all right with her studies?'

'How should I know? I'm only her mother. She never texts me unless she's on the scrounge.'

Steve made a regretful face. I pulled a mug out of the cupboard and set it down on the breadboard. 'You could always go up there and visit her.'

'To t'university? Brrr. I don't reckon it's my cup of tea. Full of students. They'd make fun.'

'Don't talk soft.'

'It's all right for you, you're clever.'

'Looks like it.'

'Please, Karen. I'm trying—'

'What?'

'Look, I knew you'd be fed up today so I wondered if you fan-cied a little spin?'

I nearly dropped the lid of the tea jar. 'On your bike?'

'Yeah.'

'Do I look insane?'

'I thought it'd give you a boost. You get a real buzz at top speed. Clears your passages right out.'

'I don't want a buzz. Anyway, I've no helmet.'

'Now, well, hang on a minute. Ta-daa!' He shook the carrier bag at me, then laid it on the fridge top and peeled down the crinkly plastic. What emerged was a silver and pink crash helmet with flames airbrushed down the side and a lightning bolt across the brow. Steve patted the crown admiringly.

'Oh,' I said. 'You really shouldn't have.'

'It didn't cost me owt. I did an exchange with a woman at the club, Lusanna. Means now you can hop on whenever you want. Yeah? Come on. Just a spin round t'block, just down Vickeridge Road and then back up the high street. You'll have to have a try sometime. Five minutes, we'll be. Honest, Karen, you'll love it. You'll be set up for t'day.'

'And who'd look after Will?'

Steve jerked his thumb towards the lounge. 'How about Valentino Rossi in there? He'll sit with the boys while we nip out, won't he?'

Before I could stop him, he'd opened the door and stuck his

head round. 'Hoy, Eric, can you watch the kids for a bit? I'm taking Karen for a quick ride.'

I saw Eric glance up, startled, then jump to his feet. 'I was going to say, actually. I was hoping you could have Kenzie for an hour this afternoon, Karen. There's a job in Bolton needs pricing and I said I'd call today and check it out for them. In fact, I'm late now—'

Steve folded his arms.

'So if it's OK with you, Karen,' Eric was already in the hall, 'I'll be back by three but I have to get off or I'll be ... Oh, did you know there was a card stuck behind your door curtain?'

He bent and retrieved it, held out the bright blue envelope to me. I took it, and the next second he was gone.

'Fool,' said Steve.

'Aw, he's OK,' I said, turning the envelope in my hands and wondering at the London postmark. 'Just a single dad trying to juggle everything.'

Steve went back into the kitchen and I heard the rustle as he stuck the helmet back inside its plastic bag.

'I didn't mean him,' he said. 'I meant you.'

Gemma was making a chilli for us all. She had the big pan out and a shedload of peppers, a pack of economy mince and four bashed-up tins of beans waiting on the drainer. She looked too glam to be cooking, though, in her boat-neck top and red nail varnish. She'd applied her black eyeliner in wings, like a French film star. I wondered if she had a girlfriend yet but I was too shy to ask.

'Do you think Roz'll be down for this?' she said, rinsing pepper seeds off the blade of her chopping knife.

'I'm not sure.'

She opened the cutlery drawer and rooted about. 'What was it they argued over anyway? Did she say?'

For a moment I was stumped; I'd forgotten my own lie. 'Oh. No. Something completely trivial, I expect. Gareth can wind her up pretty easily. God, what's Walshy doing?'

Through the kitchen window we could see him running around the yurt, hitting the canvas sides with a long whippy twig. After a few seconds, Daniel's head poked through the entrance flap. He said something that made Walshy laugh uproariously, then ducked back inside. Walshy began what looked like a tribal dance on the lawn.

'Operating as normal, I'd say. Hey, Charlotte, chop an onion for us, will you? I don't want to ruin my mascara.'

I came and stood beside her to work. Thought of Nan teaching me to peel an onion under a running tap, saw her pressing pastry into the bottom of a pie dish with her knuckles, blowing on the flames at the back of the grill to get them to ignite. There's nothing so nice as cooking with your grandma when you're little. I could tell Mum had felt let down when I'd said I wasn't going home for the anniversary, but I missed Nan the whole time, not just one date on a calendar. Besides, to be completely truthful, I just couldn't face a day watching Mum screw herself further and further into her own grief.

Walshy and Daniel emerged from the yurt again and began to examine one of the guy ropes. It was funny seeing them standing next to each other like that, Walshy so upright and well-formed, Daniel hunched and with legs that were too long and skinny for his body. If only he'd stand up straighter, that would help. And if he'd do something about his hair. Then I thought, How shallow am I? Not half an hour ago I'd imagined committing myself to this man for all eternity, forsaking all others, etc. God, I was a crap girlfriend.

The boys finished their inspection or whatever it was, and began to slope across the lawn towards the kitchen. When Walshy got to the window he made a pig-nose against the glass. We both ignored him.

'You know he's dating a barmaid at the moment,' said Gemma. 'Well, I say "dating".'

'What happened to the sociologist?'

'Oh, her? Vanished, weeks ago. Like thistledown in the wind. Then there was a Spanish student, briefly.'

'That's quite a fast turnover even for Walshy. Do you think he's trying to prove something?'

She laughed. 'To me, you mean? Nope. I think that's just him. He can't help it.'

From the back porch came the sound of boxes being shoved out of the way and empty bottles clinking, then the boys appeared.

'You like our new tent, then?' I asked Daniel.

He sat down at the table and clasped his hands in front of him as though he was about to say grace. 'I do, actually. Very much so. Impressive capacity, robust construction.'

'Easy erection,' said Walshy.

'Well, that's always a bonus. But I'm thinking seriously, something like that'd be ideal for the *Twenty-First Century Rocks* event because it's so much easier to handle than a traditional marquee. It depends on cost. And size. I'll get Amelia to look into it.'

Amelia again. I put on a slight sneer. 'An expert on yurts, is she?'

'She knows a bit about marquees because they had one put up in the grounds for her sister's engagement party.'

'Ooh, get her. The *grounds*?'

'Of her house.'

'Lah-di-dah. So they're too posh to have a garden like every normal person?'

Daniel flopped back in his chair, annoyed. I didn't care.

'Does she live in a mansion, or what?'

'I don't know.'

'You don't have grounds unless you have a bloody great house.'

'Well, yes, then, I expect she does. I expect her dad's a baronet and she wears a tiara to eat her supper every night.'

Walshy and Gemma were exchanging glances.

'Well, does she?'

'I have no idea. She could bed down in a dog kennel for all I care.'

'But she doesn't, does she? She has *grounds*.'

'What on earth's the matter with you, Charlotte?' asked Daniel.

'It just sounds so pretentious. "In the grounds".'

'"Garden", I meant.'

'You said "grounds".'

I knew full well I was behaving badly. But suddenly I was sick of it. It all seemed so unfair. Who was this Amelia to waltz into my life with her well-heeled family, her cheerful charity work, her uncluttered, child-free background? The darling of Mrs Gale. *Oh, I meant to say, Dan, Amelia popped round with some copies of* Country Life *magazine for me, isn't that sweet of her?* Sometimes it felt as though she'd been sent specifically to make me feel inferior.

Walshy reached for the radio, turned it on and got Britney Spears. 'Oops, I did it again,' he sang, pursing his lips and rolling his shoulders. I watched, scowling, as he took the knife off Gemma and began to dance her against the sink. Daniel was sitting across from me with his eyebrows raised – waiting, I suppose, for some more reasoned response. Let him wait. I thought of Roz upstairs, weeping over her traitorous body, and of my own fucked-up life. No tiaras for me. No marquees on our scant lawn. Lucky if you could fit a couple of Portaloos on there.

Because by now I was convinced Amelia was after my boyfriend, the number of invitations she seemed to be throwing his way, all the post-meeting drinks, the strenuous flattery of his mother. And my fear was that Daniel was simply going to gravitate towards his own kind. Who could blame him? Mrs Gale would be on her knees with relief if he traded me in.

'What's Amelia think of me, then?' I persisted. 'When she found out your girlfriend was a single mum from a northern pit village. I bet that made her lip curl. I bet she's got me pegged as a right freeloader.'

'We haven't talked about you,' said Daniel.

'You mean you've kept quiet, out of embarrassment?'

'No. When I see her we discuss arrangements for the gig. You don't figure as a topic of conversation.'

'Then don't you think it's time I did?'

Daniel raised his palms in a 'can't win' gesture. At the same moment his phone began to ring. He flashed me a wary look but reached for it anyway, pressed it to his ear. His face stiffened.

'What's up?' I said. 'Is it Will?'

He waved me to be quiet. Then my head cleared and I thought, Idiot girl, why would anyone be phoning Daniel about my son? They'd ring me, wouldn't they? And my mobile was by the tea pot, lying silent.

'In the stairwell?' Daniel was asking. 'How long for? And she's OK otherwise? Does she need to get up to A and E?'

'What is it?' I mouthed.

This time he turned away, shutting me out. I waited till he'd finished, jiggling my leg under the table with impatience.

Finally he closed the phone. 'My mother's had a fall and we think she's sprained her ankle. She's in one piece but shaken, so I need to get back over there.'

'Who was it calling?'

'Amelia.'

I knew it. 'And what was Amelia doing round your flat again?'

'I think she called to pick up some flyers. Look, Charlotte, that's really not the most pressing issue I have to deal with right now. My mother's had an accident and she wants me home.'

I backed off sulkily. It was only a sprained ankle, for God's sake, and almost certainly the result of a drunken stumble. I didn't see the need for an immediate mercy dash. Especially with Amelia on hand to soothe her brow.

'So you're going right now?'

'Yes. I have to.'

'When will I see you again, Dan?'

'We'll arrange something later. I've really got to get off.'

I did walk him to the front door. Just before he left he said, 'What went wrong today? It was great earlier on, and then you went cross all of a sudden.'

I shrugged.

'Don't let's part on bad terms, Charlotte. I knew you were going to be near the edge with it being your nan's anniversary, and obviously it's—'

'I'm fine,' I said tightly.

'So, yeah – I'm sorry for whatever it is I'm supposed to have done. I'm sorry you're upset. We'll talk when things are calmer, yeah?'

Part of me wanted him just to go, part of me wanted to throw myself on the carpet and beg his forgiveness for behaving like a brat. *I'm sorry for being a stroppy cow and I'm sorry about your mum* is what I needed to say. *Tell me you're not interested in Amelia. Tell me I'm better than her.* I could shape the words in my head; why couldn't I get them out? Roz's misery vibes leaked through the floorboards and filtered down into the hall around us.

He hesitated, then grasped the door knob. 'I'll ring you, let you know how I get on.'

'Yeah.'

'See you—' Then he was gone.

'Bloody hell, Chaz. What was that even about?' said Gemma, coming up behind me.

'And does Eric babysit for *you?*' Steve fixed me with a beady stare.

'Not yet. But he will. Anyway, you can't talk. How much babysitting have you done lately?'

'I had Will last month, when you went for that tooth out. You're not being fair, Karen. It's you who dunt want to leave him with me.'

'Blame Charlotte for that. She bothers because you've no stair-gate, and no cupboard locks, and you live in a tip.'

'Aw, geroff. I'll have him if you want me to. While I'm off work, anyroad. You know, we never had any of these safety gadgets when I was a kid. My mother just used to plonk a chair on t'landing at night to stop me wandering. I never came to any harm. You were trusted not to go sticking your head down t'toilet or your hand in t'fire. And guess what? We didn't, and we lived to tell t'tale. Funny, that, int it?'

But I'd stopped listening. I was staring at the card and envelope in my hands. A cheap thing, embossed beige-flowers on the front, one corner bent over. When I opened it, words that made me almost stop breathing. *LOVE FROM YOR MUM.* The writing was nothing like Mum's had been, that loopy, quavery style so many old ladies use. This was heavy-handed, laborious. It reminded me of the way some of our Special Needs kid write. I checked the postmark again, my whole body trembling.

'What's up, Karen?' I heard Steve say. 'You look a bit peculiar.'

'Why don't you give him a ring, apologise?' said Gemma, rinsing her hands under the tap. 'Better than stewing all night.'

'I can't.'

'Why?'

Walshy was back outside, playing Frisbee with himself. The radio was playing 'Too Many Broken Hearts'.

I said, 'He'll come round. He always does.'

'If you say so.'

I looked at the clock.

'I'll give my mum a call. She'll appreciate it today and I need to hear a friendly voice.'

I turned on my heel and ran to the back door. I flung it open, jumped down the step, wrenched the lid of the wheeliebin open and stuffed the card under a slop of spaghetti hoops rejected the previous day by Will. I closed the bin and counted to ten. Then I counted another ten. I felt so sick and angry I barely knew what to do with myself. Finally, my legs still shaking, I went back inside.

'Is it a migraine or summat? Have I to get you an aspirin?' said Steve. I stared at him, hearing the words but not able to take them in. At the edge of my vision, Will strained and scrambled after the plate of biscuits on the table.

My mobile began to ring.

Steve picked up and went, 'Oh, hiya, love – yeah, yeah, all right – well, up and down, you know – I don't think so. Look, I'll pass you over. Charlie,' he mouthed at me. He held out the phone and I took it automatically.

At the exact same moment I put the phone to my ear, Will dropped with a thump between the table-edge and the arm of the chair. He landed face forwards, banging his chin and nose on the carpet. The screaming started immediately.

I threw the phone onto the sofa and ran to pick him up. His jaws were wide open in a yell; I could see there was blood in his mouth where he'd bitten his lip, but no other obvious damage. With one hand I felt over his skull for bumps, then I ran my fingers up and down his limbs the way Sylv's shown us at school. At last I gathered him into a cuddle and sat on the floor, rocking him.

'Hurts, Mummy,' he said. 'Hurt my mouth, Mummy.' His little body shuddered and heaved against me.

'Ssh, no,' I told him. 'Grandma's here. Shush. Shush.'

Take your eye off the ball for one single second, I was thinking, and you invite disaster. That is literally all it takes.

And I could hear Will howling in the background for bloody ages before Dad picked up again. I had no idea what was happening, I was frantic.

'Aw, he took a tumble off the chair, that's all. He'll be right as rain in a minute. No need to worry.'

'He's not damaged himself?'

'No.'

'You don't think it's worth taking him up to the Health Centre for a check-up? He might have concussion.'

'Nah. He didn't hit his head. Banged his nose, give hisself a fright. Aside from that he's champion. Honest, love. Don't fret.'

'You're sure?'

'I'm sure.'

My heart was hammering against my ribcage.

I said, 'Tell me one thing, Dad. Who did he just call "Mummy"?'

KAREN: What can you tell me about Grandma Fenton?

NAN: Lily Fenton?

KAREN: That's right. Your dad's mum.

NAN: Oh, well, she were in service. It's her as brought back that ladle.

KAREN: What ladle?

NAN: You know. That bonny ladle wi' a shell bowl.

KAREN: No, I don't know.

NAN: It has a bit of brass round th' handle. Like a brass collar.

KAREN: Honestly, Mum, I don't.

NAN: You do. Like a big serving spoon, a shell-shaped bowl.

KAREN: Hmm . . . I think I dimly remember it.

NAN: I used to serve peas up wi' it, and mash. It's in t'drawer.

KAREN: Which drawer?

NAN: Under t'big cupboard. In t'kitchen.

KAREN: Is it? Perhaps it's dropped down the back. I'll have a look tonight. So, what – did she pinch the ladle or was she given it?

NAN: Given it, I think. Mind, that weren't all she got, neither.

KAREN: How do you mean?

NAN: Well, we never knew who Harold's dad was, but we think it was her employer. After she left, he sent her money, regular. She never went short.

KAREN: Oh, I see.

NAN: But nobody ever said it outright ... That might have been why Harold was such a monkey, because he didn't have a father around to knock him into shape.

KAREN: You mean the way he messed your mum about, and having other women?

NAN: Aye. We met one of 'em once, at t'bus stop. My mother just went, 'Get on this bus, quick,' even though it were t'wrong one, she were in that much of a state. He broke her heart, did Harold Fenton. And then one day he were run over outside t'Corn Exchange in Manchester, and that were that.

KAREN: Awful.

NAN: Aye.

KAREN: But he was good with you?

NAN: Oh aye. When he was around. He brought us brandy snaps and bags of currants, sometimes toys he'd made. He thought the sun shone out of our Billy.

(Long pause.)

KAREN: Tell me more about Grandma Fenton.

NAN: Oh, well, she were a nice woman, a bit of a folk healer. You know, if you couldn't afford t'doctor, you'd go to her. She had this pantry full of jars and bottles, knitbone and Friar's Balsam, goose grease, brimstone and treacle. Laudanum.

KAREN: Laudanum? That's poison!

NAN: Aye. They took it in cough mixture. I don't think as

she killed anyone. I remember one time a neighbour come running in with a big hornet sting on t'top of his head – he were bald, like – and she put a vinegar poultice on for him. Only, it were vinegar out o' t'beetroot jar, and he went round all day wi' a bright purple crown. We were two-double laughing.

KAREN: But you said she was frightened of electricity?

NAN: She didn't understand it. She'd allus had gas-lamps, you see. Just after she moved in wi' us, we caught her standing on th' eiderdown, trying to blow out t'light bulb. She used to say, 'I see you've one of them lights in a bottle.' (Pause.) Now I look back, I think she had trouble keeping up wi' life after she lost her son. It was like, she couldn't be bothered wi' it. Do you know what I mean?

CHAPTER 6

On a day in June

'Tell me, who do I have to see to withdraw from the course?'

I plonked myself down across from Martin and pushed my bag out of the way under his antique desk.

He closed the book he'd been reading. 'One of those weeks, is it, Charlotte?'

'This time I'm not joking. I've had enough. I want to leave.'

That made him sit up.

'OK,' he said. 'Let me pour you a coffee and then you can tell me all about it.'

I waited while he took the jug off its stand, filled two cups, turned down the Baroque music he'd had playing in the background. Telemann again. Nowadays it was one of my favourites. I knew if I lived to be a hundred, Telemann's Allegros would always transport me back to Martin's office.

'All righty,' he said, placing a cup of evil-smelling Java in front of me. Then he settled back to listen.

So I told him about Will calling my mother 'Mummy'. 'It was horrible,' I said, 'like someone slicing my chest right open. I couldn't believe it. To call *her* his mother. Her! What does that make *me*? I *knew* it wouldn't work, me being away so much! It's all gone wrong the way I said it would, and *nobody* listened.'

Martin considered.

'Are you certain that's what you heard? You might have got hold of the wrong end of the stick. What you heard might have been him calling for you. In effect, "I want my mummy."'

I shook my head. 'Yeah, I bet Mum would have tried to argue that if she'd got the chance. But Dad blew it for her. He went, "Oh aye, Charlie, he's done it a couple of times now. We've tried telling him."'

'Ah.'

'And then Mum came on the phone and spun me this line about language development and how it was natural for toddlers to confuse names, and how once he'd called a man in a shop "Granddad" just because the guy had a moustache. She went, "Anyway, you used to mix up parrots and pirates. You could never remember which one sat on the other one's shoulder." As if that had anything to do with it. She said to me, "It's just words, it doesn't mean anything."'

Martin frowned, tapping his forefingers together while he marshalled his thoughts.

'Well, if it's any consolation, Charlotte, my four-year-old godson calls his parents Xander and Rowan; no one's ever used the handles "Mummy" or "Daddy" in that house, but he has no doubt who they are and what they mean to him. So while I can certainly appreciate why you're upset, I agree with your mother on this one. Terminology's not that important. Will's feelings for you won't have changed.'

'You honestly think? God, I was so angry I could barely speak.' In fact, I'd put the phone down on her in the end. It was easier than trying to explain the riot of misery charging through my veins.

'Are you still angry?'

'I don't know. I don't know! It's so complicated. I mean, I wanted her to look after him properly, to love him, it would have been awful if she hadn't. So of course he sees her as a mum-type figure. In practical terms that's what she is, most days. It's not like she set out to steal him from me or anything.'

'And some women in her position might be tempted to do that.'

'Yeah, I know.'

'So you're not blaming her.'

'No. Although I'm jealous of the time she gets to spend with him. I can't help myself.'

'Have you told her that?'

'There's no point. It wouldn't change anything, plus I know I'm being irrational. This is the most practical set-up, we agreed. Meanwhile she gets to tuck him in at nights, give him his baths, set his daily rules and routine. The result is, I feel like I haven't forged that crucial bond with my own child. Or maybe I did and I've let it come apart. It's my fault. I meant to be the best parent, and I've turned out to be rubbish. And do you know why?'

Martin waited, knowing I was about to answer my own question.

'Because I think part of me's holding back from him. He might only be two and a half but he already senses that. It's not just the being away from home – although that's obviously a major deal – it's that inside, I'm sort of at war. I love him, I love him utterly. Utterly. There's no question of that. I'd die for him. But I can't help resenting the way I have to arrange my life now. It's exhausting. I'm forever in the wrong place. There's never a moment's mental peace,

I can't be the person I want to be because half my mind's always somewhere else. And I don't want that kind of relationship with Will. I want him to grow up knowing his mum loves him, full stop, without other stuff leaking in.' I leaned forward and rested my elbows miserably on the desk. 'The most awful part is, I suddenly GET my mother. I can see it now. I understand why *she* was so resentful of *me*. Which makes me the same as her. I wanted so much to be better.'

The music had slowed to an Adagio. Martin took a pen and began to doodle little cages on his notepad.

'She wasn't such a bad mother, was she?'

I hesitated. 'Well – she constantly used to blame me for cutting short her opportunities. I mean openly, say it straight out in front of me. "Oh, Charlotte, what I could have been, what I sacrificed for you." How's that supposed to make a kid feel? Then, as I was grow-ing up, it was all the pressure to achieve the targets she missed. Compensating for her so-called failure. She isn't a failure at all, actu-ally, she teaches children to read. I'd say that's a pretty worthwhile job.'

'She encouraged you to do well.'

'That's true. But it didn't feel like encouragement. It wasn't how your middle-class parents do it, you know – "You go for it, Charlotte, we believe in you, yay." It was more like continual jabbing with a sharpened stick. And I don't know whether the success she was after was for me or for her. And when I got pregnant, God. She went spare. Threw stuff, broke ornaments, threatened me and Nan. She was like a woman possessed. Then of course afterwards there was this complete weird turn-about. She'd been away on a break having some meltdown on her own by the seaside, and by the time she came back I was in labour. Suddenly she's full of maternal remorse, can't do enough for me. Cries her eyes out at the birth. Instantly dotes on Will, when months before she was cursing him.'

'Babies have been known to trigger Damascene conversions. I think it's to do with witnessing a new life. It makes people take stock.'

'Or something happened while she was away, some mental crisis got resolved. Who knows. What matters is, the resolution didn't last. Since my grandma died – well, I'd say we're currently at a pretty low point.'

I noticed that Martin's cages were forming into stacking patterns, and that some of them looked to have branches or hands sticking out of them. To be honest, they looked a bit sinister. I was about to make some comment on them when he pushed the pad away and stood up. I glanced at the clock: it was coming up to noon. Had my time run out? Was I about to be dismissed? This was a busy man with lectures and tutorials to give, departmental meetings to attend.

But he didn't go for his briefcase or tap his watch. Instead he wandered over to the sash window and wiped his jacket cuff across the glass. He said, 'Have you been to the Railway Museum lately, Charlotte?'

Strange question, I thought.

'No. Not since Freshers' Week.' Walshy had visited at the start of term, but only to make mischief. He'd had this idea of planting a rude figure in one of the model-train layouts – a tiny plastic flasher he'd carved out of a Dungeons and Dragons druid – but when the day of installation came it turned out he'd made him the wrong gauge. What he'd actually created was a flashing giant. A shame, really, because he'd spent hours with a heated craft knife, carving and tweaking his miniature pervert.

'Well, if you're around that way, it's worth having a look at one of their engines,' said Martin. 'I don't mean the trains, I mean the actual engine mechanism. They have one in a glass case so you can study the component parts.'

'Yeah?' I still didn't get where this was leading.

'If you watch an engine in motion, you'll see that for some sections to rise, others have to fall. There's a harmony even to a simple piston. You have to have the up and down movement, the cyclic, the forward and backward, for energy to be produced. So if you'll allow me the analogy, this is dynamically how a relationship works. How could it be entirely positive, entirely on one note? It would be unproductive. It would stall. And that applies across the board, to you, to your mother, to me, everyone. We all experience our low points and our high, times we're close and times the momentum of living carries us further apart. That's normal.'

'Is it?'

'What I'm saying is, things will come round again. You just have to keep the lines of communication open. Really, try and talk to your mother, bring her nearer. Explain to her about this "Mummy" business, that it's made you feel vulnerable. Stress that you're not blaming her. Ask for reassurance.'

I thought of the days after Will was born, how it seemed as though we'd finally reached a new understanding. How even the way we spoke was different, mum to mum. And in some ways they were dark times: I'd struggled like mad to cope with a newborn, and she was busy beating herself up at having to put Nan into a home. But we supported each other. We confided, we listened. I remember joking with her about her boss Leo Fairbrother always hanging round, and about Dad being his usual shifty-charming self. In that tough year Mum and I grew closer than we'd ever been. Was it possible to get back to that level of tolerance? Right now it seemed unlikely. Mum was just too far away, and weary. Sometimes it felt as though she was living at the bottom of a deep, deep well and the rest of us were shouting down to her.

'I could try, I suppose. I still think I need to pack in the course, though, Martin. The bottom line is, you just can't be a decent parent at a distance.'

He turned back from the window and his expression was grave. 'Can't you?' Our eyes fell at the same moment on the photo of his daughter. 'Well, if that's the case, then a great swathe of us are doomed.'

Meet me at 12.30, Eric had texted me.

Straight away I'd got myself into a dither: was this a sort of date, or what? How should I dress? For a school day I normally wore flat shoes and trousers because, as a classroom assistant, you're half the time squatting on infant-sized chairs and half the time on your feet. All us adults have backache at the end of the day. My hair I tended to keep clipped back out of the way of glue, sand, snot, headlice, etc, and I never wore much make-up because who was there to appreciate it? This morning, however, I'd got up early and washed my hair and tonged it, and put on a bit of lippy. I'd chosen a long skirt and a summer blouse and shoes with a bit of a wedge. I knew that by mid-morning the lipstick would most likely have slid off – those big windows heat the classrooms like a greenhouse – and there was every chance I'd have caught my skirt on a chair leg and ripped it. But it felt nice to make an effort for once, and anyway, nothing ventured.

When the dinner bell rang I gathered up my stencils and

went to wash poster paint off my fingers. Some horrible child had put dirty fingermarks on my white sleeve, which was a blow, but I turned the cuff up and that more or less hid the damage. I reapplied my make-up and smoothed my hair with wetted fingers. Sylv shouted after me as I sneaked across the foyer.

'Ooh, you look nice, Karen. Going somewhere special?'

'Smear test,' I called back. That shut her up. This was one bit of gossip she wasn't having off me, not yet. Not till I'd an idea myself of what I was walking into.

'I'm sorry,' I said. God, if I could have climbed into a hole and shovelled earth over myself, I would have done. 'I didn't mean to suggest you couldn't be a good father unless you lived in. Like, when I told you before about my dad's set-up and how it worked fine for us, I wasn't lying. Obviously you're a fantastic parent. I know you are.'

But he only smiled. 'I think you've just defeated your own argument, Charlotte.'

'Yeah, that's right. Because I'm sure you're terrific. I've said before—'

'It's OK. There's no need to apologise. Just think it through logically. Regular, consistent and committed contact is what counts, not some specific number of hours. Yes, the type of parenting you and I have to manage is perhaps more difficult, it's certainly more complicated logistically than what happens in a traditional nuclear family, but it's not poor or inadequate. Not by default, anyway. We're simply parents who do our best in not-always-ideal circumstances, and there are millions of us in that camp.'

I didn't know how to respond, but he didn't wait for either validation or argument.

'Now, to go back to the degree for a moment. Have you considered how helpful it's going to be to Will if you abandon the course at this stage?'

The kind expression in his eyes pierced right through me. 'Martin, I'm not going to lie to you. I really, really want the degree, you know I do. I've worked so hard for it. I love the course, I chose it because it was one of the best, set my heart on it before I ever got pregnant. I've been revising like mad for these exams. But the bottom line is, you don't need a degree to get a job.'

'I'm not talking about jobs. I'm talking about a sense of fulfilment, completion. Completing who you are. If you break off your studies now, you're always going to feel that loss. Will might come to feel it too. You said how bitterly your mother regretted not finishing her education, and the effect that had on your growing up.'

'I would never make Will a scapegoat like that!'

Martin left a pause before he carried on: *You might not intend to.*

'Let's look at this pragmatically. You're already two-thirds of the way through the degree. You've got your dissertation sketched out, haven't you? Ready to tackle in the autumn. We were going to draw up a reading list so you could cover some background research over the holidays. Would you really bin all that effort at this late stage? It's your decision. You have five weeks till we break up: why not stick it out till the end of term, then decide during the summer? Talk it over with your boyfriend. He's supportive, isn't he?'

'Let's not go there,' I said.

'All right, leaving that aside, it really is a situation you need to think through in a considered space, not something you should leap at. Of course you can terminate the course whenever you want to – you're an adult, you're here of your own free will. But personally speaking, Charlotte, I'd be *very sorry indeed if you left.*'

He strolled back across the room, ignoring his chair and instead leaning against the side of the desk so he could refill our cups.

I felt slightly shaky with gratitude. Daniel used to joke sometimes that I had a crush on Martin. I wondered if he was right.

'OK,' I said at last. 'I need to think about this some more. But thank you for taking the time to listen to me.'

'My pleasure.'

Then, with barely a pause, he went on to the subject of this extended reading list he was compiling for me, how he'd grouped the texts not by simple chronology but by stylistic development, so I'd appreciate how each author drew on previous writers for inspiration. 'Nothing comes from nothing,' he said. 'Everything begins before itself. There'd be no Romantics without the Augustans.'

I said, 'Haven't you another student to see?' And he said no, he had a meeting but he'd decided he'd have a more interesting and productive time talking to me instead.

By the time he'd finished going through the list, my brain was alight with ideas. I wanted to run to the library and start straight away.

'I can lend you the Mandeville,' said Martin, reaching for his bookshelves. 'My own copy. Keep it as long as you need it.'

I took the book reverently.

As I flicked through the pages he smiled. 'Not that I'm putting any kind of pressure on you to stay, Charlotte.'

'Course not. I haven't been bulldozed at all.'

'I'm glad you see that.'

The *Adagio* finished; we were back to the brisk and busy *Allegro*.

'Martin?'

'Yes?'

'One last thing. Since we're speaking so honestly.'

'Uh huh?'

'Do you mind if I don't drink the coffee any more? Only it tastes like bitumen.'

He laughed and patted the back of my chair. Then he turned the music up and we sat for another couple of minutes in companionable silence.

I'd have stayed there the whole day if I'd dared.

For once it wasn't raining. I crossed the playground and went out through the gates, a right turn onto the main street with its unlovely mix of Victorian and 1960s architecture. All my history was laid out in the length of this village, like the Bayeux Tapestry. Here was the top of the road where Steve nearly ran me over on his push bike so that I dropped my satchel and my pencil case burst open and my O level science book fell in the mud. Here was the chip shop I used to visit on a Friday night when I was first married. This building on the right was the library where I'd come during the day when Charlotte was a baby, to try and keep warm. Because, God, we were skint in those days. We had this rented room over the newsagent's, and the gas fire would go on for three hours each evening and that was it; getting up to feed Charlotte at night was freezing torture. Everything we owned came from car boots or charity shops, although even charity shops were sometimes too dear. Our cupboards were stocked with value labels, and I'd often buy a bag of stale rolls off the baker at the end of the day and freshen them in the oven. One particular memory I have is of me crying as I tried to wrap Christmas presents with cheap paper off the market so thin it ripped if you looked at it twice. I even used to squash the toilet rolls out of shape so they released fewer sheets per tug. That's how poor we were.

Here was the chemist where later on I'd queued endlessly for Mum's prescriptions, and the Wool Shop, also one of her favourites, and now the post office where a pre-teen Charlotte once stopped to stroke an evil-eyed Westie, only to have it nearly bite her finger off. I caught sight of my reflection hovering over a display of Hallmark cards, and paused. My face wasn't actually too knackered from a distance, but when I moved in closer I could see there were two deep worry-lines between my eyebrows. I forced my muscles to relax and the lines grew fainter. That wasn't bad, if I could stay like it. Mum always said people ended up with the face they deserved.

Five minutes later found me pushing at the saloon door of the Feathers. Eric I spotted immediately. He was at the bar, denim jacket hanging open and brick dust staining his T-shirt.

I nodded at the state of his front. 'I see you've brought some work home with you.'

'That's me, always do a thorough job. What are you having to drink?'

I went mad and ordered wine. The air in the pub felt close and thick, and I had to pick up a menu and fan myself with it.

'Aye, it is warm,' said Eric.

I watched as he peeled off his denim jacket. Builder's arms he certainly had, lean and brown and nicely muscled. Manly arms, the kind of arms which could fold you in and hold you tight. The hairs on the skin above his watch were golden rather than dark, which was surprising. Perhaps he'd been working outside and they'd bleached in the sun. On his left-hand middle finger he wore a signet ring. There was a white scar across the knuckle of his right thumb, a recent cut at the base of the palm.

'– and out of nowhere this damn bucket landed on my foot,'

he was saying. 'So there's mortar spilling everywhere, me hopping about. Don't think I'll lose the nail, but it wouldna be the first time.'

'Oh, no, awful.' I was going to have to pay attention. 'Don't you wear special boots?'

'If I remember to load them in the van.'

The drinks arrived and we took ourselves to a corner table.

'You're very nice today, very summery,' said Eric.

I blushed. 'Normally it tips down here eleven months of the year, but we seem to have had an amazing run since you moved in.' God, now I was talking about the weather. It was stupid of me to get wound up. We'd chatted easily enough before, with Kenzie and Will ferreting about in the background. If only this room wasn't so hot.

'Nothing to do with me, hen. I grew up in Dumfries and Galloway. I tell you, Scotland can out-rain England any day of the week.'

'Bet it can't. Year Five were doing the water cycle this morning. I had to help them stencil weather symbols and I thought to myself then, there ought to be a special cloud with a scowling face on it for Lancashire rain.'

'Do you enjoy being a teacher?'

'Classroom assistant.'

'Same thing, isn't it?'

'No. It pays a lot less, for a start, but then I work fewer hours and I don't have all the marking and planning to bother with. Which at the moment is a blessing, admittedly. I would still like to be a full-time teacher, get on a training course, see if I could pass the right exams. But you know what life's like. Fate tends to knock you off your tracks.'

Eric tutted as if he knew exactly what I meant. 'I bet you're good, though. With the wee kiddies. I bet you're patient. More patient than me, anyway.'

'I wouldn't claim that.'

'Ach, I ended up shouting at Kenzie this morning. He wouldna put his shoes on, wanted me to do it and I know he can manage perfectly well himself, I taught him over the summer. It's as if he wants babying, as if he's going backwards. And I canna be waiting on him hand and foot.'

'Well, it's hard when you're on your own.'

'It is.'

Our table-mats and cutlery arrived.

I said, 'Do you mind if I ask: is there no sign of Maria coming back? Has she not been in touch at all?'

'Nah.' He cast his eyes downwards. 'It just happened out the blue. Told me one day I wasna right for her, she wanted more, then the next day she'd packed up and gone. No forwarding address. Trying t'explain to the lad . . .'

My indignation flared again. What kind of mother just drops her child as if he's an inconvenience? She ought to be hunted down and hauled home.

'That must have been awful.'

'To be honest with you, Karen, it cuts me up to be talking about it.'

I nodded sympathetically. 'Kenzie's such a sweet boy, as well. It's lovely to watch him play alongside Will. He likes colouring in, and drawing, doesn't he? He did me a beautiful sun the other day. Will just scribbles. He'll scribble on anything if you don't watch him – magazines, letters, the skirting board. His own legs one time.'

'You wait till he discovers scissors. Kenzie's done for my shaver cable. Two minutes, I was out the room. Mopping up a drink he spilled.'

At the edge of my vision I could see two middle-aged women very obviously checking Eric out. They swivelled in their seats and leaned together, whispering. One of them had maroon-streaked hair and the other needed her roots bleaching; both wore skirts like pelmets. I thought, Well, at least I'm not dressed like mutton. I look 'nice and summery': he said so. I sat up straighter and smoothed my blouse.

'No, you can't afford to take your eyes off toddlers for a second,' I said. 'And I'll tell you something, it's worse when the child you're in charge of isn't your own. It puts you in an impossible position. I've lost track of the number of things I'm supposedly doing wrong with Will. The latest is, Angel Delight's not a fit and proper pudding, even though Charlotte ate her way through vats of it when she was his age and I don't recall her being struck down with nutritional deficiency. And I cut his hair too short, that's another bone of contention. What I say is, she can take over when she comes home for the summer, she can be the one to hold him down in the barber's chair while he screams his head off and chokes on his own clippings.'

Eric was nodding like a man who understood.

'Although, as it stands, our Charlotte's not even speaking to me,' I went on.

'How come?'

'Oh, a stupid misunderstanding. Something she heard over the phone. I'm not stressing about it. She'll come round. Basically the problem is, she wants control over Will but she's not here to enforce it.'

'That's too bad,' said Eric. 'She should be on her knees thanking you for what you do.'

'Ha! Dream on. Anyway, next on the horizon it's potty training. Charlotte's read up on the topic, reckons if you stay firm then it's a doddle. But I remember what a demon she was at that stage, and how many pairs of knickers we'd get through in a day.'

'Our Kenzie still wets the bed.'

Now that doesn't surprise me, I thought. Nervous little scrap. I wondered if it had started when his mum left.

Our dinner arrived and I found I was very hungry. Eric watched me tucking into steak and ale pie. 'I like a woman who enjoys her food,' he said. I suspected he might be eyeing up my cleavage, but I was well into my second glass of wine by then so my judgement maybe wasn't pin sharp. I did notice that when he got up to go to the Gents, several women clocked him cross the room, clocked the neat bum in faded jeans, the slight swagger of a man happy with himself. Yes, ladies, he's with me, I thought. Get over it. I remembered Sylv, suddenly, and felt mean: maybe I should go out with her sometime. A spot of salsa might get the blood pumping again. *You need to loosen up*, she'd said. At the same moment I realised I had sky-blue poster paint all round the nail-bed of my little finger. How had I missed that? I put my finger in my mouth to see if I could suck it clean. I didn't want Eric to think I was growing mould.

And as I nibbled, a different memory popped into my head, of Steve licking my fingers after we'd eaten Chinese ribs one night: that was in the months after I became a grandma and I'd almost had him back. I was glad now I'd held out. Even at the time I knew I was just feeling sorry for myself. I half-closed my eyes and tried to imagine that it was Steve who'd any minute be walking across the saloon towards me, how I'd feel, how those women sitting at other tables might react. I doubted he'd provoke much interest from any quarter. He wasn't an ugly man, my ex, but he was skinny, slouched his shoulders as though he was permanently battling through hail, and then there was that damn moustache.

There was a time in my early thirties when it seemed a terrible embarrassment that I'd ended up divorced and single. So I'd run around dating various gits and losers, while Charlotte sniggered from the sidelines. The year Will was born there'd been that funny half-flirtation with my boss, Leo, only in the end I'd walked away because however kind someone is, if you don't fancy them then the relationship's going nowhere. Last year there'd been a bit of excitement when I was asked out by one of the dads at school. Twice we went for a drink and once he took me to Rufford Old Hall Gardens for afternoon tea. And he was OK in himself but his son was a little sod, loathed by everyone in the staff room. I couldn't bring myself to hook up with a man whose child liked to smear his own face with Pritt Stick and then press his chin into pencil shavings.

Since then there'd been naff-all in the way of romantic activity, unless you counted a dozen or so fumbles with Steve. Which I didn't.

And now here was Eric, dropping into my life out the blue, landing practically on my doorstep, with his easy manner and interested face. I couldn't help being stirred. He just had that way with him.

I sneaked a glance across at Maroon-Streak and Brown-Roots. *They* were out on the pull, they obviously felt entitled to a sex-life. The trouble was, ordinary routine swallowed you up, made you dull and mumsy. Grandmumsy, in my case. There didn't seem much left over for erotic adventure. Or was I being defeatist? Was I all washed up, or only in my prime?

By the time he came back I was on my third glass of wine and I'd unbuttoned my blouse a notch.

'How old are you, Eric, if you don't mind my asking?'

'Thirty-two. Why?'

Thirty-two! Thirty-two was OK. 'No reason, really.'

'Aye. I'm as old as my tongue and a little older than my teeth, as my granny used to say. Have to keep checking I've no bald patch coming.' He patted the top of his scalp cheerfully. 'So far so good. Although if Kenzie keeps on misbehaving I might start losing a few hairs.'

I said, 'Not every man could have coped in your situation. You do better than you think. You do, I've seen you with him.'

'He's not a bad kid. I wish he was tougher, though. Like your Will, y' ken? Nothing fazes him.'

That was true. You wouldn't have caught Kenzie poking an Alsatian with a stick, or taking off on his own across Menses Park after a stranger's football. 'No, but he's two. He's fearless because he's immature. A bit like Steve and his ruddy bike.'

Eric sipped his pint, studying me.

'Do you see much of your ex, Karen?'

'Not a lot. Not since he turned into Easy Rider.'

'You get on OK, though?'

'He's all right.' I thought about it. 'Yeah, he is.'

'When did you split up?'

'Oh, ages ago. When Charlotte was tiny. It was me, really, Steve would have stayed the course. But we were too young and we had no money and I suppose I blamed him. Not that I'd call myself materialistic, but it grinds you down when you haven't enough to cover the basics. He kept walking out of jobs, mucking about. It was just a grim start to a marriage and it spoiled things between us. I hadn't even wanted to get hitched in the first place, it was my mother who persuaded me. "Make a stable home for the baby," she said.' I pictured Mum standing on the doorstep that day I'd come home, her hands clasped against her bosom. 'Not that I blame her. She meant well. After the split it was Mum who took us in and looked after us. And it did come right eventually. Because no matter how bad a break-up is, you get through it in the end.'

It must have been the wine talking because I suddenly heard myself say, 'Can you ever see yourself dating again?'

Eric put down his glass thoughtfully. Even through the veil of drink I could see I'd been less than subtle.

'Well, there's a question,' he said. 'Put it this way: I hope one day I'll find someone I can trust again, who won't let me down, who talks to me if she's unhappy instead of bottling it up. Someone who'll be nice to Kenzie, who he likes. It's the thought of that keeps me going.' He gave me a lovely conspiratorial smile, one single parent to another. 'But that's for the future. Let's say for now, I'm not quite on the market yet.'

And there we were. Wherever that was.

Across the room, Brown-Roots raised her eyebrows at me. I just looked away.

After I'd seen Martin, I went back to the house and did two hours' straight revision. Then I took Roz into town for a spot of window shopping. I thought that was better for both of us than sitting in our rooms and brooding. Lately she'd been either clingy with me or miserably aloof – I never knew which I was going to get when we met each morning over the toaster. Meanwhile Gemma and Walshy were wild to know what was up with her, and I kept having to pretend I didn't know. It was a crap place to be.

'So what *is* the plan?' I'd asked her two days ago. She knew straight away I meant about the baby. 'I'm keeping it,' she'd said. 'I'm telling Gareth next week.' I'd given her a hug and she'd had a little cry. Since then she'd been like my shadow.

Now we were cruising down the baby aisle in Boots, and Roz was goggling at all the shelves of gear stretching along both sides. In the milk section alone there was Cow & Gate, Aptamil, SMA and HiPP, in cartons, bottles, tins, travel sachets; there were sterilisers and warmers and breast pumps, teats and spouts and cleaning brushes and trainer cups, pouches and pots of baby food, soft plastic spoons and grip-base bowls. Bibs came in rigid plastic or floppy cloth, singly or in multipacks, alongside wipes featuring mice, rabbits, hippos, chicks and crocodiles. There were banks of nappies in all sizes, and cotton-wool pads and scented plastic sacks and self-seal bins; shampoo and lotion and bubble bath in Gentle, Calming, Sensitive and Regular. Roz paused in front of the Baby Safety display. She reached past a rack of thermometers and picked out a socket cover.

'It looks bloody complicated, having a baby,' she said, her voice wobbling a little.

'Well,' I said, 'there's a lot to do at first, when they're newborns. But you get loads of support. It's not like you're dropped and left. I mean, with me, the baby's dad wasn't great ...' Understatement of the century, that was.

'I've no idea how Gareth's going to be.'

'No, but what I'm saying is, other people always step in. In the first weeks I had Will, my mum changed more nappies than I did ...'

I trailed off because of the look of horror crossing her face. Obviously she hadn't broken the news to her folks yet, either. 'Plus there are professionals queuing up to help, midwives and health visitors and your GP. Someone pops round every few days, and they'll answer any questions or worries you have. You won't be on your own, I promise you.'

Roz nodded bravely, but I could see the terror in her eyes. For a distraction I pointed at a photo of a model pasted on the wall near the tills. 'Hey, have you seen? Doesn't she look like Gemma?'

Roz squinted. 'Prettier than Gemma.'

'She's got the same-shaped jaw, though, and her haircut's similar.' It was somewhere near the truth.

'I still reckon she might fancy you, Chaz. When you were watching TV last night, she kept looking over. She did.'

I gave Roz a mild shove. 'Get off.'

'No, I'm serious. Just when you aren't expecting it, she'll pounce.'

That made me laugh. 'You make her sound like a Bengal tiger. For God's sake, being a lesbian doesn't turn you into a raging sex maniac, casting about for anything in a skirt. You like men, yeah? But you don't fancy every bloke you meet, do you? You don't fancy Old Dogbreath in the corner shop, or that postman with all the nostril hair. You don't fancy John Prescott.'

'You're not the equivalent of John Prescott, though. You're more ...' She paused to flick through a few likely candidates. 'I dunno. Walshy.'

'I bloody am not.'

Roz pursed her lips.

'I'm not like Walshy! Not in any way. And Gemma isn't on my case. Sheesh, I've enough on my plate with the exams next week, I don't need any extra distraction.'

'OK, OK. Chill out.'

And how about you, Roz? I wanted to say. *How's YOUR revision going?* That would have brought her up short. Not a lot of note-making and open textbooks to be found in her room, as far as I could see. But she was on Planet Motherhood right now. I remembered that feeling of being behind a glass wall and watching others, at the same time fascinated by the smallness of their concerns and irritated to death. She couldn't help it. And maybe once the pregnancy became common knowledge, her tutor would step in and offer support, salvage something out of the degree.

'Hey,' I said. 'How about we go seek out a bit of mindless distraction? Do you fancy playing tourists for an hour?' I took Roz's hand and pulled her towards the exit.

Eric gave me a lift back in his van. I had some fun climbing up into the seat, what with my heels and my trailing skirt, and the footwell being full of papers and empty Coke tins. When it was time to get out, though, he came round my side and opened my door for me like a gentleman. Then he offered a hand down. I couldn't ever recall anyone doing that for me, and it made me blush. Tragic, isn't it? My whole life I've been starved of gallantry.

'Will's booked into nursery till three,' I said. 'Do you want to come in for a coffee?'

Eric slammed the passenger door shut. 'Can't. I've to be back at work.'

'What have you done with Kenzie?'

He nodded vaguely in the direction of the bypass. 'He's at Little Beavers nursery, over in Radcliffe.'

'Radcliffe? Blimey, that's a fair hike for you.'

'I know. Useless in an emergency. But it's where he was before we came here and I daren't move him. It took Maria months to settle him as it was. That's why it's so good he likes coming round to yours. What would we do without friendly neighbours, eh?'

'That's right. And, likewise, I know I can always leave Will at yours if I need to.'

He jangled the keys of his van at me. 'Course you can, Karen,' he said easily. 'Any time.'

'This may be your idea of fun,' said Roz out of the semi-darkness, 'but it's making me feel sick.' An assistant had helped us into one of the little open carriages, there was a whirring sound, people giggling in the car behind us, and then we'd been jerked backwards into the past: the Jorvik Time Travel Experience. Down through Victorian York, Georgian, Stuart, Tudor, Norman. At the end the car did a three-point turn to face forwards and there we were, surrounded by Vikings.

If you're in need of entertainment, York isn't short of attractions. Roz and I could equally have taken ourselves to the Minster with its Great East Window and inspiring Gothic lines, raised a prayer to the vaulting and bought a fridge magnet from the gift shop. But that place was off-limits because of Walshy last autumn, hurtling like a man on fire out of the Lady Chapel and shouting into the crowds, 'A miracle! A miracle! I was blind and now I can see!' I had no idea holy people could get so cross.

We could have gone and cheered ourselves up at the Dungeon, but memories of that place were tainted also, this time by Gareth who'd been caught flicking nuggets of chewed-up paper at the model of Dick Turpin to see if he could get them to stick like warts.

We all got chucked out of the building that time, even though I'd just been a spectator.

But you didn't fool with the Vikings. Jorvik was a weird enough experience without the need for any mucking about. Here was the Viking village with a thatched hut, creepy mannequin children playing outside, a mannequin crone inside and what looked like a real stuffed rabbit hanging from the doorpost. The charcoal fire flickered electrically and a smell of soot wafted over. Viking voices muttered in the background. A cockerel crowed.

'Your little boy would like this,' said Roz.

I nodded, though I wasn't sure. He'd more likely find it nightmarish, what with the subdued lighting and strange, dungy smell. Some of the figures seemed to be watching us back.

The narrator over the Tannoy told us this was Lothin the wood turner, and we craned our necks to see.

'Have you ever brought Daniel to this place?'

Lothin was indeed turning his wood. In the cars we were treated to a whiff that reminded me of pencil sharpenings and fresh sawdust. I thought about Daniel waiting for me to say sorry. Closing the front door behind him, his face sadder than sad.

'No. Never got round to it.'

'You could drop in next time he's here.'

Before I could reply, the narrator started to speak again, telling us about the importance of fishing to Viking communities. We moved into a tableau of men hauling nets, silver herring glistening under varnish, buckets of oyster shells at their feet. One of the fishermen had wiry hair like Daniel's. *Next time he's here.*

A whole week he'd kept me hanging before he'd phoned – God, I was so keyed up I nearly broke first. A week! We'd never left it so long without talking. There'd been texts, of course, tight-lipped, polite enquiries passed between us. *How is ur mum? – Ok. Hows revsn gng?* I still hadn't managed to apologise. I was saving it till after the exams, I told myself. Till I could see him face to face.

We trundled past Thorfast the bone carver and Snarri the jeweller. In one of the huts a baby cried and its mother sang to calm it. 'Sweet,' I said to Roz.

Svein the leather worker smelled of ammonia. 'Piss,' Roz said, clamping her hand to her face in disgust. 'And worse. Oh, gross, is that someone on the toilet?'

Above the top edge of a wicker wall, a man's face strained.

'I suppose even Vikings used the loo.'

'I don't want to see it. Seriously, Chaz, I think I might be sick.'

'If you're going to hurl, wait till we get to the midden at least, then no one'll notice. In fact, it'll add authenticity to the exhibit.'

'Thanks for the sympathy.'

You're going to have to deal with a lot of toilet-stuff when the baby comes, I felt like saying.

Someone in the seats behind us went, *Eew, do you think they come to life at night?* and it gave me the jitters because I'd been playing with that idea myself. It was hard not to when the flickering half-light made some of them look as if they were moving. Svein's eyes glittered back at us from under his rat-tail hair, the brazier cast a glow across the muscles of his arms. What would they think of us, these Vikings, if they could see us trailing past, gawping? If they could somehow spy on our glossy modern paraphernalia, our mobile phones, computers, TVs, our motorways and air travel? Our shining high-tech hospitals. The vast fields we have these days with their agricultural machinery scooping up industrial-scale crops; the container ships crossing the oceans with their satnav. Our space rockets, our weapons. How far we'd come. And yet, behind the hut, hardly visible unless you squinted, two ninth-century lovers embraced against a tree. Her face seemed tilted to his and he was smiling down wolfishly, one hand pressing against the bark above her head. Was it a secret tryst? Was he honourable? Was she safe? Perhaps if I came back here after closing time and waited long enough, I'd see them argue and one of them walk away.

Over the stench of ammonia now came hay, roasting meat and cloves. Roz was making gagging noises beside me.

'Don't you think,' I said, 'that really we're all alike? I mean, for all these guys are less advanced than we are, they're just human beings with the same worries and stresses and triumphs and grief. A few hundred years makes no difference. That's what the exhibition's telling us: it's as if we're them and they're us. Only they pooed in pits and we have flushing toilets.'

Roz made a show of pinching her nose. 'You must be kidding. We've come a bit further than that.'

But when I looked down, her hand was resting on her belly, the unconscious pose of a mum to be. Mum-alone, mum in trouble. Her dilemma was the oldest one in the book.

The post was waiting on the mat. Our new postie's nice but he's slow, likes to chat and wonder aloud about what he's handing over. I only see him on Saturdays because by the time he delivers I've usually gone to work.

I picked up the pile of letters and went into the lounge. Eric's van was just swinging onto the Working Men's car park for a U-turn. I waved but he didn't see me.

One by one I dropped envelopes – a bumper crop of rubbish

today – onto the table. Two special offers from catalogues, a flyer from Sky, a suggested tariff change from British Gas, a leaflet about swimming classes, a Dear Occupier and a letter from Social Services asking if I wanted to join in this autumn's Carers' Events. Still I get this stuff, even though it's three years since I looked after my mum at home. You get onto some database and then it's like trying to scrape chewing gum off your shoe.

The last was an envelope – pink this time rather than blue – another greetings card. The writing I knew.

My heart began to thump. *Don't open it!* went my sensible side. *Put it straight in the bin.* But sometimes your hands don't do what you tell them to. I put a finger under the flap and ripped.

FROM YOR MUM IN LONDON it said. Painting of some Venetian bridge on the front, smudgy biro print on the inside lower right corner. I vaguely thought, That'll be useful if I have to go to the police. Then I shook myself out of it. I wasn't going to dignify this nasty-minded mischief by contacting the law. The best way to meet it was with a blank.

I forced the card back in its envelope, took it by its edges and ripped ripped ripped till the pieces were the size of cornflakes. Then I swept them into a cupped hand and carried them outside to the wheeliebin. The only mum I'd had in London was a five-star bitch and I'd rather have put my own eyes out than let her anywhere near my family.

As the carriage trundled out into the light, Roz went, 'You know, I can't imagine being a mother. Do you think I'll be a good one?'

'You'll walk it,' I said.

Just because a lie's well-meaning doesn't make it any less of a lie.

Afterwards I went and stood at the bottom of the garden for a while. I was safe here, I had nothing to worry about. No one was coming for me. And say she did turn up, I'd simply march her off the premises and then call the cops. I wasn't frightened. Just bloody angry.

The sun was strong and I had to shade my eyes against the glare coming off the stone flags. I scanned the lawn, taking in the patches of browning moss and cat scrattings. Mum's hydrangeas were in full flower now, and her Michaelmas daisies, and I thought how pleased she'd have been to see them. I remembered playing in front of these bushes as a child – Dad kept a pile of builder's sand here for a while – and watching Mum as she bustled down the path that ran behind the rest of the houses in our row. Some errand she'd have been on, visiting an elderly neighbour, or trimming back the verges beyond our gate. Sometimes Chalkie would be following her. In this bed by the fence were her flowering currants, now coming into fruit. I stood and breathed in the scent of the leaves, not because it was especially nice but because it was one of those smells that took me back and calmed me, like privet and grass clippings. Lux soapflakes used to do the same.

Bloody hell, though, what was this? Broken stems and snapped-off daisy leaves, green leaves squashed into the dark soil. I bent to examine. The damage was slight, but annoying. Pringle, that would be, landing badly off a jump, or rolling about in the sun or pushing his way through on some catty mission. Little sod. Could he be any more of a nuisance? I'd have to stake some of these taller plants, see if that would protect them. Maybe I'd get some citronella sticks. Beat him about the head with one.

On the other side was the wilderness of Eric's garden, gone to weed and featuring a pile of decorating debris on the grass, broken furniture and paint-splotched rags. Well, not everyone was a gardener, and when did he have time to bother about flowerbeds? He obviously had enough on, sorting out the interior. I wondered what had changed since I'd last been in the house, on the day of Mr Cottle's death. I craned to see.

Downstairs, the blinds were drawn so I couldn't look in. But across an upstairs window I thought I saw something move. I stared for half a minute: nothing. Only the sky reflected. It must have been the image of a bird flying past.

KAREN: What was it like when you were a girl? Did you have a happy childhood, would you say?

NAN: Aye.

KAREN: You don't sound so sure. (Pause.) Are you tired? Shall we leave it till another day?

NAN: Aye. We used t'play piggy. I've shown you a piggy, hant I?

KAREN: There's one in the box under the bed, it must be yours. Did your dad whittle it for you?

NAN: Aye.

KAREN: And a wooden top, you know, for a top and whip.

NAN: Oh, that were Jimmy's. My dad made that. He said he'd mek me one an' all and he did, but not for about a year after, and when it come I didn't want it. I swapped it for some ribbons. (Laughs.)

KAREN: He carved you a boat, didn't he?

NAN: He made Jimmy a boat. It had a mousetrap inside it

and when you pressed t'side, th' whole thing flew apart. I wonder what happened to that.

(Pause.)

KAREN: And you sang playground rhymes?

NAN: Oh aye.

KAREN: Can you sing some now?

NAN: No. I can't remember.

KAREN: (chanting) 'Karen Cooper is no good, chop her up for firewood. When she's dead, jump on her head—'

NAN: 'And then we'll have some currant bread.'

KAREN: See? I knew they were still there. What was that one about toffee?

NAN: Oh. 'You're daft, you're potty, you're made of treacle toffee, I like treacle toffee but I don't like you.' (Laughs.)

KAREN: And you knew some about Charlie Chaplin?

NAN: Aye, a few. (Chanting.) 'Charlie Chaplin, meek and mild, swiped a sausage from a child, when the child began to cry, Charlie socked him in the eye.'

(Both women laugh.)

NAN: Eeh, I dunno.

(Pause.)

KAREN: And what else do you remember?

NAN: Cards, we used to mess about with, sometimes. Jacky Ollerton, he had a pack and we'd go in t'Labour Club back porch and play there.

KAREN: Play what?

NAN: All sorts.

KAREN: For money?

NAN: No. For a flirt of your nose.

KAREN: What do you mean?

NAN: Like a flick. Come here, lean over. Like this.

KAREN: Ow!

NAN: So if you won, you flirted t'other person's nose.

KAREN: Flipping heck, Mum. That's brought tears to my eyes.

NAN: Aye, it did sting. And when your nose got too sore, you'd play for a flirt o' th' ear.

KAREN: (Blows nose.) I can't see there's much fun in that. Would it not have been easier to play for something else? Matchsticks or stones?

NAN: I suppose. We didn't, though. It was just, that was our game. That's how we used to play.

KAREN: They must have built you tough. Crikey. (Blows nose again.)

NAN: Aye, I think they did. Hey, Karen, your eyes are really watering, did you know?

CHAPTER 7

On a day in July

Last day of Second Year and I was gathering up my stuff to go home. Ends of term always make me slightly sad, even though I'm on my way back to Will and ecstatic about that. I suppose there's an element of nostalgia – we've had some laughs in this house, I've been as happy here as I could have been. But probably the root of it's that I'm frightened. This time next year I'd be finished as a student, packing up for the last time. And then what? Panic, that's what. Limbo, the hideous wideness of the world.

Mind you, however wobbly I was feeling about the future it was nothing compared with Roz's state of dread. I'd sat up with her till the small hours talking through how her parents might react when she got home and told them she was pregnant. 'Do I show?' she'd asked, getting up and standing sideways on.

'No,' I said. 'You wouldn't guess, not yet.'

'Thank God for smock tops.' When she lifted her shirt, the top button of her jeans was undone.

'If you buy some maternity trousers, they expand with you. They fit you when you're slim and when you're fat.'

She'd looked appalled at the suggestion. 'Maybe next month, when I really start to change shape.'

She said she was going to confess to her mum first because she was the calmer of the two. 'If I can get Mum on my side, Dad'll come round. Then we can talk about how we're going to manage things at home. And I'll tell them about you, how well *you've* coped.'

'Right,' I said, embarrassed.

'Then I'll break it to Gareth.'

'I bet he'll be fine, once he gets over the shock. He loves you, Roz.'

'Did Will's dad love you?'

'You know he didn't. Not ever. Don't even go there because it's just not the same.'

To get us finally to bed I'd come out with all the usual stuff, about how everything would turn out right in the end and how everyone loved babies once they were here. She'd hugged me very tight and told me how sorted I was. I admit, it did give me a bit of a kick. 'And when you come back next term,' I said, 'we'll have a chat about birth plans and equipment. It'll be great. You'll have a proper bump then, yeah? Everyone'll be so excited for you.'

Her face had fallen about a mile.

I dropped the lid on my big suitcase and opened up my little one ready to pack all my dressing-table stuff. Daniel was picking me up at midday and it would be the first time we'd seen each other in over a month. Never, since we'd started dating, had we spent so much time apart. We'd both been mired in exams, of course, so the gap wasn't sinister. Or possibly it was. He hadn't come with me during my last visit home, but then it wasn't fair to drag him away from his revision. The way his course works, his exams count for more than mine. And it's no bother for me to hop on a train once in a while.

I paused to check the room; considered the hair-crimpers. We'd all be coming back to the house next term so I could leave a few items if I wanted. The vase of peacock feathers I wouldn't bother with, for instance. No point carting that home only to have Mum throw a superstitious fit over it. My posters were staying up on the walls (Bette Davis in *Jezebel*, two freaky fractal images courtesy of Daniel) along with Nan's kitten picture, Will's scribbles and a selection of postcards Mum had sent in my First Year featuring Views of Industrial Lancashire. I was only taking half my CDs.

That made me think I'd like some music on, so I fired up the laptop and selected some Oasis to load. 'Where Did It All Go Wrong?' suited my mood this morning. I wanted to be soulful and resigned. Only, when the screen loaded, I saw that Walshy must have sneaked in at some point yesterday and changed the wallpaper to a picture of himself with cartoon goggle eyes and a speech bubble over his head saying 'Happy Holidays!'.

'You knob,' I said out loud. Poking about on my hard drive: what if he'd seen something personal? I'd have to change my password again.

A movement on the landing outside my room.

'Roz?' I called.

'It's me,' said Gemma, stepping forward.

'Oh. How's the packing going?'

She cast her eyes about as if she was embarrassed. 'I'm nearly done. Hell of a job but I wanted to do a stock-take, check I wasn't hanging on to any books that weren't mine ...'

'And? What's the matter?'

'It's a bit awkward. I've realised I'm missing a couple of things.'

That made me sit up. What was she saying? Did she think some-one in the house had been thieving?

'What things, Gemma?'

'Oh, some notes on Thomas Cromwell. A book on the Reformation. A Ventolin inhaler. An earring in the shape of a fish.' She counted them off on her fingers.

'Interesting selection.'

'I know.' She laughed and shuffled her feet. 'I think they might be in Walshy's room.'

We both cast a glance across the corridor towards his closed door. 'It's been months since you broke up with him, Gemma. Didn't you notice you were missing stuff? I mean, I'd have thought you'd need the inhaler.'

She shook her head. 'Nah, it was only a spare. The earring I kept thinking would turn up. The book and notes, I haven't been doing that period. I'd like it all back, though, if I can find it.'

'Well, go ask if you can look.' I didn't see what the problem was.

'I can't. He's left.'

'Ring him.'

'I did. His phone's switched off.'

'Just go in, have a quick poke about, then. He won't mind.'

Gemma looked doubtful. 'Do you think?'

'He's been in here this morning fiddling with the settings on my laptop, so I wouldn't say he's in any position to take the moral high ground. Listen, I give you permission to go search his room. Will that do?'

'Can you come with me? I'll feel creepy if I do it on my own. Mad-stalker-ex type scenario.'

Her expression was so anxious, so unlike her usual laid-back self, it made me smile. 'Give me ten minutes to shift these magazines and I'm all yours,' I said.

This time, I saw the card as soon as it came through the letter-box. I was combing cat hairs off my cardigan when it dropped onto the mat. My neck prickled straight away. Don't tell me how, I just knew there'd be a London postmark before I even picked it up. As if I'd ever want to get back in touch with that bitch.

I walked straight out through the kitchen, opened the back door and threw the card in the wheeliebin. When I came back inside I washed my hands. Silence, I knew, was the best way forward here. Meet any communication she sent with a blank. That way I stayed in control.

Will was at the table playing innocently with a new set of Play-Doh that Maud had bought him. His cheeks were very flushed. Tooth coming through was my guess. I'd equipped him with a small plastic knife, a toy rolling pin and a tractor for making wheel patterns.

'Look at you,' I said. 'You're busy.'

'Make a sausage?'

'If you want.' I took up a ball of yellow, ready to knead.

'No! No!'

'All right. Don't snatch. I thought you were asking Grandma to do it for you.'

The dough squidged out under his palms. 'Cut it.'

'Are you cutting it, you mean?'

'Yeah. Cut-cut-cut-cut-cut.' He chopped the plastic knife-blade along its length, biting his lower lip with the effort. 'There. Put this one here.'

'What have you made?'

'It's your dinner.'

'Is it? Yum. Are you having any?'

'This is mine.' He prised another chunk off the table-top and put it to his lips.

'You mustn't really eat it. It's only pretend.'

Will glanced at me scornfully. 'Another colour now.' The knife clattered down.

'Which colour?'

'Make a shape. Make a man.'

'Which colour?'

'Blue.'

'You're starting to know your colours, aren't you? Clever boy.'

The blue was stuck in the pot and he had to claw it out. His lips parted and his tongue moved slightly. It was one of his little habits that made me smile. And I thought, How *can* anyone hurt a child? How can anyone want to harm something as precious as that? You couldn't begin to understand. Yet all across the country it was happening every day. There'd been a story in the news this morning.

'Grandma, see.' Will was holding up another fat sausage length. 'Make this a man.'

I shook my head to clear it of unhappy thoughts. 'What, do you want to do it?'

'No. You.' He slapped the dough into my hand then sat back, waiting.

'Oh, OK.'

Quickly I pinched out a couple of legs and arms, and folded the top over to make a blobby head. It was rough as you like but my grandson watched as if I was performing top-flight magic. 'There. How about that?'

He laughed with delight and took the tiny model off me. His cheeks were still bright and hot.

'What do you say?'

'Please.'

'Who is he, your man?' I asked as Will laid the figure flat on the table. 'Is it Fireman Sam? Is it Station Officer Steele?'

'It's Grandma.'

Then he took the toy tractor and began to run its wheels over and over the soft body. 'Oh dear,' he said. 'Oh dear.'

It was strange, crossing the threshold of Walshy's room again. The windowsill was still fluorescent green, the curtains still paint-marked and also mottled where I'd tried unsuccessfully to bleach out the remaining splotches. You'd think he'd just have called his dad and put an order in for some more, but instead he'd hung them back up cheerfully and seemed not to notice that they made the place look like a squat.

'Eew.' I sniffed the fuggy air. 'He hasn't even stripped his bed. Are you sure he's gone?'

Gemma was walking round the room picking up rubbish. 'Yeah, I waved him off. He gave Roz a lift to the station. Which could come back to haunt him.'

'How do you mean?'

'Well, with this crush she's brewed up on him. I presume it's that that's been making her all mopey lately. 'S'OK, Chaz, I won't pry, I know she's sworn you to secrecy. But it's got to be that. And one day Gareth's going to notice and there'll be trouble.'

You have no idea what trouble we're in for, I thought. 'Have you got the other earring so I know what I'm actually looking for?'

She rummaged in her pocket and drew it out: a flat leaping

salmon hanging off a silver hoop. It was pretty. I could see why she wanted it back.

'And the history book?'

'That and the notes should be together. It's small, standard paperback size, with a blue spine and a painting of a throne on the cover. The title's something like *Reformation and Religion*.'

We set to, clearing the floor, moving light furniture, returning all manner of objects to their homes. The clothes were at least clean but they all wanted putting away. 'I'm not hanging his shirts up for him,' said Gemma, 'I'm not his charlady.' So we laid them across the duvet out of the way.

The inhaler we found pretty quickly. It was inside the cardboard base of a promotional cut-out for *End of Days* that Walshy had blagged from HMV: Arnie in a long coat grasping an unfeasibly large weapon.

'How did it get there?' I asked as Gemma shook the inhaler till it rattled and tried out a test spray above her head.

'Got kicked, I should imagine.' Tiny droplets hung in the space between us. 'Hey, I got a kiss off her this morning.'

'Who? Roz?'

'Uh huh. Took me completely by surprise. I was in the kitchen, helping myself to a slice of bread, when she launched herself.'

'What was that in aid of?'

Gemma began to root through a box of DVDs. 'She said she was sorry she'd been so miz these last few weeks. She said it was all going to work out OK.'

'What did you say?'

'I said of course it was. Although I'd no idea what we were talking about. Well, half an idea. It's good she's getting away from Walshy for a few weeks, give her a chance to de-crush.'

I shuffled over to the bedside and peered at the dark space beneath the frame. 'Now, do I look under here or what?'

'Go for it,' said Gemma.

'It'll be porn mag city. Oh, in fact, here they are, yum. *Razzle*, *Knave*, *Fiesta*. Lovely.' I levered them out with the toe of my shoe.

When I looked across, she was gazing out of the window and frowning. 'Anyway, the point is, she's been so jumpy near me, it's nice to think she can actually – you know, *mwah*. It's a big step forward.'

'I told you she'd come round.'

'Is it really that big a deal, though? Is it?'

'Well, it was a surprise. To be honest, I've felt a bit awkward at times.'

Gemma turned back to me. 'You, Chaz? How so?'

'I mean just because I'm in uncharted waters, that's all. Like, you're the only lesbian I know.'

'Bet I'm not.'

'All right: the only lesbian I *know* I know. And mainly I don't want to show up my own ignorance. I don't want to come out with anything that's going to hurt your feelings – you're my friend, that's the last thing I'd want to do. But I'm aware there might be all kinds of stupid stuff that non-gay people spout without realising it. Sweeping assumptions, like thinking all lesbians must know each other. I don't want to end up an angry anecdote in a pub, *My Ignorant Flatmate*. That's all.'

'So, ask me.' Gemma tucked her hair behind her ear, businesslike.

'Ask you what?'

'Whatever it is you want to know.'

'Don't want to run the risk of sounding nosy.'

Gemma picked up a scrap of paper that was lying by her feet, scrumpled it into a ball and lobbed it at me. 'You are a daft bat, Chaz. We're all nosy in this house, we live together. It's the human condition. If I was seeing some bloke, you'd ask about that, wouldn't you?'

I nodded.

'Well, then.'

On the cover of *Readers' Wives Special* a blonde girl in a baseball cap simpered up at me. I pulled one of Walshy's shirts across to cover her toplessness. 'OK. Well, for a kick-off, did you always know you were gay?'

'No. Some people do; I didn't. It was a swift conversion.'

'Like getting religion.'

She raised her palms, fingers spread, a mime of revelation.

'What happened?'

'I met a girl. Off my course.'

It did feel weird to hear her talk like this, but it was only the unfamiliarity of the situation. She was right. If it had been a man I'd have been gagging for every detail.

'And did you date her?'

'No. She already had a partner.'

'Were you upset?'

'At the time I was. She helped put me in touch with some other people, though, so I could talk things through.'

I remembered Roz saying darkly, *They have these clubs, you know.*

'Are you dating now?'

'I am. Just. We've had a few things to sort out but yeah, I am dating.'

'What's she like?'

'Funny. Tall. American.'

'When do we get to meet her?'

'Not yet. Not till I'm a bit surer where I stand.'

'Fair enough.'

So much for Roz's theory that Gemma was after me, then. I knew it was bobbins.

'You've told your parents?'

'That's a job for the summer holidays.' She peeled a limp grey thing off the carpet, might have been a sock. 'I'm pretty sure they'll be OK. They've always been cool about boyfriends so I can't see they're going to be any different about girlfriends. Mum put me on the pill at fifteen.'

'*Fifteen*?'

'She said it was for acne but we both knew it wasn't.'

I felt a pang of envy. Oh, to have such an open, liberal household. No wonder Gemma always seemed so confident in herself.

She began to pull a chair across to the wardrobe so she could investigate what was on top. I laid myself flat on the carpet in an attempt to see what was going on under the bed.

Down in the under-mattress world was more porn, I discovered, and some falling-apart trainers and two stinky kitchen mugs and a bag containing a tracksuit. There was quite a lot of electrical goods packaging, the remnants of expensive gifts he'd had off his dad. There was a Davy Crockett hat, a box of Quintero cigars, an empty guitar case, an abdominal exerciser bar. A biscuit tin full of McDonald's Happy Meal toys. A picture made of flowing sand held between two glass plates. A riding hat (*riding hat?*) full of CDs. A *Magic Eye* calendar. A box of toy air-gun caps. Some foreign coins inside half a coconut shell. An opened packet of Trebor mints. A toothbrush with its bristles dyed saffron yellow, a half-made racing car kit. A pair of shin-guards, a giant ampersand nicked off some shop-front or other.

'Found my book!' Gemma cried happily. 'Notes inside, perfect.' She blew away a coating of dust from the cover and stood looking at it.

'Don't give yourself an asthma attack. If I hear you start to wheeze, you're going out.'

'Uh huh.'

It was impossible to settle. The card had upset me and I couldn't stop thinking about it. What I really needed was to get out of the house and be on my own for a bit, but this was Saturday and no nursery, and Charlotte wasn't due back till the afternoon.

Will was under the table, barefoot and playing with a punnet of gooseberries Ivy had dropped off earlier. Neither of us like them but she will keep bringing them. My fault for pretending we do, I suppose. I don't seem to be able to open my mouth these days without a lie falling out.

A gooseberry rolled and hit my shoe. I lifted up the cloth. 'So, lad. Have you made Grandma that goosegog pie yet?'

Will shook his head. There was squashed fruit down his T-shirt and in his hair and smeared into the carpet. 'Jam,' he said.

'I see. Mummy's coming home today. Mummy, your mummy. That's nice, isn't it?'

He snorted as if this was the funniest thing he'd ever heard. 'Jammy jam.'

'Yes, all right. Sinky sink, washy wash. Now. Otherwise your mother'll wonder what the heck I've been doing with you.'

I watched as he scrambled forward, accidentally kicking the punnet on its side. The last of the gooseberries spilled out, and when he raised his head to assess the damage, the young skin of his cheeks was completely perfect.

The bad thoughts were gathering again. Where could I go? How could I escape?

'Tell you what. Shall we go see if Kenzie's about?'

For answer, he reached forward and pulled at his toes.

'I know, shoes and socks on. But I'll hose you down first. That way we maybe stand a chance of finally being invited in.'

A cobweb clung to my face and I shuddered, wiped my cheek on the carpet. To my right was a box of lens-cleaning wipes, some felt tips and a balled-up T-shirt. The T-shirt I drew out and unfurled. *100% SURFER* said the logo on the front. As if there was a whole lot of surfing to be done in York. Then I thought, Wouldn't it be handy if we all went around ready-labelled. Not with naff boasts like this one, but with key info that was otherwise tricky to drop into intro-ductions. *I HAVE A TODDLER AT HOME*, mine would read. Job done, everyone in the clear. No angsting in the union bar over when to let that snippet fall, no wondering whether friends were quietly filling in my background to strangers. Get the reactions out in the open. If people wanted to be funny, let's have it over with straight away. Gemma could have *100% GAY*. Roz – well, Roz wouldn't be need-ing any T-shirt to announce her pregnancy before too long.

'If I could just find this damn earring,' said Gemma.

I reached towards the bottom end of the bed and found a mobile phone with a broken screen and a book about archaeology. There was also a ball made out of rubber bands, plus two unfletched arrows and a headless soft toy. The toy, a rabbity thing, I recalled Walshy finding stuck on a spiked railing on his way home from the pub. He'd dismembered it for its squeaker, sawing into its neck with a bread-knife, while I'd scolded about some child somewhere crying itself to sleep. He'd just squeaked back at me, annoyingly.

I was aware of Gemma climbing off the chair and opening the wardrobe door. Right under the end of the bed was a video camera Walshy's dad had sent him so he could try and get one of us on *You've Been Framed*. God knows what footage was on there now. Best not to think about it.

As I backed out from the under-bed space and gulped some air I realised I'd been taking these little shallow breaths, not wanting to take in lungfuls of Walshy and his train of girlfriends. All those dead skin cells piling up.

'Looks as though we've drawn a blank on the earring,' I said.

'They were a present from my mum,' pleaded Gemma. 'Sterling silver. I can't go home without them.'

I got to my feet and started to push the various displaced items back under the bed. The magazines slid into place obediently, but the shin-guards got jammed and I had to shove. When I moved the cigar box, it rattled. I thought, Cigars don't rattle. So I opened it.

'Oh, wow!' Gemma's voice was excited. 'Oh, yes! I don't believe it – yes, I've got it. I've got it, Chaz. See? It was hooked in the hem of this sweater he'd rolled up and shoved at the back . . . he used to let me wear it sometimes. Oh, that's brilliant. It's not bent or anything. Thank God. Phew. See, I'm sticking it straight in my earlobe then it can't go anywhere. Excellent. OK, now, all we've got to do is put everything roughly back, there's no need to be tidy. In fact, if we were, that'd probably just confuse the hell out of him. What have you got there, Chaz? You need some help? Like I say, just kick it under, yeah? God, I'm so relieved.'

Her voice carried on and on, happy and high, but I wasn't listening. What I was looking at was a box of me.

*

Even from the drive I could see the back garden was in a worse state than ever. That central pile of debris, broken wood and old furniture, was now of bonfire proportions. The grass was long, the bushes near his fence were squashed out of shape and the fence panels themselves were really sagging; I'd have to look into getting them propped up from our side. I could see he'd still not taken the cat-flap out. 'Trouble is,' Eric had said last week, 'when you're decorating, everything looks worse before it looks better. And the inside needs straightening before the outside.' Which was true, except why bother doing up a place you're only renting? 'Because I can,' he'd replied. 'Because I want it nice for me and the lad.' Well, I could understand that. It gets you down, living in a hole.

As I rang the front doorbell, a Cabbage White butterfly landed on a knackered old wall unit and spread its wings wide against the sun.

For a minute or two I heard nothing, then Kenzie's small shape appeared through the frosted-glass panel. I saw him run from one side of the hall to the other and back again, like a man on the deck of a storm-tossed boat. Eric came up behind him and lifted him out of the way.

I thought, I so need you to invite me in. If I could have half an hour even, standing with a coffee in his kitchen, or sitting in the lounge where I'd last seen Mr Cottle stiffening among his Carol Vordermans. Trivial chat was what I needed. Tune my head back into everyday matters. I wanted to rest my eyes on a pair of nice muscly arms. And there was something else at stake, too: Charlotte had been getting at me lately, asking why I was providing all this free childminding for a man we barely knew. (*She* barely knew. *I* saw him plenty.) She said, 'Do you not mind that he just sees you as a babysitting service?' I said, 'It's hard for him. I have your dad down the road, Maud and Ivy at a push. He has no one. I'm doing a neighbour a good turn, that's all.' But her words had niggled away. Twice I'd asked Eric to take Will while I popped out, and each time he'd been ready with an excuse. He was taking Kenzie to a birthday party, they were late for a hair appointment. OK, these things happened – I'd had to say no myself one afternoon when Will's shoes fell apart and we were forced to make an emergency dash to Bolton. The fact remained, in all the weeks I'd known Eric, for all the talks and cuppas we'd shared, I hadn't actually set foot in his house yet.

The door opened. 'Karen!'

'Are you busy?'

'Well, you could say. I've just this minute finished knocking plaster off the ceiling in the back bedroom, and it's everywhere.'

'Oh.'

'We're in an absolute state. One of those jobs you think, Oh, it'll be easy, this, and then you get intae it and you wish you'd never started. Dust, filth, awful. Is it in my hair?'

'Can't see any.'

'My baseball cap must've caught most of it. Anyhow, I've done the worst, it's pretty much all off, but there's a load of tidying up. Poor Kenzie's been stuck in the front room all morning with only the TV for company.'

Obviously I wasn't stepping over the threshold today. I thought fast. 'You're going to be around all morning, then?'

'Aye, I've to scrape it up and bag it—'

I grabbed Will's shoulders and thrust him forward. 'Look, I really need you to have him for an hour. I need to go somewhere.'

'Honestly, Karen, I would if I could—'

'I have to go now.'

'He'll only get himself filthy . . .'

'I've got an emergency.'

'Why? What's up?'

My head was ringing with garbled snatches of panic: that vile greetings card, I must make sure when I went back that I buried it deeper down the bin, didn't want anyone seeing that when they took out the nappy sacks. And in six hours Charlotte would be home, I had the house to tidy and the bed to make up and all her foods to get in, her Edam slices and her Tunnock's Tea Cakes, and how long would it be before we rowed about Will, how long before she started picking holes in the way I'd been feeding him or dressing him or our night-time routine? Which suddenly broke a dream I'd had last night that I'd found Pringle dead under Will's bed, and I was trying to squeeze the corpse inside a little sandwich bag without him seeing. Then I remembered a true scene, Mum holding Chalkie's body, wrapping it in a towel after Dad brought him home from the vet's and that was the first time I'd seen my dad cry – what a shock because till then I'd thought tears were the preserve of us children and I couldn't believe a grown man could weep. Snatches of angst my mind compressed into a few seconds, like the dial of a radio tuning up and down the different stations. I heard myself say, 'It's Pringle.'

'You what?' Eric's gaze swept over me.

'He's swallowed poison.'

'Eh?'

My face bloomed with heat. Why in God's name hadn't I just said I needed a break? That it was his turn to babysit? *Just bloody take him, Eric. Take him and let me go.*

'I put some slug pellets in a dish on the kitchen shelf and he might have eaten some so I need to pop him to the vet's for a check-over. They do an open surgery on a Saturday morning. I can't take Will, it'd be too upsetting for him. But if I get up there straight away . . .'

'Slug pellets?'

'We've had an outbreak round the sink. Yesterday there was a great big brown one climbing over the drainer. I thought it was a splash of gravy till it moved.' That bit was true.

'Sounds odd. How are they getting in, Karen?'

'Where the pipes come through? No idea. Now's not the time, I need to shift.'

'I didn't even know cats liked slug pellets.'

'Normal cats probably don't. Pringle'll have a go at anything, remember.'

Will, bored with waiting, ducked past him and tottered down the hall, Kenzie following. I had no option but to finish, and run. 'Anyway, I'll be home soon as I can.'

I turned my back on his doubtful frown and began to sprint down the path, my mobile bumping in my cardigan pocket.

No one else looking into this cigar box would know what it was about. Any of Walshy's girlfriends might have opened it and seen only a collection of rubbish, maybe trawled from the bottom of a car-door pocket or tipped out of a rucksack lining. The sticker off an apple I'd made him wear on his forehead like a bindi, a jellybean we'd kicked all the way back from town, a beer mat I'd doodled flowers over, a flyer for a band we'd been to see at the union. In one corner was a tiny shrivelled bit of green that I recognised as a clover he'd split for me to make it four-leaf, and I'd told him cheating like that would bring bad luck. There was a red button off my coat sleeve – I'd wondered where it had got to – and a stripy feather I'd picked up near the Walls, that was quite recent.

I put out a finger and stirred the contents round wonderingly.

'I really hate untidiness, don't you?' said Gemma from a hundred miles away on the other side of the room.

Steve met me on the corner of Aspull Road, between the church and the chippy. He roared up on his Kawasaki like some cut-price Hell's Angel and sputtered to a halt on Saint Mary's car park. Watching him dismount was a spectacle in itself. Since I'd last seen him ride he'd invested in a full set of leathers and they were clearly on the stiff side.

'You walk like John Wayne,' I said as he drew near.

He gave me the thumbs-up and began to lever his helmet off his face. After an effort it came free. 'You what, love?'

'Nice outfit,' I said. 'Are you not cooked?'

'A bit. Aw, this is champion, though. I can't believe you're up for it.'

His face was bright with anticipation. I held up the bag containing my own helmet and he nodded approval.

'There's a spare jacket for you in the pannier, and gloves if you want them. Now, I won't go too fast. The main thing is—'

'Go as fast as you like.'

He raised his eyebrows slightly. 'OK, whatever. Main thing, like I said, is don't be scared. I know what I'm doing. Only you have to remember to lean when I lean – you know, see the corner coming up and lean into it the way I do. Well, you'll feel me go. You'll have your arms round me.'

'Oh, I will, will I?'

'Course. How else are you going to stop from sliding off?' He saw my expression. 'OK, you can hold on to the grab rail if you want. But you still have to lean.'

It took me a while to get the helmet fastened, and I had to remove the leather jacket halfway through and then put it on again because it was too snug round the shoulders for me to move my arms. The gloves I waved away. I nearly said to Steve, *This must be what it's like to be mummified.* But there was no speaking any more. Like a bloody scold's bridle, this helmet was.

He motioned me to get on the bike, so I did. Once astride I felt as well as heard it start up, the vibrations from the engine running right through me and making my teeth rattle. Or that could have been nerves. The seat felt slippery under my bum and I fought against the constraints of the jacket to reach the rail behind me.

And then we were off. Before I'd even got myself into position Steve was steering us through the concrete bollards of the car park entrance and bumping onto the main road, into a stream of traffic.

At first we went pretty slowly because we were following a bus and a lorry. But the bus halted to let off passengers, and there was a sudden surge of power as Steve swung the bike out and round, then overtook the lorry, nipping past where a car would never have risked it. I closed my eyes. When I opened them, we were coming out of Bank Top and about to join the bypass.

'I thought you weren't so keen on the bike,' Steve had said when I rang him. 'What's changed your mind?'

'Can't explain,' I told him. That's the difference with an ex, I suppose. No need to make up fancy lies for Steve. All I understood was a sudden desire to be outside and travelling very fast, tarmac blurring beneath the flesh of my knees, the wind thundering. Blow the badness out of my head. Feel as though, for a few minutes anyway, I was on the verge of escape. We turned onto Grimstone Lane and then he put his foot down. The Kawasaki shot down the straight and under the motorway bridge, then up, climbing towards Rivington and the countryside. His hips pressed back into mine as the bike angled to the incline.

'This is fantastic!' I said, knowing he couldn't hear me. I wondered how fast we were going. I craned my head to see the speedo and the needle was hovering on 60. Not that fast, then. It's just that you felt so exposed on a bike, connected to the contours of the road in a way you weren't in a car. Ahead of us were the colours of the moor, browns and greys and greens and purples, merging into a grey-white mottled sky. I wanted to ride into the horizon, ride and ride.

'Sod you, Jessie sodding Pilkington!' I yelled into the engine's drone. 'Sod you and whatever it was you wanted!' What could my birth mother be after? Perhaps she was dying and she wanted to try and make her peace with me. Perhaps she had an inheritance to pass on, or another horrible family secret she wanted to dump on my shoulders. Perhaps she'd got religion. I couldn't imagine what would make her suddenly pursue me when less than three years ago she'd slammed the door in my face. Whatever it was, I wanted no part of it. 'Bitch!' I yelled. 'If you come after me or mine, I'll make sure you regret it!' Then I took in a deep breath, filled my lungs and howled into the fabric of the helmet. I howled till I had no breath left, till my lungs were emptied. The wind was drumming round us, fierce and cooling. I took another huge breath.

Time passed, I have no idea how much. My head was now giddy with too much oxygen. But I became aware of Steve shifting and half-turning to me, trying to tell me something, and I spotted the dip in the road ahead and the tight left bend immediately following it. 'Lean,' I remembered him saying. I nodded to let him know I'd seen it, I was ready. As we approached, fields and stone walls whipped past us. The bike seemed to speed up till we were nearly flying. Then we swooped down and into the curve, and without even thinking I let go of the grab rail and fastened my arms round Steve's body, holding him tight as I could. Because of the leathers it wasn't a normal hug, there was no warmth to it. This was more how embracing a tree might feel, stiff and solid, an up-and-down trunk shape. Impersonal. We angled together as a unit, slanting ourselves against the bend and balancing out the bike's momentum. Round the bend, the road curved right – another lean, to the other side – and then we were on the long bridge, zipping over the reservoir with shimmering water stretching out on either side.

This was the direction of home, though. Was my time up? Surely not yet. *I bet you've had enough, haven't you, Karen?* I imagined him saying. *Shall I take you back to Will, let you get your feet on solid ground again?*

No, I urged him silently. *Please don't let us be going yet. Please let me stay out here just a little bit longer.*

But to my joy, instead of heading west, Steve flicked the indicator then turned and headed off round the bank of the reservoir and back up the hill into moorland again. Telegraph poles blipped past. A flock of birds peeled away from the hedgerow. Without taking his eyes from the road he lifted his arm and gave me the thumbs-up. I signed it back.

Way in front of us, over the horizon, clouds piled high and clean. We were zooming away from trouble, into green space.

I never wanted it to stop.

I guess my head was at least half-full of Will, as it usually is on the drive home. I tend not to say a lot anyway till we're on the M62. Usually Daniel witters on about the latest biochemical discovery or some piece of weirdness that's been in the news, and I do my decompression thing and turn slowly back into a mum. Today my thoughts were also whirling with the discovery of Walshy's box, and what it might mean. Essentially the question was, did he have similar collections for his other girlfriends? But I'd pretty much been through his under-bed supplies with the attention of a foren-sic scientist and I hadn't come across any. And if he didn't, must that therefore be a sort of proof that I was special to him in some way? Maybe even that he was a little bit in love with me? If he was ... Jesus. How was I supposed to feel about that? Mixed up, that's what. Churned, like a washing machine. Excited. Amazed. Appalled.

Because even though our pre-Christmas fooling filled me with shame and horror, that couldn't dampen the fizz still between us, the little shiver that passed across the room sometimes. However I'd tried to hide it, there was something, undeniable. Even when he was at his most irritating. But what about his take on it? What if that night had really meant something to him? 'You know, Chaz,' he'd once told me as we trundled round the supermarket together, 'you're the only person who understands me.' I'd dismissed this as blether because at the time he was wearing a Bill Clinton mask and also he stank of beer. But none of us *ever* knew what Walshy really thought about anything because he just talked bullshit and flirted all the time. Under all the posturing there might be any number of emotions we'd never guessed at. Imagine if he *was* burning for me all those months, since the snog, or even before that. It made my chest squeeze with anxiety to remember.

Again I played back that drunken walk home, the out-of-nowhere kiss on the front step, the fumble on the stairs and then on his bed. Only the bleep of his phone saving me from myself and making me leap up and run to my own room, lock the door. Tramp that I was. Shame on me. At least, thank God it was the holidays now, and an end to temptation. But what about next term? Where did I stand?

True to form, as we passed over the Pennines it started to rain. Daniel turned on the windscreen wipers and upped the volume on the radio to compensate. 'Isn't She Lovely?' sang Stevie Wonder. Isn't she shabby, more like. Isn't she devious, shifty, cheap. I fought to banish those images, to focus instead on Will and how pleased he would be to see me. 'Mummy', he'd call me, for definite. We'd been training him up using the photo album. There wasn't going to be any more confusion there. Mum was also on at me to start his potty training and get his hair cut, go through his wardrobe, have his hearing checked. Plus apparently I hadn't to make the letterbox 'talk' to him again because he'd trapped his fingers in it after I left last time. I knew there'd be a barrage of demands as soon as I walked through the door. But this is a mother's world, chores and tasks stretching off to infinity. It's what I signed up to.

I was thinking of Will, and then Walshy, then Will again, when Daniel suddenly turned off the radio and said, 'What exactly is it that bugs you about Amelia?'

'Nothing,' I said at once.

'Come on, Charlotte.'

I rolled my eyes. 'You really want to know? Pff. Only that she's had it all on a plate. I bet she's never put a foot wrong in her short sweet life.'

'You don't know a thing about her.'

'I know she lives in a mansion.'

'No, she doesn't. Her parents own a four-bedroom house in Wiltshire, I asked her. Six years ago they bought a small field off the farmer next door to save it from developers. That's all. And stop being an inverted snob. Would you like it if someone judged you on the size of your house?'

'Oh yeah, I've remembered what it is bugs me about her: the way you always defend her, like you're doing now. That's seriously annoying.'

'I don't "always defend her". I offer an alternative viewpoint when you're not being rational.'

I'm your girlfriend, I thought. You should side with me.

'Well, I know your mum thinks she's the best thing ever, and wishes you were going out with her.'

'That's ridiculous.'

'It's not! Bloody hell, Dan. Every time we're round your flat, she finds a way to drop Amelia into the conversation. You must have noticed. Amelia brought her some honey for her sore throat. Amelia's family live near where your mum grew up. Amelia's been admiring her William Morris cushions. I said, "Hey, Mrs Gale, I love William Morris stuff," and she gave me such a patronising smile. *You? Get back to your Woolworths tea towels, dear.*'

Daniel's fingers twitched on the steering wheel. 'You could argue that Amelia makes an effort with her.'

'God, I try my best, Dan. Your mum's not the easiest.' If he only knew the strain involved in just keeping my mouth shut whenever I was with the sozzled old witch.

'My mother feels comfortable with Amelia. They come from a similar background.'

'Yes, and doesn't she let me know it.'

Lorries in both neighbouring lanes now, hemming us in. I wondered, if you added them all up, how many hours I'd spent travelling this damn motorway.

Daniel said, 'Are you jealous? Is that the problem?'

'No!'

'How about this, then. Would you like to meet her?'

That caught me totally off-guard. 'Meet Amelia? Where?'

'Anywhere. I thought you might like to see her face-to-face.'

'Why?'

Daniel raised an eyebrow slightly.

My temper flared. 'I've no interest in the woman. Why would I want to trail over to meet her? What's so fascinating about her, anyway?'

He said nothing for a while. I turned my head away and stared out at the moorland and the misty outline of the hills. *Can't bloody stop talking about her, can you?* I imagined saying. But I couldn't face another row. All I wanted was to get home.

'Can we have the radio back on?' I asked, reaching forward for the button.

'No.'

Again I was wrong-footed. 'Huh? Why?'

'Because we need to talk. Well, we do, don't we?'

'Does it have to be now?'

'I'd say so.'

'OK,' I said, without enthusiasm. Not more shit, I was thinking. Not more strife to go burning round my head.

The car slooshed past a coach filled with old ladies. They looked happy, off to some pensioner-attraction, no doubt. Nan used to go on these trips with the Over Seventies, the Edinburgh Woollen Mill outlet store, the Tower Ballroom, Harry Ramsden's, and she always had a whale of a time. Cup of tea and a bun and her day was complete. I thought how nice it must be to be past it, untroubled by the urges of youth.

Daniel said, 'How many of my uni friends have you actually met, Charlotte?'

I thought about it. 'Well, I've spoken to Julian on the phone. I took a message from him. We had a really long chat. He seemed nice.'

'So, none, then.'

'I've seen loads of photos. I feel like I know them.'

'Uh huh.'

'Aw, come on. It's difficult. You know it is. If I have a free weekend I need to spend it with Will. That's the way it has to be. Obviously.'

'Obviously.'

'So are you saying I shouldn't? Daniel, I've got to see my son. I hardly see enough of him as it is. You of all people should understand that.'

I thought I'd clinched the argument with that, but no, he wasn't stepping down.

'I'm not asking you to see less of him.'

'What, then?'

He set his jaw stubbornly. 'Just to respect me more. Think about it, Charlotte. The bottom line is, you don't take any real interest in me—'

'Bollocks.'

'In my Manchester life, in anything I am outside what I do for you. You've no real idea who my friends are, and we never talk properly about what I've been up to.'

'Gerroff. You do tell me. You told me about Julian dyeing a rose blue for his girlfriend, and Professor Jamieson talking that student down off the roof. And you're always banging on about science-y stuff. I know so much about what's going on in your lab I reckon I could have sat your end-of-year exams and scraped a pass.'

'But you don't *listen*!' His voice was suddenly loud in the confines of the car. 'I talk, yes, but you don't listen to me. I see you zoning out. Yes, you do. You never ask me anything back. It's as if I'm giving a lecture.'

I laughed. 'Glad you said that and not me.'

He let out a kind of stifled groan. 'For God's sake. You see, you're not even listening now. This isn't funny, Charlotte. Always I'm in second place with you. I *know* you have a child, and before you start it's not about that. I love Will, he's top of my chart, too. I know he takes up your time. But this is about you taking and taking and not giving back. I run round after you and what do I get in return? Bad moods. Your eyes glazing over when I tell you about *my* world. You don't *think* about me. Sometimes it's as if my words don't even register. The whole of our relationship's based on me supporting you. I'm like a – like a bloody clothes prop.'

This time I didn't dare even smile.

'I suppose I've always known it,' he went on. 'That was the basis on which you let me be your boyfriend, right from the word go. Right from that day in the sixth-form library when I asked you out and those girls were giggling on the table behind and you were looking at me as if I was completely mad. But you were kind to me when you could have laughed in my face. You became the first real friend I had at that bloody school. My best friend. You shared your secrets, you asked my advice. And then when we started seeing each other properly, it was like everything came right for me. My parents warring, it didn't matter. We had each other. You made me laugh. You were beautiful, you were clever. It was a privilege to be by your side, and if people wondered what someone like you was doing with a geek like me, I didn't care. I was just on top of the world. So if there were times I worked a bit harder in the relationship, I was prepared for that, it didn't seem too bad, you know? There's always one person in a couple who does more accommodating. It was OK. Until lately, and this ridiculous reaction over Amelia – don't, let me finish – that brought it home how little *respect* you have for me. It's as though I can't have friends of my own unless you approve of them, even if you never actually take the time to meet any of them. Suddenly you decide to take a dislike to someone I mention, what, once or twice, and then every time her name comes up, it's open season.'

'Well, you shouldn't go on about her so much.'

'I don't "go on about her". I don't mention her in any other context than *Twenty-First Century Rocks*, and the reason I talk about that is because I'm enjoying it, it's taking up a lot of my time, it's important to me. That's all. Do you think I fancy her or something?'

I shrugged.

'For the record, Charlotte, I don't. I like her a lot, she's fun, she does an efficient job, that's as far as it goes.'

'What if *she* fancies you?'

'It makes no difference. Sheesh. I can't believe you genuinely consider her a threat. And lately it's struck me how bloody unfair things are between us. See, I would never tell you who to hang round with, or sneer about them, or question your motives. Your friends are your friends. I trust you to choose them and I'm happy for you to get on with it.'

A picture of Walshy flashed up before my eyes and there I was, skewered on my own hypocrisy. *Yes, that's the reason you're so twitchy about Amelia*, went my conscience. *He trusts you and look how you've repaid him. Trying to judge him by your own slack morals. Trollop.*

'Honest, it isn't like that,' I said feebly.

'But it is, Charlotte.'

Where the hell had all this come from? Ten minutes ago we were bowling along as normal. Suddenly, out of nowhere, he'd brewed up a crisis. I just hadn't seen it coming. Daniel didn't really do Angry, it wasn't his style. Stoic, he was. Level. Constant. For as long as I'd known him.

'This sniping at my mother,' he went on.

'She snipes at me.'

'Get over it.'

Now I was righteously indignant. 'Hang on a minute, she started it! She's always looked down her nose at me. I was never good enough. And I hate the way she acts with you, she's too controlling. Banging on the floor every time she wants you, and you springing to your feet and running up to her flat straight away. For God's sake. You need to stand up to her more.'

'She needs support.'

'Yeah, stop her falling over drunk.'

He swallowed. 'That was low, Charlotte.'

'She is an alcoholic.'

'You think I don't know that?'

'Then why pretend everything's OK? Why not *do* something about it?'

'What do you suggest?'

'There are groups. The AA.'

'Oh, thanks. That never occurred to me. When I get home I'll just strap her to a gurney and wheel her to the nearest branch against her will, shall I?'

I'd have protested but he carried straight on.

'All right, she's over-reliant on drink. But look at what she's been through. She's not a strong woman. You're so much stronger, and you have so much more in your life than she does. You could afford to be generous, let the odd jibe go. Because ask yourself how I am with your family. Ask yourself about the effort I put in with your mother, with your father, with Will, your nan.'

Again he had me. It was all true. His treatment of Will alone made him a saint, never mind the way he fielded my bloody mother. I was officially the worst girlfriend in the world.

'So what are you saying, Dan? What do you want me to do?'

'I'm saying, I deserve better.'

The knife twisted in my guts.

'I don't think you love me,' I said outrageously. It was the clumsiest kind of emotional blackmail but I was getting desperate. I only wanted him back to normal, back to his usual mild and tolerant self. Why wouldn't he behave? Why now all this resentment and chafing? I looked at him, willing him to tell me it was actually OK. If I wished hard enough, perhaps any minute now he'd sigh and say he'd had a bad morning, or he just needed to get things off his chest, and then I'd come in with some concessions of my own.

All right, I'll come to Manchester with you. I'll miss a precious weekend with Will and I'll meet your friends. I'll listen more carefully when you tell me about neurons and stuff. I'll try and be pleasanter with your mum. I won't make fun of your marvellous – no, not that – I won't make fun of Amelia any more, I'm sure she's very nice. Obviously you have to have a social life. And I do trust you, I'm sorry if I got it wrong. The problem is, I get so stressed over missing Will and everything else slides out of proportion. It feels as if there's not enough of me to go round. As if I'm failing on a dozen fronts.

He'd nod, he'd smile, the row would be over. We'd pull in at motorway services and share a muffin.

'Daniel?'

His expression stayed grim.

'Don't you love me?' I said. A tiny moth-sized flutter of panic had started in my chest.

'God, Charlotte. More than you have any idea.'

His voice sounded bleak and lost. Across the horizon in front of us, dark clouds gathered and the sky flashed with sudden summer lightning.

When we pulled up outside my house I found I was shivering all over and my teeth were chattering. My hands, when I tried to take off the helmet, were numb and useless.

'You're never cold?' asked Steve incredulously.

'Frozen,' I said. It was easier than trying to explain the exhilaration still coursing through me. Every fingertip tingled. I hadn't felt so alive in years.

'So, do you get it? Do you understand why I needed this bike?'

'Suppose.'

That was enough for Steve. He beamed proudly. 'Champion. We'll make a biker of you yet. Hey, and I nearly forgot. I were talking to this old gimmer in t'warehouse last week and he was telling me about his daughter doing this teacher training course actually in a school, you know, working and getting paid for it. How smart is that? I don't know if it was legit but he reckoned it was. She didn't have a degree or anything, and she's older than you. So I thought it might be worth looking into.'

'What's it called, this course?'

'Dunno. I can find out. Do you want me to?'

'Well, yes.'

I dragged off the jacket, aware that my blouse underneath was patchy with sweat. I needed to get inside and take a shower; what's more, if Steve showed any sign of wanting to join me, I wouldn't say no. Not today. My whole body sang like a guitar string, joyously tense.

'Oh,' he said as I opened the gate and stepped through. 'By the way, I'll need that back. The jacket.'

'What?'

'It int mine. I borrowed it.'

I looked down at the thick leather bundle. I'd assumed it was mine to keep, like the helmet had been. Feeling foolish, I held it out to him. 'Fine. Have it.'

'Ta.' He rolled it as best he could to tuck under his arm. 'It's Lusanna's. It's her spare.'

'Lusanna.'

'The girl from the Kawasaki Club. You know. As swapped me your helmet. She loaned me the jacket this morning, after you rang.'

'Ah, right. That Lusanna.'

Steve thinks he's Mr Enigmatic but I can read him like a book. The reason Lusanna was able to hand her jacket over immediately was because she was with him when I rang; or rather, he must have been round at hers because you don't cart spare jackets about with you for no reason. And he never rises before ten on a Saturday, which meant he'd stayed over.

I said. 'Are you seeing her?'

He gaped, then shut his mouth and came over shy. 'Yeah, like, sort of.'

'That's great.'

'Well.'

'No, it's good. It's good.'

''S'only casual. Nowt, really. Don't say anything to our Charlie yet, eh?'

The face of a healthy, unpoisoned cat appeared at my upstairs window, meowing to be let out.

'I wouldn't dream of it,' I said. 'None of my business. Anyway, tell her thanks for the jacket. Tell her it was a bit loose on me but it did the job.' I laughed lightly to show I wasn't being a bitch by saying that, but no one was fooled. We both knew that, if anything, the jacket had been on the snug side.

'OK.' He sighed and looked down at his massive boots. 'Anyroad, Karen, I can probably blag you a jacket of your own from somewhere, if you're interested. Shall I? We could go out again sometime. I mean, it was a blast, yeah?'

'I'll see you around,' I said and closed the gate between us.

KAREN: What I wanted to know about was my dad's side. I haven't really got anything there except names. (Pause.) I know there was an Aunty Annie somewhere, my dad's younger sister. She moved down south, didn't she? With her husband? (Pause.) Did you keep in touch? (Pause.) Were she and my dad close? Did you have much to do with her? (Pause.) Well, we're getting nowhere fast today. All right, Mum, tell me about your uncle Jack. I know he went to Mesopotamia during the First World War and he came home poorly. Didn't he catch malaria? And he never fully recovered. You told me he was always cold, and you were in

trouble if you left a door open near him because he couldn't
bear draughts.

(Sounds of someone coming into the room.)

CARE ASSISTANT: Now, how are we doing?

KAREN: She's incommunicado today.

CARE ASSISTANT: Oh dear. Are you not feeling so bright,
Nancy? She had a bad night, I think. You couldn't get off,
could you? Shall I get you some tea? Are you ready for a
cuppa and a biscuit?

KAREN: Mum? Did you hear? Is she OK, do you think?

NAN: Uncle Jack's dead.

KAREN: I know, Mum.

NAN: Jimmy's dead, Bill's dead, my mother and father.

(Pause.)

KAREN: But we're here, Mum. Me and Charlotte, and Will.
We're all still about. I'm bringing Will tomorrow for you.
He's cut another tooth. You said he was teething, didn't
you?

NAN: I shan't mind, when it's my turn.

KAREN: Oh, don't say that. Come on, now. Come here. Oh,
Mum. (Pause.) Sita's going to bring you a cup of tea. You'll
feel better after you've had something to eat and drink. You
will, I promise. (Pause.) Sita, could you turn that tape-
player off, please? Just, that red button. Thanks.

CHAPTER 8

On a day in August

I swear there's a special circle of hell reserved for mothers who repeatedly ask about their daughter's love-life. Two weeks into the summer holidays and I felt chewed to bits.

By day I had Mum making ever more earnest enquiries about when she was going to see Daniel again, how we were getting on, was I being *nice* to him. Meanwhile, for every one of the fourteen nights I'd been home, Will'd had me up with nightmares or just fancying a play in the small hours. 'Mummy,' I'd hear him shouting through the wall. 'Mummy, come!' 'It's your own fault,' Mum said when I complained I was exhausted. 'He's been sleeping through for me. But you get him all excited at bedtime and then he can't settle.' Obviously I'm not supposed to have fun with my child post-5 p.m. Not supposed to cuddle him after dark, either. 'Look, if he wakes up and there's nothing really wrong, then tuck him in and leave him,' says Mum, all sanctimonious. 'Don't lift him out of bed and start chatting, or make his teddies talk or read him a story. He's not going to want to sleep after that, is he?' I said, 'So now I'm not allowed to comfort my own son? Is that how you used to treat *me* when I was little?' And she went, 'Why do you always have to twist my words, Charlotte?' In the end I told her, 'Decent mums don't mind getting up in the night. It's our job.' But she switched on the hoover and drowned me out.

So this early light found me sitting on the floor of the front box room, resting my neck against the wall with my lap full of teddies, while Will bounced up and down on his duvet.

'This used to be my room,' I told him. He took no notice, obviously: like I had any kind of a life before him. But I *did*, I wanted to tell him. I was a child once, without any cares, with a mummy and a nan who arranged everything for me. I sailed through my days, gold stars in my schoolbooks and clean plates at the table. 'A good girl', I'd hear people say.

It was when I grew up and struck out on my own that the trouble started.

By the crack of illumination under Will's curtains and the glow of Bedtime Bear I could make out the wardrobe mirror I'd stood in front of the day it dawned on me I might be pregnant. Will had been nothing more than a little tiny grub-thing wriggling about inside me when I'd put my hands on my stomach and wished him away with all my might. Three months later and blown up like a cushion I'd sat on the bed sharing Mintoes with Nan while Mum raged about us, screaming how I'd ruined both our chances. In the corner, where nowadays Will's nappy-changing unit lived, I used to have a bean bag. Daniel had once sat on it and listened to me angst about whether I still loved my baby's father or not. But it was the room next door – Nan's old room – where Dan and I had our first real kiss. That was where we'd begun. The beginning and the end. From outside of us I could see the whole shape of our relationship, the highs and lows, the points where we'd been closest and where we'd drifted apart. Probably Daniel could draw a graph of it, labelled axes, the lot.

I deserve better, Charlotte.

Had somebody fed him that line? I'd been replaying his words for a fortnight, waiting for the pain to hit. After all, this was my best mate in all the world, the biggest part of my adult life after Will, closing the door on me. Basically I think I didn't believe it.

'What do you want me to do, Daniel?' I'd said. 'You knew I had baggage when we got together.'

'It's not the baggage. It's how you see me. It's like you've been gradually disconnecting yourself all year, I don't know why. Not through lack of effort on my part, that's for sure. I try and do everything to suit you. And now I'm tired of being in the background, taken for granted.'

'I don't take you for granted.'

He just looked at me. In the end I'd had to lower my gaze, away from the lie.

The light under Will's curtains was growing stronger, now casting a bar across the duvet and carpet. Next to me Will rolled and kicked his legs out sideways, battling the bedclothes. 'Mummy,' he said. 'Stuck.'

I turned sideways to unravel him and he snuggled into me, butting his head against my breastbone. What about you, you poor fatherless ferret, I thought. When will you realise Daniel's not around any more? Will it matter to you? How much do the under-threes remember? That hurt, the worry that my fucked-up love-life might be damaging my own child. It cut deep.

'I can't do this any more,' was what Daniel had said.

And somewhere in the middle of my disbelieving panic, Walshy's shining face was rising up between us, his choppy fringe, his laughing eyes. Walshy in boxer shorts and sunglasses, standing on a plastic garden chair singing 'No Sleep Till Brooklyn'. Walshy, the man I thought I wanted right up until the day he was mine for the taking.

I'd got it so wrong.

'Mummy,' whispered Will down my ear. 'Need some juice.'

Here I was in the nursery, cold and stiff from sitting on the floor. Charlotte Cooper, single mum again.

'Shall we go downstairs?' I could make a hot drink and stick the gas fire on. Watch a video. Text Roz and ask how she was doing. I had a driving lesson at nine. No point trying to go back to bed now anyway.

Life sails on, whether you're ready for it or not.

Banging drawers, running taps. Half past bloody five in the morning, and I think it started up earlier than that only I refused to open my eyes so it could have been any time. Don't want to wake up. Feel old and unloved and fatty-fat fat. Big blobby whale like the ones you see on the news, stranded on beaches. Done for. Jiggered. Yesterday, I tried on a blouse I bought two months ago, and it's too tight across my bust. Ripped when I tried to take it off. Bastard buttons, bastard bloody useless thread. Cheap rubbish, that's what it is. Keep thinking about Steve. I don't want him, not really. Keep thinking about Eric.

God Almighty! She can't half slam a door, can my daughter. I've told her till I'm blue in the face to leave Will during the night and he'll settle himself, but oh no, she's on this mission to prove she's Wonder-mum. 'I'd never turn my back on a child who needs me,' she says. No one can do pious like our Charlotte. Well, she can get on with it. Good luck to her.

Bloody birds singing. Shut up.

Opened some daft magazine article last night, *Reclaim Your Zing!*. Assuming you ever had any zing in the first place. Mine ran out about 1980. *Sniff a pine cone*, urged this article. *Buy a fresh duvet cover. Change the way you part your hair. Cut out sucrose*. Never read such bobbins. Cut out sucrose? White sugar's been one of the truest friends I've had. White sugar in tea. Wish someone would bring me tea in bed. Open that door now with a tray, slice of toast, flower in a vase—

Bloody cat trying to claw his way in now. How's he managed to break out of the kitchen? Scratching at the wood, miaowing. Really odd miaow that cat has. Doesn't sound right. Sounds like someone pretending to be a cat. Sometimes he says 'meringue'. That's not normal, is it? Bloody shut up, Pringle, or I will feed you slug pellets.

Oh, bugger it. Duvet back, swing legs down, connect feet with carpet, unseal eyelids. There, see? Sun's barely up.

Grope for door. Forehead against panel for a moment.

Open door a tiny crack. Look, flea-bag, if I let you in, will you stop your racket? Right. Come on, up, yes, curl up on the pillow next to me and go to sleep.

Eyes closed again.

Pringle loves me, at least. Curl up, Pringle. No, not padding about with your bony paws all over my face, Lord knows where they've been. Or showing me your backside. Euff. Settle down. Settle. Down. Bloody mog.

Not that this bed's going to see any other kind of action for the foreseeable future.

God, cat, I'm going to open that window and chuck you out. I will, too. Wrap you in a pillowcase and drive you to the canal. Should have done it months ago. Meringue? Never mind meringues. Will you LIE DOWN?

Mum's voice in my head: *No rest for the wicked.* Mum wrapping a worming tablet in mince for Chalkie. Mum boiling up rhubarb on the stove; explaining how to roll pastry; showing me how to put on my first pair of grown-up tights.

Cat going mental. Where's the damn bedside light switch gone? Who's moved it? There! Nothing. Bulb's gone. All I bloody need. Push cat off bed, thud.

Peace. Lovely.

No. Dazzled! Someone must be holding a floodlight over my head. Ow, ow, too bright. Have to shade my eyes to be able to see.

And it's the damn cat again, jumped on the windowsill and pushing the curtain open. Sun breaking over the horizon right in my face, full on. I'll never sleep like that. Bloody, bloody animal. Off to the RSPCA with you tomorrow, lad, get you re-homed. You can go 'meringue' at someone else.

Stagger up, flailing, grab for the curtain. Only, what's this? What's going on in my garden? Who in the name of Jehovah is that lurking by my fence?

I might be a rubbish girlfriend but by God I'm a good mum. I am.

I pulled back the curtains on what looked like another sunny day. Amazing how warm it's been, actually. The cleaners from the Working Men's Club set up deckchairs on the car park yesterday.

Next I helped Will dress – no nappy today, we're living dangerously – and carried him downstairs. I set him on the kitchen floor while I went to splash cold water on my face and rinse my mouth with Listerine. When I came out again he'd broken into the bottom cupboard and was cradling the biscuit barrel hopefully.

'Come here,' I said, and took it off him. I prised up the lid, snapped off a sliver of digestive and handed it to him to gnaw while I made his porridge. Smart mums compromise (I read that in a magazine).

I have to say, it's a sight easier navigating our kitchen since Nan went, but it's also less exciting. No chance of finding sausages in the bread bin, or half the morning's post stuffed inside the toaster. This neat drawer where Will's cutlery and bowls live used to contain sachets of ancient bread mix and wildflower seeds, hair nets and plastic rain hoods, Atrixo, crepe bandages, mousetraps, drawing pins and half a draughts set. The little pantry, which was where Nan stowed her laundry paraphernalia, now houses Mum's herb pots and features a gingham café-style curtain and a set of much-prized Cath Kidston tins. I know Mum would love to go the whole hog and rip out the old kitchen, have fitted units in a nice farmhouse pine, but she won't part with her savings. 'They're ring-fenced for your education,' she says in tones that range from martyred to downright angry.

'I'm not going to put that sort of pressure on you,' I said to Will, who was busy smearing biscuit paste across his clean-on-five-min-utes-ago top. 'Although if you could let me know about the potty today, that would be good.'

'Yuk,' he said, dragging at his T-shirt.

'Potty?'

'Nah.'

We'd see. If the books were right, I'd most likely have him con-tinent by the end of the week. And that meant, hooray, no more changing mat and nappy sacks and zinc oxide cream and air freshener and hand sanitiser and trips to the wheeliebin in the middle of the night. End of an era, in fact. Nothing stays the same in motherhood. You just get your head round one routine and then it's all change. This toddler-porridge I was making (half a cup of water, stir hard, stick dish in microwave) would be replaced by something else in a month or two. I'd come home from uni and find Mum was feeding him Frosties or scrambled eggs or possibly even Kit Kats and milk in a bowl.

I turned to look at Will where he sat, legs spread out in front of him on the lino, the top of his head lit by a ray of sun. He was so beautiful. The morning was beautiful.

'Hey, you,' I said. 'Come outside.'

The best mums see an opportunity and just take off. I hoisted him up – he's a bloomin' weight these days – and settled him on my hip. Then I opened the back door onto the glistening lawn. By now it was properly light, the ridge tiles on Eric's house and one side of our hedge illuminated red. Over the other side of the sky, the pale moon sank towards Rivington.

'See?' I said, giving Will a squeeze. 'See how amazing the world is. There are glow worms and thunderstorms and live music and the seaside, hot-air balloons and magicians and Toblerones and mosaics and snowboarding. Loads of cool stuff. And it's all out there, waiting for you. There's so much you can do, there's so much you can be. There'll be change, and loss, people you care about who'll leave you, but you mustn't be scared. You must run out there and jump straight in. You must go after what you want. Because you'll always have me behind you, supporting you. I love you so much. Do you know that? Do you understand?'

Will snuffled against my neck. His body felt hot next to mine. How do I ever manage to go away from you? I thought.

'Because you're everything to me, and I promise, promise I'm going to make your life better than mine. We'll have so much fun together. I'm going to take you by the hand and lead you through all the happy times and the sad ones. Whatever unfolds, I'll be right by your side, and I'll rejoice in your joy and not whinge for no reason and get disillusioned and start to pick holes in everything you do. You can be who you want to because I'm not going to force you into any kind of mould. You were always a blessing, not a millstone, and I'll never make you feel anything other than a hundred per cent wanted. Whatever wrong turnings I've made, you were never one of them. I really need you to know that. And if I ever do make mistakes, I'll 'fess up straight away and try and make it right again. I make you that vow. I'm going to come at you with a great towering wall of love, a tidal wave of it, and you won't have any choice but to love me back and be happy.'

Out of the blue, a memory of Daniel jogging round the garden with Will shrieking on his shoulders . . .

There was a clunk as the back door opened and I heard my mother's voice.

'You know you've knackered the microwave, don't you?'

I let Will slither gently to the ground. 'What?'

'You set it for thirty minutes, not thirty seconds. His porridge exploded. His ladybird spoon's melted. This is what happens when you go round half-asleep.'

She marched up to us and peered into my face. 'Where's your red scarf gone?'

'What red scarf?'

'You were wearing a red scarf.'

'When?'

'Five minutes ago. I saw you from upstairs.'

'No, I wasn't. I don't own a red scarf.'

Her colour was high, and there was gunk in the corner of her eyes. I wondered if she was going a bit mad. She's so near the edge these days.

'I *saw* you,' she said. 'You were rooting about in the bushes.'

'You must have dreamed it.'

'I ought to be able to come up with better dreams than that.'

There's no arguing with her when she's in a mood. I said, 'I was showing Will the sunrise. Isn't it fantastic? I couldn't let him miss it.'

She dismissed the glorious sky in a glance, then pointed triumphantly at a dark patch on the side of my T-shirt.

'Looks like you did a good job, anyway. He's wet himself with excitement.'

Within three hours we'd had a sight worse than wee. Thank God his trousers had elasticated ankles. Of course by this time Madam's swanned off for her driving lesson, so it was all for me to deal with.

I took him to the bathroom, in fact I stood him in the bath, and peeled off his lower clothes. Lord, where to start.

'Why didn't you ask for the potty, Will? It was right by you, under the table. Mummy showed you.'

He cast his eyes round the room as if he was considering.

'Will?'

'A big crocodile lives there,' he said, pointing at the plughole.

'What? Who told you that?'

'Mummy. It goes snap! Snap! Snap!'

Oh brilliant, I thought. That'll be another screaming fit round about bedtime.

'Don't be silly, love. How would it get through that tiny hole? Crocodiles are big. Bigger than you. Could you fit down there?'

'Snap!'

'You couldn't fit down there, could you?'

'Snap you up for dinner.'

'Can you stop jigging about, at least?'

I set to work with the toddler wipes but it was hard going. There was poo on his socks, for heaven's sake. How could one small child produce so much? And as I scrubbed and flushed, scrubbed and flushed, I was thinking, You know, I've done all this once. My life's moved on. My time for this is past.

'Snap! Grandma. Snap your leg.'

'So next time you're going to say, aren't you? Next time you need the potty. Don't wait. You know where it is, you can just go.'

'A lion in there.'

'What?'

'In there. Rarrrrr.'

In the airing cupboard now. Well, that was great. What other beasts had Charlotte installed around the house for him to panic about? As if we didn't have enough tension in the air without generating imaginary stress factors. 'No, there isn't. Hey, those trousers are getting pretty thin on the knees. We'll have to buy you some more. Shall we do that? Nice new trousers?'

'He comes out at night.'

'Who does?'

'Lion.'

I began to dry off his legs with a towel. 'There's no lion in the cupboard, Will. I promise you.'

'Mummy said.'

'Mummy made a mistake. Look, we'll open the door now, shall we? You can see for yourself.'

I lifted him out of the bath, gave him a quick dust of talc and set him on the mat. He'd become distracted by a silver moth which had flown out of the curtain and was dithering about by the mirror. But I didn't want to let the lion business go. I knew it would rear up again, and the very last thing we needed during the trauma of potty training was for him to develop a phobia of the bathroom.

'Shall we see?'

Will shook his head.

'It's fine, love. There's nothing there.' I pulled open the airing cupboard and stuck my head in as far as I could get it, which wasn't that far because of the lagged bulk of the boiler. 'Will, look. Are you looking? Now, how could a lion fit in here? There isn't even room for Pringle-cat.'

Frowning, he strained forward and nodded at the tank. 'In there.'

'No. No lions in there, love. It's full of water. Lions can't live in water. And there isn't a way in or out. Only this thin pipe. A great big lion couldn't get through a little narrow pipe. It couldn't, could it? And this water gets very hot. The lion would be cooked. He'd be boiled, like your egg.'

I thought this barrage of logic would have convinced him, but I forget he's not even three. In the World of Two, anything's possible. 'There,' he said, pointing to the shelf above the tank.

'That's towels.'

'He lives there.'

Bloody hell, I thought, I'm going to strangle your mother when she gets home.

'Right,' I said. 'Wait.'

I nipped back through to the lounge and picked up a chair. This I carried to the bathroom and placed in front of the cupboard. Then I clambered up onto the seat and started pulling out the towels one by one. At first I tried to throw them so they landed neatishly across the sink, but they soon slipped off on to the floor. Will watched for a moment, then jumped into the middle of the pile.

'Can you see,' I called down to him as he rolled about, 'no lions. Not one. No animals at all, unless you count a little spider.' Just a battered tenor horn case right against the wall, and a box of candles and a possibly antique first aid kit. I climbed down again, intending to hoist him in my arms so he could inspect the space and declare it lion-free. Only he'd wrapped himself in towels like a mummy and didn't want to be freed, so I had a bit of a battle on there, and then in all the kerfuffle he did another wee, and I was just starting to get to crisis point when the front doorbell rang.

I left him where he was and ran to peep out of the window. It was Eric on the step.

'Hang on,' I yelled into the hall, then scuttled back to the bathroom. While I was away Will must have rolled against the sink pedestal because he was sitting up with a red mark on his forehead, crying. He was still entirely naked from the waist down. His stinky trousers, socks and pants festered in the bath waiting for me to deal with them. I didn't dare check myself in the mirror; I had a fair idea of the state I was in.

'Right, you.' I picked up my grandson, gave his head a quick rub and then dragged him into the lounge where his potty was. 'Sit there for one minute, don't move, and you can have a Kit Kat. Yes?'

He sat without argument. I dashed back to the bathroom and picked out the dirty clothes. For a moment I considered hurling them into the washing machine, but really they needed a scrape and also I couldn't cope with the smell any longer. So I nipped out the back door and just slung the lot in the bin. Then I came back inside, gave the place a frantic blast of air freshener, stuck my hands under the tap and finally went to greet Eric.

'Are you busy?' were his first words. Kenzie clung to his hand.

'I've one or two things on.'

Eric pulled a pleading face.

'Do you need me to look after him?' I said.

'Would you? Would you really? You're such a star, Karen. I wouldn't ask only it's a job, y' ken, and you can't keep turning down work, can you? Not these days. But we should be done in a couple of hours – say, by midday.' He relaxed his grasp and Kenzie stepped confidently inside.

'OK.'

'And then,' he paused for effect, 'I'm taking you out.'

'Out?'

'Pub lunch.'

'Oh. Well, that's nice.'

'My treat. You deserve it. Although I'm thinking, we'll have to go somewhere with a playbarn, that place on the bypass, so we can get a bit of peace while we eat.'

I knew the pub he meant. We'd been to a birthday party there. They had a plastic ball pit and slides and a soft play area for under-threes. Weary mums and dads sat at nearby tables and forked out an endless stream of cash for sweets, slushies, Simpsons keyrings, hairbands, helium balloons, Postman Pat rides. Pop music boomed from all sides, cranking up the hysteria. Meanwhile the kids flung themselves about and every ten minutes there'd be some collision requiring the mopping of tears and the buying of further junk. It's torture for adults, basically.

'We could,' I said. 'But I've an even better idea.'

'Aye?'

'Yeah.'

He smiled and I thought, Why do you have to be so damn handsome.

'I'll put myself in your hands, then,' he said.

I had literally not closed the front door behind me when Mum announced she was leaving me to babysit someone else's kid. That's terrific, isn't it? Foist whoever you like on me, 'cause I've nothing better to do. And really I needed five minutes to come round because down by Cobbs Barn I'd made a complete hash of parallel parking, got myself stuck against the kerb with my front wing poking out, rev-rev, everyone looking, plus there was a bunch of scuzzy kids on the corner all laughing at me. Bastards. Towards the Wigan end of the village they do go a bit feral.

So I walked into the house and the first thing I see is Will, sitting on the sofa in a T-shirt only and with a towel under him. Kenzie's next to him but fully dressed, thank God for small mercies, and Mum and Eric are canoodling in the corner. Well, I say canoodling; they're leaning over a newspaper together. It looks way too familiar, anyway. Mum goes, 'Yeah, so the kids have eaten and we're popping out for some lunch, won't be long, and I've got my mobile phone.' She didn't even have the decency to phrase it as a request.

I said, 'Where are Will's trousers?'

She said, 'In the bin. They're beyond redemption.'

'Beyond redemption? Gemma bought him those, he's only been

wearing them a couple of months. What's he done, spilt nitric acid down them?'

'What do you think he's done?'

I said, 'Any luck with the potty?'

She laughed nastily.

I asked her where exactly she was going in case there was a problem or emergency. She went, 'I've got my phone,' again and winked. It wasn't an answer at all. I hate the way she goes all arch when there's a man around she fancies. It's so embarrassing. Christ knows what Eric thinks, although as long as he's getting his free childcare I don't suppose he's bothered. I call it a colossal cheek, them leaving me with a strange child to look after. Exploitation, it was. When Mum came back we were going to have it out.

I started by turning off the TV. Will immediately flared into temper mode and threw a cushion, but Kenzie just slouched back, watching me. There's something odd about that child. He's too quiet, for a start, and his eyes are permanently wide as if he's searching for something right inside your soul. It's unsettling. I can't warm to him.

I said, 'Let's get the folding table out and do some drawing. I'll join in. It'll be fun.'

Will kicked the towel onto the floor. I thought, Don't get cross, Charlotte. Be positive, be bright.

'Hey, I know. Will, how about a little wee-wee before we start?'

He buried his face against the back of the sofa, his small white bum poking upwards. Making the point, I suppose. *It's my bottom and I'll do what I like with it.* He was like a bomb ready to go off.

Of course, when you tell people you're potty-training, everyone has some surefire piece of advice to give you. Start early; start late. Cheer your child madly all the way; play the whole business right down. Make him sit and don't let him move till he performs; never force him. Offer rewards and treats; never bribe him onto the toilet or he may grow up plagued by weird associations. One point everyone seemed to agree on, though, was that once you'd started, you had to see it through to the bitter end.

'Come on, sweetie.' I picked up my son, intending to set him down next to the potty. 'Give it a go.' But when he saw where I was headed, he suddenly went all floppy-at-the-shoulder-joints so he was slithering down my body and out of my arms. I released him in a gentle heap onto the carpet.

I gave up and went to fetch the folding table, and paper and pens. These I set up in front of Kenzie, while my son rolled his head back and forth against the edge of the rug and giggled insanely. I wondered about shoving the towel under him again, but thought that might be courting failure.

'OK,' I said, grabbing a couple of sheets off the table and two felt tips. I knelt down next to Will, the potty at my elbow. 'I'm going to draw the biggest snake in the world. What are you going to draw?'

That caught his attention. He sat up, swiped the red pen and pulled off the cap.

'Snake.' He began scoring his own paper energetically.

'Look at mine. Mine's enormous.' I trailed my snake all round the outside edge of the paper, winding his length in spirally. 'See his long tongue and his zigzag back.'

Will ignored me. He still holds the pen like it's a dagger, his fist curled tight. I've told Mum to try and make him grip it correctly but she never bothers. Maybe I'll have a word with nursery.

Above me, Kenzie sneezed. I glanced over to check he was all right and saw he had his head down, concentrating on his picture.

See? I thought. He's holding his pen right. Then I remembered he was four and not far off starting school, just tiny for his age. His clothes would fit Will, near enough. And that reminded me of the lost trousers and got me cross again. I'd definitely be fishing them out of the bin and washing them, if only to make the point to Mum. You didn't chuck clothes away because they had a tiny bit of poo on them, for God's sake.

Will pawed at my arm. 'My big snake.'

'He is big. Where's his tongue?'

'There.' Will made a blind stab at the top of the paper.

'Where?'

'*There.*'

'Right-oh.'

I reached across and got a clean sheet, laid it on the carpet in front of Will. 'Can you draw me a cat?' There was a kid in his group at nursery who'd managed a cat; the picture was on display in the hall near the coat pegs. OK, we're not talking much detail here, but it had a head and body and eyes and ears. One of the staff had written *Bobo* underneath.

'What you need to do is hold the pen like this.' I tried to mould his stubby fingers into position round the barrel. But as soon as I took my hand away, the pen flirted out of his grasp and hit the fireplace. I went and retrieved it from where it had rolled under the TV, and while I was up, cast an eye over Kenzie's progress. He was drawing some kind of figure with no legs, an oblong body, very long arms and spiked fingers. At the top of its head he was adding exuberant coils of orange hair.

'Who's that?' I asked.

'Mummy.' Kenzie carried on with his tight little circles and I watched half-admiringly, half-irritated at his fine motor skills. All at once he paused mid-stroke, stiffened and looked at me. 'Not Mummy. Not Mummy. That's not Mummy.'

'OK.'

'*Not Mummy.*'

'You said.' I sank back down to see how my son was getting on. Really, I couldn't be doing with Kenzie, he was too freaky. Will meantime had done another scribble, this one more expansive than before, some of the lines heading off onto the carpet. I'd have to have a scrub at those with a wet cloth before Mum came home.

'Just try a cat, for me, yeah? Concentrate, Will.'

But he'd lost interest in artwork and was playing with his privates.

'God, you so need some pants on,' I snapped. What the hell's so fascinating about willies that men have to fiddle with them all the time?

The view from the bridge where we parked was like a holiday poster: *Come to Lancashire, County of Brimming Reservoirs.* The sun was strong but the air breezy; the sky was covered in mares' tails. The water was blue and choppy. On the way up here I'd made him stop at Greenhalgh's while I bought two meat pies, two Chorley cakes and two tins of pop, everything we'd need for a happy afternoon. Then we'd come up Rivington.

'It was good of your daughter to have the kids,' said Eric as we ambled towards the shore.

'Will's her son.'

'I keep forgetting that.'

The water was a sheet of sparkles and I had to squint against the brightness.

'I've some sunglasses in the glove box, if you want.' Eric nodded towards the car.

My instinct was to say no so as not to be a nuisance, but then I thought, He's offering. He's showing some concern. 'Thanks,' I said, and he ran to get them.

When he caught up again I said, 'You must be some kind of sun-god, I reckon.'

He grinned. 'Aye?'

'You always bring the weather with you. It normally rains on pretty much everything I do, but this summer, since you moved in, it's been like the Med.'

'Oh, that's me. A god. Watch, I can make stones walk on water.' And he picked up a flat pebble from the scattering by his feet and sent it skipping across the reservoir surface in four jumps. 'I tell you, when I was a kid in Moffat it would rain like you've never seen, for days on end. Us kids would just pull our coats on and go play out in it because if you'd waited for the dry, you'd never have left your house. The fields would flood regular, there'd be ducks and geese in the middle of them.'

'I thought it was just me with a soggy upbringing.'

'The Lord sends rain on the righteous and the unrighteous, as my granny used to say.'

'You don't talk much about your family, do you?'

'Nope.' Eric nodded at the ripples his stone had left. 'Want a go?'

'I've tried before, I'm useless.'

Eric shook his head and scanned the shore for another pebble. He selected one, turned it over, weighed it in his palm and handed it to me. 'Here,' he said. 'This one's perfect.'

'I know the theory. It's the practice I fall down on.'

He came and stood behind me – tingle-tingle went my skin – and drew my arm up and back. 'Have it between your fingers, like this. Then bend your wrist so when it flies, it flies with a spin. Keep it horizontal. If it tips it'll sink.'

Suddenly I felt silly and awkward. 'I can't.'

'Here.'

He held my arm level for me, and I swung and let the pebble go. It sploshed into the water at first contact.

'Oh,' he said.

'See? I told you.'

'It's practice. That's all it comes down to. If you spent half an hour, even, you'd crack it. Watch me.'

He crouched again, searching the ground. I was able to really study his shape, the solid, well-formed muscles of his back and arms and thighs. How different he was from spindly-limbed Steve. All bone and sinew is my ex. This Lusanna would eat him for breakfast.

The image that popped up, of them in bed together, made me shudder. I shook it away crossly. *Skip, skip, skip-skip-plunk* went Eric's stones. Across the reservoir, white gulls joined black rooks, circling.

At last he emptied his cache and turned back to me, his jacket flapping in the breeze. 'I'm sorry to say some of my skill comes from winging pheasants.'

'What, chucking rocks at birds?'

'Not rocks. Wee stones. And not to hurt, only to surprise. We liked to make the birds explode out the ground, squawking. There wasn't a lot else to do when you lived out in the wilds.'

We wandered over to the stone wall and sat on it.

'What was it made you move to England?'

'Maria.'

'Would you go back?'

'I might, one day. Depends how life unrolls.'

How nice it must be to take yourself off somewhere fresh and start again.

'Penny for them,' said Eric after a bit.

I said, 'Oh, nothing. I was thinking, our Charlotte's been mustard this holiday. I feel like sending her back to York. Don't know if it's because her boyfriend's not around.'

'Aye? Where is he?'

'Abroad, apparently. He's taken his mother to France or somewhere.'

'That's decent of him.'

'I'll say. I can't imagine Charlotte ever taking me away anywhere. Do you know, the last holiday I had was ...' I paused, realising horribly that the last time I'd had a break from home was when I stormed out and went looking for my birth mother in London. '... a stopover by the coast, three years back. And that wasn't much fun.'

'Tell you what, hen. If I come up on the lottery, I'll buy you a holiday,' said Eric, passing me one of the cans.

'Would you?'

'I would, too.'

Even if it was a joke it was a kind joke. A bubble of warmth rose up inside me. I thought of the envelope that had come for me this morning from London, from Jessie, a different handwriting on the front that had fooled me into half-opening it, and the rage which made me rip it straight in two, unread. I thought of Charlotte stomping about, of the chaos and sulk that would no doubt be there to greet me when I got back.

I said, 'Do you ever wish you were really old? I mean, so old you didn't have to do anything except sit around and watch TV and have food brought to you? Have someone drape a nice blanket over you in the morning and pop a cup of milky tea at your elbow. Then just leave you alone to rest.'

Eric laughed. 'Ach, no. Do you?'

'Sometimes. When I'm really tired. It's just the idea that you could close your eyes and drift, and not be worrying about a dozen deadlines before the end of the day. No responsibilities, no one depending on you. You could shed the lot. Just sink down into your bones and sleep and sleep . . .'

'Ha. It'll come to us all soon enough.'

I checked myself guiltily. 'God, sorry. It's awful of me to even say something like that. Especially after what my poor mum went through towards the end.'

Mum, lost inside herself, unsure of the days, of who was alive and who was dead.

'You're still finding it difficult, aren't you?'

'I am, yes. I wish you'd known her, Eric. She was so balanced and good. This memory book I'm making, I thought it might help – meet the grief head-on – but I'm not sure it has. And no one else understands. Every day I think it'll be better and sometimes it is a little bit, but not much.'

'Might be worth having a word with the doctor. Maria was on Seroxat before she left.'

'The answer isn't pills. I know what the matter is and there's no pill on earth can help.'

He waited respectfully for me to carry on. There was something so honest and straight about him, with his strong jaw and wide, capable hands.

I said, 'Funny, I used to come here with my dad sometimes and look for mussel shells. When I was a kid, you know.'

'Aye?'

'He was the best. He died when I was a teenager and it was awful. Everyone thought the world of him. Only, he wasn't technically my dad. Like my mum wasn't technically my mum. I was adopted. I didn't discover that till a few years ago and it was a hell of a shock.'

'My God, I bet it was. Does your daughter know?'

'Uh huh. Not that she's especially interested.'

'How did you find out?'

'Mum let it slip one time when she wasn't herself; she didn't mean to. Initially I didn't believe her, but then I wrote off for my birth certificate and that proved it.'

'Were you upset? Is that what's bothering you?'

I hesitated for a moment, trying to answer truthfully. 'Not the being adopted itself, no. Though I'll admit, first off I was very, very shaken. Something like that knocks you totally off-kilter because your basic assumptions about who you are, your roots, turn out to be wrong, and you're left going, Who am I, then? Where do I actually come from? It goes to your core. And I was angry that I hadn't been told, because it was my life, I should have had that information. I felt it wasn't right to keep it from me. I couldn't believe Mum had done that. But then once the news had sunk in, I became excited. I thought I could go and meet this other mother and maybe – I know how this sounds but I'm trying to stick to the truth here – maybe claim a better life for myself. I suppose you could say I had ideas above my station.'

'She was wealthy then, your birth mother?'

'I didn't know anything about her except she'd moved to London. From where I was, though, that seemed quite glamorous. I was thinking Harrods, and people in suits, Carnaby Street. I know it's not all like that, but I just had this – instinct –

she might have made something of herself. That turned out to be so wrong.' I looked down at the wheels of yellow frilly lichen decorating the wall next to us, wondering whether to carry on, tell him everything. 'Listen, Eric, no one knows this next bit. Not even Charlotte. Especially not Charlotte. She has to be protected from what happened. You have to promise me, promise you'll never breathe a word. Can I trust you?'

'Of course. I promise.'

'Never tell anyone. Ever.'

'I promise!'

His expression was so earnest. I longed for the relief of confession at last.

'OK. Well. I did go and track her down.'

'I see. And?'

Again I hesitated. 'Like I said, I've not told a soul. Actually, I don't know if I can tell you.'

He nodded, then slid off the wall so he was standing in front of me. 'Come on, let's walk.' And he held out his hand.

The shore was uneven with loose stones and patches of soft sand, tussocks of grass. The water level was low and some of the rocks we walked over were green with dried-out weed. His fingers felt hot in mine.

I said, 'To cut a long story short, it didn't work out. I found my birth mother and she wasn't a nice woman. She didn't want me and I didn't want her. So I came home. I thought that was it and I'd be able to get on with my life. I tried to make up for – for my disloyalty – by appreciating Mum more. I thought, She doesn't know where I've been, I haven't hurt her, it'll be all right. But I didn't realise what damage I'd done to myself. See, Mum had given me such a secure childhood, and effectively what I'd done was throw it back in her face. That's what it felt like to me, anyway. Like I betrayed my mother, and I got punished for it.'

Some of the gulls over our heads were crying, a seaside sound. Days out in Blackpool and Formby, that sound meant, novelty rock and the thick sliced nougat that Mum always called 'nugget'. Dad winking at me over his potted shrimp.

'Ach, come on,' said Eric. 'There's nothing wrong with you wanting to know about your roots. I mean, that's human nature, needing a mystery solved, y'ken? Who wouldna want to hear about their own past? God, *I* never think about it, I take it for granted because I've always known – the house I grew up in, my mum and dad's marriage, my grandparents. All the family stories, where, when, who. If I didna know this stuff, you can bet I'd be hoaching to find out. It would really bother me. You did nothing wrong, Karen. You just asked the question ninety-nine per cent of us would have done.'

'You think?'

'I do. Did you ever hear from this woman again?'

I swallowed. 'Sometimes she sends me these cards. I throw them away.'

'Are you worried she'll come after you? Is it that?'

'She wouldn't dare. I could – I could cause a lot of trouble for her. She knows that. I'm safe as long as I don't reply. Only, seeing the handwriting brings it all back and churns me up for days after.'

'Must have been some meeting between you.'

I had meant to leave the story there, he'd heard enough to understand, but now the rest came pouring out, unstoppable.

'You've no idea. No idea. She was *so* cruel. Not just to me, because you could understand that – the shock of me turning up out the blue might make her defensive. Aggressive even. It wasn't that. It was a lot worse. I saw this social worker-type person while I was down there who told me … there was something she did. Basically that she hurt someone and was sent to prison for it. More than hurt. Somebody died because of her.'

And here it came, forming before my eyes: a head-and-shoulders shot of a little girl in a check dress and cardigan, smiling for the camera. How many times had I called up her image after I came back from London? Hundreds? Thousands? So many it drove me nearly mad and I had to train myself to stop. Now, when she shimmered at the edge of my consciousness, I pushed her away. Stood up, walked about, pinched myself on the arm, sang out loud. Anything to block the memory. Some knowledge is just unbearable.

'It was – I'm sorry, it's too horrible to think about. I have to keep blotting out the detail.'

'Jeez.' Eric's voice sounded a long way away.

'So I knew what sort of a woman she was, but I went to her house anyway. I thought there might be some kind of explanation for what she'd done, I thought – I don't know what I thought. And I got there and she opened the door and screamed at me to go. The whole visit was a nightmare, from start to finish. I don't think about it now any more than I have to. It's boxed up in my head, shut away. If I do start to remember, then I immediately make myself concentrate on something else. Mostly it works. Except for the sense of guilt, and Mum.'

'Karen. That's terrible.'

'Yes.'

His hand was still round mine, his thumb stroking and soothing. We carried on along the shore, crunching shingle.

After a while he said, 'But look, what your birth mother got up to's no' your fault. And as for your mum, your adopted mum, did you love her before you went to London?'

'Of course I did.'

'And when you came back, did you love her any less?'

I laughed bleakly. 'No! I loved her more, because I appreciated what a lucky escape I'd had. I realised how Mum had been keeping the past a secret to protect me. And I saw how much she'd done for me while I was growing up, the trouble she took just in ordinary ways. I became a lot more patient with her, and grateful for what I had. With Charlotte too, and Will. It was as if we'd begun again. A proper fresh start.'

'Well, then.'

'Yeah, but I keep coming back to *How would she have felt if she knew I'd been to London?*'

'Don't you think she'd have forgiven you?'

'Yes, yes, I think she would. She definitely would. But—'

I couldn't meet his eyes, so I fixed my gaze on a patch of sky above his head and a cloud shaped like a stretched-out rabbit. The cloud thinned, the rabbit's head and ears broke off and became a beak. Mum up a stepladder sweeping a broom round the picture rail; me on the bottom step sucking a stick of black Spanish. Happy kids don't realise how blessed they are, they just assume happiness is their right. Which is as it should be. I felt as though I was shifting with the shapes I watched, changing form. Memories broke apart, dissolved, reformed.

'Then don't you think it's about time you forgave yourself, Karen?' he said.

I left the boys to their activities and ran upstairs for clean trousers. I brought them down, persuaded Will into them, and switched the

TV back on. Then I went outside to fetch the trousers Mum threw away.

To my relief, as soon as I opened the bin lid I could see an embroidered giraffe motif. I remembered how touched I'd been by the gift, that Gemma had even thought of Will, let alone spent her own money on him. 'I saw them in a window and just thought they were so sweet,' she'd said.

I took hold of the tiny section of material on show and attempted to drag out the rest from under the rubbish. Sod's law, though, the waistband caught on a piece of plastic packaging, and in tugging I dislodged a stack of vegetable peelings and mouldy fruit that showered onto my feet. A gust of wind nearly blew the lid shut on me; I flung it back angrily. Something horrid flew off and splashed in my eye. In the past I've laughed at Mum for believing inanimate objects gang up on her, but right now I could have kicked that bin to within an inch of its life.

Finally the trousers came free and I shook them, turning them this way and that. They were pretty caked; Mum had been right, damn her. But nothing a hot wash wouldn't put right. I'd show her.

I was about to drop the lid back in place when a picture caught my eye: a glossy picture of a baby, Photoshopped so its face was at the centre of a giant sunflower. I'd seen the image before on greetings cards, there's a whole range of them. Babies dressed in ladybird suits, babies peeping out of flowerpots and seed pods. I think they're yuk but Mum thinks they're cute. I couldn't imagine why she'd throw such a card away and not have it out on the sideboard. Idle curiosity made me reach down and ease it free.

It was soggy, of course. Our junkmail always is. Mum drops it in the sink to soak for half an hour before slinging it, then that way no one can steal our identities, though what poor bugger would want to be any of us I can't fathom. But there was more than water damage here. Now I looked properly, the card had been ripped almost in two across the middle of the sunflower. The crown of the baby's head had been removed.

I laid the trousers on the ground and concentrated as best I could on peeling the ruined card open.

What I saw inside made my mouth fall open. *Jessie* it said at the bottom, and a wiggly arrow pointing to *New Address* in London. The biro handwriting was rounded, a bit childish; above it was the end of the printed greeting, something about Sunny Days. There'd been a message at the top of the left-hand side too, but that section looked to have been added in felt tip and was now too blurred to decipher.

I stood there for half a minute, squinting at the ghosts of words. I knew who Jessie was. The last time I'd seen that name was on my mum's birth certificate, uncovered three years ago when I accidentally broke Nan's kitten picture. I remembered the certificate falling out from between the frame and the glass, then Paul Bentham and me unfolding the yellowing strip of paper and trying to make sense of it. The shock as the penny dropped. Mum not who she thought she was, Nan not my nan. Jessie Pilkington my grandma, wherever she was. Then: did it matter? Did I care? Did it change anything, day to day? What about Mum, how would she cope if I told her? Hugging the knowledge to myself for weeks, and then it turning out Mum knew she was adopted anyway because Nan had apparently blurted it out in a moment of confusion. Other more immediate events – Will's arrival, Nan's stroke – overtaking us so the discovery shrank pretty much to nothing. For me anyway. For Mum too, I'd thought. She never said much on the topic, even when I asked her. I'd assumed she'd turned her back on that avenue. Now to find out Jessie was writing . . .

The back door banged shut, nearly giving me a heart attack. Mum must have come in the front and created a through draught. For a moment I stood and dithered, then I slid what was left of the card into my pocket to examine later, and picked up the smelly trousers between my thumb and index finger.

When I got in, the bathroom was occupied so I was forced to rinse the trousers in the kitchen sink. What damned lie had I texted to Roz that morning? *Being a mum is fun!!!* I slung them in the washing machine, scrubbed my hands again and went through to check on the boys.

It was sitting on its side on the lino, propped against the skirting, waiting for me. I bent down and picked it up with trembling hands. 'Mum?' I said.

Both kids were back on the sofa. The (empty) potty was upside down and Will had draped the towel over his head. Pens lay scattered across the floor.

'Just waiting to say cheerio to your mum,' said Eric from the doorway, making me jump.

I nodded, and went to right the potty.

'She had something in her eye, she's gone to wash it out.'

Busting for a pee, more like, I thought. The mysteries we women have to preserve.

I said, 'Kenzie's done a lovely picture. He'll want to take it home with him.'

'Aye?'

I thought Eric wasn't going to even bother looking, but after a few seconds he seemed to change his mind, stepping forward to glance at the orange-haired, stick-fingered figure. The reaction was not what I was expecting. 'Jeez,' I heard him say under his breath.

Oh, give the kid a break, I thought. It's not bad for four.

The next moment he'd snatched up the paper and folded it roughly. 'Hoy, you, come on,' he barked at Kenzie. 'Home.'

'Are you not waiting for my mum?'

He shook his head and took hold of Kenzie's arm. The lad wriggled off the sofa obediently. I heard the toilet flush.

'So I'll tell her you said goodbye then, shall I?'

'Aye.' In four stiff strides he was out of the room. Weirdo son, weirdo dad.

Will flopped backwards into the empty space left by Kenzie and I went to the window to watch them. Eric's free hand was working in his pocket as if he was mashing up the folded paper there.

'Oh, has he gone?' Mum's voice sounded disappointed, but when I turned to look it was worse than that. Her mouth was twisted and her eyes wide, maddish. She looked like someone who's had a terrible shock.

'Bloody hell, Mum, what's up? What's he done to you?'

She shook her head. 'It's nothing to do with Eric.'

'You come home from a date with him, straight away lock yourself in the loo, and then emerge all upset? Give me some credit.'

'I'm not upset.'

'Could have fooled me.'

'You wouldn't understand. You never understand.'

'Try me.'

'This. See.'

She held out a photo to me, one I'd not seen before. It was obviously old, the black and white fading to sepia, and it featured a wedding group where the bride wore a hat rather than a veil, and a dress with long, tight-cuffed sleeves.

'Is it Nan?' I asked, knowing it was even as the words came out. Her rounded young face was aglow, while the groom on her arm smiled modestly. Making up the party was an awkward teenage girl in round spectacles and ankle socks, a very tall bridesmaid, a laddish best man, and two fierce-looking old biddies in long, funereal coats.

Mum blinked a few times. 'It was in the bathroom when I went in just now. Just under the sink. You didn't put it there for me, did you?'

'Nope.'

'My God, then.'

'*What?*'

'If you didn't put it there ...'

'No big mystery. It'll have fallen out the airing cupboard. You probably pulled it down with those towels you cleared.' She was that freaked, I was trying to be helpful.

The moan that escaped from her was like something collapsing. She shifted her bulk round the corner of the sofa and sat down heavily by Will.

'*Why*, Charlotte? Why? Why do you always have to be so mean?'

Honestly, it was just a photo. It had been lost and now it had turned up. That should have been a nice thing. She could stick it in her history book. What was wrong with the woman?

I started to gather pens and lids, while on TV a cartoon owl asked over and over, 'Where's my mummy?' I felt useless, as though everything I said and ever had said and ever would say was poisoned.

On the seat next to her, Will went quiet and a dark stain spread out across the cushion beneath him.

Bless Eric, oh, bless him. I didn't care how often he babysat, any of it. He'd more than paid me back. Because Charlotte was wrong. That photo wasn't an accident. This was the message Mum had been trying to send me: that she wasn't troubled by anything I'd done, she was just happy now to be with Dad. Why would my mother ever have wanted me to be miserable? I could stop beating myself up. I could let it rest.

This was the forgiveness Eric had told me would come. This was what happened when you let yourself trust someone.

CHARLOTTE: I've got a question.

KAREN: Go on.

CHARLOTTE: What do you remember about Mum as a baby?

KAREN: (Whispers.) Careful, Charlotte.

NAN: Oh, she were a little love, everyone at church said. I put her in a great big pram – I had that off Connie Settle and your dad fixed it up and mended t'wheel – and we used to walk up and down t'village, people stopping and saying how bonny you were. We'd tried for years t'have a baby, you see. I thought as I were too old . . .

KAREN: It's OK, Mum, if you don't want to talk about it.

NAN: And you had a yellow crocheted hat wi' ribbons, 'cause you had no hair till you were nearly two, and I were worried you'd catch cold. Little yellow mittens. Whenever I went into t'butcher's he'd say, 'Well, Mrs Hesketh, I've never seen a finer baby in all my life.'

CHARLOTTE: And was she good?

NAN: Like a lamb. She loved to hang over t'pram side and laugh and laugh at people's feet.

CHARLOTTE: Yeah?

NAN: Enjoyed her food, allus cleared her plate.

CHARLOTTE: No change there, then.

KAREN: I can remember that bucket you made into a chair so I could sit at the table.

CHARLOTTE: What, you sat on a bucket?

KAREN: Not on one. In one. My dad cut the front low and made a couple of holes for my legs to fit through. The bucket was tied to a dining chair to stop it falling off. And it worked fine, didn't it, Mum?

CHARLOTTE: I can't imagine you so tiny.

NAN: And do you remember that time a mouse ran up your bedroom curtains and you came to tell me and I thought as you were codding me?

KAREN: I don't, no.

NAN: You came into my bed one night and said, 'There's a mouse climbing t'curtains,' and I told you you'd dreamed it.

KAREN: I really don't remember. Was there a mouse, in the end?

NAN: Oh aye. About a dozen of 'em. My dad were trapping 'em for weeks.

KAREN: *Your* dad? We had mice a few years back, that bad winter when Charlotte was—'

NAN: And what about that time as you fell into t'farmer's midden? And we had to hose you down in t'yard.

KAREN: I don't think that was me.

NAN: Florrie were furious.

CHARLOTTE: Who's she talking about, Mum?

KAREN: I'm not sure.

NAN: And t'farmer had a mare as'd break wind if you threw a stone at it. I said to Jimmy, 'Don't hurt it.' But he only ever chose little stones – pebbles, really. It used kick its back legs up and do a great trump. We thought it were t'funniest thing ever. Do you remember?

KAREN: No, but it doesn't matter. We like to hear you talk.

NAN: Aye. They were grand times. You were a grand baby. You were a blessing, you were. Honest, I've never been as happy.

CHAPTER 9

On a day in September

I knew it was a risk. But oh, if it paid off. After a year of getting everything wrong, from velvet jackets to ghostly photos, I'd suddenly be the hero of the hour. Even finding out about the Daniel business wouldn't matter in the face of all the comfort and joy I was going to deliver to Mum's door.

What I'd thought was, I'll get the train down to London and phone from there. That way, if Jessie's up for seeing me, I can nip straight round before I lose my nerve. If she isn't, I'll take myself across to Oxford Street and do the shops instead.

Mum I'd fobbed off with a tale about needing to get back to York for a few hours so I could reserve some books for my dissertation. She wasn't pleased – maybe she'd had plans for the day, I don't know – but I just went, 'Look, do you *want* me to pass my degree or what?' That always shuts her up.

Not that I liked going behind her back.

If we were the sort of mother and daughter who were able to talk, I'd have already said to her, *You can't go on like this, Mum. I miss Nan loads, of course I do, but life goes on. It has to. You can't let the absence-of-someone swallow up the people who are still here. It's not healthy and it's not fair. Look at me, look at Will. This is your life.* And I might have been able to say, *There's more family to find, if you want. There's another mum out there. Do you not think it might be useful to go see her? Give her a chance? I know she's not Nan – who could ever replace Nan – but you ought to meet this woman, just touch base with her. Then you could have a good chat, she could see how you'd grown up and you could tell her about me and Will and teaching and all the rest of the stuff you've done with yourself over the years. It might be nice to hear a bit about where our genes came from. And I bet she'd love to hear. I mean, she gave birth to you. OK, yeah, she did give you away, but they were different times and anyway people change. Having a baby completely mashes up your head. I should know. So she might have really regretted it straight after and not been able to do anything. She might have been pining for years. Crying on your birthday. Imagine that. You could help her and she could help you. It could be exactly the boost you need.*

When I went over it like that, to myself, it made total sense.

I had tried on a few occasions to discuss the adoption: never got very far. Once, when Will was only a baby, I'd asked if she ever wanted contact with her real mum. First off she'd got in a strop because I'd said 'real', when Nan was 'every bit her real mum, always was and always would be'. But then she said it 'all happened too long ago' and that she 'didn't have the time or energy to cope with the disruption'. Mainly, though, her argument was: what did she want with another mother when she had Nan? She was happy, she said. Nan had kept the adoption a secret because she didn't think it was important. Well then, if Nan felt that way, then so did she. Let sleeping dogs lie.

I said, 'Perhaps when Nan did tell you, it wasn't a mistake. She meant it to come out. A Freudian slip.' Mum's eyes had filled up and she'd said, 'No, Charlotte, she was ill, she didn't know what she was saying.'

I hadn't dared push any more.

And now the train was already past Milton Keynes, and less than an hour away from Euston.

How can you be sure she hasn't already spoken to this woman? went Daniel, always the annoying voice of reason even though he was only in my mind. One blink and there he was on the seat opposite me, his wild hair squashed against the velour head-rest.

Because, I said to Imaginary Daniel, I asked her straight out last week, with Jessie Pilkington's secret card burning a hole in my pocket, and she told me she hadn't. I said again, 'Did you ever try to contact your birth mother?' and she said, 'No. Don't you think I've enough on my plate right now?' She was having to shout over the din of the washing machine and Will hitting his potty with the TV remote.

I could see Daniel's eyes narrowing. *She threw Jessie's card away. What does that suggest?*

Only that she's stubborn as hell. The way Mum works is, she makes a decision and then, bang. Done. No budging, ever. She's been that way as long as I've known her. She believes changing her mind is a weakness. As a kid I learned pretty fast that if I wanted a certain toy and I got a no, there was damn-all point asking again. Once a no, always a no. So, when Nan was alive, Mum made the decision not to go looking for Jessie, and even though Nan's out of the picture, Mum won't shift from that position because she's

Bromsgrove Library

Tel 01905 822722
Thank you for using Bromsgrove Library

Borrowed Items 02/08/2019 12:35
XXXX8764

Item Title	Due Date
Bad mothers united	23/08/2019
My husband's wife	23/08/2019

Amount Outstanding: £3.06

Items listed are just those borrowed today
Remember to remove security lock
from borrowed DVDs
If you would like your child's library card
updated to the new design children's card
please ask a member of staff

Bromsgrove Library opening times
From 1st September 2016
Monday 9.00am - 7.00pm
Tuesday 9.00am - 5.00pm
Wednesday 9.00am - 5.00pm
Thursday 9.00am - 5.00pm
Friday 9.00am - 5.00pm
Saturday 10.00am - 4.00pm

decided and that's the end of it. Plus, even if she *did* reconsider, she hasn't got the drive or the confidence now to pursue it. She's really low. I think she'd be worried she's too vulnerable at the moment and wouldn't be able to cope with the emotional upheaval. Even if meeting her birth mother might be her saving grace.

Yet you're prepared to risk that on her behalf? Dangerous, Charlotte, dangerous.

It wasn't, though, not really. The risk was all mine. I'd be the one to sound Jessie out, and if I thought she'd be good for Mum, I'd get them together, a heart-warming reunion. Like Cilla on *Surprise Surprise*.

And obviously if things weren't looking too promising, if I didn't think Mum'd take to her, I'd just come home again. End of story. Jessie knew where we lived: if she was going to cause trouble, she'd already have caused it. I didn't see there was anything to lose.

I'm not stupid, whatever Charlotte thinks. This holiday we'd had one excuse after another as to why Daniel hadn't been round. His term finished later than hers; he had to stay on to help set up a charity concert; he'd promised to take his mother away because she'd not been well. I swallowed it at first, but by the time we got to 'his flight home was delayed', I knew I'd been had. Which meant one thing only – she must have given him the boot. Wild horses wouldn't keep that boy away otherwise.

When I finally accepted the state of play I found myself so angry I couldn't actually confront her. Have you ever been like that? Scared to start in case you can't stop. I didn't know what words might fly out of my mouth. That lovely lad, like a father to Will, and her passport to something better if she was smart enough to see it. Yet she messes up again. How many times! How *many* times?

I could imagine how the conversation had gone. She'd have told him it was time to move on, that she needed someone more exciting. No tact, my daughter. I should know. I've had years of her cutting comments. She probably had a new boyfriend lined up already, and given her history it could be any brand of rubbish. God help us all if it was another Paul Bentham. Throw out the doctor's son, the boy who stood by you all through your pregnancy, who runs you about like an unpaid taxi service and plays with your child, even changes his nappy sometimes. That's right, you chuck him and see what happens. You dozy girl! It's as if you sabotage your chances deliberately. I despair. And who is it's left to pick up the pieces, eh? Who can it be? I'll give you three guesses.

Anyway, she'd swanned off to York after some textbooks, so she claimed. Gone after a boy up there, more like. I was sure it was that, she was shifty as anything when she went to catch the train.

Which left me, Will, and an uninterrupted morning. I'm not one to interfere, I'm really not, but something had to be done.

Tweenies were running frenzied circuits round the TV studio. I laid a Kit Kat on the arm of the sofa; I knew that would buy me at least fifteen pester-free minutes.

I was going to pick up that phone, dial Daniel's number and see if I couldn't sort things out.

Soon as I alighted at Euston, I tried ringing her. It was noisy, what with the crowds shoving past and the station announcements coming over the Tannoy, but it seemed noisier still at her end.

'Jessie?' I shouted over the babble. It sounded as if she might be in a pub.

'This is Jen,' said a woman's voice, sharp, unfriendly. 'Who's this speaking?'

I tried to stifle my panic. What had I done? Copied down the wrong number?

'It's Charlotte. Karen's daughter. Your granddaughter? From Bolton.'

There was a pause and then the line went muffled, as if she was covering the phone with something. I strained to hear.

After a few seconds she came back on. ''S all right. You took me by surprise,' she said.

'Is it Jessie?'

'I call myself Jen now.'

'Oh, right. Sorry. Jen, then. I'm so excited to be talking to you. Long-lost family! I mean, wow. It's just brilliant. Are you, do you know who I—'

'Let me go outside,' she said. 'I can't hear nothing in this place.'

Her accent was a funny mix of flat northern vowels and Estuary. I tried to picture how she might look, but in my stressed state could only call up Pauline Fowler off *EastEnders*.

'There,' she said. 'I can hear meself think.'

'I need to come and see you.'

'That's right, course you can, love. When?'

'Now. I'm in London.'

'You're here?'

'Yeah.'

There was a long pause.

'Right,' she said. 'Here already. OK. D'you know which tube you want?'

'I'm – I'll get a cab.'

I'd thought it through in advance: because I didn't want the hassle of trying to work out maps and lines and stations on top of all the other anxiety, I'd sneaked some cash from our special savings account. An unforgivable act. If Mum found out before I could top it up again, she'd go ballistic. Some of the banknotes were tucked into my jeans pocket where I could get at them straight away, and another lot were stashed in a zipped compartment inside my purse. I thought it might be safer that way. Around me people hurried by, checked watches, hugged, swore at suitcases across their path, craned to see the departure boards. I laid my hand against the doorway of Sock Shop to steady myself. It was vital not to panic.

'Come right over, then, sweetheart,' said Jessie, Jen, whatever her name was. 'I'm dying to see you.'

'Really? Are you really?'

'Oh, yeah. Get yourself here as quick as you can. We've a lot to catch up on, you and me.'

I tried Daniel's mobile number first because, for all I thought Charlotte was lying, I couldn't be completely sure he wasn't on holiday somewhere. The phone rang for a while then cut out.

Next I tried the landline. I wasn't interfering, I only wanted to find out where I stood so I could act in Charlotte's best interests.

The phone rang and rang again, and I was about to end the call when the receiver was picked up.

'Hello?' A woman's voice, posh, a bit slurry.

I said, 'Who is this, please?'

She went, 'Who are *you*?'

I said, 'It's Karen Cooper. Is that Mrs Gale?'

'Oh, Mrs Cooper,' she said.

I have spoken to Daniel's mum before, at Speech Day. Oh,

and once when Daniel slammed his finger in the door and wasn't able to drive Charlotte home so I had to go and collect her from their Victorian villa (I think Dr Gale must have been out on call that night). Daniel's dad I quite like, but I've never warmed to Mrs, mainly because she looks at me as if I've crawled out from under a council grating. Perhaps she thinks if she turns her back, I'll rob her. Not that they have a right lot worth nicking any more. Nowadays they live in separate flats on different sides of the city, and Mrs G's flat is over the top of Daniel's. Funny arrangement, if you ask me.

I cleared my throat. 'Would it be possible to speak to Daniel, please?'

'He's not in.'

'What time will he be back?'

'Not till tomorrow, I'm afraid.' She sounded smug. I wondered why she was in his flat. Had I interrupted her nosing around or had she heard the phone and come down? 'He's out with his girl-friend.'

'Girlfriend?'

'Yes.'

I knew it was a trap but what choice had I? 'You mean Charlotte?'

'Oh no. That's been over for weeks. Didn't you know?'

And there we were. So I was bloody well right again, but wishing I wasn't, and out of the corner of my eye Tweenies danced as though they were possessed by demons and Will giggled and kicked the sofa. No Daniel. Daniel gone, moved on, lost forever to the family along with all the blessings of his goodness and patience and sanity. The young man who'd been part of our lives for three years. Someone who never talked to me as though I was a fool or a nuisance, who was happy to tackle an awkward light bulb or nip up to the chemist to get Nan's prescription for me. Gold, he'd been. A treasure. And she'd driven him away and some new girl had snapped him up.

Though my hand was trembling, I managed to make my voice stay calm. 'Obviously not, Mrs Gale. But thank you for letting me know.'

My throat felt too strangled to say anything else. I pressed *End Call* and threw the mobile at the armchair.

One by one the decent were abandoning me, leaving only the duplicitous behind.

The taxi passed out of the station through streets of tall old buildings. Outside one a modest demonstration was taking place, six men in anoraks and lumberjack shirts holding placards. I tried to read the slogans but a red bus came between us and blocked them out. A pigeon passed low in front of the windscreen. Someone bibbed a horn.

I'm going to meet my grandma, I could have said to the driver. The back of his head wasn't encouraging, though, and he had the radio on. It didn't matter. Every so often I'd give myself this metaphorical prod – *I'm about to discover a new branch of the family!!!* – and try to gauge the reaction. Because although I was excited and curious, and giddy with righteousness, I couldn't quite process the information. The idea of Jessie/Jen didn't yet stir any biological tug. Would that change when we came face to face? I wondered what we'd do. Hug? Or not? Kiss? Shake hands? Damn, I should have brought flowers, I realised. Too late now. Bloody *EastEnders* music was going round and round my head, sending me nearly mad. 'I'm dying to see you,' was what she'd said.

It would be OK. There was bound to be some connection between us, even if it wasn't instant. We were flesh and blood, after all.

I dragged Will round to Eric's so fast his feet barely touched the pavement. It seemed like the only way to stop myself ringing Charlotte and screaming down the phone at her.

'She's only gone and chucked her boyfriend,' I barked in his face as he opened the front door. Without waiting to be invited in, I barged past him down the hall and into the lounge where I parked myself on the sofa. No way was I emptying out this rant on the doorstep.

Kenzie was playing with Duplo on the carpet, and Will squatted down nearby to watch, his thumb in his mouth. Even in my stressed state I took in how tidy the room was: amazingly tidy for a man, and when you considered the chaos in his garden and his van. The floor was freshly vacuumed, Kenzie's toys stored neatly in a vinyl mesh bin, his and Eric's shoes lined up under the sofa. No loose DVDs on the floor or plates of half-gnawed toast balancing on chair arms. The decor was still Mr Cottle's though. Eric's programme of improvements hadn't reached this room, unless you counted the pub-style baseball mirror over the fireplace and a new net curtain at the window.

'Are you OK?' Eric asked cautiously, from the lounge doorway.

'No. No, I'm very much not. Charlotte's chucked Daniel and never told me. I've just had the news off his snooty mother. Made a right idiot of myself, because my own daughter doesn't think I'm worthy of her confidence. Never said a word to me, and I *knew* something was wrong. I said to you, didn't I? Hell. I can't believe it. Well, I *can*. Stupid, stupid. I'm that angry with her!'

'So I see.' Eric stayed where he was. I wished he'd come and sit down with me.

'Because I think the world of that lad. He's sensible, he's grown-up. You can have a decent conversation with him. I'd banked on having him as a son-in-law one day ...' Will, strangely shy this morning, manoeuvred himself a fraction nearer the bricks. 'No chance of that now, of course. Someone else has already snapped him up, according to his mother, damn woman.'

On the floor above, something went thud. Both of us jumped.

'The back bedroom window slams shut sometimes,' said Eric, recovering himself. 'I'm going to have to mend the latch.'

'Oh. Daniel mended the latch on our pantry,' I said mournfully. 'He was just so helpful round the house. Carried bags of shopping, washed up. Reached things down off the top of the cupboard for me. Unblocked the hoover pipe. Helped bolt Will's new bed together. And he was always lovely with Nan, even on the days she talked nothing but rubbish. And polite. Politer than our Charlotte. No eye-rolling or sighing, it was always a nice greeting, always a smile.'

There was a clatter from the kitchen and the next second a cat shot across the hall. I did a double-take. 'Dear God, is that who I think it is?'

Eric stepped back out of sight and reappeared in the doorway holding Pringle uncomfortably round the middle, the way you'd carry a squashy pillow.

'It is. He comes every day or so. Don't you, laddie? We've shut the food away but it's made no difference. Last week we found him on the drainer, drinking washing-up water.' He opened his arms and Pringle dropped to the floor, shivered his tail and stalked off. Something in the cat's imperious manner reminded me of Charlotte.

'Sorry,' I said. 'He has his own water bowl at home, Whiskas twice a day.'

'It's no' your fault. You canna train a cat.'

At last Eric left his station by the door and came and perched on the chair arm opposite me.

I said, 'I'm sorry. I don't mean to just land on you and moan, only I really needed to sound off. It's been such a shock.'

'That's OK. It's just that I have to go out soon. A job over in Bolton.' He tilted his head in Kenzie's direction. 'Via Radcliffe.'

Will had finally edged over to the Duplo box and was sorting through the tub of bricks after the little figures. Kenzie was building the green wall of something.

I ploughed on.

'See, the problem with Charlotte is she's never appreciated what other people put in. I'm not saying she doesn't work hard – she does – only she doesn't think about the effort everyone else is making. And you can tell her till you're blue in the face. She's still no idea what a battle it was for me, bringing her up on my own. You know what it's like, Eric, don't you? Sitting in night after night with no one to talk to, having to deal with every crisis and no one to share the load. It's hard, isn't it?'

He nodded.

'I didn't have the kind of freedom Charlotte's enjoyed, waltzing off and living the high life while someone else holds the baby. Not that I resent it – well, I do . . . It's vital she gets that degree, only she's sat there like a queen bee while we've all buzzed round her. I'm not jealous. I want her to do well. It's this, this *self-sabotage*, that's what I can't deal with. I'd have given my right arm to have a boyfriend like Daniel around. The way he took on another man's child, treated him – well, he was just wonderful with him, and I've watched her all this time and she's not been *grateful* enough. We owe Daniel, all of us.' I glanced down to where Will rummaged. 'And my worry, my big worry, is what's *he* going to think when Daniel never comes back? Because that's the nearest he's ever had to a dad, and you need a dad, or something like one. How much say has my grandson had in the matter? None, that's how much. It's not just her own life she's spoiling. She needs to sit down and think about it.'

At my feet Will grasped a plastic man in each fist and banged their heads together. I let my gaze linger on his rounded cheeks, his clean silky hair. His eyes were wide and long-lashed, heart-melting. Charlotte didn't deserve such a beautiful child. But then, when had she ever appreciated what she was given? Barbie dolls I'd saved for, left out and rained on; her school PE kit lost I don't know how many times. Six-month-old bike forgotten in the park, nicked by the time she went back for it. Careless, she was. Memories sparked off memories: my daughter, aged eight, sitting in a Southport café, scowling and stabbing at a dish of spaghetti as if it was alive. Some row about something. A glittery cowboy hat with the crown stamped flat.

'It's like, no matter how you try and smooth her path, she throws rocks into the middle. I'm sick of it, sick of it!'

Will looked at me for a moment, but then carried on playing. Eric cleared his throat.

'Ach, people break up and get back together all the time. She might change her mind, and then if he's still keen . . .'

'No, because his mother said he was already with someone else.'

'She might be lying.'

'You think?'

'Scoring a point. You said she was stuck-up. *You* don't know if he's got another woman, and I bet she doesn't, either. Not for definite. Lads don't tell their mums anything, take it from me.'

The little spike of hope I felt at his words made tears well up. I lowered my face and patted my pockets for a hanky. 'God, what a state to get into.'

'It's OK, Karen.'

'Last thing you want, neighbours turning up and weeping on your sofa. I'm such a fool.'

'You're not.' Eric shuffled forward and lightly rested his fingers on my knee. 'Come on, it'll work out.'

'How, though?' Another wave of self-pity broke over me. 'She's that perverse! You know, all I've *ever* wanted, from the day she was born, is for Charlotte to have a better life than I managed. Realise her potential. I've worked so hard for that. Learned her spellings and tables with her, always turned off the TV so she could do her homework, helped her revise for exams, bought her the right course books. Cut back on things for myself so she could have what she needed. Not that I mind, she had to come first. And she did pass her exams, so that was a relief, and then Daniel turns up and I really thought I'd got her onto the right track. I thought, Yes, Karen, in the end you have done a decent job and all that struggle's been worth it. And OK, the fact he was a doctor's son did make me glad because it's a step up the ladder, isn't it, and if thinking that way makes me a snob, I'm a snob. But I'd have loved him if his dad had been on the dole. A diamond, he was. And she's chucked him away.'

I buried my face in my hands. After a pause I felt Eric come and sit next to me and place his arm across my shoulders. I let myself lean into him, exhale, and it was so lovely to feel the support of his hard, muscly body against mine and smell his spicy aftershave. This was what I'd come round for. I could sense the small shifts in his limbs, hear his breathing, hear the clatter of stirred Duplo, and Will's nose whistling because he needed to blow it. Kenzie was humming softly and I found myself thinking, It's strange how little that lad has to say for a four-year-old; our Charlotte was never quiet at that age. Maybe he had glue ear like Joe Evans in Year Four. I recalled Joe sucking a cushion in the book corner; a young Charlotte sucking her thumb under the table during a fight I'd had with Steve over a bill not paid. Steve on our wedding day, the cuffs of his jacket hanging halfway down his hands. I pictured Steve with Lusanna, racing up Rivington on his bike and then afterwards, in his bed. Would he compare my body with hers? Would he rate the sex as better? The world around me churned and buckled; nothing was the same as it had been. The rules were all changing.

Go on, went my inner demon, *turn your head now and give Eric a kiss. I dare you. I know he said he wasn't on the market, but that was weeks ago. Things have moved on. Think how he was at the reservoir that time. Held your hand like a boyfriend would. All you have to do now is tilt your head and put your lips against his skin. Easy. While he's here, next to you. Don't miss the moment that's being offered to you.*

My heart began to thud.

This is why you came round. To be held, to be kissed. He's right there, right by your side. Just do it, do it. Quick!

'Need a wee, Grandma,' Will broke in, piping and urgent.

I jerked back guiltily.

'Potty, Grandma.'

'Oh, OK.' For a second I'd been in too much of a dither to process what he'd said. 'I haven't got the potty here. Can you hold on till we get home?'

Will clutched the front of his trousers and pulled an anguished face. 'Need it now.'

'You haven't still got Kenzie's old one knocking about, have you, Eric?'

'Nah. We slung it ages ago.'

'Right, well. It'll have to be the toilet, then, like a big boy.' I remembered old Mr Cottle's chemical commode, tucked behind the stairs. 'Where is the bathroom? Upstairs?'

'You can't. It's too untidy.'

'As if that matters.' I grabbed Will and made for the hall.

'Use the garden. It's nearer.'

I glanced back in surprise. 'I'm not going down that route. Otherwise he'll be pulling down his trousers in the street and just widdling anywhere.' Ivy's grandson had once been forced, during a motorway traffic jam, to pee into a bottle. For months afterwards he'd refused to go in anything that hadn't previously held Coke or 7UP.

I lifted my grandson by the armpits and ran for the stairs with him, top speed. 'It's the door straight ahead,' Eric called from behind me.

The bathroom door was the only one open anyway. We charged in and I flung the toilet seat back, yanked Will's trousers down and held him so he was above the bowl. After a moment's pause an obedient stream hit the pan. 'Just in time,' said Will, mimicking my intonation.

'We were, weren't we. Good boy.'

While he finished off, I gazed round the room, trying to calm my thundering nerves. The place was shabby, yes – wallpaper half-peeled off, some of the brown and blue patterned tiles cracked and all of them needing a re-grout – but it was a long way from unusable. The suite itself was a nasty turquoise. I imagined old Mr Cottle proudly picking it out of a showroom thirty years ago, back when he was still fit enough to manage the stairs. Aside from the suite, there was a bucket of Kenzie's bath toys in the corner and some value toiletries ranged on a shelf, nothing really. Nothing to hide. *You nearly kissed Eric*, went my head. *Oh my God! What if you had? What then?*

'Wash hands, Grandma.'

'That's right.' Shakily I set Will back on the floor and left him to deal with his own trousers. As I stepped away, though, something odd caught my eye. The turquoise sink was streaked on the inside with blood, a single thick drop and then a line of it running down and pooling about the plughole.

I stared, confused. Had Eric been wounded in some way? Or Kenzie? Neither of them had looked to be damaged. My brain flicked through the various accidents I'd witnessed at school: a burst nose, a cut lip, a tooth knocked out, that boy who came into class having sliced open the heel of his hand on some corrugated iron. The memory made me shudder.

Quickly I turned both taps on full and sluiced water round, swilling it against the sides with my palms. The blood seemed sticky and persistent, and in the end I took toilet paper and wiped it off that way. I dropped the paper down the loo, closed the lid and flushed so Will wouldn't see and ask questions I couldn't answer.

Tucked under the outflow pipe was a small plastic step which

I presumed was for Kenzie's use. I pulled it out and Will, his waistband more or less back in the right place, climbed on. Together we dabbled our fingers under the cold tap. The water was now perfectly clear. Perhaps the bleed had been caused by knocking off a scab, an old injury you wouldn't think to mention. Eric must get injured at work. He dropped that bucket on his toe a few months back, didn't he? *Almost kissed him! What's the matter with you? He's a friend, that's all. Don't spoil it, don't mess this one up as well.*

'Karen? Karen!' I heard his voice from the hall. To me he sounded anxious and annoyed, or maybe that was my embarrassment I was hearing reflected back at me.

Will climbed down off the step and headed for the stairs.

'Wait,' I said. 'Let Grandma hold your hand.'

He paused in the doorway and I reached out to him. But at the same moment, the mobile in my pocket started to ring. I fastened my hand round Will's cuff, opened the screen and held the phone to my ear.

What I heard in the next ten seconds blasted any thoughts of Eric – of nearly everything – right out of my head.

Fairly soon we'd left the grand streets and we were out into a grittier urban landscape. The road became an expressway, crossing the Thames, ducking under flyovers. Then we were moving through streets packed with high- and low-rise flats, back-to-back terraces, 1930s council semis like mine. I saw parades of shops, bookies and off-licences, kebab houses and launderettes, warehouses, lorry parks, leisure centres, occasional playing-fields. We passed a schoolyard where children in blue sweatshirts queued in lines; an ornate church that was now a carpet-fitter's. All these people going about their normal days. Eventually the taxi pulled up by a tyre-fitting yard. The driver pointed across to a row of stone bollards.

'Pedestrian precinct. Can't go no furver. But that's the road you want.'

My legs went weak. I scrabbled in my purse and extracted from the special zipped compartment what felt like a huge amount of cash (Mum was going to do her absolute nut when she saw how much I'd taken). I offered no tip, though. Our eyes met in the mirror but I stared him out. Something told me to keep tight hold of every penny I had.

As the driver pulled away I panicked again, this time at the sensation of being left alone on a strange street. But then Jessie – Jen – would see me right, wouldn't she? She'd give me a lift back to the station, after I'd travelled all this way. 'I'm dying to see you,' is what she'd said.

I stood for a moment, getting my bearings. Around me was a modern estate with flat-roofed buildings, concrete balconies and walkways. A metal pedestrian bridge, painted blue, flaking metal garage doors. Murals, graffiti. Not a lot of greenery going on. I followed the house numbers till I came to a three-storey block, plain and functional. The balcony directly above me had a folding chair set out on it and the one next door was being used to dry baby laundry.

And here I was. This was Jessie's place. I rang the bell for the ground floor and stepped away. Daft, I told myself, to get worked up when it was all going to be fine. This was a good thing I was doing, for my mum. Across the street two teenage boys in sweat-tops slipped out of an alleyway and watched as I rang once more.

By the time she opened the door I was a bag of nerves. I pretty much fell into the dark little hallway, and began babbling immediately about what sort of journey I'd had. She stood it for thirty seconds, frowning, then nudged me into the lounge and got me to sit.

First impressions: I wasn't in a nice place, it didn't look very cared for. For a start there was hardly any furniture, not even a TV on top of the TV unit, which meant you could see every scuff on the walls and every mark and dent in the carpet. The wallpaper under the window was peeling and even where it was in decent nick the colour scheme was pretty rank, a lot of burgundy and gold and blue, stripes and swirls, Mum would've had a fit. And the light-shade had a loopy fringe that was lower on one side than the other, and on top of the gas fire was a lone crappy ornament, a china pig cuddling a duck. Skank. Tat-orama. And then I thought, For God's sake, stop being so mean, Charlotte. Jessie's only just moved in, hasn't she? It takes time to get a place straight, install your stuff. Half a pot of wallpaper paste and a go with a steam cleaner, it'd come up a different room.

And still I couldn't stop talking, spilling my life out in one big gush. Where I was at uni, how I adored my tutor, how I missed Will, the Daniel situation. Meanwhile I was drinking in Jessie and trying to see Mum's face, or mine, in hers. She was a smallish woman with brown hair, though you could tell it was dyed because there was a good two inches of grey at the parting. The eyes were similar to Mum's, the same creases in the corner and the same-shaped forehead, but Jessie was quite a lot more wrinkled. Her lips were thinner; she was thinner all over. Her hands had gone a bit clawed, big knuckles pushing against chunky resin rings.

She sat down opposite me, crossed her legs. The jeans she wore had sparkles down the seams.

'Well,' she said.

I knew it was time I shut up so she could get a word in. But there must have been something wrong with me because I just carried on rabbiting. Paul Bentham, I now found myself describing, and how it hadn't been my fault I got pregnant in the first place but I was so glad Will was around, not that I'd ever judge anyone who didn't keep their baby, it was such a hard call, you had to do what you thought was best, and Mum had taken a while to get over the shock of Will but now she was fine with it. Jessie's brow creased. What the hell's up with this girl? I guessed she was thinking. Is she on drugs, or what?

It was my ringtone that shut me up finally. I jumped as if I'd been shot, grabbed the phone, dropped it, retrieved it from where it had spun under the sofa, checked the screen and it was Mum. MUM! Jesus. I switched the mobile off, shuddering.

'All right?'

'It was no one. No one important.' I looked up shyly. 'You know it's funny, I can't think of you as "Jen".'

'Well, I am. That's who I am. That other was a different time. Do you understand?' She sounded quite fierce.

I nodded. Don't we all have periods of our lives we'd prefer to gloss over?

We stared at each other for a moment. Then she said, 'Have you come on your own?'

Again I nodded.

'You've not brought her with you?'

'You mean my mum? No. It's a secret. I've come in secret.'

'She's not sent you?'

'She doesn't know.'

'I thought she'd sent you.' Jen frowned, as if I was being deliberately obstructive.

'I reckoned it'd be a surprise when I went back home and told her.'

Something flickered across her face.

'How long have you known about me, then?' she said.

'Three years. I accidentally saw her birth certificate. But we haven't talked about it much. She did tell me you were young when you got pregnant and you couldn't cope. That's all she said, though. I don't think she knows any more details.' I waited, expecting Jen to start filling in some gaps. 'It must have been a rough time for you.'

'Damn right it was. The worst.' She sat back then, her lips a tight-closed line. Whatever had happened in the past, it didn't look as though I was going to hear about it today.

'So I don't really know anything about you!' I said. 'But I'm excited to meet you, "Grandma".'

That made her laugh finally, a kind of croaky chuckle. 'Yeah,' she said. 'I suppose I am. No one else is ever gonna call me that, for sure. So, are you stopping for a cuppa?'

While she disappeared with my bag and coat, I wandered round the room, too wired to sit any longer. I'd hoped there might be a few family photos I could check out, but the only framed item on display was a naff foil print of a howling wolf. The smell of air freshener was making me want to sneeze.

'Anyway, your mum,' she said when she walked back in. 'Tell me what's going on there.'

She sat down on the sofa and patted the seat next to her. I came and rested on the edge of the slippery vinyl.

Where to start? I wondered. How truthful should I be? *Well, she threw away that card you sent, left it to stew under tea bags and toddler wipes.* Best not. I said, 'She's the reason I'm here. I couldn't really tell you the whole thing on the phone, but what it is, she's really down at the moment, missing my nan, she can't seem to get over it and I thought ...'

I hesitated, not sure how to put it.

'What?'

'I thought you might be able to help.'

'How's that, love?'

'I'm not sure exactly. I suppose, lift her, bring her out of herself. Stop her dwelling on sad stuff. Give her a new focus. That kind of thing.'

Jen just looked at me. The china pig went on cuddling the china duck. There was something malformed about the duck's beak, as if prior to the cuddle the pig might have smashed it in the face. Then she said, 'Your mum don't want to see me, sweetheart. I've been writing to her for months and not a peep – ah, you didn't know that, did you? I can tell by your face. She really hasn't told you anything, has she? So then you ring me and I think, Oh, she's coming after all. Only she's not, it's just you turns up. In secret, you say. Without telling her. But she must've showed you the cards I sent?'

'No. I found one, by accident. How did you know *our* address?'

'I had a friend who used to be with Social Services. She fixed it for me. Wasn't supposed to, like. But I made a nuisance of meself till she gave in. I'm an expert at that.' Jen gave another wheezy chuckle.

I tried to picture Mum and Jen together, hugging on the doorstep or poring over a photo album.

I said, 'The problem is, she hasn't got much confidence at the moment. And since my nan died last year, Mum's been adrift. And I want her to move on. I'm pretty sure she would like to meet you, at least once, except she hasn't felt up to it. That's why she hasn't been replying. Not because – well, I don't think she's let herself acknowledge you in case it gets too complicated for her to cope with. But honestly it would do her good to meet you, ask you some questions, hear some family history. She enjoys stuff like that. Sort of filling in the past and a new start at the same time.'

How much of this was Jen understanding? Her eyes were needle-sharp, as if she didn't trust me. I suppose when you've been hurt, you do put up a few barriers.

'What do you think, Jen?'

She stood up and walked towards the window, her mouth working as if she might be about to spit. I saw how hollow her cheeks were, and the harsh lines around her mouth. Everything about her looked dried out. At last she turned and spoke.

'I was always going to leave it, see. Let the past stay the past. You know? But then lately I thought . . . It don't matter what I thought. I sent a few cards but I weren't going to bother again. I know a closed door when I see one.'

This poor woman, I thought: how utterly bloody awful to be parted from your child for years, believe you're going to be united at long last and then end up rejected. Watching the post every morning, and nothing. Silence. If that was Will and me I'd literally die of a broken heart.

'The door doesn't have to be closed,' I said warmly. 'I can act as go-between. I can help you get back together, if that's what you want. We might have to tread carefully, 'cause Mum's quite fragile right now. I think I can swing it, though. What do you say?'

I got up and went to her and put my hand on hers, and it was chilled, the way Nan's always used to be.

I held the phone away from me for a second because I didn't recognise the voice and I couldn't for the life of me take in what this strange man was saying. The screen showed Steve's number.

Will wriggled free and began to tackle the stairs himself.

Fortunately Eric ran up to help him. I suppose he must have seen the shock on my face.

'Sorry, can you repeat that?'

'I'm a paramedic,' said the voice. 'Your husband's had a road traffic accident and he's quite badly injured.'

There was a scuffling noise and in the background I could make out Steve shouting, 'No, I'm not. I'm all right. Tell her.'

The paramedic said, 'I'm going to put him on, OK?' And before I could respond, Steve was speaking in my ear.

'Karen?' He did sound shaken.

'What the bloody hell's happened to you?'

'I've come off my bike.'

'What have you done to yourself?'

'I've – I've broken my arm—'

'Oh, you noodle. What happened? Were you going too fast?'

There was a scuffling noise and a groan. The paramedic came back on. 'Mrs Cooper, he's on Grimstone Lane, do you know it? Two hundred yards before the motorway bridge. The road's blocked off but if you speak to the ambulance crew, they'll let you past.'

I said, 'We're not married any more.' Which was a stupid thing to come out with. I wasn't thinking straight.

'No, but you're his next-of-kin,' said the paramedic. 'Could you get to him, please? Quick as you can.'

Next thing I knew, Jen had dragged her hand free and started a coughing fit. I found myself stepping back as she heaved and retched, her eyes watering.

I said, 'Can I get you anything?'

She shook her head. I supposed it was the shock catching up

with her. She was old, after all; older than her years. And she didn't
look in tip-top health and this place felt damp.

When she could get her breath again, she motioned towards the
door. 'Shall I make us that cuppa, sweetheart? You must be gasping
after your journey.'

'OK.'

Jen's kitchen turned out to be on the poky side and well knackered. Those TV makeover programmes would have had a field day.
I mean, our kitchen's dated, but Mum always keeps it fairly clean
and neat. The units here were shabby and covered in a weird dark
blue veneer; one of the doors hung wonky and there was dirt in the
grooved edges. At the corner of the ceiling black mould mottled
the wallpaper. The steel sink was stained down the sides, one of
the taps bent forward and dripped constantly. The hob was coated
in gunk. I was about to ask how long it had been since she moved
in when, without a word, she ducked out of the room and left me
to it.

I waited for a minute, then filled the kettle myself and began to
hunt for tea bags and cups. A biscuit wouldn't have gone amiss
either. I cast about for a likely-looking tin, but aside from a sauce-
smeared plate, a pair of trainers, a bunch of keys and a pile of
newspapers, the work surfaces were clear. Cautiously I hooked my
fingers under a cupboard door and pulled it open. No biscuits here,
only a packet of cereal, five or six assorted cans of beans and soup,
a jar of lemon tea granules and a handful of pasta screwed up in
polythene. The top shelf held the end of a loaf of bread. I closed
the door and tried another: this one housed a few mismatched
plates and bowls and half a dozen drinking glasses. The first base
unit I tried contained two pans, a balled-up tea towel and a bucket,
and the one next to it an overflowing bin. Last chance was the

modest-sized fridge where I hoped there might at least be butter or a lump of cheese. In fact, two of the racks were empty and the third was occupied by lager, Lucozade and a lone egg.

Where was all the food? Didn't this woman eat at all? Normal shopping aside, our kitchen at home was stuffed with emergency supplies, tins and packets and plastic containers of easy-to-prepare food, all the fall-backs of the busy working mum. There was always a stock of rice-meals and dried milk, tinned meat and fruit, cartons of custard, sachets of porridge. In the event of Armageddon, we Coopers could survive for months.

My stomach whined. I should've eaten something on the train but I'd been too stressed. Now my fear had subsided, I was ravenous. As I contemplated nicking a slice of dry bread to keep me going, I heard the toilet flush. Jen reappeared.

I said, 'Is there anyone else I could meet? I mean, has Mum any other relatives round here?'

She took two mugs from the cupboard and spooned lemon tea into them. 'No. There's no one else. 'Cause my parents are dead and – yeah, that's it.'

'Mum's father?'

'Him too. Just me, that's all there is. 'Cept for Dex, he's my boyfriend and he's not a blood relation, obviously. He wants to meet you. He's gonna pop round in a bit, say hello.'

To be truthful, I wasn't that fussed about seeing any boyfriend. It seemed ungracious to object, though. I checked my watch. 'OK. I can't stay much after three. Will you be able to give me a lift back to the station?'

'Course, sweetheart.' Her thin lips curved upwards. 'I'd say that's the least we can do.'

*

It's not something I want to witness ever again.

I'd got it into my mind that when I arrived, Steve would be sitting on a verge holding his arm and looking rueful. Instead, once I'd got past the lorry they'd used to block the road, I could see he was lying across the tarmac with a pool of blood under him.

'Come through,' said the paramedic. He had hold of me by the elbow which was just as well because my legs felt like water.

They'd taken off his crash helmet and cut his jeans up to the thigh, and that knee was splinted and strapped. I didn't like to look at it too much. That's where the blood was coming from. I crouched down and called his name. At first his eyes were closed but when he heard my voice he opened them. I'd forgotten his irises were so blue.

I said, 'Oh, love.'

He gave a weak laugh. 'Hit a sodding brick in t'road, that's all it were. A sodding brick. And look at t'state of me. Only just started at t'warehouse, can't even claim for sick pay. What am I like?'

When I glanced to the left, I could see a bone showing through his arm and I nearly cried out with horror.

'Are you in a lot of pain?' Daft question.

'It nips a bit. How's my bike?'

Sod the bike, I nearly said. But he seemed genuinely concerned so I got up again and went to check. The Kawasaki was laid out by a hedgerow, in one piece but with the front forks bent and the fuel tank dented. The speedometer case was cracked and the front wheel buckled. He'd want to know whether it was salvageable, and I had no idea. As I stumbled back to him, I found a silver dial lying near the white line which I thought must be the bike's clock. I waited till the paramedics moved away, then I crouched back down and showed him. I had to hold it in front of his face because they'd braced his neck.

'That's not off the Kwacker, that's what's left of my watch,' he said.

'Oh, right.'

I made myself keep my eyes on his face, though the temptation was to glance down and see what state his wrist was in.

'How is she, anyway?'

'The bike looks fine,' I said. To be fair, I didn't know whether it was the kind of damage a lump hammer and a bit of determination could straighten out.

'She flipped right up and threw me off, caught me as she came down ... It were all over in seconds.'

A spasm gripped him. His good hand came up and groped about for me. I could hear the ambulance men on their radios and a swell of helplessness came over me. What were they playing at? Why wasn't he on his way to hospital right now?

As if he'd read my thoughts, one of the paramedics came over. 'We're waiting for a helicopter.'

'A helicopter?'

'It's the best way with accidents like this. Mr Cooper, we need you to keep very still and tell us if there's any sudden change in sensation or pain levels, OK?'

Steve licked his lips. 'I'm not going anywhere, mate.' Then his eyes closed.

'You'll be all right,' I told him. 'You're going to be fine.'

'Yeah.'

I noticed the pool of blood had crept nearly to the edge of my shoe.

'Will somebody radio that bloody helicopter to hurry up?' I shouted.

Then, over this tea that tasted of lemon Fairy Liquid, she began to tell me her own history. And what a train of misery it turned out to be: how her mother had persuaded her to move to London to escape the shame of being a single mum, how she'd changed her name because after all the upset she wanted to start again. Her years with a man who beat her (and held her arm against a hot stove and burst her eardrum and mashed her foot so badly with his boot she had no big toenail there). How afterwards she'd had a breakdown and spent several years in a sort of hospital, recovering. When she came out she'd married a nice man but they'd only been together two years when he got knocked down by a drunk driver and died on his way to hospital. For a bit she worked in a clothes shop, till one of the other assistants took against her and lied to the boss that she was stealing so she got the sack. Then she met another man who seemed decent and kind, only he turned out to have a drugs problem and stole money out of her purse and pawned her jewellery. In one particularly grim week she lost her job, her flat and her boyfriend. There were some bleak months hooking up with any bloke who offered so she'd have a bed to sleep in that night, and then by luck she wangled a job in a friend's café, which is where she met Dex. 'He saved me,' she said. 'Because he understood. He's had troubles of his own. Terrible troubles.'

Dear God, please don't start unpacking those as well, I thought. Now she'd opened up, I found it a bit overwhelming. There seemed almost an element of competition, of boasting. *See my hard-knock life*, she was saying. *Haven't I suffered?* I hardly knew how to respond. I felt dragged down under the weight of all her past woes, my face was stiff from sympathy.

I said, 'Don't you want to hear about Mum?'

'You've told me, sweetheart.'

'I mean about her growing up and Nan and everything. There must be a hundred things you want to ask.'

'Yeah, there are. Course there are. But I want to hear about you, too. Tell me more about this boyfriend who's giving you gyp.'

Suddenly we heard the key in the lock and the front door banged open. Two seconds later a man burst into the room. He was short, bald, wide, excited. Dex.

'Has she brought it?' His eyes glittered as they fell on me.

'Brought what?' I said.

'Shut up,' said Jen quickly.

Dex's smile slipped a little.

I said, 'What am I supposed to have brought?'

'Nothing. Excuse us.'

I watched in dismay as Jen hustled him out of the room. 'Idiot!' I heard her hiss. Whatever was going on, it didn't feel right. Was she upset because I hadn't come equipped with a photo album or some special memento of Mum's? That didn't seem likely. So far she hadn't even seemed that interested in Mum, had reacted really weirdly when I suggested a meeting. The whole atmosphere was beginning to make me anxious.

Partly to relieve my jittery legs I got up and went to stand in the hall. From there I could hear Dex's voice quite clearly, even though it was coming from behind a closed door. 'You were the one reckoned it would work,' he grumbled. 'You said she'd cough.' Then Jen cut in, too quiet to make out words but very angry, I could tell from her tone. Then Dex again: 'It's not my debt, is it? Go back to friggin' Archie's, see how happy he is to give you another week.'

There was a strange noise, a kind of strangled groan or yelp.

'Yeah, but what choice we got?' said Dex.

And finally I understood. I pushed down the door handle and walked in.

They were standing on either side of a bed, except it was really just a mattress with a duvet on top. Around the room were piles of clothes and assorted odd bits of junk: a computer keyboard propped against the corner, the parcel shelf off a car, an orange plastic planter split down one side, half a fireguard. One wall had been stripped down to plaster and the curtain was held up with drawing pins. There was no carpet. I thought, This isn't the shambles of someone half-moved in. This is actual poverty. This is all they have.

Jen froze when she saw me. 'Give us a minute—'

'You thought I was bringing you money.'

'No!'

'Course we did,' said Dex. He sounded defensive, as if the problem here might be mine.

'So those cards you wrote to my mum were begging letters. When I said I was coming to London, you thought it meant she was sending me with cash.' No response. My heart swelled with indignation. 'For God's sake, what makes you think we're rich?'

She hung her head, but Dex stared me out. 'I bet you've more than us, love.'

I opened my mouth to protest, then stopped. He was right. For all we'd had our lean times, I'd never had to live with bare floors and no TV.

I said, 'What is it you need money for?'

She gave a bitter laugh. 'What don't we need money for? They're bloody queuing up.'

'What, are we telling her now?' said Dex.

'She might as well hear. I owe somebody, Charlotte. Well, I owe a load of people, but there's this one man. He's not so patient as the others. He's—'

'He's gonna fuck us over. We're out of time, basically. Finished.'

'We've moved twice but they always find us. And it's all right saying, "Ooh, don't go down that route," but you get a bit behind with your rent and that, and then someone offers you notes in your hand. You'd have to be Mother sodding Teresa to turn them down. A month later they're taking the door off its hinges.'

Loan sharks, then. I'd seen a drama on TV a couple of months ago about one and it had given me nightmares. One woman they'd pushed so she was leaning right out of a window, another said they'd set fire to her son's school bag. There'd been children screaming, mothers on their knees. Jesus, if it was pigs like that shouting through the letterbox, no wonder she was wound up. No wonder she was so keen to see me. A walking cash dispenser, I must have looked like. My conscience hovered between pity and outrage.

'Listen,' I said, 'I might be able to give you something. Just a small amount. Out of my own money.'

'Yeah?'

'Maybe twenty.'

Dex snorted.

I said, 'It's all I can manage. I need the rest to get back home.'

'Waste of time.'

'Where did you put my bag?'

Jen shot Dex a look. 'I tell you what, sweetheart, how about you just loan us the cash. I can see you've got a few notes in your pocket there. Make it a bit more than twenty and we'll pay you back. Promise.'

'Where's my bag?'

'I'll post the money to you. Soon as I get straight.'

'Enough.' I slapped my hand against the thin wall. 'I'm going to go now, right? Give me my stuff or I'm calling the police.'

That made her laugh. 'And tell them what, sweetheart? You've mislaid your handbag? Your old granny's asked you nicely for a few quid to see her through the week? Like they'd even come out.' She saw me reaching for my mobile. 'Oh, for fuck's sake, it's in the loo.'

I turned on my heel and ran for the tiny bathroom, locking the door behind me.

This was the rattiest room of the lot. No window, naked light bulb, gouged-up cork tiles under my feet. The bath had a line of grot going right the way round and a load of what looked like dirty bedding bundled down at the plug end. I didn't dare check the toilet.

At first glance there didn't seem anywhere to hide a bag, unless she'd stuffed it in the cistern. But when I used my foot to shift a pile of clothes from the corner, underneath was my coat and a plastic bin with my bag in it. I grabbed it and held it to my chest, heart thumping. Outside I could hear Jen and Dex still arguing. Dex didn't look to be in great physical shape, but he was angry and desperate. He could probably just take my money off me if he wanted. Or worse. A swell of panic sent me giddy and I had to clutch the sink for support. Idiot, Charlotte! What a total and utter idiot I'd been ever to come here in the first place. Swept in on a tide of arrogance, and now see the state of me. No one knew where I was or who I was with. God, I'd have given every penny I possessed to be back in Bank Top with Mum and Will, bickering over TV channels. Even to be on the platform at Euston.

I had to get home.

A deep breath, and I undid the lock.

I think what happens is, straight after a crisis, your brain function splits into two halves to protect you. There's this brief period where you go onto auto-pilot and deal quite coolly with all the small practicalities, even though part of you wants to be throwing yourself on the ground and howling. For instance, I remember the day Mum died, the Health Centre rang about Will's MMR and I was able to hold a perfectly rational conversation with them about suitable dates for his jab.

It's later that you let yourself fall apart.

When the helicopter had taken off I first of all tried Charlotte's phone, no bloody reply, bloody selfish girl, then I got back in my car and drove to a petrol station because I knew the tank was down to fumes. Next I stopped off at Iceland because it was the quickest way I could think to get my hands on some ready cash, stood in the centre aisle cradling a catering pack of spicy chicken wings – and Lord knows when we were going to eat those – managed to pay for them OK, even exchanged a line about the weather with the girl on the till. I collected Will from Eric's and foisted him instead on Maud, who was so shocked at my news I thought she was going to have a heart attack. Finally I took myself to hospital.

There was a bit of waiting around and then the surgeon led me into a side room. By that point I was nearly dead with fear.

'It was a very bad accident,' he began.

I fingered Mum's crucifix round my neck, managed a nod. *Tell me something I don't know.*

'Steven's injuries are multiple and serious. He's fractured his left shoulder, elbow, wrist and hip, and also his right knee. The shoulder and knee are particularly badly damaged. He's going to need several operations in the short-term. There will be longer-term issues, too.'

I found my voice. 'Will he walk?'

'We think so.'

'Will he lose a limb?'

'I can't rule it out at this stage. We'll know more when we operate. Now we've completed the X-rays we're taking him straight down to theatre. The good news is, his skull and spine are intact. His injuries are life-changing, but not life-threatening.'

'I see.'

'Have you any other questions?'

'About a million, only they're all swirling about ... I can't think straight.'

He waited for about half a minute, and when I didn't speak, he stood up and put his hand on my shoulder. I didn't want to delay the man, but I wasn't ready to be left just yet. 'How long will he be in hospital?'

'We're looking at months rather than weeks. And when he comes out, he's going to need a lot of looking after.'

This time I didn't say we weren't married. What did it matter? I wondered who was going to tell Lusanna.

I should have said no, but Dex insisted.

'Jesus, girl. You was asking for a lift earlier,' said Jen. 'And it'll be ages before we can get you a taxi. They're all tied up with school runs this time of day. So if we don't take you now, you'll miss your train. Be stuck here. With us. Imagine that.'

'We'll go straight to the station?'

'Course we will.'

I knew they weren't being honest only I didn't feel I had a choice. It's hard when you're in a strange city and everyone you love is two hundred miles away.

We all climbed into his stinky Saxo and set off down the back streets. I was holding my bag so tightly my finger-ends had gone numb. Sure enough, five minutes in and Dex began saying we should call round at his son's because we were pretty much going past and he needed to drop something off. I said that would make us late. Jen sat in the front and stared out of the window. 'I'll ring my mum,' I threatened at one point, and I saw her shift in her seat, half-turn towards me. Her eyes held a kind of spiteful triumph.

'Like fuck you will. Like you're going to tell her you were *ever here.*'

And I knew that what she said was absolutely true. Mum must never know I'd been here and met this evil-minded cow.

Without warning the car swerved up onto the kerb and Dex pulled on the handbrake.

'Why are we stopping?' I said. 'My train!'

He pointed to the row of shops opposite, and the bank. 'See that cashpoint? Yeah? Just nip across and draw us out fifty, will you?'

I gaped at him stupidly.

'Go on. Then we'll take you straight to Euston and you'll never hear from us again.'

'And if I don't?'

Dex sighed. Jen had shut herself off from the whole proceedings, fixing her gaze ahead and saying nothing.

My hand groped for the door handle.

'Or seventy,' said Dex.

I leaned hard on the door and it flew open. I stumbled out and, legs wobbling, made it across the busy road. From there I walked past the bank, and into the newsagent next door where I stood in full view of the window, facing the car. Then, slowly and clearly, I retrieved my phone and switched it on, holding it up to my ear so Dex could see.

After a minute the car drove away.

I closed my eyes in relief and, at the same moment, the mobile began to ring.

They let me say goodbye before they wheeled him away, but I don't really think he had a clue. On my way out a nurse gave me a plastic carrier bag of his clothes, and then I went outside to ring Charlotte. And if she wasn't answering, by God, I was going to keep pressing redial till the damn button fell off.

KAREN: I've been clearing out the front room for Will. Have you any idea how many tins of food I found in the bottom of that wardrobe?

NAN: (laughs)

KAREN: Why do you hoard so much, Mum? Is it because of the war?

NAN: (laughs)

KAREN: Anyway, they're all pre-decimal so I'm afraid I've whizzed them.

NAN: Aye.

KAREN: And there were eight false moustaches. Eight! All in different styles and colours. Those were from your Mothers' Union plays, I presume?

NAN: That's right. I were allus chosen for th' hen-pecked
husband, and they'd put me wi' Molly Higham or Gertie
Speak, somebody big, as my wife. Th' audience'd start
laughing before we even spoke.

KAREN: You enjoyed acting?

NAN: Oh aye. We did some grand plays. Comedies, mainly. *A
Tuppenny Tale*, *The Lost Slipper*, *Down the Primrose Path*.

KAREN: Can you remember any lines?

NAN: No. It's too long ago. (Pause.) Did you find my ladle in
t'wardrobe?

KAREN: The one with the shell bowl? No. I found an old
carpet-beater and a bag of donkey stones.

NAN: I wonder where it went?

KAREN: What's so special about this ladle?

NAN: Nowt, really. Only it were a nice thing and I had it a
long time. I used clean up after t'dog wi' it.

KAREN: We never had a dog.

NAN: Your dad did, briefly. Took it in for a neighbour when
she fell sick. But it were a whippet and very flighty. So
someone at t'paper mill had it off us. I think he ended up
racing it. It could run like the clappers.

KAREN: You never told me about that.

NAN: Didn't I? We only had it a month or two. Sammy, they
called it. Lightning Sam. So anyway, this ladle come in
very handy.

KAREN: I thought you said you used it to serve vegetables?

NAN: I did, later on.

KAREN: Are you winding me up?

NAN: It were properly disinfected. Mind, I did used t'think,
Imagine their faces if they knew where this ladle'd been.

KAREN: Good grief.

NAN: (laughs) But what folk dunt know won't hurt 'em.

KAREN: You reckon?

NAN: Aye, I do. I do.

CHAPTER 10

On a day in October

It was ludicrously early, not even light outside. I'd crept downstairs after an upsetting dream I couldn't remember, and stuck the TV on low so as not to disturb Walshy or Gemma. For the first half-hour I'd watched a programme about a dance school and a bunch of nervy anorexic teens who studied there, which was mildly interesting. But that programme had finished and now it was snooker and I was too weary even to bother switching channels. The screen showed a close-up of coloured shiny balls jammed inside a triangle, then the frame was lifted away. Seconds later the formation was smashed apart. The balls sprang in different directions to ricochet off the table-edge or each other, scattering themselves across the green cloth. And I thought, That's how my life is right now, blasted.

Back in another county, Dad was laid out on a hospital bed with actual metal screws driven into his skin, and a tangle of tubes going in and out all over. One tube was morphine, I knew because the nurse kept having to come and change the cartridge. The one at the foot of the bed was for holding wee. I tried not to look at that. Mum had said before I went in the first time that it was really important I didn't freak out in case I upset him. She kept stressing that. God, though, it was difficult. I've never seen anyone so bashed up. With respect to my mum, I reckon I could have said pretty much anything to him, waltzed round the HDU in a ballgown, and he wouldn't have turned a hair. He was too drugged up. Yet Mum was adamant, in the face of all the evidence, that he was going to end up OK. I wasn't convinced her definition of OK was the same as mine. I'm pretty sure she just meant Not Dead. After that initial visit, I'd texted Dan – more to head him off than anything, I didn't have enough strength left to deal with him turning up in person – and he'd been shocked and kind and let me speak to his father, which helped a bit. You have so many questions and there's never anyone around on the wards who seems able to answer them.

Obviously the next thing I'd done was put York on hold. Final year or not, there was no way I was leaving Dad in that state, and also I was needed to look after Will while Mum hung round the hospital. But, three weeks down the line, she'd persuaded me to go back because we were winding each other up and because it was crucial I didn't blow my degree on top of everything else. By then we'd had so many offers of babysitting she was able to draw up a rota stretching for months. Colleagues from school, parents of kids she taught, the massed ranks of the over-seventies, everyone wanted to help. 'It is amazing how people step up in a crisis,' she said. 'I didn't know so many people were bothered about me.'

Meanwhile, in an entirely separate nightmare, I spent every spare second sweating over the Jessie/Jen woman: the possibility of her trailing after me, pursuing me for cash, threatening to reveal to Mum how I'd sneaked behind her back. Ringing our front door-bell, barging her horrible way in. What kind of bitch had I unleashed there? How far might she push? I still wasn't sure if she was mad, desperate or plain criminal. Should I have given her money? Or might that have opened the floodgates? Even though I'd told her no, she could come. And then Mum, already so near the edge, would tip right over. *My God, Charlotte, who is this woman? What the hell have you been up to?* Again and again I went over the information I'd let slip whilst I was in Jessie's flat – our daily routines, the places we visited, so many different ways she could smash her way into our lives. Random details – the smell of air freshener, a pile of dirty bedding – brought back the visit with sickening clarity. That godaw-ful train journey home, replaying Mum's message on my phone, having to lie to her that I was coming back from York. Not knowing whether Dad would be alive when I got to him. The overwhelming sense that Fate was punishing me for my deceit.

What the hell had I been thinking when I took myself to London? Some tangle of selfish logic about how Mum being mis-erable was mainly a drag on me, and how superior I was to her when it came to rolling up my sleeves and sorting out problems. Trust Charlotte to take charge. Charlotte'll make it better. Hah. It hadn't been my business, it wasn't my mystery to piece together.

What would Daniel have said? I tried to conjure him up, but this time he wouldn't come. My fault for telling him to keep away, I sup-posed. All I could visualise was his bedroom wall, the poster of Einstein I'd bought him, the case of scarab beetles below it. I must have lain in his bed for hours, staring at his ranked insects while he explained to me the biological function of iridescence, the proper-ties of chitin, the differences between katydids and cicadas. An ache of longing pierced me. What was he up to now? Who was he with?

A sound on the stairs made me whip round. Here came Walshy, pale and ruffled in his ridiculous Chinese robe.

'Fuck's sake, Walshman,' I said. 'You nearly gave me a heart attack.'

'I am incredibly threatening.' He slouched against the doorframe. The robe fell open.

'Make yourself decent, at least.'

'Some might say you shouldn't have been looking. What you doing up at this time?'

'Trying to unravel the knots in my head. What about you? You don't normally grace us with your presence till gone eleven.'

'Gotta be off to Stranraer in a couple of hours. Dad's girlfriend's mum's funeral. If I'm late for that, Dad'll come after me with a shot-gun.'

'God, I'm sorry. I didn't know. Are you OK?'

He rubbed his eyes. 'I never met the woman. I'm only going as a show of family support, show Dad I'm behind him, blah blah. Though obviously it's a shame the old biddy's dead.'

'I hope they're not relying on you to give the eulogy. Oh, you might need to shave before you set off, too.'

'Yeah, I know I look like shit. I've been up all night, which doesn't help.'

'How come?'

'Talking the night away with Gemma.' He swung across and flopped down next to me.

Gemma and Walshy? That took me by surprise. Had I missed something while I was away?

He laughed at my expression. 'Yeah, that's right. She decided to become un-gay over the summer and we're back together.'

'You're not!'

'Nah, we're not. She's just having a freaky time right now and wanted someone to moan at. I came down for an aspirin around midnight, she was in the kitchen. We got chatting, drank a shed-load of coffee and the next thing you know it's nearly morning. She's gone off to bed but I've this funeral to get to, so I thought I'd make some toast, crank up my energy levels for the day. You want some? I can even scrape the fur off the jam.'

'Go on, then.'

I followed him into the kitchen and he flicked on the light. I said, 'Aren't you tired at all?'

'Nope. I run on adrenalin. I'm like a panther.'

'There's not enough meat on you to make a panther. Weasel, maybe. So what was up with Gemma? Can you say?'

Walshy set the toaster off, then settled at the table opposite me. 'She had a bad summer. I mean, a *bad* one.'

'Did she? How come? She texted she was fed up one time but she didn't go into details. I thought she was just bored.'

'I think the situation wasn't reducible to text-speak.'

'So what's happened?'

'Basically, her mum's giving her a load of grief about coming out, and her dad's just following the same line because that's what he always does. They've been fairly shitty about it. Wouldn't let her tell their friends. Monitored her calls, tried to find out who'd "turned" her so they could "take action". Wanted her to go and see a psychiatrist in case she could be "straightened out".'

'No way!'

'Apparently yes.'

'Jesus. I'm amazed. I thought they were cool. Gemma told me at the end of term she was pretty sure her parents would just accept it.'

Walshy rubbed his eyes. 'If I told my dad I was a woofter, he'd go into meltdown. Chuck me out, disinherit me, the works. Mind you, I say that: perhaps he'd be OK after it had sunk in. Who knows? I guess it's one of those calls you can't judge till it happens. You tend to lose perspective here because the uni's so liberal, but out in the real world there are nutters setting off bombs outside gay bars. Society's phobic, by and large.'

'Depressing-Thought for the Day.'

The toast popped up.

I said, 'I wish she'd confided in me.'

'She would have done, sooner or later. I think she was concerned about your dad and stuff, didn't want to lay on any extra hassle. Anyway, I've told her she can move her girlfriend in if that'll help. I presume you're OK with that?'

'Girlfriend?' I hadn't seen that coming.

'I thought you'd be fine. This is Gemma we're talking about. Your mate.'

'Yeah, yeah. Sorry, course I am. Of course. Anyway, it's your house, blimey, you invite who you want. It's just, we've never even met her, and Roz might not be that comfortable with it. Which I know is Roz's problem, but then again she was here first and we all have to live alongside each other ...'

As I was speaking, Walshy got up and began to assemble crockery, knives, spreads. 'Roz isn't here any more.'

'What?'

'She's gone.'

It took a moment for me to process the information. 'You mean, isn't part of the house? Eh? How have I missed this?' It was true I'd not seen her since I'd been back, but that was less than a week and I'd assumed she'd just been round at Gareth's. The door of her room had been closed so I had no idea if she'd moved her stuff.

'We haven't wanted to bother you, what with things being so crap at home.'

'Well, you should have! She's not chucked in the course, has she, gone back to her parents? Shit, is the baby OK?' I'd blurted it out before I'd realised.

'It's all right, she told us. We know.'

'And what? What's happened?'

'There is no baby, Chaz.'

The news fell with a thud across my chest.

'How?'

Walshy came back to the table. He set the plates down carefully.

'She couldn't go through with it. She went home, had a chat with her mum – didn't tell her dad, he still doesn't know – and talked it over again with Gareth. In the end she decided on an abortion.'

'When?'

'Middle of the summer. She came back here to have it, away from the village, from people she knew.' He paused to bite into his toast.

'But we were *texting* then.' I tried to remember what messages we'd exchanged. Some of mine had gone unanswered, I was vaguely aware. I'd assumed she was busy, hadn't thought too much of it. Then there'd been a gap, then Dad's accident, and now it dawned on me, nothing for weeks. 'Jesus. I can't believe she didn't say anything.'

'She's been too frightened to tell you. Well . . .' He saw my expression. 'Not frightened. Worried. About how you'd react.'

'Me?'

'Because of Will. You having done the whole birth thing, she thought you'd be angry with her.'

I swallowed. '*No*. Angry? No! Where is she now?'

'Gareth wanted her to move in with him. Which is something she's been angling for, so that's kind of worked out. I saw her last week, at the union. She's coping OK and she says to tell you hi. And sorry.'

Sorry. I stared at the toast and felt sick. Frightened of me! How could she ever have thought I'd condemn her over something so difficult? Oh, Roz.

I grasped Walshy's sleeve, the silk slippery and cool under my fingertips. 'Did you *say* I wouldn't judge her? Did you say "Charlotte's a friend, she wouldn't think that way"?'

He nodded, his mouth full of toast.

'Because this is awful. I have to talk to her, let her know she got me wrong. I wish she'd rung me. I'd have come over. God, what a thing to have to go through on your own.'

'She wasn't on her own.'

'Did Gareth—?'

'It was me, actually. I took her to the clinic.'

'You?'

He shrugged. 'It wasn't planned. I was around anyway. Dad's girlfriend was being spectacularly annoying, so I'd come back to York to get out of the way. Then Roz turned up in tears. Gareth was supposed to be taking her but they'd had a big fight. She didn't want to go alone. I offered. That's it.'

'That can't have been it. How did she cope? What was the clinic like?'

'Like, you know, a clinic. All *I* had to do was sit and wait. Then I drove her home and supplied room service for the rest of the day. Afterwards Gareth came round and they made up and he took her back to his. No big deal.'

It bloody is a big deal, I thought, because never in a million years would I have put you down for a mission like that. Sensible, supportive Walshy? I've had you so wrong. Beneath all the backchat and posing, you're actually pretty solid and it's creeping me out. Go back to being flip, you bastard. Then we all know where we stand.

'And is Roz really OK? Was she very upset? Has she let her tutors know? I can't believe nobody told me what was going on. Walshy, I've got to see her.'

He shoved the plate of toast in my direction. 'Go round there today.'

'I can't. It's Will's birthday. I've to be in Bank Top by dinnertime.'

'That's you scuppered, then.'

'I could ring. I could call her from the train. Or text and say I'll be round tomorrow and wait for her to reply. Check out how she sounds. She will want to see me, won't she? What do you think?'

Walshy stretched and yawned extravagantly. 'God, you girls do get yourselves in a tizz. Course she'll want to see you. Just save her a party bag and a balloon. Bit of cake and coloured icing. That should fix it.'

And I thought, Yep, that's the Walsh we're used to. Normal crassness has been resumed.

They moved him off the HDU and onto a general surgical ward, which I suppose was progress. Everyone else in the annexe was having hip replacements, into theatre one day and tottering about the next, home within the week. Meanwhile my ex-husband's lying there looking like death. 'How long before he walks?' I'd asked the consultant when I finally managed to collar him.

'It depends,' he said.

'On what?'

'On whether he gets an infection, how he responds to physio, how well the bone grafts take, how well the artificial joints bed in. Many factors.'

Hedging their bets at every opportunity. I couldn't get a proper tale out of anyone. But I used to watch these old gimmers hobbling gamely up and down and I thought, How's Steve ever going to use crutches when he's only got one good leg and his arm's buggered?

This morning I'd popped into the hospital early because I'd all Will's party food to organise and his presents to wrap and the house to make decent. Madam wouldn't be turning up till most of the work was done. Half the night I'd lain awake going through my lists, fretting. Truth be told, I hadn't slept right since the accident. Nevertheless, this hour was Steve's. I'd sit and read the paper to him and cut his nails, trim his moustache, anything he wanted.

There was a trolley coming through as I walked into the ward. I flattened myself against the wall to let it pass. Then, would you believe it, another trolley appeared coming in the opposite direction so we had a minute of negotiating which one was going to back up and how that might be achieved in the narrow space available. I stood pinned between the nurses' desk and a mobile drugs unit, and turned my gaze respectfully away from the prone old man in front of me. His shrunken frame under the waffle blanket reminded me too much of Nan. Instead I squinted across to Steve's bed to see if there were any medics in attendance or if the curtains were drawn.

What I saw made me catch my breath. A woman – forties, big-boned, blonde, leather-jacketed – was sitting in the visitor's chair, holding Steve's hand. Lusanna, it had to be. We'd exchanged a few words on the phone but I'd never met her in the flesh.

Immediately I felt my heart speed up. She was talking away and she kept smiling, that weak, fake smile you see all round hospitals, people straining to hide their awkwardness. I'd used it myself.

Steve's eyes were open but he didn't seem to be saying much back. I watched Lusanna bend to pick something out of her bag, saw the slight crepiness of the skin at her cleavage.

All at once the trolley rolled past leaving me exposed and panicked. Without stopping to check if I'd been noticed, I turned and hurried back to the waiting room by the entrance, closing the glass door behind me.

Get a grip, I told myself. *Just go over there and say hello. This is stupid, hiding. What reason have you got to hide, anyway?*

And I had no answer to that. Except for, mentally and physically, I was at rock-bottom, stressed and tired with permanently ratty hair and no make-up and some infuriating break-out of spots – spots! Like some bloody teenager! – on my chin. So I hadn't the energy to be bright and polite to this strange woman, whatever she was to Steve. Heck, it was taking everything I had simply to keep up with the ordinary day-to-day trauma.

It wasn't that I was jealous, it wasn't some competition. Of course his girlfriend could come and visit him now he was on a public ward. I was bound to run into her sooner or later. She could take some of the strain off me because quite frankly I was meeting myself coming back. Passing Will from pillar to post, fielding phone calls. It was hellishly time-consuming, visiting every day. Let Lusanna run some of his errands, buy him his lip-salve and prune juice and bike mags and wet wipes.

Then suddenly, dear God, what a shock, there was her big pale face peering through the glass panel of the waiting-room door. She spotted me and grimaced. I gripped my newspaper.

She was coming in, and I would have to deal with her.

Close up I thought she too looked tired, with puffy skin under her eyes and the tell-tale signs of yesterday's mascara. She was slightly shorter than me and wore her fair hair loose and girlish. It didn't suit her.

'You know who I am,' were her opening words.

'Yes, I do. Nice to meet you at last. I'm sorry you couldn't come before. It was close family only on the HDU, that's the rule. The nurses are dead strict.'

"S'OK.'

'What I'm saying is, you know, it wasn't anything against you. You can visit whenever you want now. Give me a break. Steve'll like that. It'll make a change for him. I bet he's fed up of staring at me day after day.'

I'd expected her to go, 'No, no, I'm sure he isn't,' out of politeness, but she just shuffled her feet. We stood there, eyeballing each other. Her leather jacket creaked in the quiet of the room.

She said, 'I'm not great with hospitals.'

'Neither is he, if it comes to it. Mind you, the first few days he was so poorly he didn't know where he was. They had him so drugged up he was convinced they were stripping down motorbikes next to his bed. It'll be better for him when he can sit up and watch TV, distract himself.'

'I'd only been dating him a few weeks.'

'Yes, I know that. He was very fond of you, though,' I said, amazing myself at my own generosity.

'Was he?'

'Absolutely.'

'Oh. He's been telling me what you've been up to, Karen. How you never miss a visit and you always bring something to cheer him up. That you've washed his hair, put his deodorant on for him. Personal stuff.'

'Well, it had to be done. You can see that, can't you?'

'But you're good at that kind of thing. I know you looked after your mum for years. He said how devoted you were.' Her eyes kept sliding over my face, then away again. 'Like, you know, some people are born to be carers.'

'It's not something you choose.'

Outside in the corridor someone was battling a coughing fit.

'No. But the thing is, I don't know if I – I think you have to be *a certain type of person.*' These last five words she dragged out with a kind of angry emphasis.

Ah, hang on, I thought. I get it now. I understand what you're after. And no, I'm not going to help you spell it out. Let's see if you can do that on your own, let's see if you have the guts to tell me that you're out of here, that you plan to walk away from him just when he needs every friend he's got.

'Yes, Lusanna?'

'Well, what it is – you know when he's discharged? How bad's he going to be?'

'They're not sure. He'll be in a wheelchair, that's definite; they won't say how long for. He won't be able to use his arm. What's your house like? Is it suitable for a disabled person?'

Her eyes widened in alarm. 'It's old. Narrow. A wheelchair wouldn't fit through the doors.'

'Don't worry about that. You can get special lightweight ones.' I deliberately made my tone bright, matter-of-fact. 'Steve's pretty slim, so there won't be an issue there. Social Services'll provide one. Plus they'll come and fit ramps and grab-rails for you, toilet frames. They'll do an assessment. Or alternatively, you could move into his place. Whatever suits you best. You work from home, don't you, so it should be manageable.'

'No. I can't do it, Karen.'

'Can't do what?'

'I can't take him. I can't be looking after him when he's discharged. I'm sorry, I can't.'

'Oh, right. So where does that leave him?'

'Could you take him on?'

'Me, love? No. I've a young child to care for. It's impossible.'

'He could go in a home or something for a bit.' She looked uncertain. 'I just can't do it.'

'So you said.'

Something in her face hardened. 'You're the one. It's you he thinks of as his wife. The whole way he goes on about you. You're the only person he can really stand to have around him right now. You're the one he wants.'

I think I understood from the moment I saw him spread-eagled in the road that he'd be coming home to me. Still I fought her. I was so disgusted by her attitude. 'Lusanna, we're divorced. I've a toddler to bring up, a job to go back to, a college course I want to apply for. Steve's not my responsibility.'

'Well, he's certainly not mine!'

God, I could have smacked her for that. In fact, unconsciously I tensed my arm muscles ready, and a rush of adrenalin washed over me.

She was quicker, though. Now she'd said what she needed to, she whipped round and grabbed the door handle.

'What are you doing? Running away?' I said as she blundered out. I followed, furious, shouting down the corridor after her: 'We could all run away, love.'

She jabbed at the lift button, then abandoned the idea and headed for the stairs.

'And don't think I'm going to tell him for you,' I called. 'Tell him you've chucked him because he's disabled.'

She never looked back. The fire door slammed behind her, and even through its thickness I could hear her boots skittering down the steps. I imagined her hurrying through the main entrance, across the car park, fumbling for her keys. Driving home to a silent house.

The lift pinged open; no one got out. I realised the newspaper I'd been holding was limp with sweat.

You can exit Bank Top station via a concrete slipway that leads onto the back streets of Harrop. Quicker, though, if you're village-bound, to head in the opposite direction and cut diagonally across the fields where Nan used to take me blackberrying. Unless it's raining this is quite a nice walk: past the willow pond where Ginny Greenteeth the water-witch hung out, past the golf course where we once saw a man get hit on the back by a flying ball, over the stile which one spectacular summer was covered in ladybirds, and out onto the bypass. You can do it in ten minutes, though it used to take me and Nan about an hour by the time we'd filled our plastic tubs with fruit.

As I got down off the train I wasn't paying much attention to anything. My mind was occupied mainly with Will and the trike I'd bought him, and how this year, at three, he'd be unwrapping his presents with purpose and understanding. I thought of his little beaming face and how cute it would be to watch him learn to pedal. Perhaps Mum could borrow the school video camera again and film the attempts I'd miss. She could even take it into hospital and show Dad. I must remember to ask her about it.

I was about to shimmy through the kissing gate when I became aware of someone from the slipway end of the platform shouting my name. I turned round and, unbelievably, it was Daniel, striding towards me on his long stork legs. A shock went through me. I had to blink a couple of times.

'What are you doing here?' I asked when he came close enough.

'Sorry, I know you said – I thought I'd just swing by on the off-chance.' He grinned nervously and adjusted his glasses. Then there was this awkward hovering moment where in the old days we'd have hugged but now we very much didn't.

'Is everything all right? Shit, you haven't been sent to break some bad news, have you?' The way my life was at the moment it wouldn't have surprised me.

Daniel frowned. 'I'm here to drop off a gift for Will. And – if I'm invited – to say a quick hello to the birthday boy. Is that OK?'

'How did you know which train I'd be on?'

'Guessed. There aren't that many.'

'Oh. Sorry. Yeah, of course.'

'Look, I appreciate I've sprung myself on you. Say if you'd rather I disappeared.'

Daniel at Will's party. 'I'm not sure.'

'Is it better if I leave?'

'No.'

'What, then?'

I had no reply, so he took my rucksack for me and we began to walk along the platform in the direction of the slipway.

'I suppose I could do with a lift,' I said.

I picked Will up from Maud's – dread to think what she'd been letting him do because his hands were covered in sticky fluff – and brought him home to get ready. I'd pretty much kept it simple, filled two carrier bags at Aldi with sausage rolls, crisps, mini-muffins and a ready-iced birthday cake. But I wanted to lay it out nicely. I was using Nan's flowery cloth and the polka-dot crockery.

At twelve Eric came round with Kenzie and helped me plate up some of the food, while I went upstairs and retrieved the trike from the bottom of Charlotte's wardrobe. I don't know if you've ever attempted to wrap a trike in sparkly paper. I'll be honest, I've tackled easier jobs. Before I went back down I took five minutes to spruce myself up, couldn't recall the last time I'd bothered with lipstick or eye-shadow. Then it was a run round the carpets with the vac because a couple of the mums from nursery were coming and no one judges the state of your house the way a strange woman does.

While I hoovered, I tried to imagine where on earth I might put Steve's bed and associated paraphernalia, where a grab-rail might work best, whether a wheelchair would fit between the armchair and the china cabinet. I knew from Nan's visits home how much clutter comes with disability. Would I be able to leave him on his own? Could I work *and* look after him? How would he call for help during the night? The thought of everything I'd need to sort out nearly made my brain collapse. And how long had I got to make up my mind? Surely we were talking months.

But maybe not. They kicked people out of hospital way earlier than they ever used to.

I paused to switch off the vac, and through the kitchen doorway I could see Eric reach up to switch on the extractor fan, crouch to pull out a serving bowl, and step easily over the cat. He looked so healthy and whole. It bloody wasn't fair, my life. Not on any front.

Even though I was longing to see Will, I asked Daniel to drive up to the reservoir and park the car for twenty minutes. I was shaking, I don't know why.

We sat looking out over the grey water.

He said, 'How are things?'

I laughed flatly. 'Pretty damn awful.'

'Yes, they would be. What's the latest on your dad?'

'Waiting for his next op.'

'My father says to tell you that the shoulder joint your dad's having fitted is the best on the market, state of the art. How's your mum coping?'

'More or less holding it together.'

Daniel hooked his index fingers over the bottom rim of the steering wheel. 'And you, Charlotte. How are you doing?'

Without you, I thought, drowning. I miss you. Seeing you now's sent my heart into freefall. I want you to take me in your arms and tell me it's going to be all right. Then it will be.

I said, 'I find it hard when I go in and see him. I've only been allowed on the ward twice in case I upset him. Because I can't seem to be as calm as Mum, and they say that's not helpful if I'm crying all over his blankets. But he's my dad, he's supposed to be fit and strong and look after me. I've never seen him weak and helpless. It's just wrong. You know, his knee's so mashed they can't even fit an artificial joint, there's nothing to attach it to. They've had to put in a mesh cage and inject ground-up donor bone. It's just awful.'

Up till then Dan and I had avoided eye-contact, but now I turned to him, appealing. *Hold me, comfort me.*

And then, miraculously, his arms were round me, and he was squeezing me and patting my back and making soothing noises. Relief just flooded through me. I wriggled across the seat so I was closer, laid my head on his chest.

'It will get better, Charlotte.' His voice vibrated through his breastbone. 'I promise.'

'He'll never be the same, though. I heard Mum on the phone say the surgeon couldn't promise more than a forty-five-degree bend in his leg. He won't get full movement back in his arm, either. He's wrecked two limbs out of four, basically.'

Daniel went on patting. 'Consultants always try and cover themselves, they always err on the pessimistic. Often recovery's much better than they dare predict. And my father says bones continue healing for years after a major trauma, so your dad could be improving for ages after he comes home.'

'Do you think – could I have another talk with your dad sometime? It's just, Mum holds stuff back and there are questions I don't like to ask her.'

'Of course. He'd be happy to.'

We stayed as we were for another minute or so. I could hear seagulls crying faintly, and the hum of traffic passing. Sticking out from the car mat, I noticed, was a tatty leaflet left over from the *Twenty-First Century Rocks* event. I wondered how the concert had gone in the end, whether Amelia had been satisfied. How they'd celebrated afterwards. But I wouldn't let my thoughts go down that route; it was pointless.

I said, 'Look, while I'm here, there's something else, too. I really need to tell you something.'

He tensed very slightly in my arms.

'What it is, Dan, I've done a terrible thing – God, I can't keep it in any longer. I might have started something really bad and I don't know how to stop it.'

Still he said nothing, but the silence sounded sympathetic.

'Can you keep a secret?'

'You know I can, Charlotte. And for what it's worth, I'm sure it's not so terrible, whatever it is you think you've done. You're very fragile now.'

'No, it is bad. I've got to offload. I've had no one to confide in. Please.'

'Tell me, then, if you think it'll help.'

I pulled myself away and faced the windscreen, focusing on the rippled surface of the reservoir because I didn't dare watch his face while I was speaking. Then I began to tell him about Jessie.

By the time I'd finished, the car windows were steamed up, as if we were a courting couple. When I was at school we used to go a bit stupid if we saw a car parked like that. We'd bang on the windows and bonnet, then run off. What a laugh. If anyone tried that now I'd jump out of the car and nut them.

'Wow,' said Daniel in the pause that followed my story.

'Should I have given her money, do you think?'

'Absolutely not.'

'She was really poor.'

'Sorry to be harsh, but that's not your problem.'

'I might have been able to save her.'

'From what?' He shook his head. 'You don't know the real situation. You only had her version of events and for all you know she could have been exaggerating. Perhaps this Dex can take charge. Or she can go to someone else. There must be other people, closer people, she can appeal to. The authorities, as a last resort; Citizens Advice. In any case, it's her responsibility if she mixes with dodgy characters.'

'Cash might have guaranteed she'd stay away,' I said gloomily.

'I think if you'd tried to buy her silence, it could well have started an unhealthy pattern of contact. Could you see her settling for a one-off payment, honestly?'

No, I couldn't. And that was one relief, at least. In my mind I'd many times played out just handing over my purse, Jessie's possible reactions, whether a single grand concession like that might have straightened everything between us. It was good to hear Daniel squash that particular dream.

'If this woman still comes after us, though, that's my family blown apart, just when we're least able to cope. I've been so fucking stupid.'

When I dared look across he was tapping the wheel, considering. 'You may never hear from her again.'

'But if I *do*? She is a whack job, so it's quite likely.'

'OK. You've met her, I haven't, remember. We need to think through a strategy then.'

'There is no strategy, unless I can rewind time. I've ruined everything.'

'Don't say that. Look, let's think up a worst-case scenario plan. Even if you don't use it, it'll make you feel more in control.'

'What kind of a plan? What can I possibly do here to make things better?'

He steepled his fingers in exactly the same way Martin sometimes does during tutorials. If I hadn't felt so rubbish it would have
made me smile. 'Well, first, if she contacts you directly, threaten her
with the police.'

'Would they be bothered? She said they wouldn't.'

'What have you got on her? Attempted blackmail, potentially;
harassment; theft. I should think so.'

That last bit was certainly true. When I'd got home, amid all the
chaos of Dad's accident, I discovered Jessie had helped herself to
fifty quid from the back of my purse. No idea when that went.

'God, she'd be livid, though.'

'So what, if it stops her in her tracks? Actually, you could write
down an account of what she did and have it ready to hand over as
a statement. Do it soon, while it's fresh and you're still fairly calm
because it's hard to recall detail under pressure, that's been proven.
Also – and you won't like this but you need to try it – rehearse what
you're going to say to your mother if she does find out you went to
London.'

I covered my face with my hands. 'No way. I can't.'

'You can, Charlotte. Sketch it out now. Come on! One: you were
trying to help. Two: you're sorry how it turned out. Three: you're
prepared to do whatever you can to minimise the damage. That's
basically what you need to tell her. And then what's the very worst
your mum can do? Be cross. Well, she's been cross with you before.
She'll get over it. But the upside of her knowing is that, if this Jessie
does decide to make waves, you'll be able to tackle her together.'

I could see he was right. The idea was hideous to contemplate,
though. I mean, yeah, we'd had our battles, Mum and me. Years'
worth, stretching as far back as I could remember. Worst by a
mile had been how she was over my pregnancy, but I'd stood my

ground and in the end she'd been fine, more than fine. So I wasn't afraid of her anger. I could cope with another bout. That wasn't the issue. What I couldn't cope with was how much it would hurt her that I'd blindly interfered, hooked us up to a really nasty piece of work.

Daniel said, 'The approach to take here is, you may not be able to change the past but you can shape how the future pans out. Yes?'

His eyebrows were raised encouragingly, his glasses glinting, his curly hair sticking out in random directions. And I thought again how much I'd missed him. Whatever had happened between Dan and me, we had this bond. That hadn't changed. We would patch things up between us, he would have me back. Maybe not today, but soon, when he'd had the chance to mull it over. I just had to convince him.

'Yes, you're right. I can see it. I need to let the ideas percolate.'

'It's not going to be easy, but if the worst happens, you'll manage. You will, you know.'

A rush of love overwhelmed me.

'God, Daniel. You're so calm, you think stuff through so clearly. I owe you *so* much.'

He fiddled with his glasses, then started to speak but he didn't get the words out because next thing, I'd leaned across and fastened my lips on his. His skin was soft and warm. *Oh, Dan*. I was home, I was safe.

'Charlotte—' he said when I broke away.

I shushed him. Let the moment stand.

Twenty metres in front of us, waves lapped angrily at the shore. The sky was darkening, the wind was getting up.

As if on autopilot Daniel reached for the car keys, slotted them in. A couple of times he glanced across in a baffled way. Finally he swallowed and spoke.

'Charlotte, I have to say this. I can't take you back. I'm sorry.'

'What? What do you mean?'

'I mean I don't want us to get back together.'

'You *do*. I can tell. The way you kissed me.'

'No.'

'You do love me! You came specially to see me, you put your arms round me. You let me tell you personal secrets.'

'You wanted to talk.' His shoulders drooped. 'Please, Charlotte. Please don't stir everything up again. There isn't time, anyway. We have to get to Will's party.'

I stared at him but his mouth was set firm.

'So why did you come today? What was the point?'

'To check you were OK. I've been worried about you. And to see Will.'

'See Will? You must be joking.' Anger fought with disappointment, humiliation. 'Why should I let you see Will? How's that going to help anyone?'

'Because I care about—'

'Stop it, stop it there. Don't say you care about him, or about me, not in the same bloody breath as telling me we're finished. You can't have it both ways. Caring isn't jerking people around, making them think one thing and then doing another. If you didn't want to raise my hopes, you should have kept away. Why didn't you stay away? And Will needs to get used to you not being there. It's cruel to keep appearing and disappearing. You have to let us be. That's part of the package. That's what ending a relationship means. Start the car and take me home, Daniel. I need to be with my son.'

He held himself very still while I finished, then he fired up the engine, revving it hard.

I thought the car would implode with misery before we reached the end of the road.

I was in the back kitchen trying to defuse a bottle of pop Ryan Marshall had been shaking but I heard her come in, all loud and jolly. I swore under my breath and eased the bottle cap as carefully as I could; even so, dandelion and burdock spurted down my arm and dripped onto the floor. He's a little sod, that Marshall kid. His mother hasn't a clue.

I stood the bottle in the sink and wiped round, then I went through to say hello. Charlotte was pulling off her jacket, her cheeks all red and her make-up smudged. She was wearing black tights and daft ankle-length socks over the top, and her skirt was far too short. She's going to have to smarten up when she goes job-hunting, that's for sure. As I watched, Will came bowling up and she straight away flung herself down on her knees, started mauling about on the carpet with him, rolling about and banging into table legs. You could see her knickers and everything. I caught Ryan's mum looking at Drew Tipton's mum, and smirking.

'She studies at the University of Central Yorkshire,' I said. Who were these women to dismiss my daughter at a glance? That's the trouble with kids' parties, the mothers who hang around and pass judgement.

'And does she have a boyfriend?' asked Mrs Marshall.

'No,' I said firmly. I wasn't even going to think about that today. I'd given up grieving over Daniel; any grief-energy I had was going on my ex. It is amazing how one crisis can completely eclipse another.

Eric, meanwhile, was squinting out of the window. 'Did some-one give you a lift, Charlotte?'

'No,' she said. 'I walked it.' She was tickling Will and I couldn't see her face because her hair was hanging down.

There was a plastic bag on the sofa. I said, 'You've not been buying him extra, have you?'

'It's only something I picked up along the way, Mum. Stick it on the pile.'

Now she'd come we could at last let the birthday boy loose on his presents. The trike was meant to be held back as the grand finale, but he went straight for it and tore away the top layer of paper before we could stop him. Then he lost momentum, dis-tracted by a sparkly pompom I'd stuck to the gift tag. Eric had to lean in and finish the job, and by the time he had, Will had broken into a box of Smarties. 'Look,' everyone was going, 'look at your lovely trike.' Will just carried on stuffing Smarties into his mouth. Ryan made a determined grab for the handlebars but Drew's mother distracted him with a party blower. When it was clear that progress had completely stalled, Charlotte knelt to help. She undid the parcels one by one, showed them to Will and then to us, and piled them in the far corner, away from Ryan. Maud had sent a children's prayer book, short-sighted Ivy some liqueur chocolates. Debbie, who used to clean for us back in the days when I was Mum's carer, had posted a dinosaur nameplate for his bedroom door. Leo had sent a parcel of Enid Blytons and Sylv a new ladybird dish and spoon. Charlotte's impulse-buy turned out to be a light-up map of the stars. God knows what possessed her to get him that, it was way too old for him. Mrs Marshall had bought him a toy trumpet (evil cow), and Mrs Tipton a jigsaw alphabet.

Eric had got him a football. 'I hope he gets on with it better than our Kenzie,' he said. 'You throw a ball in his direction and he just flinches. He's not remotely interested, are you, son? Oh, hang on, where's he disappeared to now?'

We all looked round but he wasn't anywhere obvious.

'Well, he can't have gone far,' I said. 'He's in the house, for definite. He's too small to reach the front-door latch and the back one's locked. I'll check the loo, shall I?'

'I don't want him wandering about,' said Eric.

It had crossed my mind he might have sneaked off to my bed-room to stroke my velvet scarf – he'd developed a bit of an obsession with it last time he was here and in the end I'd let him wear it round his shoulders like a cape. There'd been tears when he had to part from it. In fact, I'd said to Eric he could have it if it meant so much, but Eric flat-refused. I suppose it did make the lad look a bit camp.

Kenzie wasn't in the bathroom, so I came back through to the lounge thinking my suspicions were confirmed only to find everyone crowded round the armchair by the window.

'Come out, love, you're missing the party,' Mrs Tipton was saying.

'We saw the curtain moving,' said Mrs Marshall. 'I think you might have to pay a visit to the dry cleaner's in the near future.'

I pushed through and knelt on the chair. Squashed up against the wall behind it, the material well scrunched in his chocolatey hands, was Kenzie. My lovely chenille curtains were smeared to beggary.

'Oh dear,' I said, trying not to sound pissed off. 'Is someone feeling a bit poorly?'

He didn't respond, so I bent over and tried to pull him out.

'Let me,' said Eric. I assumed he was going to lift his son up and give him a cuddle, but instead he barked, 'Get out of there now, you wee maddy! Why do you have to keep letting me down?'

It did the trick. Kenzie moved immediately, slithering past the arm of the chair, and out. I took the opportunity to give him a quick wipe as he passed, and in return he stopped and wrapped his arms round me, his face against my skirt. 'Have you got tummy ache?' I asked.

He shook his head.

'Come sit with me, anyway. We could have a look at Will's jigsaw, yeah?'

As I settled us onto the sofa, I caught sight of Charlotte's face. *Say what you like, that kid's well weird*, her expression said. I looked down at his tender, buzz-cut scalp and it was true. You could feel the need coming off him in waves.

'Some children can't always cope when someone else is getting the attention,' Mrs Marshall was saying in a poor imitation of a whisper. Then she went, 'Were you playing hide and seek, Kenzie? You have to tell us so we can join in next time.'

Just because she owns a four-bed detached house with a cobbled drive and views of Anglezarke, she thinks she is somebody.

'How's your Lucy doing?' Mrs Tipton asked her.

'Oh, still at Bristol. Started her post-grad training.'

'Did she get sponsorship in the end?'

'She did, she heard at the start of the summer. Which means she's been able to put down a deposit on the flat as well as set a date for the wedding. It's all fallen into place for her.'

'It always seems to, doesn't it?'

'It does.'

I said, 'Watch Ryan doesn't hurt himself on the grate.' Really I meant, *Never mind boasting about your daughter, take control of your bratty son and stop him picking fake coals out of my fireplace to lob at the cat.*

Across the room Charlotte and Will had squashed themselves into the other armchair and were sharing a sausage roll. Will was laughing and she was jiggling her feet as if she was stamping out bugs on the carpet. Her hair draped over his chubby arm, his cheeks glowed with happiness. And I thought what a nice picture that would make if I'd happened to have a camera in my hands instead of a gloomy infant picking sugar blobs off Iced Gems.

As I stared, she raised her head and her eyes met mine.

'Thanks, Mum,' she mouthed.

In the middle of the party stress, it was such an unexpected moment that something kindled inside me and I came over all maternal, whoosh. Funny how that sometimes happens. I thought, Well, we don't do so badly between us, do we? Will's happy. Not like Kenzie, scared of his own shadow, or that mini-thug Ryan. My grandson's growing up, looking more and more like his mother. It's wonderful to watch, there's something new from him every day. If Mum could see him now. Her lovely Nan. You know you gave her such joy, Charlotte, when you left Will here. You've no idea what he did for her in those last few months.

In my mind's eye I could see Mum so clearly, as she had been when Charlotte was small: plump, capable, never fazed by a houseful. I remembered birthday parties then, the way she'd calmly set out each crimp-edged cardboard jelly dish, make chocolate-finger log cabins and funny-face toasties. She liked traditional, but she knew how to spin things to make them fun. It was her idea to turn 'Pin the Tail on the Donkey' into 'Stick the Bandana on Axl Rose', and hold dressing-up races using my old lipsticks, beads, hats and heels.

Kenzie wriggled, burped, then slid off my lap. Across the room Charlotte was still laughing, blowing at Will's hair now to make it stick up, and the mums had decided to rearrange all my plates on the table. Behind the TV, Pringle retched quietly. Ryan and Drew were taking it in turns to jump on a mini-roll which had fallen off the table. And it struck me, for the first time since she died, that I'd been recalling Mum with simple love and pleasure, without that automatic flood of guilt I'd become so used to.

A warm hand on my shoulder. 'OK, Karen?'

I glanced up and it was Eric, standing behind the sofa. I am OK, I thought. Thanks to you. Charlotte had been right, of course. The old wedding photo I'd found under the bathroom sink had only fallen out of the airing cupboard. No ghostly hand had planted it there. Yet it still had been a sign: a sign I needed to banish forever the idea that Mum was somewhere looking on, hurt. Why does pain sometimes feel the need to latch onto more pain? I imagined my guilt as being like a kind of smothering ivy, quick-germinating and rampant, a parasite, dragging me down. Then along had come Eric, an outsider, to tear it clear with his big strong arms. So what if he never offered to babysit? How did that matter, in the scheme of things? Friendship wasn't an accounts sheet, two columns to be balanced. The peace of mind he'd brought me was worth a thousand hours of childcare.

'I suppose I'm a bit tired,' I said.

'You must be.'

He reached down and began massaging my shoulders lightly.

The contact was so unexpected I blushed like mad and shifted forward in the hope my position might hide from the others what he was doing. I knew obviously what I should do was pull away, spring up and offer a round of coffees or attend to the various carpet disasters. But what the hell. It felt glorious. I deserved it. Eric might never be my boyfriend, there was no way that was going to happen now, but I'd take whatever came next down the list.

So I relaxed my muscles and let my eyes focus on the fireplace, tried not to think about the mums looking on, or Charlotte, or the voice inside my head going, *What the hell is this?* Hospitals, potties, shredded wrapping and pet vomit: the rest of my sorry life would be waiting for me when I came back down to earth.

Christ knows what was going on there, Weird-kid's dad pawing at my mother while she pulled a face like a vicar in a trance. In my opinion the middle-aged ought to keep their hands to themselves. It's not pretty and it's not clever.

I did think about commenting on the incident later – what's it mean for Dad, apart from anything? – but Eric was still hanging about and anyway, once the mums had cleared off and we'd binned all the half-eaten food, I suddenly realised I was pushed for time. I think it helps to leave in a hurry because that way you're not tempted to cling or get tearful, you have to keep the goodbyes brisk. I was strung out enough as it was. I didn't want Will picking up my gloom. I left him rolling a pickled onion back and forth across the chair arm while *Pingu* played in the background.

Once on the train I fished my phone out and stared at it. I burned to text Daniel, to have the last word. Shout, or cry, or beg, I wasn't sure which. Make him come back, strike him down. Across the aisle from me was a woman with a baby in a sling, and for a moment I was distracted by its splayed fingers and kicking feet. Will once had some bootees like that, with bobbly pads on the soles. Had he ever been so small? Oh, that age of innocence. How had the time since he was born gone so bloody fast?

The next second, my phone was ringing. I snatched it up and held the speaker to my ear.

'Daniel?'

'Charlotte, yes.'

Instantly I was in a temper. 'What? What do you want?'

'I wondered if you were OK. When you left—'

'I'm fine. Thank you.'

'Right.'

'Was there any other reason you called?'

'Will. Did he have a nice party?'

'For fuck's sake, Dan. Yes, he did. Thank you for his star map. OK, are we through now?'

There was a pause.

'Look,' he said. 'I've been thinking.'

'What about?' The blood was thudding in my ears.

'The Jessie business. One of the things you're worried about is the missing cash, isn't it? The cash you took out of your savings, what your mum'll say if she finds out.'

'*When* she finds out.'

'Yes, right. So tell me to get lost, Charlotte, but if you need it, I can lend you the money till you're in a position to pay it back. That is something practical I can do. If you want.'

'You're offering me money?'

'I know things are difficult right now. I thought that might be one less worry for you.'

My mind reeled with nasty retorts. *How can I possibly take your money now? What do you think you're playing at? Waving your wallet around, turning up with presents for a kid who isn't even yours. You say we're finished: well, if we're finished, stop calling, let me go.*

He said, 'I just hate to see you so upset.'

And then I thought of the way he'd listened while I explained about Jessie, and his brilliant dissection of the problem and his check-list of damage limitation. When had I ever had such a friend?

'Where are you, Dan?'

'In the supermarket. Mum needed more aspirin.'

I took a chance. 'Look, is there any way you could come over to York next weekend? Or I could come over to you. Just to get things straight between us. Give it another try. I want to. Please.'

His shallow breaths down the receiver.

'No, Charlotte.'

'Why?'

'I'm sorry.'

'But why?'

'Because it's not right.'

'It's Amelia.'

'No.'

'It is. Your mum said.'

A sigh. 'That was my mother stirring. I apologise on her behalf.'

'Truly?'

'Truly.'

'So, what?'

'You don't really want me back. You're lonely and down, that's all. And, Charlotte, if I let you break my heart again, I'm not sure it'll ever function properly. I can't take that risk.'

I pictured him standing in some supermarket aisle with his wild hair, his anxious frown, a wire basket over his arm. How could he not be mine any more?

He said again, 'I'm really sorry.'

Sorry? *Sorry?* Disappointment made me a bitch. 'OK, then listen up. You shut the door now and you shut it forever. If you're so sure you want to finish, let me spell it out: I don't want you in my life, or in Will's. I have to protect us. So I never ever want to hear from you again. I might be having a tough time, yes, but I'll manage on my own. I can do that, you know – I am capable, and there's no need for you to worry about me or feel upset. Understand? This is it. No more contact. *Ever.* Got it?'

I waited for an answer that never came. Eventually I ended the call and snapped my phone shut. The woman across the aisle with the baby was busy pretending she hadn't heard.

My nose was running and I was shivering, as if I had a cold coming on. Who did he think he was, finishing with me and then turning up out of the blue, saying it was over and then ringing me? Bloody game-player. He could bloody well keep away in future, from me and from Will. Leave him to his snotty girlfriend and snottier mother.

I switched my phone right off and dropped it in my bag, then groped around for the packet of tissues I knew Mum had stuck in there. Even that was bloody mucking me about, bastard. I managed to stab my finger on a pointy nail-file; something tacky stuck itself to my palm. Eventually I just tipped the bag up on the table, not caring about the incriminating crap that might fall out. What slid onto the table in front of me, along with my scarf, essay notes, a copy of *Washington Square*, diary, lolly stick, voucher for Superdrug, packet of mints, tampons and lip balm was the *Twenty-First Century Rocks* leaflet I'd sneaked from the car. It was lying back-cover-up and there was a photo of the events team near the bottom. I should just have screwed it up, but some masochistic streak made me take a closer look. The photo was captioned and there was Amelia's name.

She stood shoulder-to-shoulder with Daniel, a healthy, glossy girl with strong but well-groomed eyebrows and a peachy skin. Straightforward, smiling. God. No wonder he didn't want to come back to me when there were girls like that circling. There was a confidence about her too: *Dan might not be mine yet, but he will be soon*. Once again I heard Mum going, 'You don't appreciate that lad. One day someone else'll snap him up, you'll see.'

And I'd laughed at the idea. Now it looked as if the joke was on me.

After they'd all gone home Will really crashed, and I only just got him into bed before he was sparko. I, on the other hand, was buzzing, couldn't settle at all. I wondered whether a Horlicks might help – that was always Nan's drug of choice – so I took myself to the kitchen.

It was dark outside already. I'd have quite liked to do some therapeutic tidying but Eric had cleared every surface and there was nothing left to put away. So while the kettle boiled I stood by the window and looked out at the garden. The moon was full and bright; you could pick out the groove in the lawn caused by Will's trike wheel, and the row of clothes pegs he'd stolen and planted in the side border. Come tomorrow I'd have to go out and dig those up. And drag the wheeliebin round the side, and scrape up the cat poo by the gate. Now the cover of leaves was coming away I could see that the back fence had sagged more than ever; it was so low you could have stepped over it. Which meant that would need sorting at some point. Not now, though. There were more important things to fix than a larch lap panel.

Once upon a time I might have taken the broken-down fence as a sign about me and Eric, the state of our relationship. But that dream was past. Across the other side of Bolton my ex-husband lay on a metal bed and waited for visiting time to crawl round.

I made my Horlicks and drew down the blind. I still had Will's cards to Sellotape round the mirror.

As the train pulled into York I tried Walshy, but the phone just rang out. Obviously he'd have switched off his mobile because of the funeral, maybe forgotten to switch it back on again. I reconsidered. Roz was off-limits for a moan till I'd seen her face to face. Gemma sounded as if she was in bits already; I wasn't going to bother her. Who else could I talk to? Not Mum – all I'd get there was a guaranteed bollocking which I didn't need on top of everything else. Not Dad, obviously. Not Daniel. Who was there left to save me from the wretchedness of my own thoughts?

The carriage door swished open and an old woman came through. She must have let a draught in with her because the things on the table began to stir; my essay notes lifted and the voucher flipped over and the paperback slid off the heap of scarf and fell on the floor. I bent to pick it up before she trod on it, and something fluttered out. It was a postcard of a Dalmatian dog wearing a bowler hat. I recognised it at once. Martin had sent it at the start of the summer, I suppose to cheer me up. He'd written simply,

Between the optimist and the pessimist, the difference is droll.
The optimist sees the doughnut, the pessimist the hole.

It had made me laugh, it had worked. Martin always knew what to say. I always felt better for speaking to him.

Suddenly I realised where I needed to be this dark and lonely night.

KAREN: I found this under the kitchen cupboard yesterday. Is it your ladle, Mum? Mum?

CHARLOTTE: It's not. She said it had a shell bowl and brass round the handle. This is plain nickel.

KAREN: Is it, Mum? Put it in her lap, Charlotte.

CHARLOTTE: There you go, Nan. What do you think? Do you recognise it?

NAN: You're a bonny girl.

CHARLOTTE: (laughs) Thanks.

(Sound of spoon dropping to the floor.)

CHARLOTTE: Stay where you are, I'll get it.

NAN: My granddaughter's in York.

CHARLOTTE: Is she?

NAN: She's very clever. They're all very pleased with her.

CHARLOTTE: That's good to hear.

KAREN: I think you're tired today, Mum?

NAN: Aye, I am.

KAREN: What are you having for your tea? It's Saturday, so what do you have here on Saturdays? Isn't it Sandwich Selection? That's your favourite, I think? And fruit cake or plain sponge.

CHARLOTTE: Sounds yum!

(Pause.)

KAREN: Did the vicar come this week?

(Pause.)

CHARLOTTE: I brought you some flowers, Nan, did you see?

I've put them on the windowsill. So you won't knock them over.

(Pause.)

KAREN: Bertie's just gone past, wagging his tail. You like Bertie, don't you?

(Pause.)

CHARLOTTE: (whispering) God, she's bad this afternoon.

KAREN: She has these blank days. She could be different again next time I come.

CHARLOTTE: Let's hope so. Look, I'm just nipping downstairs, get a Twix out of the machine. Do you want anything?

KAREN: No, I'm fine.

(Long pause.)

NAN: Eeh, it's a struggle to keep my eyes open today. (Pause.) What time is it?

KAREN: Coming up to four.

NAN: Aye.

(Pause.)

KAREN: What is it?

NAN: (sighing) I don't remember who you are, but I know I love you.

KAREN: Well. That'll do for now. We'll sort out where we are tomorrow, I expect.

CHAPTER 11

On a day in November

He was in better fettle than I'd seen him since the accident. When I stuck my head round the door of the ward he was actually sitting in a wheelchair, trying to turn the pages of a magazine using his uninjured hand. It turned out they'd earlier had him practising transfer from bed to chair and back again, and though the effort had taken it out of him physically, mentally he was on a high.

A nurse appeared carrying a sheet of paper. She attached it to his clipboard, then turned to me.

'Before he goes home, Mrs Cooper, we need to know he can get himself on and off the toilet and in and out of bed independently. Otherwise we're not allowed to release him.'

'I see.' I felt as if I was standing in the path of an advancing steamroller. Just because it was still a way off didn't mean it wasn't going to flatten me eventually.

'Release me back into the wild?' said Steve.

'Only if you behave and do your physio like a good boy.' She picked up the empty pill pot on his locker, then bustled off and left us to it.

'All right?' I said.

'Oh aye, champion. Never better.'

'What hurts the most?'

'My shoulder. Definitely.'

I cast a glance at his leg which was splinted and about twice the size it should have been. 'Really?'

He nodded. 'Don't get me wrong, Karen, I'm in pain all over. But the shoulder's agony.'

They'd fitted him with a replacement steel ball joint, like the Terminator.

'What do they say about the knee?'

'They've managed to keep it free of infection, so it doesn't look like they'll have to amputate. I won't be able to bend it much, though. I'll never be able to run, or kneel, or go down the stairs one-two, one-two, you know.' He mimed a walking action with his fingers. 'Physiotherapist woman reckons I'll have to do exercises every day to get any movement back in the joint at all. Which would be OK except for the fact it nearly kills me.'

'Don't the drugs help?'

He beckoned me closer and I leaned down to him. 'I tell you what *would* help.'

'What? What is it, love? Just say the word.'

'If you came in here with that thin white shirt and no bra on.'

I sat back. 'Clearly not everything's broken, then.'

'Oh, not by a long shot.'

'Bloody hell, Steve.'

'Aw, come on. Would you deny an ex in distress? I've missed you, stuck in here. I don't know what I'd do if you didn't come and visit me. Anyway, it's not as if Lusanna's going to be walking in on us any minute.'

The moment I'd dreaded. I glanced round the ward. 'She's probably been too upset to come in. Not everyone can cope with hospitals. Do you not remember when our Charlotte was in here having Will? I more or less had to drag you across the car park and shove you through the doors.'

"S'all right, Karen. I know the score, I know she dunt want to see me. She texted me.'

'She *texted* you? She broke up with you in a *text*?'

He shuffled uncomfortably in his chair. I could see the pain lines etched on his face. 'To be honest, I weren't that surprised.'

So he'd already got the measure of her, had he? Heartless bitch. You didn't walk away from folk you cared about when they were damaged. That was the time you stood by them, if you had any decency in you.

He said, 'Thing was, she'd been through it before. She'd had this boyfriend six year ago, came off his bike and he were in a coma, and she was praying he'd recover and then he woke up and the doctors thought he were sound. Sent him home, everything back to normal on t'surface, and then it turns out he's completely changed. It's like he's had a personality transplant. Moody, violent, he'd go for days without speaking a word to her and then explode over nowt. Put his fist through a window, kicked a neighbour's bird-table over. Started hitting her. One night he pulled a knife so she threw him out. It broke her heart. She said she couldn't go through it again.'

Lusanna's lips tight with unspoken words. The sound of her boots on the hospital stairs as she ran away.

'Well,' I said, 'I'm sorry for her. But none of that's true in this case, is it? You haven't changed. You're still you.'

'Am I?'

'Yes! Never mind your dodgy limbs. What matters is you're still Steve.'

He looked hopelessly at his splint, then at his sling. 'It's nice of you to say so, Karen. But this is going to be a long haul. However they manage to patch me up in t'finish, I'm not going to be t'same daft bugger I was before. Stands to reason.'

Across the ward an elderly man tried to manoeuvre his feet into slippers. It was impossible to think of wiry, active Steve hobbled, confined. That would be hard for him to bear. I remembered his jaunty walk as he came down our front path, the way he'd do a little skip up onto the doorstep. Gone forever, that had.

'You never know, the crash might have knocked some sense into you.'

'You reckon?' His hand reached out for mine, grasped it hard. 'I do love you, Karen. I do need you.'

'I know,' I said.

For the first few seconds I couldn't work out where I was. I knew this wasn't my bed – not my Bank Top bed or my York one – because the mattress was firmer and the light coming in under the curtains was wrong and the smell around me was different: male, and inexplicably orangey. Next to me, his head hidden by the duvet, someone stirred.

That's when it all came back to me.

I'd been to Martin's place twice before because every year he held a social evening for his tutor group. The flat itself was part of a Georgian block, tall and elegant with arched windows and black railings round the front area. The stone doorstep was worn away in the centre, a detail that made me wonder about all the feet that must have passed over it in the last two hundred years. Martin opened the door in jeans, slippers and a jumper that looked as if it had been unravelled from a dog blanket and then knitted up again.

'I was passing,' I said. 'Can I come in?'

He'd hesitated for a moment, then stepped aside. 'Of course. Though you'll have to excuse the mess.'

Once I was in he offered me a lager, and when I refused, milk. 'Well, you won't touch my vile coffee, will you?' he said, and we laughed. I hadn't drunk milk in a glass since I was about ten. I had to pick my way across to the sofa because the floor of his living room was covered in notes and books, spread out in what I could tell was a really important order. I suppose he can do this because he lives alone, and no one's going to tidy them away or kick them around or spill juice or scribble on them. I asked what he was working on and he said it was a chapter on courtly love for an A level study guide. He said it was hard to simplify the concept enough, to make it bite-size and instantly accessible because the whole process went against the grain for him, that the study of literature was about expanding English and opening up and exploring every nuance and cadence and technique. He said, 'Synopses are anathema to me,' and postured like an actor, which made me laugh again.

I said, 'It must be hard for you having to dumb-down to your students,' and he said he never dumbed-down for me.

Still, though, he didn't ask me what was wrong even though he could see I was on the edge. And I didn't want to just launch in. The signals weren't right yet.

More out of nerves than anything I picked up a photo of his daughter and asked how she was going on.

That seemed to break the ice. Martin came and settled at the other end of the sofa from me and launched into how Isabella had been having a problem with her knee joint, and she could have an operation on it now or wait for six months and see how it developed because it might be that the bones would fill in themselves and an operation wasn't needed in the end. Except Martin wanted it dealing with straight away whereas his ex-wife thought they should hang on, and she'd gone to see another specialist without telling him and they'd had a major row about it. 'I'm afraid I haven't handled it well,' he said.

I asked him what Isabella wanted and he said, 'She's siding with her mother, of course. What nine-year-old volunteers to have an operation? Although, actually, I'm always in the wrong. She always takes her mother's part.'

I said, 'I bet she doesn't,' and I told him about how I used to play my parents off against each other, pretending to agree with whoever wasn't in the room. It was a power-thing, the thrill of being able to wind an adult up. Sometimes if I was angry with a friend at school or with a teacher or just feeling generally down, that would be the trigger to start stirring. Why do you hurt the people you love? Because you can.

I said, 'Has she got you to promise anything recently, or give her a present?'

Martin nodded. 'She has, actually. I handed over one of these Baby Annabell dolls last week.'

'Well, there you go. Ten-to-one she'll have been showing off to her mum and using dolly to make *her* feel bad. You don't live under the same roof, you don't get to see. This situation you're describing, it's not like your daughter thinks, Mum's a hero and Dad's a villain. Honestly. It doesn't work like that. From a child's perspective, parents are like a set of scales; you're balancing one against the other all the time.'

He looked at me and said, 'So young and yet so wise.' But he wasn't taking the piss. You could see he was genuinely grateful. I told him some more, about how I'd twice threatened Mum I was going to go and live with Dad, even though I'd never in a million years have moved into the junk-pit that was his house and he'd never have had me. Then Martin listed some of the gifts he'd bought Isabella since the divorce, and described how she'd always put on this total lack of interest as she unwrapped each one. 'She's like an empress accepting tribute,' he said. 'Nothing engages her. I don't necessarily ascribe it to the separation; she was becoming spoiled long before we got divorced. And I'm very aware the clock's ticking here. She's nearly ten now, which is coming towards the end of primary school, and once she turns into a teenager I shan't have a clue. I see these knots of giggling girls in the shopping centre, and frankly they scare me.'

'Sounds like Isabella needs someone to pull her up on a few things. She's old enough to say thank you, for a start. This pretending you're not important in her life, it's a bluff. Don't fall for it. And there is time, but she needs putting straight before she goes all moody and hormonal.'

'Are you offering?'

I wasn't sure if he was joking or not. Even so it felt good to be the one giving advice, sitting in this lovely book-lined room on this squashy sofa and being treated as if I actually knew what I was talking about. Taking my mind outside my own problems. And I had this flash of an idea: me escorting Isabella round the museums, coffee bars, clothes shops, letting her chat, offering wisdom and guidance. Maybe letting her play with my make-up or crimpers. She'd love that. She'd open right up. Then I could put her dad's case. And maybe – now, this was a plan – we could go out, the three of us, Martin as well, take a boat up the river, or nip over to Fountains Abbey for a picnic or something. Have a trip away from the city where she could talk on neutral territory.

Shit, did I dare suggest it? Was he really seriously asking me to help him?

I suppose it was all the tension of the last few hours building up, but suddenly the earnest tilt of his eyebrows made me want to giggle. 'What?' he said.

I tried to stiffen my face, but that only made me worse.

'I was thinking,' I managed. 'Right, if we got this boat . . .'

'A *boat*? I'm sorry, what boat, Charlotte? Have I missed something?'

That made me giggle harder. 'Any boat. Like, if we hired one and went up the river together, you, me and Isabella, I could talk to her; it would be like counselling but fun.'

Martin started laughing as well. 'Well, I'm intrigued. You want us adrift? For what particular purpose? Flotation therapy?'

'Forget the boat. We could hire bicycles instead.'

'Why bicycles?'

'To keep us moving while we chatted, because I think that can be quite productive. I've read that somewhere – no, stop it – being in motion alters your focus and makes you feel more relaxed. Or we could hire some horses. Does Isabella like horses?'

'She's potty about them. But really, me on horseback? Have you lost your wits, girl?' He had no idea how hilarious his outraged face looked.

'I'm not – you could stay behind – what I'm trying to say . . .' I fell back against the sofa, shaking with mirth. But the sofa was squashier than I'd anticipated and I found myself rolling right into him, actually bumping shoulders.

I've been in close proximity to Martin before but I'd never felt this jolt of electricity that shot through my body now. The room seemed to pitch, the laughter vanished in an instant.

'Oh. Oh my God, Martin.'

'Charlotte.' His voice was a warning note.

'No, listen, it's time, I have to tell you something.'

'I think it's probably better if—'

'Martin, this is important. I really like you. Seriously.'

Within seconds he was on his feet, staring down at me.

'OK, right. Hold it there. Don't say any more. You're muddled and emotional. You've clearly had a bad day which I guess you came here to tell me about and I didn't let you – I'm sorry, I've had rather a rough one myself and I didn't quite feel up to it – so I bear part of the blame here. I should have allowed you to vent. But strictly speaking, you oughtn't to be here. Not in my flat, not over a non-academic issue.'

At last full realisation dawned. What the hell had I been thinking? I'd invaded his personal space and totally taken advantage. I'd embarrassed us both, I'd put his job in danger. Fool, Charlotte. Selfish, selfish fool.

'Oh, God,' I wailed.

'No, don't panic. Come on. You know I enjoy our chats in the Department. Only there are protocols. It could do us both harm if we disobey them.'

'You hate me now! You think I'm rubbish!'

'Don't be ridiculous. The stress you've been under, I'm not surprised you were looking for somewhere to offload. But I'm not the right person. Not here, at this late hour. You need to be somewhere you can think straight. Perhaps the time's come to make an appointment with Student Services? They're a great team.'

'I hear what you're saying: you never want me in your office again.'

'Of course I do. I'm looking forward to our next tutorial. As always. Truly, Charlotte, everything's OK.'

'*I'm* not. Not now.'

'Trust me, you are. Go home and get some sleep. I suspect you need it.'

I stood up, and to his credit he didn't back away. 'My head's just such a scramble. Sorry. God, Martin, I'm so sorry. I don't know what I'm doing. It's been a week like you wouldn't believe and I'm all over the place. But that's no excuse. It's out of hours and I should never have come round. I'm such an idiot. Only, I've always looked up to you and I thought, I thought . . .'

'Forget it. It's wiped. It's unrecorded history. And don't waste any more angst on me or on this evening. You're better than that. Yes?'

I couldn't answer.

'Come on, Charlotte. I'm not letting you go till I get at least a nod.'

Eventually, when I'd calmed down, he'd led me to the door and let me out over that worn-away stone step. He'd watched me down the road – probably to make sure I didn't turn and run back in tears or something nutty like that – and given me a last, reassuring smile before I rounded the corner. I thought I would probably die of shame right there on the pavement. The last person on earth who'd believed I was sane and level, and I'd contrived to mortify myself in his very own living room.

So I'd gone straight back to the house and slept with my landlord.

Next to me the duvet stirred again, then flopped back. Walshy's head poked out, flushed and ruffled. He sniffed suspiciously.

'How long's it going to be before my carpet doesn't stink of Cointreau?' he said.

It was one of those mornings where the phone never stops. Sylv rang first for a general update, then it was Leo asking if he could bring my hours back up at school, to which I had to say no because I was finding it hard to manage anyway. Then I had the hospital with an urgent request from Steve to bring in another tub of prunes. Last it was Social Services letting me know that no, they didn't hold any motorised wheelchairs, only self-propelled ones, but I could put in an application to central stock and I'd hear back within a few months. I said, 'Never mind a few months, he's going to need one as soon as he comes out, which will be in about three weeks.'

The lady sounded sorry. 'The way it works is, he has to go through his GP. Get his GP to fill in a form and then your husband'll get a letter calling him in for an assessment and then they'll take his measurements. In the meantime, there's the manual chairs.'

I said, 'He doesn't need a GP's assessment. A quick glance will tell you he's only got one functioning limb out of four. Therefore a manual wheelchair's no use, is it? Look, don't take my word for it. Ring the hospital and they'll confirm the state he's in. And bloody hell, if he wants measuring, I've a ruler here.'

She said, 'I'm sorry, it's the procedure.'

This kind of shenanigan I'd been through whilst I was caring for Mum, so I wasn't surprised. Just incredibly disappointed, weary, frustrated. Normally you're dropped into these Social Services systems at exactly the time in your life when you're least able to cope with them. Hard enough to find the time to phone once, never mind ring back because the office hours have been so pared down the place is only open half the week, or call round four different organisations because everyone you speak to is convinced whatever it is you're pursuing is someone else's responsibility. I felt barely able to write my name, but here I was filling out forms left, right and centre, every one of which required at least one piece of completely obscure information which meant I'd have to take time out to go rooting through Steve's house after his private papers, and we're talking about a man whose filing system consisted mainly of sticking important letters between the pages of random magazines. It would be all too easy simply to give up, lay my head on the table and weep.

'Mrs Cooper? Are you there?' went the wheelchair lady.

I suppose it can't be nice for them on the other end, either. 'OK, send me the papers and I'll get the ball rolling.'

'I have to send them direct to your husband's GP.'

'*Ex*-husband. Oh, God, I'm not sure who his GP is. The surgery's somewhere in Harrop. Round the back of the library, I think. Big pillars either side of the door. You must know it.'

'Have you a street name?'

'No.'

'We do need a full postal address. Oh, and your ex-husband's NHS number while you're at it.'

I made a huge effort not to swear. 'I'll call you back.'

Spread across the table was a mountain of papers, scribbled

phone numbers, care brochures, benefits information. Somewhere amongst this jumble might well have been Steve's doctor's address, but I couldn't be certain. On top of it all was the Disability Living Allowance form I'd been attempting to begin on behalf of Steve, thirty-eight pages of such baffling complexity it required its own separate help-booklet. I'd only been able to fill in half of it because we still didn't know how much Steve would be able to do for himself when he came out of hospital (or how we'd work it, or whether I could pack my bags and flee the country in time).

Help with your care needs during the day (continued)

Do you usually have difficulty or do you need help with dressing or undressing?

Please tell us what help you need, how often and how long each time you need this help:

I have difficulty or need help with:

putting on or fastening clothes or footwear	*How often?*	*How long each time?*
taking off clothes or footwear	*How often?*	*How long each time?*
choosing the appropriate clothes	*How often?*	*How long each time?*

I moved a few sheets of paper half-heartedly and uncovered two Get Well cards I'd failed to take in for him, plus the contact details of the police Accident Investigation Officer. I could feel my energy draining away.

Help with your care needs during the night. By night we mean when the household has closed down at the end of the day.

Do you usually have difficulty or need help during the night?

This means things like settling, getting into position to sleep, being propped up or getting your bedclothes back on the bed if they fall off, getting to the toilet, using the toilet, using a commode, bedpan or bottle, getting to and taking the tablets or medicines prescribed for you and any treatments or therapy.

Please tell us what help you need, how often and how long each time you need this help:

I have difficulty or need help with:

turning over or changing position in bed	How often?	How long each time?
sleeping comfortably	*How often?*	*How long each time?*
my toilet needs	*How often?*	*How long each time?*
my incontinence needs	*How often?*	*How long each time?*
taking medication	*How often?*	*How long each time?*
treatment or therapy	*How often?*	*How long each time?*

Sighing, I flipped the DLA form over, picked up a pen and went out to the hall to retrieve our *Yellow Pages*. Then I remembered I'd last Sunday shoved them under Will's cushion so he could reach the big table while he did a bit of painting. At least he was at nursery this morning, that was one blessing.

I hauled the book out, lugged it over to the settee and started flipping backwards and forwards through the thin pages. There it was – S – no, gone past it – hell, bloody thing's shut itself. Come here, you bastard. Sliding off the bloody table now. Were telephone directories deliberately designed to be as awkward as

possible? *Storage Services, Supermarkets, Surveyors* – nope, no sur-
geries there. Should I look under GPs? Someone knocked at the
door. I ignored them. *Gates, Gearboxes, General Practitioners see
Doctors.* OK. *Distribution Centres, Driving Schools, Do It Yourself
Shops, Doctors.* That was more like it. *Ashfields, Broome, Clayton,
Coleman.* What was the surgery called? See, I didn't even know
the name of the road. Had I an old A-Z knocking about anywhere, anything helpful like that? Course not. It was hopeless.
I was going to have to wait until I saw Steve again. The doorbell
rang. 'Hang on!' I shouted. I'd do one last scan through the
addresses in case something jogged my memory. I put my finger
on the page and ran it down: *Park Lane, Littleacre, Millbank
Cottages, Cheshire Street, Manchester Road, Bradwell Crescent*—

Someone was banging on my front door, or kicking it. The
directory slid off the cushion and thudded to the floor, losing
my page. 'Bloody hell,' I said under my breath. 'Whoever this
is interrupting me, you'd better have something important to
say.'

When I flung the door open, to my surprise it was little
Leanne Waring and her younger sister, Courtney. I liked Leanne.
I used to do worksheets with her when she was in Year Two
because she'd had problems with her hearing and missed learning a lot of consonant sounds. Nice girl, very willing, and she'd
caught up within two terms. She was in Year Six now, a
Playground Buddy and a library monitor. Not the kind of child
who'd batter my door for devilment.

'Hello, you two,' I said. 'This is a surprise.'

But Leanne's face was mournful, and Courtney looked to be
on the verge of tears. 'Oh, Mrs Cooper.'

'Whatever is it?'

'Your cat, Mrs Cooper.'

'Pringle? What's he done now?'

'There was this van. It came round the corner while he was crossing the road. It hit him.'

Courtney started to cry. Leanne took her hand.

'Where?' I said, trying to see past them onto the street. 'Where is he?'

'He ran off,' said Leanne.

Ran? So he was alive. Thank God. 'Which direction did he go? Was he limping?'

'He was dragging his leg . . .'

They took me to the front gate and pointed to where they'd last seen him, apparently disappearing down the ginnel that leads round the back of our row. Then they showed me where the van had clipped him. There was blood on the tarmac. I wanted to cry out with horror.

I said, 'OK, look, girls, you've been very sensible coming to tell me, but I have to find Pringle now, so you take yourselves home and let me search. And for goodness' sake, be careful crossing the road.'

Leanne hesitated. I could tell she wanted to come with me, and perhaps if she hadn't had her weeping sister in tow I'd have let her. I was a bag of nerves, I could have done with the support. All I could think of was that memory of Steve lying mashed in the road, his mangled bike nearby.

I watched them safely across till they reached the Working Men's Club car park, then I hurried to the ginnel to see if he was there. No sign of Pringle himself, but there was a spattering of dark red drops on the stone flags. I craned my neck to see past the wheeliebins and a fat curtain of Russian vine. The grass verges had died back in the cold weather, leaving the path pretty clear so at least the cat's progress was easy to see: a sad row of bloodstains and, every so often, a heart-rending smear where the damaged leg had trailed. I felt sick at the thought of finding him, sicker at the thought of not.

At the end of the path I stopped and looked right, in the direction of our back garden. Where might Pringle have gone to ground? I wondered if he'd taken himself into one of the bushes, or maybe the small gap between the shed and the fence, anywhere confined and safe. When Chalkie was poorly he'd always gone and hidden in the airing cupboard.

I reached the gate and called Pringle's name, got no answer. Had he gone back inside the house? I walked halfway to the bins, but there was no blood to be seen anywhere. Nothing by the shed or under the flowering currants either. For half a minute I just stood and shouted, letting my panic flare up. Then I dropped to the ground to see if he might somehow have squeezed himself underneath the shed base. That's when I noticed more blood smeared across the sagging fence panel and crossing into Eric's jungle of a garden. Plenty of places to hide in there.

I stepped gingerly over the larch lap panel and listened. What state would Pringle be in when I found him? What would I have to do? Pick him up? Try and get him in the car? And all the time knowing he was in agony. There might be bones sticking out, like there were with Steve. I didn't think I could do it. I remembered Mum dealing calmly with Chalkie's half-kills, snapping the neck of a mangled starling so it went limp straight away. Me, I'm hopeless. Even handling turkey giblets gives me the willies.

Ahead of me through the grass was a cat-trodden path leading to the house. Of course, Eric still had his cat-flap, and Pringle
in his hour of need had simply headed for his old familiar home.
The dark staining on some of the grass blades confirmed it. I said
a quick prayer, marched up to the kitchen door and knocked.
There was Pringle-blood on the step between my feet, and
smudged across the plastic frame of the cat-flap.

The seconds ticked by and no one came. Shading my eyes
with my hand I peered through the glass and saw only empty
rooms. Damn. DAMN. I patted my pockets optimistically for my
phone but really I knew it was in my bag, hanging in the hall. I'd
have to run home, try and call Eric and hope he wasn't working
too far away.

By which time Pringle could have bled to death. Scabby old
mog that he was, I couldn't bear it. Not coming on top of everything else. If he was still able to shift himself, there was a chance
I could call him and get him to come out to me. After all, he'd
got himself through the cat-flap once. I knelt on the chilly
paving slabs and pushed open the plastic square with my hand.
'Pringle,' I called in a voice bright with false optimism. 'Din-
dins. Dinny-dins. Come on. Come and have your dinner.'

I don't know how long I stayed in that position, face squashed
up against the UPVC, knee bones grinding the concrete. Pringle
was inside but he clearly wasn't for exiting. Nothing for it now
but to take myself home and phone for help. I struggled to stand
again, grabbing the handle to pull myself upright – and to my
amazement, it gave and I heard the latch unclick. This door was
open. Eric had gone out and left the place unlocked.

I could have run back to phone him, check it was OK. But
this was an emergency – a life was at stake. There was no one to

ask. The house was empty. So God forgive me, I opened the door and walked right in.

A knock on Walshy's bedroom door made me jump.

'Hey, lovebirds,' Gemma's voice boomed. 'Wakey, wakey. Laine and I are off to a tutorial now, but someone needs to be up to let the glazier in. So put some clothes on, yeah? You don't want him to find you running around in the nude, do you?'

The window was my fault. Walshy and I had been playing catch in the hallway with a soapstone turtle.

'We OK for lunch?' I called back.

'Yup,' she said, and then I heard her thumping off down the stairs, Laine's excited American greeting.

I reached for my jeans.

'Don't go,' said Walshy. 'Don't leave me.'

'You want I should greet the glazier naked?'

'We might get a discount.'

'Pimp. Get some pants on, stir your stumps.'

'In a minute. You're really great, you know. I love to watch you.'

'Doing what?'

'Just moving about. You've got such an excellent arse, I can't help myself.'

'Oh, move it, Walshman.'

He stayed exactly where he was. 'Will the glazier be taking the boards down?'

'Er, yeah, or we wouldn't be able to see out, would we?'

'Shame. I'm going to miss Lisa Simpson.'

Gemma's girlfriend Laine had decorated the boarded-up window for us with some liquid chalk pens we'd found in the kitchen drawer. She proved to be an excellent cartoonist.

'Me too. Farewell Spongebob Squarepants. And Cartman. We should take a photo before it goes.'

'Come back to bed, Chaz.'

'I can't. Some of us have work to do.' I pulled on my sweater and scanned around for my boots.

'Like what?'

'Well, *Daisy Miller* to finish reading, an essay to start. I've to go into town later and check out pop-up tents for Will, for Christmas. Do you want to tag along? I thought, you know, with your vast yurt experience.'

'Don't mention the yurt. That was all a bit tragic.'

While I'd been away seeing to Dad, a group of students had climbed on the canvas and bust the wooden frame. I was sorry. The garden looked bare without it now. 'Yeah, but your dad'll buy you a new one next summer. I'll help you put it up.'

'You won't be here next summer. None of us will.'

'No.' I kept forgetting. 'Anyway, are you going to come and keep me company or what?'

'Trawling round the Early Learning Centre? I think not. Do I look like ELC material?'

'Don't make me answer that.' I swung his wardrobe door open to check myself in the mirror. My hairbrush, I realised, was next door, in my room; really I should buy two and have one on each window-sill. Or was that too much of a commitment at this stage? I said, 'Seriously, if you're going to date me you're going to have to embrace the world of pre-school equipment.'

There was no smart come-back this time. When I turned round he'd squirmed down the bed and pulled the duvet over his head.

'Walshy?'

He only grunted.

I closed the wardrobe door and left him to it.

The first thing I did was snap the light on and bellow Pringle's name down the hallway. Immediately I heard a noise from upstairs.

I ran to the bottom of the banister and shouted again. I couldn't see any blood trail here, but then the carpet pattern was black and brown swirls, a relic of Mr Cottle. You could have emptied a bottle of red wine over it and it would hardly have shown. It was odd Eric hadn't replaced it, odd anyway that he'd started redecorating the upstairs and left the downstairs as it was because most of us begin with the rooms that are on show. Me, I'd have been gagging to scrape off this embossed bamboo stalk wallpaper and chuck out the ruched lightshades. But then old Mr Cottle had slept downstairs for years, so who knew what state the bedrooms had been in when he died. They might have needed gutting.

'Pringle!' I called again, and once more a faint sound answered me, like something hard rolling across a bare floor. He must have knocked a vase or a tin off a shelf.

I raced up to the landing and checked the bathroom first. This was a place I'd already been in, so it didn't feel as much of an intrusion. The shower was dripping and a towel had fallen off the rail onto the lino, but no cat. Nothing odd in the sink this time, either.

The next door I tried was the airing cupboard which I checked anyway because it had been slightly ajar and I remembered Chalkie going to ground among Nan's sheets, all those years ago. There were only piles of bedding and towels here,

though, plus a cordless vac and a boxed fan-heater. Eric did keep
the place neat.

I had a swift hunt round Kenzie's room, lifting his football
duvet to peer under the bed, sweeping the curtain to one side,
prising open the mini-wardrobe door. His toys were mostly
tucked away in plastic storage crates and his small clothes hung
or folded; the under-bed space was taken up by zipped suitcases.
There was barely space for even a hamster to hide, let alone anything bigger.

Which left Eric's room. Fretting as I was about Pringle, I did
hesitate at this point. It's not nice to go poking round a bedroom
without permission. Who knows what private things you'll
uncover? But then I heard another thump and a kind of scrab-
ble coming from inside.

I flung the door open and went in.

Double bed with black and white duvet and black headboard,
one wall decorated in black and white block wallpaper. New-
looking grey carpet, paintwork all fresh, top quality lined grey
curtains. Walk-in wardrobe with mirrored doors stretching the
entire length of the far wall. However much the downstairs
might be in need of updating, this place had certainly had a
makeover. Laid across the unmade bed was Eric's navy dressing-
gown, and below the window his slippers, a Thomas Harris
paperback on the bedside table.

I got down on my knees so I was mattress-height. 'Pringle?'
Mew.

My pulse started to race. 'Pringle, love, where are you?'
Hauling myself up again, I strained to listen.
Miaow. Meringue.

He was in the wardrobe. This time I had it.

I dragged at the handle, sliding away the giant mirror along with my own harassed reflection. Inside, it was dark and half-empty, only a dozen or so shirts and jeans on hangers, work boots and trainers lined up on the floor. In the corner were some video tapes, a stack of magazines, a robotic puppy in its box, an artificial Christmas tree base.

Meringue. I could hear him, so close now, but I couldn't for the life of me tell where he was. I climbed right inside the wardrobe and blundered about, trying to watch where I put my feet. 'Pringle?' Had he got himself under the floorboards somehow? Inside the wall? I raised my hand and tapped experimentally.

Mew.

'Pringle! Pringle, love, I'm here!'

Then, 'Fuck it,' said a woman's voice, muffled but close.

I staggered out against the bed in surprise as the back panel of the wardrobe started to open, sliding aside with the same action as the mirrored front. Behind was a space roughly the width of a toilet cubicle, fitted with shelves and hooks. I saw bottles of cosmetics lined up, stylers and tongs, racks of women's shoes and, suspended against the wall like a market stall, several sets of clothing. Mainly, though, I saw a youngish woman in fleece pyjamas, standing squinting in the light. She had curly red hair, a pouty, angry mouth. I watched as she stepped towards me, first into the wardrobe proper, then out onto the bedroom carpet.

'You'll be wanting your cat,' she said bitterly. 'He ran inside, he wouldn't go. He's all ... eugh. I couldn't bring myself to touch him.'

I took a deep breath – because there'd be time for accusation and shouting later – then pushed past her to claim my pet. God, but it felt weird to walk into somebody's wardrobe. Narnia this was not: stumbling into gloom over Eric's footwear and ducking under his shirts, breathing in dust and the smell of plaster and new paint. The cupboard space behind, now I saw it clearly, was a work of art. He'd created a place to store everything, even down to her toothbrush. There were labelled plastic drawers and wall pockets, a hanging shoe tree, swing-out rails. On the wardrobe side of the door he'd nailed a bracket which he'd draped with his own belts, presumably so no one would guess it for a handle. Bloody hell. You had to appreciate the ingenuity.

Pringle was underneath one of the shelves, lying on a pale blue cardigan or coat, with his mashed back leg out at an angle. I could hardly bear to look but I made myself. Someone had to take charge. I knelt down to him and, bizarrely, he started purring. I said, 'Hey up, lad,' and he laid his head in my palm as if it was too much for him to keep it raised himself.

'Right.' I stood, assessed my route out and kicked a few shoes aside to clear a path. Then I bent and picked him up, cardigan and all, and I thought, Just let her say something, just let her. She didn't, though. She'd sank down on the bed and was holding her face in her hands.

I looked down at my pathetic bundle. 'Can you at least go ahead and open doors for me?'

And she did.

Roz linked my arm as we came out of Boots. 'How you getting on with Laine, then?' she asked.

'Oh. Laine. She's OK. She's got a lot of energy. Quite a piercing laugh. Put it this way, you know when she's in the house.'

'Gareth said that. He calls her Foghorn Leghorn.'

'Your charming boyfriend.'

Roz giggled. 'He only ever means it in fun.'

We crossed the precinct and went into Top Shop. Gemma had texted to say she couldn't make it so the afternoon's shopping and tent-hunting was mine and Roz's alone.

'Crap about her parents, though, isn't it?' Roz held up a lace dress to herself doubtfully, then replaced it on the rail.

'She's gutted, you can tell. More than anything because she was so sure they'd accept it. But they're still being horrible with her. She's not allowed to mention Laine at all.'

'That's awful. Poor Gemma. I said to her, "At least you've got us, we'll be your family till your mum comes round." I think that made her feel better.'

'So we're Gemma's family now. What a thought. I suppose Walshy would enjoy playing wicked uncle.'

A complicated set of emotions seemed to cross Roz's face. At last she said, 'Yeah, Walshy. It was a surprise, you two getting together.'

'Was it?' I remembered the secret tin of Charlotte-mementoes, hidden under his bed. I'd never mentioned it to anyone, not even him.

'I thought he annoyed you.'

'He does, a bit. It's just, sometimes I want to muck about and be young. I get sick of serious. He's fun, and there's basically a decent guy in there.'

'You don't have to convince me. I've always thought he was nice. He was brilliant with me over, you know.' Roz lowered her eyes. 'Only he gets through lots of girlfriends. That's all. And you're bound to be feeling a bit vulnerable after Daniel. That was so rough, on top of your dad and everything. Gemma and I don't want you getting hurt again.'

'Oh, you've talked it over, have you?'

'We're just concerned for you.'

'I'll bear it in mind.'

To be hurt, you have to love someone, I could have said. *I don't know what I'm doing with Walshy, but it isn't that. It's not love.*

We wandered through racks of party clothes, maxi-coats, fur gilets. Roz seemed generally brighter than she'd been for ages, girly and jokey, and I was glad for her. At one point she found me a fur hat and plonked it on my head, so I pulled a bobbly scarf off its hanger and wrapped it round her neck. It made her look very young and sweet. 'I miss you,' I said. 'Laine can cook a mean corned-beef hash, but the house doesn't feel the same. I wish we could go back to how we were at the start of the year. Or how we were in the summer – the day we put the yurt up. That was good, that. Before all the change.' Before I lost Daniel, before my dad's accident. When the end of uni seemed an age away.

'Aw. I miss you too, Chaz.'

'Is it all right at Gareth's?'

'It is, yeah. He's been dead nice to me. Not that he wasn't before, only it's different now, we're kind of more honest with each other. It's hard to explain. I know he can be a bit rough and ready but he's a decent bloke. That's the thing, when bad stuff happens, you find out how you really feel about someone.'

You never said a truer word, I thought.

'And how's your mum, Roz? Walshy told me she'd been finding it tough.'

'Oh. Yeah.' She unwound the scarf sadly. 'The problem is, Mum's trying to deal with it on her own. We decided early on we were never going to tell Dad about the – about me going to the clinic. And it's not the kind of news she'll be wanting to share with friends

369

or neighbours – that was her main fear at first, anyone finding out. So, on the outside I'd say she looks like she's coping with it, but I'm not sure. I catch her sometimes giving me these stares. She's thinking she doesn't know me any more. It's like I've opened up a world she knew nothing about, and never wanted to.'

'Mums always come round. They just need time.'

'I don't blame her. Sometimes I think about what happened and I hardly know myself. Like, it was the right thing to do, definitely. I wasn't grown-up enough to be a mother, I know that. But it doesn't make the aftermath any less tough.'

A woman squeezed past our rail with a double buggy. Inside were twin boys, about a year old, blond and beautiful. Some days there are babies everywhere.

I said, 'God, I'm really sorry.'

'What for?'

'I can't *stand* the idea of you ever thinking I'd be cross with you for what you did. I'd have helped you if I'd known. Like a shot. I could have left Will at home and gone to the clinic with you.'

'There's no need to keep apologising, Chaz. I told you, I wasn't rational. My hormones were up and down. I had my mum going on at me—'

'Because I would *never* judge you.'

'Yes, I know. I get that.'

She took my arm again and we wandered out into the precinct. Already there were Christmas displays in some of the shop windows, posters urging you to panic-buy. I remembered an argument Daniel and I once had about artificial Christmas trees versus real (which was the more middle class), and a Boxing Day where Nan mistook a lavender sachet for a tea bag.

Roz said, 'I think it was because you're such a good mother.'

I laughed out loud. 'You are joking, right?'

'No. My God, Charlotte, we don't know how you do it. We really don't. You're so ... so balanced. We're all whingeing on about essay deadlines and the prices at the union, but it's nothing compared with the hassles you have. The travelling backwards and forwards, fitting in your work, those weekend gigs you miss and the parties and stuff. You never complain about it. And we know you're crazy about Will but you don't bang on about him the way some mums do about their kids. You don't tell those long, rambling anecdotes about the littlest things he's done, or constantly shove baby photos at us. You're never boring.'

I thought, Blimey. Well, Roz, I could unpack for you right now my shoddy brand of motherhood – the clashes with Mum, the miserable goodbyes, the way I've taught myself to switch Will off when I'm not with him – so *not*-normal. But did Roz want to hear that? Did it help to know others were floundering, or was it more reassuring to believe that someone, somewhere was in control?

I said, 'To be honest, I'm not sure anyone gets the Mum Thing completely right. I used to think the reason I found bringing up Will difficult was because I was a single teenager, but actually anyone can make a hash of it, doesn't matter what age you are or your marital status or what's in your bank account. Look at Daniel's mum, drunk half the time; Gemma's telling her she isn't normal. Walshy's mum ran off when he was only about twelve, how crap is that?'

'Did she? God. I knew his parents had split but he never talks about it.'

'No. There's quite a bit of damage there, underneath all the couldn't-give-a-stuff. And it makes me wonder, where *are* these mothers who always get it right? Do they even exist?'

Roz shook her head. 'Only on TV. Actually, that reminds me of something: when I was little I used to look at kids' presenters and imagine what they'd be like to have as a mum. Did you ever do that?'

'No.'

'I did. I always fancied Yvette Fielding. Or Isla St Clair.'

'Isla St Clair?'

'Or Lorraine Kelly. Or Marti Caine. Marti Caine doing my hair for me. How smart would that have been?'

'And Isla St Clair singing you a bedtime story?' My phone beeped with a text message.

'Yeah, see, it would've been cool. Although a mum who baked a lot would also be handy,' Roz was saying as I brought the screen up. 'Someone like Delia Smith. I mean, I loved my actual mum, but she was always a bit boring, the way real life is.'

I pressed *Open* and stared.

'. . . Oh, and Johnny Ball for my dad. He could've helped with my maths homework.'

'Wait,' I said, holding up my hand.

'What is it? Oh my God, what is it, Chaz? You look awful.'

I said, 'Daniel's here. In York. And he says he needs to see me right now.'

By the time I got to the vet's, Pringle had soiled himself. I thought, She won't be wearing that cardigan again in a hurry.

I laid the cat gently on the table and the vet bent to examine the wound. I tried to read his expression but he was too professional. Did they get used to seeing animals in distress, did it become just part of the job? I recalled the briskness of the paramedic who'd treated Steve at the roadside, and the positively cheerful porter who'd taken him down for his second op. You

must have to build up a resistance to suffering when you're surrounded by it. No good if everyone goes to pieces.

'Can you at least stop the pain?'

The vet nodded. 'We'll give him a sedative while we assess
the damage. Do you want to go to the waiting room and we'll
call you?'

Out of my panicky haze I remembered Will stuck at nursery
and due for collection any minute. 'I can't. I have to get back to
my grandson.'

'That's all right. Give us a call in, say, half an hour and I'll tell
you how things are looking. We'll go from there, yes?'

'OK.' I stared at Pringle's leg again. The fur there was
drenched in blood and sticking flat down. His ribcage strained.
'It's not looking so great, is it?'

The vet pressed his lips together.

That's that, then, I thought.

'We'll do our best, Mrs Cooper,' he said.

On the way out I stopped and held the door open for a
woman holding a shoe box. God knows what she had in there.
Nothing big enough to make a fuss about. She smiled a thank-
you and I noticed she had pretty much the same vivid colour
hair as wardrobe-woman. Funny coincidence, I thought, and
then light dawned. Hair-dye. Of course! Eric's woman used red
dye. And that's what I'd seen round the plughole in Eric's bathroom. Yes. They might have thought to stash every other piece
of evidence out of sight, but she'd forgotten to rinse the sink. *It
wasn't blood, you idiot*.

I was seeing blood everywhere. Then again, there was a lot of
blood to see.

*

'Tell him to get stuffed!' Roz had said as I left her, livid on my behalf. 'Jerking you around. It's like you said, either he wants to be with you or he doesn't. Bastard.'

'No. Something's wrong.'

The way Daniel and I had left things had been pretty clear: no more contact, ever. Which meant this wasn't any kind of reconciliation, or social call. Some emergency must be driving him.

Immediately I tried ringing Mum but only got the answering machine. Next I phoned nursery, who told me Will had eaten all his fish fingers, built a train track, and his grandma was running slightly late but was on her way. So nothing amiss there. Last I rang Dad's ward expecting God knows what, but the nurse insisted everything was grand. So whatever bombshell Daniel was about to deliver, my family was safe. That was something. My mind churned with possibilities. Maybe it was to do with Amelia. Maybe he wanted to let me know officially they were going out now. If that was his news, he was going to get a beer in the face.

His text had asked me to meet him in the Crown. When I got there, the drinks were already on the table.

'What's this?' I asked, picking up the tumbler and tilting it critically.

'Whisky.'

'Why? I hate whisky.'

'Because you might need it.'

He'd had his hair cut shorter and was clearly using some product on it because it looked a lot better. I wondered whose influence that was. Loads of times I'd asked him to sort his hair out.

I took a swig of the whisky and grimaced. 'OK, whatever it is, tell me – quick. And you'd better not be playing games.'

'It's your Jessie Pilkington.'

That I hadn't been expecting. 'What? What about her?'

'I wanted to set your mind at rest. I can pretty much guarantee you won't be hearing from her again.'

What the fuck had he done? Paid her off? Taken out a contract on her?

'How?'

'This.'

He took a folded piece of paper out of his pocket and pushed it across the table to me. I took it gingerly and opened it out. It was a badly photocopied newspaper clipping, the font tiny and old-fashioned. I tried to scan it for meaning but the words blurred and shifted.

'What, though? Really, just tell me.'

'Read it, Charlotte.'

So I did. I made myself focus, and through the roaring that quickly started up in my ears, I managed to gather it was a 1971 report about a six-year-old girl who'd died at the hands of her stepfather after months of neglect. He'd gone to prison, and so had the girl's mother for letting it happen, although her sentence wasn't as long because the judge said the mother had been both intimidated and disorientated by her partner's violence. Further down the article there were details of the bruising and injuries found on the girl's body, and comments from neighbours about seeing her sometimes foraging in bins. It was utterly heartbreaking. But what made it far, far worse than a tragic tale from long ago was that I knew this mother: I'd met her, spoken to her, I'd been in her flat and drunk her sodding tea. It was Jen, it was Jessie.

I picked up the glass of whisky, drained it, then read the report through again. This time, as the details sank in, it seemed much more horrible. Emma, the girl had been called. In the grainy black and white photo she wore a gingham school dress and a cardigan. Her hair looked as if it might have been brown.

'Where did you get this, Daniel?' I whispered.

He tried to run his hand through his sticky fringe, and failed. 'I'm sorry, perhaps it wasn't my place, but I felt something wasn't right about what you told me. About Jessie's behaviour, I mean. So I did a little digging online and turned up a mention of a Jessie Pilkington in connection with this girl's death. So then I paid a visit to the Newspaper Library at Colindale and searched through their archive. And the full story was there. I did check out four or five versions but all the main facts I think are in this article. I couldn't find anything else. I don't know if there was any more.'

His eyes were anxious as I clutched my empty glass.

'Did I do right in telling you, Charlotte?'

At first I was too choked up to answer. God, her own *daughter*. How could it have happened? In the middle of a *city*. Why didn't the neighbours do anything? Call the police, Social Services? And what kind of a bitch stays with a man who beats her kid? Shit, I'd *slaughter* anyone who hurt Will. Rip their fucking head off. 'Jesus, Daniel . . . I was in her *flat*. She's *Mum's mum*. God, oh God. Why did I need to hear about this? Why did you have to drop it into my head?'

He reached for my glass. 'You've had a shock. Sit there while I get you another drink. Then I'll explain why I thought you needed to know.'

He sloped off to the bar and left me. At other tables around the room people chatted and flirted and bitched and laughed their way through their ordinary days. Meanwhile panicked, guilty voices raged through my head: *You wanted this woman to meet your mum! – Why didn't you try checking her out before you went? – Would Emma have been your aunt? – How can any mother stand by like that? – What in God's name possessed you to go turning over stones when all the family you ever needed was around you? Idiot! Idiot!*

Daniel set my drink down with an awkward clunk. His jaw was tense and his face grim.

'OK, Charlotte?'

'What do you think? Oh, Jesus. How am I ever going to move past this? It's going to be in my head forever, spoiling everything I look at. Will's little face . . .'

He took my hand and held it, and I let him. 'No, listen. The point is – and this is why you needed to hear – Jessie won't be coming after you. She's got too much to lose.'

'How do you work that one out?'

'Well, why do you think she moved to London, changed her name? She'll have been trying to escape her past ever since she got out of prison. Probably the authorities even advised her to do that. But say you were to go to the papers or the police, she'd be a target all over again. Have you any idea how child abusers get treated in this country? The public can be deeply vindictive if they decide someone hasn't been punished enough. And we're not just talking a spot of graffiti, or cat-calling in the street. I've read about people in her position who've been sent broken glass through the post, nail bombs, had petrol poured through their letterboxes. Women like her attract lynch mobs. Charlotte, you hold the power here. If she did ever make any sort of approach, try to intrude on your family, all you'd have to do would be to say you were going to the press. If you want, I can write and spell this out to her, but I'm pretty sure there's no need.'

He finished and sat back, giving me space to react. Gradually, against the turmoil in my brain, his words began to settle into some kind of sense. Because I had been tormented with the idea of her pursuing me – *If you don't give me cash I'll tell your mother where you've been* – I'd been braced for it, screwed up tight with fear. Dreamed about her landing on our doorstep with some sob-story or threat or outburst.

I said, 'Then why did she take the risk of sending us cards? Why not keep quiet about where she lived?'

Daniel nodded. 'It was a risk for her, yes. A big one. But from what you tell me, she was on the ropes. Contacting your mother was a last-ditch attempt to get hold of some cash and stave off what was becoming a meltdown situation. A situation so dire it made her reckless.'

I thought back to that scene in a London street, Dex begging me to use the cash-point. Menacing, cajoling. I'd been frightened, but Jessie had probably been more frightened than me. I wondered whether the people who were after her had caught up in the end, and what they'd done. I realised I didn't care.

'My mum must *never* know about this. You've not mentioned it to anyone else?'

'How could you even think I would?'

I closed my eyes to see if it made me feel better, but it didn't.

'Was I right to tell you, Charlotte?'

'I needed to know,' I said dully.

'Yes, because it means it's over, it means you can forget about her. Cut her out of your thoughts.'

I opened my eyes again and stared at him. 'It doesn't, though! It means the opposite. It means, whether I like it or not, Jessie's part of what made me. It's Jessie's genes sloshing about in me, in Mum, in Will. Not lovely Nan's. So where does that leave us?'

'Exactly where you were. Nothing about your family's changed here.'

378

'But it *has*. What about the DNA of it, the biological inheritance? What gets passed on and what doesn't? Come on, you're the scientist. You hear these people who research their family trees practically boasting about how their ancestor was hanged at Newgate or transported to Australia, like they think it's quite cool to be related to a criminal 'cause it happened two hundred years ago. What about if it isn't two hundred years ago? If it's only thirty? What percentage of "badness" gets handed down each time? Huh?'

Because one thing I really couldn't bear was the thought of Will being connected to that woman. Every instinct screamed at me to protect him, keep him separate and safe so he'd never ever know. My beautiful son who was more precious than my own life. What would become of him, where would he end up? Suddenly I was drowning in the smell of malt and fag smoke and cheap perfume. Everything around me felt polluted.

'You want some science?' asked Daniel. 'Really?'

'Please, Dan.'

'Right, here goes.' He spread his long fingers and began to count off his arguments. 'OK, firstly, let's look at the anecdotal evidence: have you or your mother ever given in to serious violent urges? No. And you've had your moments of provocation, haven't you? So secondly, we have to consider the wider research. And after years of investigation into the subject, across a whole host of countries, all results suggest there is no single gene for aggressive behaviour. It's possible there might be some combinations of genes that result in a predisposition to violence, but the chances of those exact combinations recurring in the next generation are minute. It's like expecting a Nobel Prize-winner to give birth to a Nobel Prize-winner. Any transmission would really be down to environment, culture, expectation. For instance, what do you know about Jessie's upbringing? There could be all kinds of abuse there, fear, violence, factors that would make the best of us turn bad. Add to that the point you made yourself, how pretty much everyone's got criminal relatives somewhere down the line if you go hunting for them. We're all genetically contaminated in that sense. But we don't have to walk around consciously carrying that burden because we're free to live our own lives. Your genetic heritage is always balanced against choice. Even if you're born harbouring a particular impulse, you always have the opportunity to resist. In this case, the fact you're aware you don't want Will to go in that direction is going to make you encourage him even more strongly to be a decent, upstanding citizen. So in that sense you might even see it as a positive factor. Although, I appreciate that may be pushing it.'

He nudged the rim of his glasses so they sat higher on his nose, nervously pleased with himself.

I said, 'I did smack Will that time.'

'Once. And remember how you felt afterwards?'

'Awful.'

'There you go.'

I thought about Will in pain, reminded myself how it felt to watch. Catching his arm on the hot tap during bathtime, how he'd yelled; the awful moment he fell and banged his forehead on the hearth; the day of his MMR jab. A heavy book tumbling off the shelf onto his bare foot. A wasp sting, a splinter off the back fence, a trapped finger. His pain was always my pain, only ten times worse. Then I remembered when I was little, Mum sitting up with me through the small hours when I was ill. She used to keep a flannel in the fridge for when I had a temperature. And I thought of her dabbing my split lip with an ice cube wrapped in a hanky, and calmly clearing up where I'd been sick. It used to nearly kill her to use TCP on my cuts; she'd suck in her breath and wince as she pressed the cotton wool on. Now I understood why. Motherhood strips us down to the thinnest layer of skin and makes us super-sensitive. It should do, anyway. And then I thought of Nan bending to button my winter coat and helping me work my small fingers into gloves, her expression of rapture when she first peeped into Will's crib. My brilliant nan. That was where my family came from, from that well of decency and love, not from some twisted stranger in another city.

I worked my hand loose from his.

'Are you OK?' he said again.

'I'm not sure. But – I suppose I should say thank you, anyway. It can't have been easy to bring me that news.'

'It wasn't.'

No. What must the discovery have been like for him, scrolling through those old newspaper reports? Then the journey here, waiting in the pub for me, watching my shock register as he talked. There'd been no need for him to suffer any of it.

'Do you need another drink, Charlotte?'

'I've had plenty, thanks. In fact, I should probably get some fresh air.'

'Of course. Do you need me to take you outside?'

'I'm not sure.' My legs felt wobbly, as if they'd never carry me anywhere again.

For a minute or so we sat listening to the juke box play 'Life Is A Rollercoaster'. Apparently the trick was you just had to ride it.

I said, 'Dad's coming home in a fortnight. That's one good thing at least.'

'Yes. Yes, it is.'

'Mum's getting a bed for downstairs. It's going to be chaos, basically.'

'She'll cope, though?'

'Oh, yeah. Mum always does.'

'And Will's OK? Am I allowed to ask?'

'He's fine. Learning to pedal his trike.'

'Splendid.'

'God, Jessie Pilkington. Will I ever feel normal again, Dan?'

'You will.'

Somewhere in the background Ronan Keating finished telling us not to fight it, and an old song came on over the speakers:

> *You are the star-sun-moon that guides me*
> *My lightship in the storm*
> *You keep me safe from harm*
> *Safe and warm*
> *Through the storm*

It made me feel seventeen again, a schoolgirl poring over her revision timetable. I used to have this tape, I could have said, 'We've kissed to this track. Do you remember?'

For a long time we sat without talking, just watching the lights on the fruit machine flash out their sequence. Gradually my churning heart settled a little, and I tuned back into the ordinary world.

'So,' Daniel said at last.

'So.'

'Where do you go from here? Can I give you a lift anywhere?'

I got to my feet. 'I'm meeting a friend at Constantine's. I'll walk.'

'Ah.'

He stepped aside to let me past and we stood facing each other for a few seconds. There was no expectation now, I understood where we were.

I said, 'I don't know how to do goodbyes with you any more.'

He glanced at his hands, thrust them into his pockets.

'I guess you could tell me to take care.'

> *The light across the sea*
> *Always guides you back to me*
> *On a path that's wavering bright*
> *Through the night*

'Take care, then, Dan. Really, I mean it. Look after yourself.'

'You too, Charlotte.'

And then there was nothing else to say. I turned and walked away, out of the pub.

Eric must have been watching my house for the lights to go on because I'd barely taken my coat off before he was knocking at the door. I put the TV on for Will and went to answer it.

'For you,' he said, holding out a bunch of carnations.

'Sod off,' I hissed, barring the entrance. 'It's been a hell of a day and I can't be doing with any more crap.'

'But I need to explain, Karen.'

'What you need to do is turn right round and go whining back to bloody Anne Frank over there.'

'She didna live *in* the cupboard,' Eric said, as if the clarification was some kind of help. 'That's just where Maria stored her stuff so it was out the way if the benefits officer came round.'

'I don't want to know.'

'I didna mean to lie to you. Not you.'

'Oh, I'm flattered.'

'No, listen. What it was, she came back to me out the blue—'

'When?'

'Not long. A few months ago. She'd been claiming for a flat, and she'd have lost that money if we'd declared it, and it was only till we got back on our feet – and anyway, Kenzie needed his mum with him. You wouldnae separate a lad and his mother over a few quid, would you?'

'Enough of this.' I tapped my watch sarcastically. 'See, single parents like me haven't time to stand chatting on the doorstep. What with being on our *own*.'

'Wait, Karen!'

'What?'

He thrust the flowers forward, pleading. 'I need to know: are you going to report us?'

I took a long, deep breath to stop the stream of abuse escaping.

'That's for me to know and you to fret about.'

And I shut the door in his broad, handsome face.

NAN: Is it night-time yet?

KAREN: No, it's only afternoon. They've not been round
    with the tea trolley yet.

NAN: I'm that tired.

KAREN: I know. Well, close your eyes, get some rest.
    Nothing's spoiling.

(Long pause.)

NAN: I keep thinking of your dad. He was marvellous with
that tenor horn.

KAREN: I know.

(Long pause.)

NAN: Will you stay with me till I get off?

KAREN: Of course I will, Mum, of course I will. (Pause.) I'll
stay as long as you want.

CHAPTER 12

On a day in December

'It's a belter, I'll say that,' Dad observed from his bed in the corner of the living room. 'I swear you could stick a saddle on it and ride it down Vickeridge Road.'

'Where the hell's it come from? That's what I want to know.' Mum, hemmed in behind Dad's perching stool, squinted nervously at the ceiling.

'Nothing to do with me,' I said.

'Well, you were the one brought in all that holly, Charlotte.'

'Yeah, but I think I'd have noticed if a spider the size of my fist had been clinging to the branches.'

A lone strand of tinsel above the gas fire shivered in the convection currents. Less than a week to go till Christmas and we hadn't managed to put up a tree yet. *Stuff Christmas this year*, Mum had said.

'Hey up, he's on the move again. He's making for the lightshade,' said Dad.

'It's that scuttling movement I can't stand,' said Mum. 'And the way they drop without warning. Urgh.'

I pointed to where Pringle slept on the wheelchair seat. 'Why haven't you been training him up to eat spiders? That'd be a useful contribution he could make to the household. Pay you back for his massive vet's bill.'

'Him? He'll be lucky if he can catch a slug these days, poor beggar.'

The way Pringle was curled up, you couldn't see the amputation at all. He could have been an ordinary four-limbed cat.

'No, I've seen him circuit the garden at a fair speed. He manages pretty well.'

'He's got more working legs on him than me,' said Dad.

The spider was exploring the light-fitting now with thoughtful interest, like a prospective house-buyer.

I said, 'Listen, when Will gets back from nursery you're not to say anything about this. Phobias are learned. I don't want him growing up frightened of everyday objects. It's irrational. Spiders can't hurt you.'

'If you feel so strongly,' said Mum, 'get yourself a dining chair and climb up after it. I'm not stopping you.'

'If I could get out of this flaming bed, I'd have him for you. Spiders are nowt, a little tickle on your skin.'

'Perhaps he was attracted in by your tache, Dad. He might think it's a mate squatting there on your top lip.'

Mum folded her arms. 'Don't worry, Charlotte. The facial hair's coming off in the New Year. It's one of my conditions as his carer. I'll empty his urinal and I'll chop up his meals, but I've decided there's no way I'm faffing about grooming a moustache. That's above and beyond the call of duty. In fact, I should've got shut of it while he was still in intensive care.'

'Oh aye?' Dad touched his top lip. 'First I've heard of it. See what I have to put up with, Charlie? It's bullying. Of the disabled. So what are these other conditions, then?'

The spider left the ceiling rose and began to trundle in the direction of the bed. We all followed it with our eyes.

'No more motorbikes,' said Mum.

'Well, I couldn't if I wanted to. I can't bend me flaming knee, can I?'

'If you ever get so you do.'

'It's not fair to blame the bike, Karen. I was unlucky. You can be unlucky in a car, or crossing the street. You can have a heart attack sitting at home watching TV. There was a chap at t'warehouse'd lost part of his hand just shutting one of them big iron gates.'

'You've lost a sight more than part of your hand.'

'I weren't even going fast.'

'Exactly.'

Dad sighed. 'See, Charlie? She gets me at every turn.'

I said, 'Watch out, it's directly over your head now. Try and lure it down. Wiggle your lip at it.'

We sat transfixed as the spider made its way coyly across the picture rail.

'Your dad's always been quite good with wildlife.'

'Has he?' I was surprised.

'Oh yes. On our first ever date he saved me from a wasp. Flicked its bottom right off.'

'Move over, Bill Oddie.'

'And do you remember that time you got mobbed by ducks, Steve?'

Dad nodded. 'In Queens Park? I do, yeah. But it was you they mobbed. You had summat on your sandwiches that was driving 'em mad. I had to rescue you. And a bloody big goose come waddling up and pecked me in the knackers.'

'I'd forgotten that.'

'I hadn't.' Dad turned to me. 'She couldn't fight 'em off herself because she were pregnant wi' you. Blown up like a beach ball, could barely see her own feet. I had to charge in and pull her out of danger.'

My brain did a little skip of readjustment as I tried to imagine the scene: Mum eighteen and swollen, rising out of a sea of angry waterfowl, and Dad spotty-faced with his hair over his collar and his bleach-washed jeans. She never talked much about that time, about the marriage full stop. I'd always assumed it was one long round of miserable sniping, but clearly that was wrong. They must have had their happy days, e.g. the duck encounter. And I looked up at the spider now, still dithering a metre out of reach above Dad's bed, and I thought, This'll become one of those little-nothing family stories too, one of those moments we recall which seem to sum up a mood or a time. Dad sitting up in bed, his bad arm strapped against his chest in a blue Velcro sling; Mum tucked into the far corner where, till a fortnight ago, the china cabinet had lived; me hovering by the kitchen door, poised for flight in case of spider attack. It had felt bizarre but also quite nice having both parents at home for once, as if I was little again, a safe harbour after all the upset with Daniel and before I had to start thinking about final exams.

And even though the circumstances of Dad's moving in were horrible, nevertheless there was something comforting about the routines Mum had set up around his disability. In the morning, before I came down, she'd empty his pee bottle and give him his tablets, and then she'd shout me and we'd all have breakfast together. Then I'd have to disappear back up with Will while she manoeuvred Dad into his wheelchair and got him to the bathroom for a sponge-wash. After that she'd leave him for five minutes' privacy, then she'd return and change the bandage on his leg and re-splint him and dress him and wheel him back to bed. At first it felt odd to be upstairs helping Will pull on his trousers while Mum was downstairs doing the same for Dad, but it's amazing how quickly your mind adjusts to a new set of circumstances when there's no alternative. Dad might be in a ton of pain, but he was so happy to be out of hospital. Mum slotted into the role of carer almost cheerfully, if that doesn't sound too strange. I suppose she'd done a lot of caring for Nan so it was like old times for her.

Meanwhile, nothing else was getting done. We weren't bothering with Christmas presents except for Will. Mum said I'd already had mine because she'd discovered the hole in our savings account and assumed I'd blown it on clothes. To say she was cross was an understatement, but thanks to Daniel's advice I'd been semi-prepared and just gritted my teeth till the rant was over. As for a Christmas present, I wasn't fussed anyway; I'd passed my driving test the week before so that was as good as anything you could gift-wrap.

Christmas Day dinner would most likely be Iceland turkey roll and oven chips, and we'd sent out no cards, not one. We hadn't even put up the ones we'd received, just stuck them in a pile on the windowsill. In that pile was a card from Gemma and Laine, who were boycotting Gemma's house and spending the holiday instead with Laine's super-cool aunty in Oxford. There was one from Roz and Gareth with a picture of Santa falling drunk over Rudolph. Martin had sent a postcard of St Mark's Square in snow, and a message telling me to relax over the holiday and eat well and read up on the *Lyrical Ballads* for our first tutorial. Near the bottom of the pile, because it had come early on, was Walshy's effort, a simple robin on a branch. *To Chazzer*, it said. *How do you keep a northerner in suspense? Tell you next term. X*

The letterbox rattled now, making us all jump.

'Go get the post, will you, Charlotte?' said Mum, her eyes glued to the spider.

I went without complaint. I'd been first at the doormat every day since I got back, just in case a letter came from Jessie that I needed to intercept. I understood really there'd be nothing more from her, but you know how sometimes you can't stop yourself doing something irrational because it feels like insurance against Fate? This morning there were four cards and a catalogue and a bank statement and two charity circulars and something from the NHS. I flicked through the cards, checked they were all local postmarks, and I was about to go back through when I heard a thump, a clatter and my dad swearing.

'God, are you OK?' I called.

Dad was still in bed, but holding aloft his plastic urinal and looking mighty pleased with himself. 'He shoots, he scores.'

'Watch, it'll climb out,' said Mum urgently. 'Put the lid on!'

Through the milky plastic sides you could make out the dark shape of the spider as it scrambled from one side of the base to the other.

'Let me,' I said, surprising myself. I went back out into the hall and opened the front door, then I grabbed the bottle off Dad and made a run for it. The urinal clattered onto the path and the spider, after a few seconds, charged out of the funnel end and disappeared into the flowerbed. As I stood watching, a filthy-looking man walked past leading a tatty wolfhound. He glanced over and nodded. 'Awreet?'

'Fine,' I snapped, as if hurling urinals about the garden was an everyday occurrence.

He gave me this yucky grin which showed his yellow teeth. Sometimes I love Bank Top, sometimes I hate it.

When I went back inside, Mum was bending over Dad. I don't want to think about what they were doing with each other.

'So even in this state I'm not completely useless, am I?' I heard him say.

While Charlotte sat and read Steve the motoring section from the *Bolton Evening News*, I went and tackled the breakfast washing-up. Some days we had a sinkful by teatime, what with everything else I had to wade through. Just getting Steve dressed swallowed up half the morning.

He was being good, though. Always said thank you for the help I gave him, always tried to think what he needed while I was still on my feet. And that's not always how caring for someone works. There was a woman at Mayfield had the nurses up and down like they were on elastic: where was her hanky, the curtain needed pulling across, her duvet wasn't straight, she'd dropped toast crumbs in the bed. I think she did it because she was bored, or for the power. Mum never demanded much. She was just pleased to see you and sad when you went.

I turned the taps on full and stared out the window at the back lawn. It was raining hard, water streaming off the coal-shed roof and puddling in the broken flags by the downspout. It had been pouring down the day Steve came home. I'd had to go out with an umbrella and hold it over his chair as they wheeled him in. But at least you know where you are with rain. It's a known factor, it's not storing up any kind of disappointment for later.

Rain doesn't show up the smears on your glass or the dust on your furniture the way sunshine does. I watched the garden spring and quiver greedily under the onslaught. At the far end of the lawn was the new row of larch lap fence panels I'd made Eric install before he left: that had been one of my conditions.

'I didna start off meaning to do it,' he'd said, finally collaring me as I wheeled the bins out through the ginnel.

'I don't want to hear, Eric, I've told you. Go away.'

But he just carried on. 'Maria really did leave me, I really had no idea where she was. That was why I moved. Then she decided to come back. Only by then she was set up, y'ken – she'd got her own flat and she was claiming housing benefit and council tax and Job Seekers' Allowance. We sat down and worked out how much we'd lose if we told the social she'd moved in again, and we realised we just couldna manage. No way. But she's Kenzie's mum. I wasna going to shut the door on her.'

'So she'd arrive after dark.'

'And leave early.'

'Not the morning I came round.'

'She'd slept in that day.'

'Nice for some! And she always came and went through the back, didn't she? Across my fence.' So bloody obvious now what was going on, but I suppose you don't see what you don't want to see.

'Not every night, Karen. A few times a week. But they call that living together and they take your benefits. They have these vans, hidden cameras. They go through your bins. They watch your house. She had to park on Pinfold Lane and walk round. Because everyone's a spy, y'ken. You'd be amazed how many busybodies are queuing up to report you.'

I could have smacked him for his self-righteousness. 'Is it any wonder?'

'Ach, come on. You know what it's like trying to cover the bills, all these demands coming through the letterbox and kiddies to clothe and feed. I thought you'd understand. Everyone cheats a bit where they can. Bit of cash-in-hand here and there. It's not the crime of the century.'

The smell of something rotting rose up from the bin, and I gripped the handle tightly with both hands.

'I'd say you've been a sight more organised about it than that, Eric. Do you know how hard I've had to fight to claim the Disability Living Allowance we genuinely need and are entitled to? I've had to jump through bloody hoops while people like you are ripping off the system. Entangling me in your lies, how dare you! How could you spin me all those lines about being on your own, a single parent? Bloody hell, I bet there wasn't even a Little Beavers nursery. You were dropping Kenzie off at hers, weren't you? Don't bother trying to deny it. In fact, why did you ever need me to babysit?'

'Because sometimes a job came in and it was short notice. And sometimes she was out—'

'Working?'

He said nothing.

'While she claims JSA? How many scams have you got going, Eric?'

'I'm just trying to scrape by, like you.'

'No, not like me! Good God. Apart from anything else, I would never take advantage of a friend the way you did. What a very low opinion of me you must've had, using me as your stooge. And I was stupid enough to think—'

Think what? That he'd had feelings for me? Most likely he just couldn't resist exercising his own charm.

'I told you, it wasna like that. I really admire you, Karen. You've been a pal.'

'Personal information I shared with you. Really personal.'

'I know, and I tried to help. I did help, didn't I?'

That I couldn't bring myself to answer.

'Karen, I'm no' a bad man. I just backed myself intae a corner.'

'I'll put you in a bloody corner,' I said, ramming the bin in his direction so he had to jump aside.

I began to trundle it down to the entrance, but he ran after me. 'Please don't report us. I'm begging you. Think of Kenzie. Me and his mum, we could go to prison.'

'Don't be so dramatic.'

'We could. They bang people up for fiddling benefits. Especially if it's not your first offence.'

There was genuine fear in his voice. I thought, He's right, I hate what they're doing, but I don't want to be responsible for separating either of them from their child.

I halted the bin and turned to face him.

'OK, right. I am thinking of Kenzie here, because somebody needs to. Straighten yourselves out – I'm not asking, I'm telling. Move Maria back in if that's what you want, but then you go speak to the DSS, adjust your finances, and give that lad a chance to settle in a normal, open atmosphere. No lies, no secrets. I don't know exactly what you've told him; he knows something's odd in the way the house works but he doesn't understand what and he's terrified to speak in case he lets something slip that he shouldn't. He's at school now, with all the pressures that brings, and it's not fair. You're the adults, you take responsibility. I'll not stand by and see a child suffer.'

'Ach, Kenzie's not doing so bad. Children are very adaptable.'

'And that's one of the biggest lies going. I won't say it again, Eric. Put yourself on the level or I will report you.'

He was trying to keep his body language casual but his face had gone pale.

'Ok, I'll deal with it, Karen, I swear.'

'You'd better.'

I'd left him leaning against the entry wall, looking shell-shocked. He could tell I wasn't bluffing.

Two days later they did a midnight flit. God knows where they'd gone to this time.

Now the house stood empty again, the grass lapping at the doorstep and the windows blank. As soon as I realised they'd left, I went round and superglued the cat-flap shut, to prevent any more Pringle episodes. At least there was nothing for me to explain to Charlotte and Steve. Eric was just gone, full stop. I thought how far I'd come since the day I tried to give Mr Cottle his windmill back, how many areas of my life had changed. Steve home, Mum quiet in my mind. No more Daniel. Things I'd never have believed, for better or worse. Every day some shift, some adjustment, even if it was only Will learning how to get the lid off the biscuit barrel himself, or Charlotte running me a bath without being asked because she thought I looked tired.

I could hear her now, giggling with her dad over some daft tale in the paper. Late last night, on her way to bed, she'd paused in the doorway and said, 'I wonder if we're one of those families who need a crisis to work properly?' And Steve had laughed and I went, 'For God's sake, don't say that, Charlotte.'

She could have been right, though. To be honest, I was too knackered to tell.

I had intended to drive – drive! – to nursery to pick up Will, but the rain slackened off and Dad started getting tetchy and tired and Mum said we should have a walk, give him some space.

'He has his mobile in an emergency,' she said. 'But really he needs his painkillers to kick in and a nap. He had a bad night.'

She'd put on one of Nan's plastic rain-hoods. I thought she looked hilarious.

'Blimey. It'll be a Pac-a-Mac next. You're turning into your mother.'

'There are worse ways to go,' she said crisply.

I didn't know whether she meant that I should be happy to grow like her in my old age, or she was happy to become Nan. Then I thought, Isn't it fantastic she just assumes that's where she's headed, how it never crosses her mind to consider the influence of that other mother, the one she doesn't know and who we must never mention. I'd studied Mum, really studied her since my trip to London, and there was nothing of Jessie in her that I could see other than the colour of her eyes, an arch to the brow. Nothing that mattered. Some nights I still had dreams about that tatty flat, about the little girl Emma, and sometimes in the dream I was trapped in a room and sometimes Jessie was crying and sorry. Then the next morning my head would be so full I felt ready to burst with the memory. I knew I'd never breathe a word, though. How much of genuine love rests in the words you hold back as the ones you speak.

I felt so protective of Mum as we turned onto Church Street that I almost put my arm through hers. I didn't, though, because then she'd have asked what was up and I'd have had to fib or come out with something soppy. We traipsed past Spar and the butcher's and the beauty clinic and the library. It started to rain again, thick blobby drops on the verge of sleet.

Mum suddenly said, 'Will you be coming back to Bank Top when your degree's over?'

I laughed because that same question had just been forming again in my own mind. Probably it was the walking past the library that had sparked a bit of nostalgia in both of us. I'd spent half my life in there as a kid.

'Well, will you?'

'I'm not sure.'

'I haven't liked to ask much because you've been that distracted. I suppose you've had a lot to deal with lately. But you do need to be thinking about it now.'

'I do think about it. All the time.'

'And?'

'Oh, useless. I get nowhere. Everyone's been telling me how to run my life for so long, and now it's "Right, Charlotte, over to you". But I seem to have lost the ability to make decisions. I've absolutely no idea what I want to do in the future. I can't *see* it.'

'Come on, Charlotte, you must have some clue. What made you choose an English degree?'

'I think you chose it for me.'

She turned, ready to be indignant. Then she saw I was smiling. 'Cheeky madam. What does your tutor say?'

'I've not asked him. He can't solve all my problems for me. I've been to the Careers Department, though, had a look at their pro-filing stuff.'

'And?'

'Nothing sounds right.'

'You always told me the beauty of English as a subject was that it could take you anywhere.'

'Perhaps that's the trouble. Too much choice.'

We passed the Health Centre and the council offices.

'Actually,' I said, 'the real issue is, I'm petrified. It's so scary, stepping out into the real world. All the things you have to manage, and how *do* people manage? Is there some kind of class you can go to, to learn things like mortgages and pensions and tax codes and how to get your car serviced? I just don't feel ready for any of it. I know it's pathetic of me.'

I waited for the lecture I was sure was coming. *Don't be ridiculous, Charlotte. You're twenty-one, that is grown-up. You've a university education behind you, which is more than I ever had. You've savings in the bank, a driving licence, the world's at your feet. Buck up.*

Instead she said nothing, only frowned and pulled the strings on her rain-hood loose, re-tying them tighter in the face of the sleet. Then she said, 'Well, I'll let you into a secret: it is scary. It's always scary, and that never stops, no matter how old you are. There's no magic age where you're finally on top of everything and in control. You think *I* know what I'm doing, day-to-day? I race about, trying to look as if I have a clue. Sometimes I feel like a pinball pinging round the place. At night I lie awake worrying and making lists. And honestly, the only way through is to get on with things. Pretend to yourself and everyone else that you're coping, and then somehow you do. But it's a scramble. I might be heading towards forty but there are moments I still want just to turn to your nan and ask her to sort it out for me.'

This time I did reach across and squeeze her arm. 'Oh, Mum.'

'Now Nan was a good mother.'

'Don't say it like that.'

'Like what?'

'As if we aren't.'

Mum snorted. 'Pff. You've called my maternal skills into question on a few occasions, if I remember rightly. Oh, yes, you have, don't look like that. At least I've tried to put things right. Every mother makes mistakes, we're all failed mothers, to some degree or other. The minute your child's born you join the club. Because there's always something you shouldn't have said, or something you should, an innocent decision that leaves its little scar. Life's too random for that never to happen. But it seems to me the best mums are the ones who admit when they go wrong and attempt to make amends. I have tried to do that, Charlotte, however it's come across to you.'

'I know.'

She stopped and stared at me, her eyes searching mine. Wet hair clung to my cheeks and my nose was moist with the cold.

'It's important you do, love, because one day all children turn round and call their parents to account. You might not believe me, but they do. And you need to have your answers ready.'

She'll be standing where I am in a decade or two. She thinks she won't because she lets Will stay up late and she makes his socks talk to each other in funny voices and she sticks spaghetti-hoop eyes on his mashed potato, everything for fun. She's so determined he's going to be 100 per cent happy. But wait till he's on her hands full-time and she's forced to lay down some serious rules. Then there'll be tears. Sometimes you have to let your child hate you a bit, even if it breaks your heart.

*

The sleet was piling down now and I began sneaking sideways glances at the rain-hood. Shoddy as Mum was, at least she was dry. That's one advantage of getting old, of course: you don't have to bother what you look like any more. I thought that might be quite nice in some ways. Let yourself go, stop worrying about boyfriends and stuff, a whole layer of hassle peeled away. My thoughts flashed onto Walshy for a moment, and I sighed. Why had I ever let myself get tangled up in that daft business? It was time on my own I needed, get my head straight, not Walsh-minding and general foolery. So there would be that to dismantle at some point. Further joy on the horizon.

We turned onto the lane leading to nursery. It was slightly more sheltered here if you kept close to the terraced houses. Mum moved in front of me to keep off the worst of the sleet, and I lowered my head and forged on. The next thing I knew, I'd run straight into her. She'd stopped without warning under someone's porch.

'Listen,' she said. 'I need to ask you—'

'Eh?'

'While we're on our own. While you're pleasant.'

'For God's sake, Mum. What?'

'Don't get stroppy with me, but I have to know. Is it completely over with Daniel?'

That very nearly floored me.

She said, 'I think I know the answer, but I need to hear it, then I can put it to bed. It's just, I was so fond of him. He was like family. And then to drop away like that. Would you not at least consider taking him back?'

I leaned against the pock-marked bricks while I tried to gather my thoughts.

'I don't want to talk about it. You'll just be angry.'

'No, Charlotte, I promise I won't. One thing your dad's accident's taught me is what's worth getting wound up about and what isn't. So tell me, please. I'm not judging, only listening. Is there any chance we'll be seeing Daniel again? I'd like to have said goodbye.'

'It's not up to me,' I said at last.

'What do you mean?'

'*He* finished with *me*.'

Now it was her turn to gape. 'Never.'

'Uh-huh.'

'But he thinks the world of you!'

'I know.'

'Whatever did you do to him?'

Straight away it was on the tip of my tongue to come back with, *See, here you go, all ready to pin the blame.* But as the grey flakes whirled around us, cocooning us in that one dry spot, I found I wanted to get it all out. Tell her and have done.

'Daniel said I wasn't interested enough in him.'

Mum's eyes widened.

'He said the bottom line was he loved me more than I loved him, and he'd realised it was always going to be that way and he needed to get out now before he got hurt any more deeply.' I couldn't meet her gaze. 'He said I should have made the time to meet his friends and be nicer to his mum and ask him more about his Manchester life. Plus there was this girl from his department buzzing round him, sucking up to Mrs Gale, asking him to various social events and generally hanging on his every word. I don't think he fancied her exactly, but he must have felt it, the way she paid him so much attention while I was all wrapped up in my own stuff. He might even be going out with her now I'm off the scene. She seemed pretty persistent.'

Again I saw that photocopied image from the *Twenty-First Century Rocks* booklet, Amelia's glossy hair and bright, clear smile.

I said, 'I tried to make him give it another go, I really did. I promised I'd see his uni friends, make more of an effort there. I said I'd be more tolerant of his mum, even though she patently hates my guts. It wasn't any use. He just wasn't having it.'

'Was there – a boy in York?' Mum ventured. I could see she was genuinely keyed up, so again I didn't snap, I didn't blurt out anything smart.

'Not one that split us up. It's true I've dated someone since, but he's nothing, which is why I haven't told you about him. He's keen on me but he's not interested in Will. Obviously that's going nowhere.'

'So you're going to finish that?'

'I am.'

'It's not the boy who you're renting off, is it?'

'Mmm.'

'Oh, Charlotte. Will he not throw you out on the street?'

That made me laugh. 'No, course he won't. Good grief, Mum. He'll just go, "Ah well, fun while it lasted," and move on. That's what he does. I bet he'll have another girlfriend lined up before you can say Millennium Dome.'

'I hope you're right.' Then she said carefully, 'I do think sometimes you were quite snippy with Daniel.'

I nodded sadly.

'I know I was. I could hear myself. The trouble is, I've just not felt as close to him this year. I feel like I've changed but he hasn't. Because, I know he cares about Will, but basically his life's carried on being more or less the same, an ordinary student life, while mine seems more and more laden down. I find it hard to relax the way he does. So, like, he tends to witter on about ordinary student things, which is OK except sometimes when I've a lot on my mind I can't be doing with how trivial he sounds. You know what he's like, you know the type of freakiness that fires him up. Super-size bacteria and bioluminescent mice. Nothing relevant. It's tiring, I don't always want to hear it. And then I get fed up with him because I think, How does any of this matter? And he thinks I'm being dismissive of *him*.'

She was frowning at me like someone working out a maths puzzle. 'It's put a lot of pressure on you, being away from home so much.'

'I've *hated* it, Mum. It's nearly done my head in. I know it had to be, and that it's nearly over, but bloody hell, it's been awful parting from Will each time. Like wrenching off a limb. Nobody seemed to understand and you all assumed I was coping.'

Rain had pooled in the creases of Mum's plastic hood, dribbling off in a defeated way onto her mac and leaving dark patches across her shoulders. For a moment I could see the old lady she'd one day become, lined, stooped, confused by the world.

'I thought we were doing all right. I did my best, with Will and that. I've really tried, Charlotte.'

'I know.'

'When you came home each time ... I thought you were just being stroppy for the sake of it. You've not really said anything.'

'What was there to say? You knew I hated leaving my son, no point repeating myself there. Plus you were so down over Nan. No, don't – I'm not blaming you for that. I miss her too.' We stood and looked at each other while the sleet dropped around us in a steady curtain. 'It's just been a really shit year, Mum.'

There was this catch in her voice that was upsetting to hear. I thought, Oh, love, it's nearly been too much for you, hasn't it?

And I've not noticed because I was so wrapped up in missing Mum, and the business with Eric, and your dad. And all that time I'd been assuming it was you who gave Daniel the push, and now it turns out to be him. Him! I suppose he must have more backbone than I gave him credit for. Unless his snooty mother was behind it, or this uppity madam from his department. Oh, yes, I bet there'd been some encouragement from the Manchester end.

Indignation flared up in me, same as it had when Ryan Marshall's mum was boasting about her perfect daughter's job and flat and fiancé. Who were these girls to hold a candle to our Charlotte? I'd have liked to see them manage what she'd had to deal with the last three years.

'And of course I've spoiled it for Will too,' she went on. 'He needed someone like Daniel in his life, a great role model, smart, loads of patience. Where the hell am I ever going to find another boyfriend as nice as him? I won't, basically. He's just about the kindest guy I've ever met. And I've blown it, like I always do.'

I pulled her closer into the porch, out of the wind.

'Look, are you absolutely sure it's finished? Only, I've never seen a lad as committed as he was.'

'He did appear out the blue a couple of times and I thought, you know, we were back on again. Then he'd turn round and say no. It was like he'd told himself he didn't want me but at the same time he couldn't completely leave me alone.'

'Did you tell him what you've just told me? Did you really explain?'

'I tried. It didn't come out very well. How could I explain, anyway, when I didn't understand it myself? I thought he was right. I thought the root of it was I'd stopped loving him enough. He said it would never be equal between us because he cared

405

more about me than I did about him. But since we've broken up I realise that wasn't true. Now I realise what I've lost. Now I get it. Believe me, Mum, if I ever had another chance I'd grab him and I'd never let go. He'd never feel second-rate again. I'd talk to him properly and I'd listen properly. No more rolling my eyes when he talks about his mum being "a bit emotional", no sighing when he goes into how DNA replicates itself. No more bad-day moodiness. I'd be the best person I could be for him. I would.'

'Then you have to go back and say that. Spell it out, if you didn't before. And as soon as you can. It sounds to me as if he could still be talked round.'

'I can't, there's no point. Honestly, this time he's made up his mind.'

'Prove me wrong. Give it one last try.'

Her mouth twisted into an unhappy half-smile. 'Hah. Because he's a doctor's son?'

'Because if you don't, Charlotte, it's going to eat you from the inside out.'

The sleet was beginning to stick where it landed on the grass verges, clumping along the tyre ruts. You could tell it wouldn't last but it carried on piling anyway, wetly.

'It's too much of a risk,' I said.

Mum frowned. 'Where's the risk? I don't see what you have to lose.'

'My dignity.'

'Right.'

'No, 'cause it'll be so horrible if I fail again. If I deliver the big confession speech and then he still tells me to get lost, I'll die.'

'And if you stay here and never ever say anything? Let it roll round and round your head for the foreseeable future?'

I thought of the nights I'd already spent, awake and fretful under the weight of my mistake. All the Daniel-free days that stretched ahead. The slender chink of hope Mum had presented.

I said, half-joking, 'Well, I can't go now. We have to pick up Will first.'

She said, 'I can get him for you.'

For a fraction of a second it seemed as if the sleet was suspended in the sky.

And then she just took off, belting down the street like she used to when she was a little girl, her feet slapping against the shiny pavement. I could see the soles of her shoes, her hair straggling behind her.

Dear God, let this one pay off, I thought.

When I got back with Will, Steve seemed brighter. I laid my coat over the back of the sofa and went to plump up his pillows.

'Hey up, Karen. Any chance of a tea?'

'Soon as I've changed Will's trousers. We're both wet through.'

'I don't know why you didn't take the car.'

'Because it was fairly bright when we set off. You never can tell how a day'll turn out.'

The Metro had gone from the front, I saw. I hoped she was remembering to drive carefully.

I took Will into the kitchen and stripped and towelled him, then popped his pyjama bottoms on because they were hanging on the maiden just by me and I couldn't be bothered to trail upstairs after fresh clothes. 'Here's two Kit Kats,' I said. 'One for you and one for Granddad, yes?' He took them obediently and trotted through to the lounge. I glanced down at my own sodden jeans; they could wait till I'd made the hot drinks.

Of course my whole mind now was filled up with Charlotte and what she was doing. The kettle could have boiled itself into oblivion and I wouldn't have noticed. I was thinking, It's so easy to get lost in motherhood. Find it blocking out the rest of you, interfering with your ability to reason, your sense of perspective, particularly if you're a perfectionist the way my daughter is. Good mothers learn to be kind to themselves, to forgive their own mistakes. But it's hard when you're caught up in the whirl of everything. I'd had a spell after the divorce where my brains just scrambled. I remember sitting up till the small hours obsessively filling in one of her magic painting books, too wound up to go to bed. And in those days, if she got so much as a spot of dirt on her clothes I made her change her whole outfit. Everything had to be just so or I got myself in a tizz. One time I lost a sock down the back of a radiator and I sat down and cried. Can you believe it? Over a bloody sock? Mum fished it out with a coat-hanger in about two seconds.

She's a lot like me, is Charlotte, though she'd hate me to point it out. I should have spotted she was in trouble, let her know I was on her side. Thank God she'd talked to me at last. I just hoped I'd done some good. *Oh, Daniel*, I prayed, *if you've an ounce of kindness in you, take her back.*

'Our Charlie gone shopping?' said Steve when I handed him his mug.

'Something like that,' I said. There'd be time enough later to fill him in. When I knew the outcome.

Will was on the sofa, thumb in mouth, staring at a blank TV screen. I reached for the remote but before I could switch the *Tweenies* on, Steve waved his hand to stop me.

'Hang about, Karen.'

'What?'

'We've summat to show you.'

He beckoned Will over and whispered in his ear. Will looked confused. Steve tried again. I watched as my grandson frowned, his eyes swivelling round the room. 'On the TV,' said Steve.

After a pause, Will trotted over to the set and reached up for the book which lay there, my family history.

'Careful with that, sweetheart,' I said.

Steve nodded, and Will slid it down, holding it against his chest to come back and stand by the bed.

'Now,' said Steve, 'watch this.'

He laid the book against the duvet and opened the pages as best he could with his one good hand, angling them so Will and I could see. The first picture was of Mum, the last we'd taken before she died. She was sitting in a wing-back chair against a bay window at Mayfield, holding a tin of oxtail soup I'd just won in the tombola. Her eyes were half-closed and she looked far away, but there was a faint smile on her lips. You could just make out Bertie's yellow tail wagging in the bottom corner.

Steve tapped the page with his index finger. 'Who's that?'

'Nan,' said Will without hesitation.

I caught my breath. 'I didn't know he recognised her.'

Steve flipped to the next photo, which was Mum and a six-teen-year-old Charlotte on the pier at Southport in a high wind. 'And who's that?'

'Mummy.'

'And?'

'Nan. Mummy and Nan.'

He turned another page, pointed.

'Nan.'

My heart swelled with pleasure. 'How?'

'Charlotte's been coaching him.'

And I thought I'd won the jackpot this morning when she'd actually told me I'd been right about something.

'So, Will, who's this?' I said, pointing at the photo of Mum by the door. I love that picture. She's standing on the back lawn wearing a lilac jumper, and it looks like she's got a bird-table growing out of her head. How we'd laughed when the print came back from the chemist.

Will left the book and came to inspect. 'Nan,' he said confidently. 'Can I watch TV?'

We put the *Tweenies* on and I came and sat on the end of the bed.

'What do you think of that, then?' said Steve.

'I haven't the words.'

'She thought you'd be suited. We know you've had a rough year. She wanted to try and make it up to you.'

I nodded. 'I'm that touched.'

'Good. We want the old Karen back. We miss her.'

'I am trying.'

'I know.'

'And I've been better lately, haven't I? Well, we've all had to shape ourselves and get on with it. It's just – it's such a shame he'll never really know my mum.'

'He will, though. We'll tell him. We'll teach him all her little rhymes, all her funny stories. Keep showing him photographs.

Play him the tapes. He'll come to know her even if she isn't here. People don't just stop being part of the family when they're not around any more.'

Out of the corner of my eye I could see Dad's tenor horn hanging next to Mum's photo.

'Steve?'

'Yeah?'

'Is there room for me to lie down?'

'Hang on.' Painfully he attempted to shift himself across the mattress.

'No, it's OK, don't worry.'

'If you want to lie down, love, you lie down. Come on.'

I squeezed in next to him.

He said, 'Fancy, though.'

'Fancy what?'

'Us. After all that's happened, me ending up back here.'

'Yes. Fancy.'

His arm came round and pulled me close. The sharp edge of his splint was digging against my leg, and I could see the angry skin below the edge of his dressing. I almost lost you, I thought. You were so nearly toast. And what now? Where do we go from here?

Steve wriggled and sighed. 'What time do you put Will down for his nap?'

'In about an hour.'

'Just time for another dose of painkillers to kick in.'

From the TV was coming an alarm sound and flashing lights. *Tweenie clock, where will it stop?*

'And then what?'

'Physio, of course.' He began to unbutton the top of my shirt.

'Physio?'

'Well, my version.'

I watched his fingers moving deftly. 'You know, as soon as you're fully recovered, you're going home.'

'Course I am, Karen,' he said. 'Course I am.'

The examiner who'd passed me on my first test said I had the makings of a decent driver. He said I was 'cautious but not hesitant', which is what they look for, apparently. He said my positioning at junctions was good and I showed a mature awareness of other vehicles on the road.

I wonder what the examiner would have said if he'd seen me hurling Mum's Metro round the back streets of Manchester that afternoon. How I didn't burst a tyre I'll never know, I hit that many kerbs. The few occasions I had been out in the car on my own I'd been nervous, but not this time. I had too much on my mind. Get there and get it over with, was all I was thinking.

I hadn't even gone back in our house in case Dad asked me what I was up to and that made me lose my nerve. I hadn't changed my wet clothes, repaired my make-up, pulled a comb through my hair. Because whatever happened between me and Dan now, it wasn't going to be decided by a slick of lipstick. He could take me as I was or not at all.

Miraculously there was a parking space along Dan's street, not too far down from the flat, but it was on the small side. Parking's the one thing I'm not so confident about, and I never attempt it without first checking to see if anyone's watching. An audience totally puts me off. I slowed to a halt, had a quick glance round but saw only two figures far, far away at the top of the road. So I went for it, heaving the steering wheel to one side and easing up the clutch, whipping my head from right to left in an attempt not to hit anything during the manoeuvre. First try I connected with the kerb, panicked, revved and shot forward, bumping lightly into the 4×4 in front. I waited for some whooping alarm to start up but luckily nothing happened. *Get a grip, Charlie*, I told myself. *It's not going to help anyone if you dent Mum's wing.* I took a deep breath and began to back up. But now I was well skewed, the front nearside sticking out and there wasn't enough room to straighten. I drove the car out and tried again. This time I had the angle better and although I still hit the kerb, I was ready for that and didn't panic. Instead I heaved the back wheel up onto the pavement, and took a moment's pause while I got my head back together.

Idly I glanced into the mirror and noticed that the two people I'd seen at the top of the road were now much closer. I squinted, trying to make out more detail. A pair of women, it was. One was tall and thin with long hair, jeans and a short beige mac, and the other was smaller, slightly broader, in an expensive-looking coat with a fur collar. The tall woman's mouth was a bright slash of colour against her pale face. That's when it dawned on me: I was watching Mrs Gale. And her younger friend? No prizes for guessing. Even from this distance you could pick up the glossy sheen of Amelia's hair, the confidence in her stride.

'Buggeration!' I said, and promptly stalled the engine.

I looked again. Had they spotted me? Mrs G was talking animatedly and Amelia was nodding, well immersed in their conversation. I thought, I can duck down and hide till they've gone past – but then they'll be in the flat with Daniel and really I have to speak to him now while my courage is up – or I can make a dash for it and see if I can beat them.

Although the car was fairly central, it was sitting with its rear end on the footpath, like a dog cocking its leg. Well, sod whether my parking was parallel or not, I no longer cared. I wrenched the gear-stick into neutral, yanked at the keys and scrambled out. I didn't dare check behind me. All I was concerned about was getting to Daniel first.

I ran full pelt for the flat, throwing myself up the brick path, and was about to ring the bell when I saw someone moving on the other side of the glass. I waved and tapped, and thank-you, God, the door was opened by one of the ground-floor Ukrainians, wearing his coat and obviously on his way out. I just gasped, 'NeedtoseeDaniel!' at him and made for the stairs. I expect he thought he'd let in a nutter.

When I reached the landing I stopped for a second because I felt sick. In the car I'd been trying to keep my head clear and not work myself into a state, even though the first song I heard when I turned on the radio had been bloody 'Seasons In The Sun'. It gives me the creeps at the best of times, that track. Then, due to the hideous lyrics, I'd had an attack of self-pity and a very short cry. But I'd managed to pull myself together by reciting Walshy's football version over the top:

> *We had goals by the ton, we had Bristol on the run*
> *but the fun didn't last 'cause the bastards ran too fast.*

Now, though, I was beyond terrace chants. It was just me and my fear.

The door to Dan's flat was shut, no clues as to whether he was in or not. I began hammering on the wooden panels and calling his name. I thought I could hear voices in the hallway below.

Suddenly the door swung open and there he was, standing in front of me.

'Charlotte!'

'Quick,' I said, slipping over the threshold. 'Close it.'

He just stood like a lemon. When he didn't move, I turned and slammed it shut myself.

'They're *coming*,' I said.

At the same moment I caught sight of myself in the mirror over his fireplace. My eye make-up was melted below my lashes, Alice Cooper-style, and my damp hair looked dark and greasy. I was in the jogging bottoms and hooded sweatshirt I'd been slobbing around in that morning.

'Who's coming, Charlotte?'

'Your mum! Amelia!'

God knows what he thought. That I was having some species of breakdown, probably.

My eyes swept round the room. Everything seemed pretty much as I remembered. Like us, he hadn't bothered with Christmas decs, though he had gone as far as displaying his cards upright. I checked again: where were the bits and pieces I'd given him over the years? The desk photo of me and Will had gone, I now saw, along with the Magic Eye print I'd bought from Bolton Scope, plus the green eco-gonk for the top of his computer. That hurt. It looked like he'd cleared me out. But no, not quite, because the bullet-shaped fossil I'd found in a charity jumble sale was still sitting under his monitor where I'd planted it last year. A belemnite, he'd called it. A tiny ancient squid. Swum its way through a million billion tides to wash up on a table in Tannerside Scout Hut.

'Daniel,' I said.

There was a sharp rap at the door.

'Don't open it,' I mouthed. 'Please.'

He stayed where he was.

The knock came again. 'Daniel? Daniel, are you in there?' His mother's voice.

I smoothed my hair nervously, wondering how long he'd hold out. How long before he'd shrug apologetically and reach past me for the latch.

'Danny?' This was Amelia. More pleading, less strident.

'Daniel, darling, open the door. We know she's in there, we saw her run in. You don't have to deal with it, don't listen to her sob story. Don't let yourself be talked round.'

My jaw dropped. Hell's bells, there's nothing like laying your cards on the table, is there? I knew Mrs G didn't like me, but to be so blatant about it.

Amelia said, 'Let us in. This is silly.'

There was another series of bangs on the door and then silence. We waited, and for a second or two I actually wondered if they might have given up, scuttled off to Mrs G's flat for a glass of wine and a bitch about me. But no, because next came a scrabbling, metallic noise that made me suck in my breath. Mrs Gale was fitting her key into the lock. She was coming in regardless.

'We're concerned about you, darling,' were her first words as she walked into the room. Amelia hovered behind, her eyes fixed on me.

'There's nothing to be concerned about, Mother.'

'It is over, you know,' Mrs Gale addressed me. 'So what do you want? Is it money?'

Even Daniel flinched at that one. I felt fury boiling up inside me, imagined marching across and shaking her by the shoulders till her teeth rattled in their sockets. I had to clench my fists till the immediate urge passed.

'Can you leave us, please,' said Daniel.

'No, I shan't. Not until I hear what's going on. Didn't I tell you we

416

hadn't seen the last of her? Charlotte, you must know you have no right to be here. You haven't brought the child along, have you? No, good, that's something. Because it won't work, this emotional black-mail. Daniel and I have talked it through and I've told him, he has no legal or moral obligation towards you or your son. I think he's made it quite clear that your romance is over, and I'm afraid you need to move on and accept the situation.'

My ears were buzzing with the effort of holding in my rage but I thought, Don't give her the satisfaction. If I lose my temper and start shouting, I'll just be playing into her hands, so she can say: 'See, darling, what a gruesome little fishwife she is when you try and cross her.'

'Please,' said Dan again, quietly. He held his arm out to indicate the door.

'I'm afraid I'm going nowhere till she leaves.'

All this time Amelia's face was growing more and more fasci-nated. I don't know what she'd heard about me, but I think I was worse in the flesh than she'd been expecting. Maybe she'd clocked my hoodie and thought I was going to pull a knife, or at the very least break into some vicious street slang. Maybe she thought I was going to offer her drugs.

Mrs G stepped forward. 'All right, let's get it over with. Say what you need to say, Charlotte, then go.'

''S'OK,' whispered Daniel to me.

Really I needed to sit down because my legs were so shaky, but I didn't want to put myself on a lower level than everyone else.

I tried to speak, managed only a rasp, cleared my throat and said, 'I'm sorry.' They all just stared at me.

And now I discovered that the whole speech I'd prepared asking for another chance, assuring him that if he had me back I'd listen more and take more interest and be less spiky and more grateful, had evaporated from my brain. How could I explain, under their critical gaze, the lessons I'd learned over these last months? How meeting Jessie had shown me what wickedness is in the world and the need to close ranks against it. To hold fast that which is good, as Nan would say. How Dad coming a-cropper demonstrated that you never know what's lying in wait for you on the road ahead. Mostly I'd learned about love watching Mum carefully cut up Dad's meals into small chunks, or each evening smooth moisturiser into his knobbly old feet. Would I do those things for Daniel if he needed me to? Yes, I would. No hesitation.

Not that I could say any of this with Witch-features listening in.

'I'm, really, really sorry,' I said again, my voice very small.

A snort from the doorway. I looked up expecting to see Mrs Gale sneering, but it was Amelia whose face was twisted in disgust.

'It's all right being sorry now, Charlotte. You had your chance, and you blew it. Danny deserves better than you. He knows it and you do too. You're not messing him about any more. I won't let you.'

'Come on,' said Mrs Gale, all brisk and buoyant now she could see I was failing. 'Time for you to go, young lady.'

But then something wonderful happened. Without looking at me, Daniel reached out sideways and took my hand. I let out a little squeak of surprise.

'Daniel!' his mother barked.

When I turned, I could see he was breathing fast and his skin was clammy. I squeezed his fingertips and he squeezed mine back, hard.

'Listen,' said Mrs G. 'If you do need cash, we can probably let you have some. Not much, but if that's what it takes, I'm sure we can come to some arrangement—'

'Move,' said Daniel, nodding them towards the door.

Amelia said, 'Don't fall for it, Danny. Don't, because you'll only end up how you were before. She'll take you for granted, she won't appreciate you. She'll break your heart again.'

'I could probably stretch to a hundred,' said Mrs Gale.

Daniel took a deep breath. 'Right,' he said. 'That's it.' And he jerked me forward so that we more or less barged the two women aside, pushing them apart, and then we were out onto the landing and running down the stairs, across the hallway, through the front door and down the brick path, still holding hands.

'Where are we going?' I asked as we turned out of the gateway and set off up the road.

He didn't answer. We passed the badly parked Metro, and a post-box, and the street sign at the corner and a Londis and a hairdresser's, and then he began to slow down, panting. We didn't stop, though. Down a ginnel he led me, across a car park, along the edge of a playing-field. Here was a trio of newly planted saplings, two of which had been snapped off and the guard-rail of the other filled with empty bottles and cans. Here was a wire supermarket basket suspended from a spiky fence. A skeletal hedge with an abandoned nest inside, a column of signs for an industrial park. I saw Christmas lights already twinkling against the gloom of the afternoon. These were Dan's streets, and I didn't know them because I'd never taken the trouble.

At the end of the next road was a garage and a bike repair shop, and some concrete steps leading to a flyover.

'Is it much further?' My lungs were on fire and my knees weren't much better.

He pulled me towards the steps and then we were hauling ourselves up a series of zigzag flights marked throughout with graffiti and water-stains and streaks of rust. Every corner and crevice was packed with litter. The traffic from the main road above us roared; I could smell diesel.

Just as I thought I was going to collapse, we reached the top. I gulped in exhaust fumes and held onto the metal hand-rail for support. Daniel walked on a little distance, then stopped and tipped his head back as if to study the sky. Above us, the clouds thickened. Sleet was on its way here too.

'Why have we come here?' I shouted. I had to raise my voice because of the lorries and vans thundering past.

He said something I couldn't make out.

'What?'

'She's not my girlfriend. She likes to think she is, but she isn't. I wanted you to know that.'

'Daniel—'

He held up his palm to stop me.

Sod this for a game of soldiers, I thought. I tucked my damp hair behind my ears and then strode over to stand in front of him. 'OK, what do you want, Dan? What do I have to say? Tell me and I'll say it, and mean it.'

'Is she right?'

'Who?'

'Amelia.'

I grasped his biceps, forcing him to look straight at me. 'No. She isn't. That's why I came, because I wanted to tell you we both had it wrong. I *do* love you enough, I *can* turn things round. Look, imagine it's a mathematical model that needed adjusting, if that helps.'

A blink.

'I can fix it, Dan. How can I prove it to you? I can't, unless you give me another chance.'

He seemed about to speak, then he broke free and started walking away again, fast. A truck bibbed its horn roguishly. 'Oh, up yours!' I shouted after it. Dan was speeding up and I could barely match his pace.

'I had it all clear in my mind,' he called back over his shoulder. 'Then you turn up.'

'I had to.'

I thought of the belemnite sitting under his monitor. Thirty pence for that little miracle of evolution. Sometimes it's hard to know how much things are really worth.

'Amelia has her own agenda. Your mum too. You can see that now, can't you? All I can do, Daniel, is promise to try harder. That's all anyone can do. But if I break your heart, I'll break mine too. I've found that out.'

He halted abruptly and turned, catching me in his arms like a kid playing kiss-chase. His expression was fiercer than I'd ever seen. Slowly he brought up his hands and planted them on my cheeks, but it wasn't a tender gesture, it was urgent, serious.

'You won't let me down?'

'Never.'

A beat.

'Then God help me, Charlotte, I'm not myself without you.'

And he drew me tight into him so that the breath was nearly squeezed out of me and my lips were squashed up against his collarbone painfully.

I don't know how long we stayed holding each other on that ugly city road. The sleet started, bitter against our necks, but he didn't let me go. Lorry horns honked, a driver shouted something crude. I imagined how we must look to all those people whizzing past in their warm, dry cabs: like a couple you'd see in a TV drama, some glimpse of careless love. Youngsters enjoying themselves before life becomes too weighted down. *Get in there, son.*

And it seemed, as Daniel clung onto me, that he and I were at the still, quiet centre of a mind-boggling whirl of activity, everyone else rushing across the surface of the planet to their grown-up destinations, to jobs and homes and partners. Any day now we'd be flung out to join them. I could almost feel the centripetal pull at my back. Where would we end up? What lay in store for us? The fear was dizzying if you let yourself dwell.

He was mumbling into my hair, his chest heaving and his arms like a vice around my back.

'Dear God, Charlotte. I thought, I thought—'

'Sssh,' I said. 'Later.'

Sometimes all that matters is the now.

Snapshots from the future

In a room with white-painted walls and striplights, Dad stands up. Not on his own, of course. They have this contraption, a kind of harness they strap round his waist and between his legs, and which buckles onto a hoist. The hoist's on wheels, so once they've cranked him upright – and it's so weird seeing him vertical again after half a year – they can start to move him forward, one step at a time.

'Are you OK?' the physio asks him. She's young and blonde and Dad likes her, which helps.

'I dunno, love.'

He's shaking, but I don't know whether that's with nerves or the effort or because his legs have become so weak. Mum says he's been doing his exercises religiously, but the muscles are still wasted. Under the baggy tracksuit bottoms you can see that his thighs are like pipe cleaners.

Another physio, a man, comes and grasps the front of the machine and begins to ease it forwards. Dad takes his first step.

'Hey, Karen, how about that? How about that?'

He looks over to the corner where Mum has her hand over her mouth, then to me. He's grinning, the physios are grinning.

'How's the pain, Mr Cooper?'

'Never mind the pain. This is champion. Hoy, everybody, see the amazing walking man! Top, int it? Let's see if I can go as far as that wall.'

Inch by inch he shuffles the length of the room. When he reaches the end, he gets a round of applause. Mum's radiant, her eyes bright and her purple velvet blazer shimmering under the fluorescent light. It's too big for her now, that blazer. 'Yes, I've been on the heartbreak diet,' she tells people who comment on her weight-loss. 'It's not one I'd recommend.' You can tell she likes it, though, being a bit slimmer; every cloud, and all that. I think the salsa classes have helped.

And now the physios are turning the machine so Dad can retrace his steps.

'Depending how you progress with this, Mr Cooper, we can start thinking about elbow crutches.'

'Fantastic.'

He's tired now, you can see it in his face. Just that very short distance has worn him out. Mum's fishing in a carrier bag for his paracetamol and for the blanket to go over his legs.

They reach the treatment table and apply the brakes. It takes a while to unstrap him and shift him from the hoist into his wheelchair. By the time we've eased him back on the cushion, he's exhausted.

'You were brilliant. Wasn't he brilliant, Charlotte?' Mum's fussing about, thanking the physios, tucking the blanket in, unpacking her umbrella ready to make the homeward trip.

'He was.' I take the wheelchair handles.

'Wait.' Dad reaches over his shoulder and grasps my wrist.

'What?'

'Are you OK, Charlie?'

'I'm fine. You were terrific, Dad.'

'Come round, where I can see you.'

I leave the handles and go to squat in front of him. I know he's hated these past months, not being able to talk to people eye-to-eye. He says he gets left out of conversations and talked over the top of. People can be crap with you when you're in a wheelchair.

'Listen,' he says. 'What you have to do is think about where I was straight after the accident, and how far I've come on since then. Focus on the achievement, not what I've lost. That's the way to see it. I was lucky. Hang onto that.'

'Yeah,' I say.

Mum puts her hand on my shoulder.

I straighten up again and we push the chair together across the lino and out through the double doors, past reception and a man on crutches.

'Would you believe it,' says Mum. 'It's stopped raining.'

My daughter is pretending she hasn't seen me. There she is, in the corner of the college canteen, sitting at a table with her mates. I can't get over how smart Charlotte looks today in a navy pencil skirt and a high-necked blouse. Like a real teacher. I did tell her ages ago she'd have to get her act together for teaching practice; you can't be skipping into a classroom wearing twenty shades of black. Especially not at big school.

Teenagers hate it when you try for cool. I said, 'You're young, you'll need to put a bit of distance between you and your students.' To which she replied, 'Since when were you an expert on secondary education, Mum?' Because I'm 'only' doing a primary-level course and my pupils stop at eleven. Therefore I know nothing. *Her* placement's bandit country whereas I just play with wooden blocks all day. I've told her, 'There's no need for snootiness: we'll both be on the same wage when we qualify.'

Now she's got a box-file out on the table and she's tapping one of the pages with a pen. The other girls are nodding in agreement. So serious! But then I knew Charlotte would apply herself once she'd decided a teaching course was what she wanted to do. She'll be up to date with her lesson plans, have done all her background reading. Every hand-out she's been given will have been filed and colour-coded in a little plastic wallet. Which makes me think, I must get on and sort out my notes, actually, before Steve buries them under car mags.

It makes me laugh, this new smart Charlotte, because they should have seen her last weekend at the boating lake, sprawled in a pedalo with Will and oblivious to the fact she was showing her knickers to everyone in the park. Ho ho, imagine if I left my seat now and wandered over to share the story with her mates. Her expression! Or alternatively I could tell them how she phoned the night before in a state of high panic because Will's school won't let him bring his blanket in, the one he's taken to trailing about everywhere and cries if it's removed. She rang wanting to know what to do. I said, 'There's nothing you can do. He'll have to leave it at home, and that's that. He'll get over it.' My advice didn't go down too well, of course. She'll always have trouble being the kind of mother who puts her foot down. But it's OK. Daniel and I are on the case.

Oh, hey up, it looks as if they're leaving. She's closing up her box-file, sliding it into her shoulder bag, standing, smoothing down her skirt. One of the other students in the group is showing round a book, another's placing the empty cups onto a tray. They begin to make their way towards the exit, heads bobbing as they put the British education system to rights. Still she's blanking me, my daughter, but I can't help following her with my eyes. She stands so straight, so beautiful, I can hardly believe she's mine. Oh, Charlotte, I think, we got there in the end, didn't we? Against all the odds. Well done, us struggling mothers.

And then, as she's about to pass through the double doors, she turns and gives me this wonderful, radiant smile. Just like that, out of nowhere. Kids: no matter how old they are, they never cease to surprise you.

God forgive me but my first reaction is, 'No, no, I can't!' Will's downstairs watching *Thomas the Tank Engine*, I hear whistles being blown and the gloomy tones of the narrator predicting collisions ahead. Dan's still at work. So it's me sitting on my own in the bathroom, staring at a positive pregnancy test.

Four terms I've been at my new job, four terms. I try and imagine the Headmaster's face when I go into his office and announce my news. Of course he'll smile and say congratulations, what choice does he have? But in his head, it'll be: *What the hell are you playing at, Charlotte Gale? We've just worked out the new timetable. I thought you were supposed to be revising the Department's library policy, and standing in for Carmen when she has her hysterectomy? It's all arranged. We were depending on you. We took you on in good faith, supported you through your probationary year, and this is how you repay us. Swanning off at our busiest time. Frankly it's the last thing I needed to hear right now. Having a baby! How selfish can you get?*

I sit down on the cold edge of the bath. The afternoon sun's streaming in through the net curtains and making a pattern on the tiles. The mirror needs a wipe and I suppose I should degunk the shower head at some point before it blocks up. Dimly I remember it's Will's hair-wash night tonight so that'll be half an hour's screaming and coaxing. I might get Dan to see to it.

I check my watch: 4.30. At least an hour till he gets home.

I get up and pace about for a bit. All the indignities and stresses of pregnancy, I'm now revising: the months of health professionals prodding and peering and measuring, the intrusive questions. The way your body expands beyond anything reasonable, leaving you in those final days unable to sit, stand, walk, lie, eat or breathe. The extreme agony of getting the baby out. All the paraphernalia you then have to assemble, the time-consuming rituals and special equipment involved. The exhaustion, the lonely night-feeds. The terrifying fragility of newborns.

Twelve hours late with my pill, I was, one time. That bloody Fertility Fairy.

In the end I go downstairs to my son. Sure enough, it turns out a blue train has smashed into an unconvincing polystyrene mountainside.

I look across to where he sits, thumb in mouth, gaze fixed on the screen, and feel a pang of something. People say he looks like his dad, meaning Daniel, which makes us smile. But in a funny way he does. Especially when his hair's due a cut. 'How would you like a little sister or brother?' I imagine asking. His mild eyes flicking across to me, full of questions. But it's too early yet for any of that.

And don't ask me who we're going to find to take over your GCSE classes, the voice of the Head breaks in. *You've only just set up the reading recovery programme with Year Seven. What'll happen to them?*

I shake him away, and instead reach under the sofa where I keep Will's baby record album. Six years since I put this book together, faithfully stuck in a clipping of his hair, his hospital wristband, the label off his cot, the copy of the Novena prayer Ivy sent me. Here's a photo of a shiny young Daniel, his hair even wilder than I remember it, waving a knitted giraffe over the Moses basket; here's Mum and Nan sitting on Nan's bed with Will across their laps. Here's a page of Firsts: first smiled, first rolled over, first clapped hands, first sat up, first crawled. Baby's first holiday, baby's first Christmas. Will clutching a multicoloured felt ball which, I seem to think, had a bell inside it that would rattle when you threw it.

I go back to the page where Daniel's holding the giraffe, recall the last, disastrous time I showed him a positive pregnancy test. Two seventeen-year-olds sitting on the damp grass in Menses Park and frightened out of their wits. I can't believe how far we've come.

I can't believe how well we did.

Suddenly I'm desperate for him to be here.

I reach for my mobile, find it's been switched off, turn it on and straight away get one of his texts: *Dropping in mums on wy hme. Dnt wait fr tea. X*

Well, isn't that typical? Bloody Mrs Gale, I suppose I'm stuck with her now. Ha ha, there's someone who won't be cracking open the champagne when she finds out. I might be really mean and insist she goes shopping for baby clothes with me.

The phone beeps again and I see it's a missed call, from Mum. Mum. That's who I want to talk to. Even as I'm dialling, I can hear her. *Oh, Charlotte, you daft ha'porth, you've got this cock-eyed. This is a baby, yours and Daniel's. You wanted another, didn't you? All right, it's landed sooner than you planned, but does it matter? There's never a right time to get pregnant. If you waited till every last thing was in place, you wouldn't get off the starting-blocks. Be glad. Think of how happy Daniel's going to be, think what it'll mean to him.*

After an age she picks up. The line's crackly and there's an odd whining noise in the background. I wonder if they've been invaded by wasps.

'What can I hear?' I ask her.

'It's your dad.'

'No, that buzzing noise.'

'That's right. He's watching motorbike racing on TV. I say watching. More shouting, really.'

'Get your arse in there, Hodgson!' goes Dad, on cue.

'Did you want something?' she says.

Now's my chance. I hug my secret to myself, my heart beating faster as I imagine spilling out the news. Mum's exclamations, Dad's mumblings, the TV maybe even switched off. Then a split second later I realise, no, much as I'm longing to share it with her, it has to be Daniel who hears first.

'You rang *me*, Mum.'

'Did I? Oh, yeah. All it was, I wanted to tell you I'd found your nan's spoon.'

'What, the famous poo scoop?'

'That's right. I dug it up under the flowering currant. It is the one. Brass collar round the handle, shell-shaped bowl.'

'Lovely.'

'Well, I thought you'd be interested. It's an heirloom. You have to keep these objects safe for the next generation. Everything's coming to you in the end, you know. You and Will. Family treasures.'

'Eight false moustaches and a gross of plastic rainhoods?'

'Don't scoff. There's your granddad's tenor horn, the barometer in the hall, the mantel clock, they're worth something. I want Will to have those.'

The buzzing's getting louder.

I say, 'Look, Mum, while I'm on, I wanted to tell you – I wanted you to know that you've been a really fantastic grandma. The best. We've really—'

There's a sudden clattering noise followed by Dad swearing.

'It's OK, Charlotte. It's only his stick he's knocked over. Ah, and the biscuit barrel and a full glass of shandy. All up the wall, marvellous. How does he do it? No, Steve, leave it. I'll fetch a cloth in a minute. Go on, what were you saying?'

'Nothing, Mum. It doesn't matter.'

'OK, well, I'll see you Sunday, yeah? I'll show you this spoon and we'll have a catch-up then.'

'See you Sunday.'

Yes. I'll tell them as we sit round the table, the family all together, united. Right now it seems an age away and I can hardly bear the wait, but it will come round.

Because that's the thing about the future. It always does get here eventually.

Acknowledgements

Thanks to: Alexandra Pringle and family, Dr Corinne Smith, Judith Strachan, Alison Winward, Sam Sinclair, Jonathan Howard, Andy Hamill, Kat Dibbits, John and Margaret Green, Lizzy Willams (@LifebyLizzy), Reena Kaur, Pam Dunnill at the CAB, Darryl Wandless, Edward Roberts, Nicky Carter (@gherkinette), Sue Marsh (@suey2y), Kaliya Franklin (@bendygirl), Pam Griffin (@_PamGriffin), Claire King (@ckingwriter), Sharon Owens (@SharonOwensAuth), @tazerbo, Anna Cassar (@oddbohemian), Jo Richards (@JoRichardsKent), Anneliese (@sluggishwalnut), Lindy Parkinson (@qubeoca), Susan Elliot Wright (@sewelliot), Phil (@GiantDespair), Helen Hunt (@hmhunt), Charlotte Ross (@ellaboheme), Rebecca Stanley (@BettyMcFab), @Ian_Kirkpatrick, @LeahFHardy, Jo Thomas (@jo_thomas01), Greg L (@natureoncam), @Martha_Williams, @BriarRidgeBooks, @PlashingVole, Jane Lawson (@BookeditorJane), Katie Fforde (@KatieFforde), Sally Quilford (@Quillers), Celia Bartlett (@ailecphoto), Naomi Alderman (@naomialderman), @bookmonkeygirl, Ian McLoughlin (@IanMcL13), Stewart Gillies, Reference Team Manager at British Library Newspapers, the always-fabulous WW girls, Peter Straus and all at RCW, Suzanne Baboneau and the team at S&S.

Bibliography

Gordon Crumpton: *Standish and its People 1900–1926*

Robin Everett, Ed.: *Lancashire: Representing the Past*

Lancashire Federation of Women's Institutes: *Lancashire Within Living Memory*

**SIMON &
SCHUSTER**

Kate Long

Mothers & Daughters

Three generations, driven apart by infidelity

Carol married young, to philandering Phil, and became
a mother young – to highly strung Jaz. But Carol put up
with Phil's infidelities. Suffer in silence and keep the family
together was her mantra. Not so Jaz. The moment she
discovers her husband Ian's errant ways – a quick fumble
with a woman he barely knew – she throws him out of
the house. She changes the locks, refuses his calls, and
bans him from seeing their toddler son Matty.

In so many ways independent and strong, where her
daughter is concerned, Carol is a coward. She cannot bear
seeing history repeating itself. When Jaz finds out that her
mother has enlisted the support of Ian's father David to try
to reunite the couple, she is beyond furious. There is only
one way Jaz knows to get back at Carol, to hurt her most:
through Carol's beloved, doted-upon grandson, Matty . . .

ISBN 978-1-84739-897-0
Price £6.99

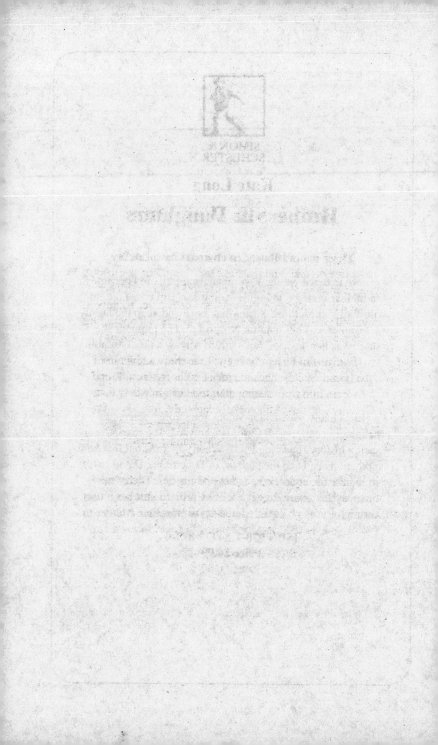

**SIMON &
SCHUSTER**

Kate Long

Before She Was Mine

Freya is torn between her two mothers. Liv, her
adoptive mother who nurtured and raised her, is earthy,
no-nonsense. The total opposite to Melody: with her
vibrant, explosive personality and extensive, brightly
coloured wardrobe, Freya's birth mother is still apt to find
herself thrown out of Top Shop for bad behaviour.

Hard as it has been for Freya to try to reconcile her
two families, it has been harder for her mothers. Proud
of her mature and sensible adoptive daughter, Liv fears
Melody's restless influence. Meanwhile, forced to give
up her baby when she was just a teenager herself,
Melody now craves Freya's love and acceptance -
but only really knows how to have fun.

Then tragedy strikes, and the bonds of love that tie
these three women together will be tested to the max. Can
they finally let go of the past, and pull together in order to
withstand the toughest challenge life could throw them?

ISBN 978-1-84739-896-3
Price £6.99